THE OTHER SHORE

SABRA WALDFOGEL

The Other Shore by Sabra Waldfogel

Copyright © 2025 by Sabra Waldfogel

Cover Design: https://damonza.com/

978-1-953354-19-8 Ebook

978-1-953354-20-4 Print

Sabra Waldfogel, Publisher

www.sabrawaldfogel.com

Published in Minneapolis, Minnesota

CONTENTS

THE SPIRIT'S VOICE

It was the voice that came to her in the twilight just before sleep. It never came because she wanted it. It came as it willed and told her what it wished.

Who? she asked. *How?*

There was a low chuckle. *You'll see*, the voice told her.

She'd first heard the voice when she fled Memphis, just after she'd stumbled into a kitchen job on a steamboat bound for Cairo. After a long day, she fell onto her pallet, exhausted but too frightened to fall asleep. The kitchen crew slept near the kitchen itself, and the roar of the engine was their loud lullaby. She closed her eyes and tried to stretch out on the pallet.

A voice said, *Don't worry. I'll help you.*

It was a familiar-sounding voice, that of a Black woman, resonant and knowing, tinged with Africa in a way that reminded her of her earliest childhood as an enslaved child in rural Tennessee.

She sat up, clutching the rough blanket to her chest,

trying to discover who'd spoken to her. But all around her, sleeping forms lay quiet under their blankets.

She whispered, "Who are you?"

The voice answered, *A friend.*

"How will you help me?"

There was a chuckle, low and musical. *You'll see.*

By daylight, she was convinced that she'd been dreaming.

In Cairo, she staggered from the boat onto the dock, blinking in the sunlight, her eyes darting as she tried to get her bearings. A Black man, with a dark, seamed face that reminded her of her uncle Moses, spoke to her in a low voice. "Where are you from?" he asked.

"Memphis."

He took her in—her disheveled hair, her dirty dress, her fear. He nodded, as though he could tell she was a fugitive. Even more softly, he said, "Get yourself on a boat to Cincinnati."

She found a steamer bound for Cincinnati and talked her way into a job in the kitchen. She got used to keeping her hands in hot, dirty water, and she also got used to sleeping near the roar of a steamboat engine. No voice, neither human nor imaginary, woke her.

Once in Cincinnati, as she walked through the streets of the Black neighborhood of Bucktown, looking for a place to lodge, the voice spoke again. *Here,* it said, when she hesitated before a three-story boardinghouse that advertised "Rooms to Let."

"Who are you?" she murmured under her breath. "And how do you know?"

The low chuckle again. *Trust me.*

The landlady was a church-going woman who fussed over her, a girl all alone, and told her about a job in a hotel downtown. By the end of the day, she had a roof over her head and the promise of money coming in.

As she fell asleep that night, she heard the voice say, *Didn't I tell you?*

She was used to working in a kitchen and she adjusted swiftly to the restaurant. If she looked over her shoulder all the time and startled easily when someone approached her from behind—well, Cincinnati was full of enslaved people who'd come there as fugitives, and no one thought it peculiar.

At first, she only heard the voice at night, just as she was falling asleep. She'd decided that it was a prelude to dreams, or the result of extreme worry and fatigue, as she'd felt during her escape. She thought she'd never hear it again, and certainly not in her waking hours.

Until she did.

One of the women she worked with was newly married, and she showed off the gold band her husband had bought for her with pride. One day, she came to work downcast. Cassie asked her, "What's the matter?"

"Lost my wedding ring. Can't find it anywhere."

In the clamor of the kitchen, the voice said to her, *Tell her to look in that clump of collard greens by her back steps.*

Cassie thought, *Why are you talking to me in broad daylight?*

Why not? Do her a good turn. Tell her.

Cassie thought, *Am I crazy?*

She heard the low chuckle. *Don't you know you can trust me?*

She thought, *If I'm crazy I'll know soon enough.* She said to the woman, "Did you look for the ring in your back garden?"

"Thought I looked everywhere."

"Do you have some greens growing by your steps?"

The woman looked at her in surprise. "I do."

"Look there."

The next day, she ran to Cassie, who had her hands in a sink full of hot, soapy water. She held out her hand, and the little gold band glimmered on her finger. She beamed. "I found it! Right where you told me to look! How did you know?"

At the sound of the low chuckle, Cassie said, "I just knew."

CASSIE COULDN'T SHAKE the feeling there was something wrong with her. No sane person heard the voice of an African wise woman who knew where the lost ring, the lost dog, the lost money was hiding. The voice was always right, and that made Cassie feel even odder.

She went to talk to a root doctor, a woman old enough to be her grandmother, whose low laugh and African-tinged speech reminded her of the voice itself. As Cassie sat in the front room of the little house in Bucktown, the root doctor asked, "What troubles you, sister?"

Cassie struggled to find the words to tell her.

She leaned forward and laid her hand on Cassie's arm. She had the gnarled, veined hands of a woman who had done hard physical labor all her life. "What scares you, sister?"

Cassie looked into her eyes, which were so dark that the pupil seemed to swallow up the iris. "I hear things," she whispered.

"What do you hear?"

Her voice even softer, she said, "I hear a voice."

"You find things, don't you?"

She nodded. "The voice tells me."

"What kind of voice?"

Cassie shuddered a little. "A woman's voice. Like yours.

Pitched low. And like someone from Africa." She looked down at her lap. "Am I crazy?"

The woman reached out to lift Cassie's chin with her roughened fingers. She broke into a smile. "No, not at all," she said. "You have a gift. You hear a spirit."

"A spirit? What kind of spirit?"

She chuckled, and the familiar sound sent a shiver down Cassie's spine. "Great, strong spirit," she said. "Ancestor from Africa. She chose you. You're lucky."

"Am I?" Cassie asked.

"Yes," the woman said.

"What should I do?"

"Listen," the woman said.

AFTER THAT, a woman sought her out after church. In a low voice, she asked, "You find things, don't you?"

"Yes," Cassie said.

The woman grasped her sleeve. "Do you find lost people, too?"

Cassie hesitated. *Yes,* the voice said. Cassie asked, "Who are you looking for?"

"My husband. Got up and left last week. Don't know where he went."

The voice said, *She won't like what you find.*

Cassie said, "I can try."

It wasn't difficult. The voice said, *Ask.* Cassie said back, "Of course I'll ask her friends." It was strange to combine the voice's suggestions with her own common sense. And sure enough, Cassie found that he was living with another woman a few streets away. She didn't need the voice to tell her not to approach him directly. She told the abandoned wife what she'd learned, and the woman said, "He ain't worth running after. We were never properly married, anyhow." She laughed. "I know about you. I don't have to ask how you found out. You just know." She looked hard at Cassie. "My grandmama was like you," she said. "She knew things. She said the spirits talked to her. Do they talk to you?"

"Yes," she said.

"CAN you find someone who is lost forever?" the woman asked.

Listen, the voice had said. She gazed into the worn, creased face and the eyes pouched with the inability to sleep, and she heard a child's cry. *Mama, mama.* Lost indeed. "I can try," she said.

Talking to the dead was different from listening to her own spirit's voice. She learned how to hear in a new way and to let a strange spirit flow through her. She learned to speak with its voice, see with its eyes, feel its emotions. As she grew more practiced, she felt its body fill hers. At first, it was a terrifying experience. But it comforted the grieving, and it became easier as she learned to anticipate it.

She asked her own voice, "Why don't I hear from my own dead?"

Because you keep them away. Do you want to?

"No."

Then they'll stay away.

Her landlady was upset by her constant visitors. She knew why they came and what Cassie did for them. Reluctantly, she climbed the stairs to Cassie's room and said, "I'm a good Christian woman and I don't hold with this sort of thing. Talking to the dead. You'll have to do that elsewhere."

As Cassie looked around her room, the spirit said, *It's time to go. You're ready for greater things.*

"In New York, perhaps?" Cassie said, and the low chuckle told her she'd guessed right.

As soon as she got off the train, she could feel the grief thick in the air. The war had taken its toll on the people of New York. The street thronged with widows missing husbands and mothers missing sons. She found a boarding-house where the landlady, a Black woman with a Yankee accent, was a spiritualist herself, and reduced her rent when she found out about Cassie's gift. The landlady helped Cassie's business, too.

Cassie discovered that New York, in addition to being awash in grief, was full of Black people with money. She modeled herself on the bearing of her new customers, matching her dress and her speech to theirs. She could speak in any voice, could she not? In six months, no one would take her for a former slave from Tennessee.

Her own dead remained silent.

It was a surprise to receive a white man in her parlor. He was tall and elegant, with an accent that spoke of having lived in many places. She was about to tell him that she couldn't help him when the voice said, *Hear him out.*

"Sir, what might I do for you?"

He said, "I'm here because there's something I might be able to do for you."

Her heart sank. She'd heard that the police sometimes bothered spiritualists, assuming they were frauds, and accepted bribes in exchange for turning an eye to their activities. She sighed. "Are you from the police?"

His eyes searched her face. They were a deep brown, unusual in a white man. "No, and I'm sorry I let you think so. I'm an inquiry agent."

"Are you here to inquire of me?"

"On the contrary," he said, doffing his hat. His black hair had the faintest coil in it. "I'm here to offer my services to you."

"Why would I employ you?"

"It might help you in what you do." He paused. "Your spiritual task."

"I don't need that kind of help."

He said, "Why not help the spirits? By finding out more about your customers' lives, their worries, and their troubles?"

She sent out a silent plea to the voice, but it was silent. She asked, "How do I know I can trust you?"

"I assume you know that appearances are deceptive," he said.

"They can be."

He smiled. "Despite my looks, I assure you that the blood of Africa flows through my veins."

Her own sons, whom she had abandoned back in Memphis, were similarly light skinned. She saw it. She nodded.

"May I offer you an inquiry? To see if we might suit? I won't charge for it."

"I can give you a reading," she said.

He was silent.

She said, "Death surrounds you."

He lifted his dark eyes to hers. "I was a soldier," he said. "You don't need to consult the spirits to know that."

He made an inquiry, and to her surprise, he was right. The information he gave her deepened the readings and made the séances easier. She didn't tell him so. But the voice, full of humor, said to her, *Let him help you. But don't trust him. Not yet.*

She thought, *I hardly need a supernatural force to remind me of that.*

His name was Randolph, Thomas Jefferson Randolph, apropos since he had ancestors from Virginia. "As well as an ancestor from Madagascar," he said, and she knew that was his way to admit to Africa.

Before the war, he'd lived in New York. He'd been a spiritualist himself, augmenting his séances with photography, trying to prove that ectoplasm existed. "I gave that up," he said, and he began to take conventional portraits instead, and occasionally pictures of crime scenes that he sold to the Manhattan newspapers.

When the war broke out, he became attached to an Ohio regiment as a newspaper photographer. "They assumed I was white, and I didn't correct them." The officers noticed his keen eye and asked if he'd like to join the regiment as a scout. "It turned out I had an ability for aiming a rifle, too."

"They never suspected that you had 'the blood of Africa in your veins'?"

"People see what they want to see." He smiled. "As you well know."

After the war, he returned to New York and put his scouting skills to work as an inquiry agent. He had white clients who thought he was white, and Black clients who knew he was Black.

"Does it tire you?" she asked. "Changing your spots all the time?"

"You know the answer to that," he said.

His suggestions helped her business. He told her, "The customers expect the theatrics you provide. They're reassured by them." Which they were. She prospered.

And even though he could never marry her—he had an angry, abandoned wife, an unmistakably Black woman, tucked away in the countryside near Utica—he became Cassie's partner in life as well as in business. Their tie remained a secret.

And then the letter came from Memphis.

~

Now, as she sat in her parlor and opened the letter, TJ asked, "Who is it from?"

"A friend in Memphis."

Ida Simmons, who was literate, wrote to her, as her own family could not. She read: *They need you.*

She let the letter fall into her lap. She heard the voice again, echoing the words on the page, strengthening the emotion that had committed them to paper. The voice, low and lazy like the current of the Mississippi River, played on her guilt. As it echoed Ida's words, the voice reminded her that her uncle struggled to make a living since the riot, that her aunt's health suffered, and that her sons—the boys she had abandoned when she fled five years ago—needed the hand of a mother.

She thought, *If it mattered so much, why didn't you tell me sooner?*

The voice had come unbidden, and it left the same way. There was silence.

She asked TJ, "What would you say if I wanted to return to Memphis?"

"I thought you'd sworn you'd never return." The flickering light of the parlor lamps cast shadows on his face. "Since you ran off under such suspicion."

She stared at the wall behind his head. "Everyone who accused me is gone now," she said.

"After the massacre?" he asked.

She turned her face to look at the face that changed according to the situation and the light, from white to Black and back again. "They aren't likely to have another, are they? Certainly not so soon."

"I don't like it."

"But you'd be with me." She met his eyes, using the luminous gaze that nature had given her.

"Close by," he said, reminding her that they could never live together openly. "What would you do there?"

"See my family. And perhaps do a little business, too."

"In Memphis?"

She asked, "Where better than in a city full of ghosts?"

THE HOMECOMING

WHEN THE HACK PULLED UP TO THE HOUSE, CASSIE DIDN'T GET out. She frowned as the driver opened the door. "Are you sure this is the right address?" she asked.

"Yes, miss. I know Mr. Moses and Miss Matilda well. We worship at the same church."

The one-story house was little better than a cabin, its boards weathered, its window frames badly warped. The front door hadn't been painted in years. The yard had been mown, but it was infested with weeds.

"Their house in Camp Shiloh was nicer than this," she said. She thought with a pang of that house, so new that it still smelled of pine boards, neatly whitewashed, with gleaming oilpaper in the windows. Her aunt had planted a tidy garden in the front yard of that house, herbs and vegetables for the kitchen and flowers pleasing to the eye.

The driver sighed. He must be new in Memphis; she hadn't known him when she lived here during the war. "A lot of people lost everything back in '66," he said.

"I thought they recovered."

"Some did, and others didn't."

Shaking her head, she paid him and, as he drove away, walked the few steps to the front door.

The door creaked open, and her aunt Matilda, her hair now completely gray, her posture stooped, broke into a smile to see her. She pulled Cassie into the house and hugged her close. "It's so good to see you," she whispered, unable to stroke Cassie's hair, which was tightly anchored under her new bonnet. She let Cassie go and regarded her with a pleased expression. "You look fine," she said. "Such a pretty dress."

Cassie felt ashamed of the money she'd spent on her new traveling outfit.

Her uncle Moses lurked behind Matilda, his face in a smile. Like her aunt, he had gone completely gray, and he seemed slighter than he'd been when she left, five years before. He'd been so angry when she left that she wasn't sure he'd be glad to see her again. But he swept her into an embrace, murmuring, "I'm glad you're home."

Her aunt shut the door and ushered her into the house. Cassie had to control her impulse to gasp. The house had a tiny front room. The floor was rough pine, bare of any carpet. The furniture was little better than kindling, old and splintered. She remembered the sturdy pine table and chairs in the Camp Shiloh house, the almost-new Turkish carpet on the floor, and she wanted to weep.

Evidently the furnishings, like the house itself, had suffered badly back in '66, and hadn't recovered since.

Her uncle said, "Will, come say hello to your mama."

Will had been a little boy of eight when she left. Now he was thirteen, nearly as tall as his great-uncle Moses. His expression was much too serious for so young a boy. He was very fair skinned, and he now looked more like his white father, the man she had hated so much. Her son held out his hand and said politely, "Happy to see you, ma'am."

Not "mama," or even "mother."

She took his hand, which was surprisingly callused and rough, as though he'd been doing a man's labor. "It's good to see you again, Will." She couldn't ask if he'd missed her. "I'm sorry I didn't come back sooner to see you."

"We know you couldn't," he said, in a tone that was eerily adult. "It wasn't safe for you."

What had they told him?

"Where is your brother?" she asked.

Her aunt answered. "Sam? Up to no good, I'm sure. Out in the street somewhere."

"I can find him," Will said. "I know where he goes."

"Don't go," her uncle said. "He'll come home when he's hungry, like a stray cat." But there was no affection in his voice, only weariness.

"If he isn't in jail," her aunt said.

Will said, "It's no trouble, Auntie Tilda. I'll bring him home."

Will slipped out the door and her aunt invited her to sit on one of the wounded old chairs.

Cassie looked around the small, bare, desolate room before she sat. "What happened to your things?" she asked, her voice constricted by her concern. "All your good things from Camp Shiloh?"

Her uncle closed his eyes for a moment. There were dark bruises of fatigue beneath them. "Burned up," he said. "Burned out."

She fell into the chair. "You can't stay here," she said.

Her aunt said, "We wouldn't if we could afford better."

They need you.

Oh, they did.

"Let me help," she said, before she could think it over.

The door opened, and Will came in, holding the arm of the younger brother, who had been just out of toddlerhood when she left. Now he was as tall as Will, and as strong.

"Come in and say how do to our mother," Will said. His voice was calm and level, but he pulled hard on Sam's arm.

Sam shook his head and struggled in Will's grasp. "Let me go," Sam said, yanking his arm away.

The house was so small that he could greet her if he turned his head. She said, "Sam—" and she held out her arms.

He stopped just out of her reach. His expression was hot with fury. He stared at her for a moment. Then he said, "You ran away! You left us behind!"

"Sammy—" she repeated.

"I hate you!"

He turned, flung open the door, and ran back into the street.

Cassie put her gloved hand to her mouth and let her eyes fill with tears.

THE NEXT MORNING, without telling her aunt and uncle where she was going, she made her way to the house of her old friend, Ida Simmons. Five years ago, Ida had run a small and discreet bordello on a side street. Now she owned a handsome two-story brick building a block from downtown. The maid who ushered her into the parlor was as beautiful as the young women who sat in the parlor itself, their complexions in every hue from very dark to ivory. They were dressed like ladies, in well-tailored dresses of fine cotton. The parlor was as genteel as any decent house, furnished in the style that had come from England after the war: heavy walnut furniture upholstered in velvet—but not red, as she would have expected—striped wallpaper, and sedate paintings of classical ruins in ornate gilded frames.

The maid showed Cassie into a back parlor where Ida sat, not on the settee but at her desk, a ledger open before her. She wore a plain dress, dark blue, as demure as a schoolteacher's. At the sight of Cassie, she shut the ledger, rose, and extended her hand, smiling.

They sat. Ida offered her coffee, and she accepted.

Ida said, "You're back."

"For a while."

"Where are you staying?"

"With my aunt and uncle. They can't stay there! It's dreadful!"

Ida didn't reply.

"And they aren't well, either of them. Is he working? Is she still washing?"

"As much as they can."

"And the boys! Are they in school?"

"Will is. Sam—" She sighed. "Sam is running wild."

"You should have told me sooner!"

Ida set down her coffee cup a little too hard and it rattled in the saucer. "Would you have come any sooner?"

Guilt surged through her. "I have to find them a proper house. And buy them some decent furnishings. They have tin plates, Ida! Like back in slavery!"

Ida said, "And what do they think of your plans?"

"I haven't told them. But how can they object? Who would want to live like that?"

"Tread carefully," Ida said. "They were proud before you left, and that hasn't changed, even if their circumstances have."

"But I can help them!"

"You ran off without a word. You stayed away for years. Tread carefully, Cassie."

Now Cassie set her cup down too hard. "You've done all right for yourself," she said, gesturing around the room.

Ida laughed. "War or peace, vice lives on," she said. "And now that there's a lot of money in Memphis, there's an appetite for quiet, genteel vice."

"I can see that," Cassie said, a little too sharply.

"You look prosperous," Ida said. "Talking to the dead must agree with you."

"It's a gift," Cassie said. "Not something to use the wrong way."

Ida leaned close. "Do you really talk to the dead? Or is it theatrics and the help of a good inquiry agent?"

Cassie said, "I can show you."

"Really?"

"There must be someone on the other shore that you—"

"Oh, hush. If I want to speak to the dead, I'll go to the cemetery to talk to my mama. Do you need the name of an inquiry agent?"

"No, I do not," Cassie said.

"You've found one already?"

"I met one in New York, and he decided to come to Memphis," she said.

"Are you planning to stay, then? To do business here?"

"I may." She wondered how long it would take to set the Hayes household in order. How long to thaw the premature adulthood in Will's soul. How long to make sure that Sam didn't end up in jail.

"Well, if you are," Ida said, "let me know. I know how to keep the police happy."

"I believe you do," Cassie said.

"Yes, that, and how to donate to the Policemen's Fund."

"Oh, that. I know all about that. The police in New York are no different."

"But you don't know who to donate to," Ida said. "I do."

Cassie said, "If you advertise as a spiritualist—no matter how discreetly you do it—the police will know to find you. If I do business here, he'll find me, with his hand out for the Policemen's Fund."

"You'll see," Ida said. "You'll need my help, as your aunt and uncle need yours."

CASSIE WALKED THOUGHTFULLY BACK to her aunt and uncle's house. Once inside, she sighed. Her aunt sat at the table, her head in her hands. Cassie knew that posture very well. It signified, "I don't know how we'll pay the rent this month."

Her aunt looked up as Cassie sat opposite her. Cassie reached for her aunt's hand, which was veined and swollen. Her aunt didn't smile.

Cassie said, "Aunt Matilda, there's something I've been thinking about."

"What is it?"

"That I'd like to stay in Memphis for a while." She glanced around the cramped, shabby house. "And do some business while I'm here."

"What kind of business?"

"Spiritual readings," she said.

Her aunt shook her head.

"Aunt Matilda, it's a real business. And a good one."

"How?" her aunt asked. "In here?"

"I'd like to rent a place where my customers can come to see me," she said. "With enough room for you and Uncle Moses and the boys to live."

Her aunt looked up, her expression worried. "You have enough money for that?"

"Yes, I do." Her aunt didn't reply, and Cassie said, "I wouldn't decide until you and Uncle Moses had seen the place. I want you to be comfortable there."

Her aunt met her eyes. Her eyes glimmered with a trace of her old energy. "You should talk to Mrs. Smith," she said.

"Miss Mahaley? Is she still in Memphis?"

"She is. Runs a boardinghouse on Beale Street. She might be able to help you."

Before Cassie fled Memphis—when she was in so much trouble she was afraid she'd end up in prison—Mrs. Smith had aided her. Mahaley Smith had been housekeeper to a planter family before the war, and during the conflict, she had kept house for General Grant himself. She heard everything that went on in Memphis, whether it concerned Black folk or white. Evidently that hadn't changed.

Cassie asked, "Beale Street? What's the address?"

Mrs. Smith's boardinghouse was a well-kept two-story structure, freshly painted white, with a pretty little garden on either side of the shaded porch. Cassie thought, *She came through all right.* The woman who answered the door hadn't changed in five years. She was still substantial and dignified, with the satisfied look of someone pleased with her place in the world. She stepped back and gave Cassie a long, appraising gaze. "Well, look at you," she said. "Risen from the dead."

Cassie wondered if Ida Simmons had told her what she did for a living, but she laughed. "No, just back for a visit," she said.

"I heard you turned into a Yankee."

"Maybe," she said. "I've been staying in New York."

"What brings you back?"

"My aunt and uncle, and my boys," Cassie said.

"What do you want with me?"

"May I come in?"

Inside, everything was new and clean and fresh. Did Black people board here? They must have some money. "This is a lovely house," she said.

"I'm full up," she said. "I can't offer you a place to stay."

"May I sit down? I have something else in mind."

In the parlor, Cassie explained what she was looking for. Mrs. Smith took on a thoughtful expression. *Just like the old days*, Cassie thought. *She's the spider at the middle of a web.*

Mrs. Smith said, "I know a Jewish lady, a Mrs. Levy, who has a building for rent, just down the street from here."

"Would she rent to me?"

"I don't see why not, because she was renting to a friend of mine, a dressmaker who belongs to my church. There's a shop downstairs and rooms above."

Cassie asked, "What happened to the dressmaker?"

"Oh, she moved to Cincinnati, where her daughter lives now. She plans to open a shop there."

"How soon can I see it?"

Mrs. Smith said, "What kind of business are you planning to run, if you move in?"

"I'm surprised you don't know."

Mrs. Smith's eyes gleamed. Cassie thought, *She'll tell everyone she knows. It's better than taking out an advertisement in the paper.* "The spirits speak to me," she said. "And they help me talk to the dead."

Mrs. Smith gave her another appraising look. "You'll do well here," she said. "This place is full of ghosts."

～

MRS. LEVY, who owned the building for rent, was a short, thin woman full of nervous energy. She swept through the property, praising its virtues with a strong German accent. Cassie took in the airy front room, the spacious area that had been a workroom, and the living space on the second story. "You like?" Mrs. Levy asked.

"I do. But I want to bring my aunt and uncle to see it, since they'll be living upstairs."

"Where do they work?"

"My uncle is a porter for the newspaper, and my aunt is a washerwoman."

"And you? What is your business?"

"I'm a spiritualist."

"You won't bring me trouble?"

Cassie said, "Mrs. Levy, are you a widow?"

The woman looked surprised. "Yes, I am. How did you know?"

Because it's clear you inherited the property when your husband died, Cassie thought. "Do you miss your husband?"

The woman's expression changed. "I miss him every day," she said.

"Would you like to speak to him again?"

Mrs. Levy didn't reply.

Cassie's voice became very soft. "Let me help you," she said.

Torn between grief and disbelief, Mrs. Levy shook her head. "I don't think you can."

"Think about it."

Mrs. Levy looked around the empty living room and recovered her commercial composure. "Bring your aunt and uncle soon," she said. "Nothing in Memphis stays vacant for long."

AFTER CASSIE TOOK THEM ALL—HER aunt, her uncle, and her boys—to see the building on Beale Street, her uncle grumbled, "Don't see how we stay here after you leave."

Her aunt had been standing up straighter since Cassie first floated the idea of a new place to live. She said, "Moses, don't you see it? We can rent out the first floor. And we can even take in a boarder to live with us."

Within a week, they had moved. Matilda, suddenly full of energy, took Cassie to find used furniture and housewares in good condition. It wasn't hard, since so many planters had sold everything they owned to keep afloat. At the rug merchant's, her aunt cried out with pleasure. "Look what I found, Cassie," she said.

It was a Turkish carpet, just a little worn in spots, the rest of it bright and cheerful, exactly like the one that used to sit on the floor of the house in Camp Shiloh.

CASSIE STOOD in the middle of the front room, thinking that it would serve well as an anteroom if she draped the windows to make it darker and more mysterious. At the rap on the front door, she turned, ready to say "The dressmaker is gone" or "I'm not open for business yet." But it was TJ, who grinned as she let him in.

He looked around. "Good location," he said. "A nice space."

She laughed. "Come in back," she said, and when they were safely out of public view, they embraced. "I missed you," she said.

He kissed her, and when he broke away, he said, "I missed you, too."

She hadn't yet sent him word about the place she'd rented. He'd been able to find out, as able a scout in the city as he'd been on the march in the countryside in Georgia.

"How have you been?" she asked.

"All right."

"Your disguise?"

He waved his hand at his pale cheek. "So far, so good." He looked around the room. "The séance room?"

"I think so."

He said, "I'll take a good look later. Figure out how to set things up."

She sighed. "You don't need to do that," she said. "The spirits talk to me, and I talk to the dead. We don't need tricks."

He said, "Whether we need them or not, they help. As the investigations do."

"Yes, I know," she said. "Once I have people who consult me, you'll hear from me. You can make your inquiry and confirm what the spirits have already told me."

He laughed. "Ah, such faith," he said. "Such confidence."

She snorted. "Have you set up your business yet?"

"Yes, and no one has seen through me. The people who consult me trust that I'm white. So far, I've looked into an unfaithful wife, a runaway son, and a servant suspected of stealing."

"And what did you find?"

He said, "The wife is sneaking away to give her brother money. He broke down after the war and can't work. The son is in Nashville, perfectly fine on his own. The servant quit when she was accused of stealing. She wasn't. Good riddance to her employer!"

She thought of the police news in the papers. "I'm surprised no one has hired you to find their lost cow."

TJ laughed. "If they do, I'll do my best to find her!"

THAT NIGHT, Cassie stretched out in the bed in her room upstairs. She felt tired but satisfied. The back room would suit very well for séances. She yawned and burrowed under the coverlet, enjoying its weight despite the lingering heat in the room.

As she drifted off, she heard a voice. It was so vivid that she sat up and listened, fearing that someone had broken in downstairs. But there was silence from the floor below.

She heard it again. It was a dead man's voice. The voice of the man whose death had driven her from Memphis.

Whether it came from the spirit world or her own laden conscience, she didn't know, and it didn't matter.

I'm not done with you yet.

THE PHOENIX

Lydia Aronson paused on the sidewalk before the school building and breathed a sigh of relief. The building was undisturbed and undamaged, as it had been yesterday evening when she locked the door. Her worry was a habit she couldn't break. Today, a quiet day in May, two years since the massacre, she still remembered watching her school—like every Black school in Memphis—burn to the ground.

The children streamed around her, calling out, "Morning, Mrs. Aronson!" She followed them inside, where the school's porter, Mr. Jasper, greeted them and sent them on their way. During the war, John Jasper had been a master sergeant in the 3rd Artillery, United States Colored Troops, the highest rank a Black soldier could reach. He had the unflappable calm and the effortless authority of a man who advised captains and colonels what to do. He was still a soldier as he guarded their door.

He had five children of his own, and he enjoyed the company of children. He was gentle with the little ones and firm with the older ones, especially the boys. He'd once told her that most of his work as a sergeant was in getting angry and rebellious boys to behave themselves.

She greeted him and he smiled and greeted her in return.

After the massacre, the Black community had strained every nerve for this school, pulling a thousand dollars from their pockets and contributing their labor to construct it. It was modest, but it spoke of their staunch belief in education. In its three classrooms, everything was new—the desks, the slates, and the textbooks. She hadn't asked the Black community to dig any deeper for those. She had shamed the Freedmen's Bureau and the American Missionary Association.

The founders had named the school the Phoenix Institute, fully aware of the meaning. The school's motto, emblazoned on the banner the children carried at the Independence Day picnic, was "Truth shall rise from the ashes."

She put her head into the first classroom, and the woman at the chalkboard turned to smile at her. Sue Ann Kinsley was tall, rangy, and lively. By midmorning, her hair would have escaped from its pins in springy curls, and her plain blue dress would be covered with chalk dust. She'd grown up on a farm in Lorain County, Ohio, a hotbed of abolitionism, and had received her degree from Oberlin College. She had arrived in Memphis in 1864, teaching at the first schoolhouse for Black children outside the contraband camp, as it was called, where the formerly enslaved settled when they left the countryside. In 1866, when the army had advised the Yankee schoolteachers to leave Memphis, she had balked at leaving, and had been escorted, much to her dismay, to the relative safety of Cairo, Illinois.

"Are you ready for the day?" Lydia asked.

Sue grinned. "Onward and upward, as our colleagues at the Lincoln School like to say." The Lincoln School was her former employer, and her best friend still taught there. Lydia had seen close attachments between women before, but Sue Kinsley's home life was none of her business. She was a wonderful teacher who loved the children, as they loved her. Lydia appreciated Sue's presence every day.

Next door, Narcissa Armstrong stood at her desk, making a neat pile of the primers she would hand out when the children tumbled into her classroom.

Narcissa Armstrong, born enslaved in rural Shelby County, had first learned her letters in a secret school on her plantation, and soon began to teach the younger children. When her family escaped to the contraband camp at Fort Pickering, Camp Shiloh, Narcissa was already a skilled teacher. At the Camp Shiloh school, she became the teacher's assistant. Once she graduated from the Lincoln Chapel, the Black secondary school in Memphis, she had been admitted to Fisk in Nashville, the nascent Black college, where she earned her certificate as a teacher.

"Are you ready for whatever the day will bring, Miss Armstrong?" Lydia asked, letting a warm, teasing note enter her voice.

Narcissa, like John Jasper, had an air of unshakable calm. She also had a beautiful, brilliant smile. "We always are."

As a Black resident of Memphis, Narcissa hadn't received an army escort to Cairo, or anywhere else. When the violence was over, she and Lydia had stood together at the site of the school where Lydia taught and Narcissa studied, staring at the ashes. Lydia had allowed herself a rare moment of despair. "How shall we go on?"

Narcissa had turned to her to say, "We'll start over."

Now Lydia walked into the back room that served as her office. Like the rest of the school, her desk and chairs were both modest and new. While she taught alongside the other teachers, her position as principal meant that she spent too much time at this desk. She kept the school's records, compiled the reports that the Freedmen's Bureau, who employed them, insisted on seeing every month, and to her surprise, wrote endless letters to raise money. The city funded Black schools, but their payments were slow and stingy, and the parents' fees were never enough. Every day, she wrote to the national offices of the missionary associations, who employed professional fundraisers. She wrote to the churches in the town where she had taught before she married for the first time, Manlius, New York. On her husband's suggestion, she wrote to the synagogue he had attended in New York City, where he grew up. The Jews of Temple Emanuel-El had been surprisingly generous. They were liberal-minded, but she knew that the influence of Elias's mother, who liked her and didn't give a fig that she wasn't Jewish, also helped.

She blotted her letter to the Temple's Hebrew Ladies' Benevolent Society and looked up at the tap on the door. It was Mr. Jasper. "Ma'am, I hope I'm not interrupting you."

"No, not at all. Do you want to sit down?"

"Thank you, ma'am."

She saw that he held an envelope in his hand. "Did that just come by messenger?"

He said, "No, and that's why I didn't tell you first thing this morning. I found it slipped under the door when I unlocked." He wasn't smiling. "Not by mail and not by messenger. By stealth, in the middle of the night."

He handed it to her, saying, "I didn't open it. It didn't seem right." He'd retained his feelings about the chain of command, too.

She took it from him and slit open the envelope. She pulled out the enclosure.

It read, *You aren't welcome here, you nasty, meddling Yankee bitches. We're watching you! Go back where you came from, or you'll be sorry.*

She sighed and handed it to Jasper, who read it. She was pleased at his literacy; she'd taught him in one of her first classes for adults at Camp Shiloh.

Their eyes met. She said, "As though we'd have no idea who sent it."

"I can hazard a guess, ma'am."

She thought of the Ku Klux Klan, led by General Nathan Bedford Forrest, lately of the Confederate army. The Klan had been alarmingly active in the countryside. There were bad reports from rural Shelby County.

She said, "So can I." She reached out her hand and he returned the paper to her. "I wonder if the other schools have gotten anything like this. I should talk to Miss Kidder at the Lincoln School." She sighed again. "And to Mr. Barnum."

Joseph Barnum, the superintendent for the Black schools of Memphis, had been a teacher all his professional life. He was an Ohio man, a white Oberlin graduate who had been raised in its crucible of abolition. He had not served in the Union army and arrived in Memphis in 1867, sidestepping both the war and the massacre. Under the auspices of the Freedmen's Bureau, he oversaw the Black schools of Memphis. He also sat on the board of trustees of the newly established Fisk College of Nashville, and in addition, he was active in the party of General Grant, which meant that he knew her husband, Elias, also politically active.

Mr. Jasper said, "And the Bureau, too."

She tried to laugh. "As though the agent doesn't have enough to do already." Still holding the paper in her hand, she said, "Miss Armstrong and Miss Kinsley should know," she said. "I'll talk to them after school. You should join us, Mr. Jasper."

After classes ended, her two teachers assembled in Lydia's office, accompanied by Mr. Jasper, and she read the letter to Sue and Narcissa. Sue frowned, and Narcissa's face took on a dark expression.

Sue said, "I understand where they want you and me to go, Mrs. Aronson, but where do they think Narcissa should go back to?"

Narcissa said, "Slavery, I'd guess."

"I hate this," Sue said.

Narcissa looked at Lydia. "Do you think it's the work of the Klan?"

"Probably," Lydia said. She added, "Whoever wrote it was too cowardly to sign a name to it."

This reassured no one.

Sue asked, "What should we do?" She looked at Mr. Jasper.

Lydia said, "Mr. Jasper, Sergeant Jasper, tell us. Should we be worried?"

"It never helps to worry, ma'am. But we should be alert."

After they left, Lydia sat alone in her office. She remembered the days of 1863, when she had helped Elias Aronson, then aide-de-camp to the commander of Fort Pickering, investigate the murder of a Union officer. She had been in danger then, and alert for it all the time. When the investigation ended, she began to carry a pistol.

She reached for her reticule and drew out the gun, a derringer with a mother-of-pearl handle. A ladies' gun, small enough to fit easily into a reticule or, in a practical dress, in a pocket. It had been a gift from Elias during the investigation. She curled her fingers around the handle and rested her finger on the trigger.

It was a pretty little thing, as ornamental as a bracelet, but it was lethal at close range. As she well knew.

She shook her head and put the gun away.

THE ARONSONS LIVED in the house of a pre-war planter who had also been a lawyer. The locals still called it by the name of the previous owner, who had retreated to his plantation after the war. Lydia, an abolitionist from upstate New York who had grown up on a farm, felt every day the irony that she and her husband, also a New Yorker and a Union man during the conflict, now lived in the house of a ruined Reb.

Elias was already home, seated in his favorite chair in the parlor, his cravat off and his collar loosened. He had a glass of claret at his elbow.

As she took off her bonnet, she teased him. "Drinking alone? You couldn't wait for me?"

He rose and swept her into his arms, kissing her with an ardor not often seen in the front parlor. He smelled of eau de cologne and the faint tang of sweat, and his lips tasted of the wine he'd sipped.

She stepped back to smile at him. The past five years had left their mark on him. His eyes showed the faintest sign of crow's-feet, and his hair was slightly threaded with gray now. But his smile was as welcoming as ever. When they first met, she'd been a widow for less than a year, and once she fell in love with him, she had the audacity to speak as no maiden could. She told him her only regret about her marriage was that she and her husband had spent too little time in each other's arms. "I don't want to make that mistake with you," she'd said, and she hadn't.

Still holding her, he said, "You look tired, my love. And a little worried, too."

"Ah, it will keep. You look pleased. Do you have good news? It will cheer me up."

He guided her to the settee, poured her a glass of wine, and settled back into his chair. He raised his own glass. "Progress," he said.

"A case?" Elias had been a lawyer before the war, and once the war ended, he mustered out and returned to the practice of law. His bread and butter was the legal business of the Northerners who had flocked to Memphis, but he dedicated some of his time to defending the interests of Black people who had no money for a lawyer.

He took a sip of the claret and set the glass down. "Yes, and I think there's a chance it will go to court. A Black man came to see us. He'd been shot by the police and wounded in the shoulder, badly enough that he was laid up for three months. He told us he was angry enough to accuse the policeman who shot him."

She said, "That's a fool's errand."

"Oh, I know. I told him so. But James had an idea that was a stroke of genius. He recommended that the man file a civil suit for damages. His lost wages. I looked at James and said, 'That's something we can get into court.' We'll file as soon as we look into it."

James Dorsey was Elias's colleague, a Black man born free in Virginia before the war. He was also an Oberlin graduate —their acquaintance in Memphis was full of them—and he'd been a law clerk in Washington, DC, moving to Memphis in 1866. He was very light of skin, and he wore a long, jaunty, upturned mustache instead of a beard. While they couldn't be business partners, they often collaborated on cases involving civil rights.

Lydia lifted her glass. "Progress indeed," she said.

"If we win it," Elias said, a little ruefully. "But tell me what has gotten you upset. And don't deny it."

He knew her too well. She sighed and took the letter from her pocket. "This came to the school last night."

He read it and frowned. "Have the other schools received anything similar?"

"I don't know yet. I'll inquire tomorrow."

He shook his head.

She said, "Of course it's the work of the Klan. If not someone who wears a white hood, someone who agrees with those who do."

"What does Mr. Jasper think?"

"Oh, he was in full master sergeant form today. He told us not to worry but to keep our wits about us."

He sighed. "I won't lie to you about the possibility of danger," he said.

"You couldn't. Not after what we saw two years ago."

"Whatever the Klan is doing in the countryside—"

She shivered.

He took her hand. "They don't dare try the same thing in Memphis."

She looked away. She was remembering the massacre, and he knew it.

"Not in a city full of Black Union veterans, all armed. Not in a city where the army still has a strong presence. Not under the eye of Governor Brownlow, who has no love for the unreconstructed Rebs. My love, I believe that with all my heart. It isn't just to reassure you."

She looked up, not reassured. "I worry about you, too," she said. "Every time you attend a political meeting. Even though you go there with a phalanx of men like Sergeant Jasper. The Klan is underground in town. But the streets are full of angry Rebs who walk around armed, too, and do reckless things when they drink."

He said, "We should both follow Sergeant Jasper's advice. Not to worry, but to keep our wits about us. I would feel easier if you took a carriage to and from the school, just for a while. Would you mind?"

"No, that's only prudent." She sighed. "And I trust you'll take care when you attend the next ward meeting?"

He nodded.

She said, "Elias, do you ever feel weary of the burden? Not just this particular trouble. But the whole burden of making sure the war stays won in the South."

"Because it isn't won. Not yet."

She sighed. "Sometimes I wonder why we stay to keep fighting."

The sun had almost set, and the room had darkened. In shadow, Elias's face betrayed that he was weary, too. "My father used to tell me that God made burdens, but God also made shoulders."

"What if your shoulders are tired?"

He put his hands there. His touch was warm and sweet. "Then you must let me help you," he said, his eyes bright.

She knew that gleam. It was desire, and she had never been able to resist it. She covered his hands with her own. "Yes," she said, rising. He came with her, and she smiled as he led her up the stairs to their bedroom.

THE NEXT MORNING, Lydia wrote to Miss Kidder, principal of the Lincoln Chapel School, about the note she'd received. She was slipping her letter into an envelope when Mr. Jasper tapped on her open door. "There's a lady here to see you," he said.

"Did she give her name?"

"Said it wouldn't mean anything to you. She's a lady of color. Has her two boys with her. Says she wants to enroll them in the school. I'm inclined to trust her."

"Are the boys old enough to look after themselves?"

"Yes, they are. I'll settle them in the hallway and show her in."

Lydia hoped that her visitor would be able to pay the boys' fees. She rose, getting ready to take her visitor's hand, as the woman walked into her office.

The visitor had the air of money and taste, which Lydia had seen in her mother-in-law, a wealthy Manhattan matron. The visitor's dress was dark blue silk, but it was far from plain. Her bearing was composed and self-possessed, like the Black orators and politicians of Memphis; Lydia wondered if she had been a lecturer or had spent time on the stage. Under her fashionable bonnet, her face gave the impression of striking beauty: smooth skin, high cheekbones, beautifully shaped lips.

One thing about her hadn't changed. Her luminous eyes were the same as they'd been five years ago, when she'd been the key witness in the murder of a Union officer and the primary suspect in the death of a Rebel planter.

Lydia had never expected to see her again. Stunned, she sat down. "Cassie Andrews," she said.

Cassie was better at containing her shock. "Lydia Owens," she replied. "So you're the one who married Lieutenant Aronson."

"Yes, I did," Lydia said. She took a deep breath, stood, and extended her hand.

Cassie touched Lydia's fingers with her own, encased in a very fine kid glove. "I'm Mrs. Auburn now," she said.

Lydia gestured to a chair and they both sat. There was a moment of silence. Lydia asked, "What brings you back to Memphis?" As though they had met at a church picnic.

"My family," she said. "My aunt and uncle needed my help, and so did my boys."

"Will you be here for a while?"

"I may," she said.

"And you want to enroll your sons in school."

She nodded. "They used to attend the Lincoln Chapel, but the elder had to leave to go to work for a while, and the younger—well, he's a handful."

From the hallway came the sound of Mr. Jasper's deep voice and of boyish laughter. Lydia said, "We'd welcome them, but why didn't you take them back to the Lincoln School?"

Cassie smiled. "Where better to make a fresh start than the Phoenix?" she said.

Lydia anticipated Elias's response if she told him that Cassie Andrews was back in Memphis. That was no fresh start. That was an old entanglement that he hoped to be free of for good.

THE OTHER SHORE

CASSIE SURVEYED HER FRONT ROOM WITH SATISFACTION. SHE'D arranged it as a parlor rather than as a shop. Near the entrance, she'd placed comfortable chairs to wait in, and farther back, where the counter had been, stood a table where she could transact business, so to speak. She always made it plain that she didn't take money for her services, even though she graciously accepted gifts.

The exterior didn't advertise her services. She didn't need to. She had Mahaley Smith for that.

The door opened—she had removed the little bell that jangled—and she smiled at the woman who came in tentatively, as though she couldn't believe she was actually here. Her black dress was faded at the seams, and her bonnet was trimmed with a worn black ribbon. Her face was lined with the marks of prolonged grief.

"Welcome," Cassie said. "Would you like to sit down?" She gestured toward one of the chairs.

The woman sat on the edge of the chair.

"I know this is difficult for you, coming here," Cassie said. "But I hope that you feel you can take your ease."

She didn't relax as much as crumple. She reached into her pocket for a handkerchief and held it tightly in her hand, as though she knew she'd need it and hated the thought.

Cassie sat in the chair opposite. Very softly, she said, "My name is Mrs. Auburn." She didn't want to prompt Mrs. Amstrong's memory of Cassie Andrews. She used the name she'd taken in New York. "Who am I addressing?"

"Armstrong," she said, in a small voice. "Mrs. Armstrong."

"Welcome, Mrs. Armstrong. How can I help you?"

She looked up. Her eyes were red-rimmed. She whispered, "Miss Mahaley said you can talk to the dead. Is that true?"

"The spirits have come to me, yes."

Mrs. Armstrong raised her handkerchief to her eyes and held it there for a long moment before she returned it, now crushed in her fist, to her lap.

Cassie said, in a soft, caressing voice, "Mrs. Armstrong, tell me about your loss."

She struggled to get the words out. "My son." She looked up. "My eldest boy."

"Did he die in the war?"

"No," she said, unable to raise her voice. "He died in the massacre."

Cassie reached for the woman's hand. Her skin was dry, as though grief had sucked the life from her, too. "Tell me all about him," she said.

LATER THAT DAY, she summoned TJ. They sat in the back parlor, which was suitably dim and eerie for a séance, the windows swathed in purple velvet curtains, the floor softened by a thick carpet. The oval table, also covered in velvet, seated six, and the chairs that surrounded it were uphol-stered in velvet and easy to sink into. By candlelight, the room looked and felt opulent, a quality that reassured her sad and worried clientele.

TJ said, "I won't smoke in here, much as I'd like to." He gave her hand a squeeze. "I don't know how the spirits feel about it, but I know you hate it."

Cassie snorted.

TJ removed a little notebook and a pencil stub from his inner coat pocket.

She said, "Don't you trust the spirits to come to me?"

"I trust in you absolutely. But it doesn't hurt to give the spirits a little encouragement."

She said, "And I thought you were a spiritualist yourself."

"I have been," he said. "And I might be again, if this earthly inquiry doesn't do well." He poised the pencil over the page. "Tell me what you know."

He listened and scribbled, and when she was done, he said, "I think I have enough to go on." He looked up at her. "Did you meet the daughter? The one who teaches at the Phoenix School?"

"How did you know that?"

"Miss Armstrong is well-known in Memphis," TJ said.

"And you already found that out."

He smiled. "Yes, I did."

"Mrs. Armstrong came alone."

"Meet the daughter before you invite them for a séance," he said. "Let me know what she has to say."

THE NEXT DAY, late in the afternoon, a young woman of color opened Cassie's door. The visitor was tall and slender. Her dress was dark blue, with a narrow, practical skirt. She wore her hair in a neat bun, without a fringe or a curl to be seen. She met Cassie's eyes in a forthright gaze and held out her hand. "Miss Armstrong," she said, in a low, resonant voice that could carry to the back of a room. "Miss Narcissa Armstrong. I believe you've met my mother."

"Miss Armstrong, it's a pleasure to meet you," Cassie said. "Would you like to sit down?"

She sat in a smooth motion, her back straight, genteel and resolute at the same time.

Cassie said, "How may I help you, Miss Armstrong?"

"I'm concerned about my mother," she said. "She's still grief-stricken about my brother's death. Nothing has helped her, and I'm afraid that she's grasping at straws in meeting with you."

"I can see how she's suffered," Cassie said, her voice sympathetic. "But I hope I can offer some assistance."

Miss Armstrong said, "I would hate to see anyone take advantage of her."

"Is that what you think of me, Miss Armstrong? Is that what you think a spiritualist might do?"

"I don't know, since I've never met one."

"Are you a believer, Miss Armstrong?"

"I'm a churchgoer, yes. And I believe, against all proof, that people can act for good as well as evil."

"You must know that the dead linger."

She blinked. "I loved my brother very much," she said. "I love him still. I miss him every day. Yes, I know how the dead linger."

"Would you like to tell him so? Once again?"

She lifted her eyes to the ceiling and back down again. "I think he knows," she said.

"Come to the séance," Cassie said.

"I don't believe in such things," Miss Armstrong said.

"Bring your disbelief. See for yourself." Cassie had long since learned how to disarm a skeptic.

Miss Armstrong blinked again, as though the soft light in the room was suddenly too bright. "Is it true that you don't charge for your services?"

Cassie met Miss Armstrong's eyes, one forthright woman to another. "Yes," Cassie said. "That is absolutely true."

"Then I won't argue with you. Or keep my mother away from you."

"You'll come to the séance?"

"Yes. To satisfy my curiosity, if nothing else."

TWO DAYS LATER, at seven in the evening, Cassie ushered the Armstrongs, mother and daughter, into her back parlor. She had made careful preparations in this room. The velvet curtains, drawn against the lingering sun, had been brushed. The table was freshly laid with a white linen cloth, its only ornament two lit candles in silver sticks. The windows had been closed to muffle the sound of the street, and the room smelled of lavender and very faintly of sage.

TJ stood next to the table, his face ghostly in the low light. She said to both women, "This is Mr. Randolph, who assists me. He is an accomplished spiritualist himself."

Mrs. Armstrong murmured, "How do," and Miss Armstrong, her face firmly skeptical, nodded in greeting.

Cassie seated them at the table across from one another. She took a seat between them, and TJ took the empty chair.

Cassie said, "Are you comfortable?"

Miss Armstrong said, "Does it matter?"

"The spirits come more readily if you are easy and calm in your mind and your body."

Mrs. Armstrong said, "This chair is very comfortable." She leaned back a little and let out a tiny sigh.

"Join hands with me," Cassie said. "As in church."

Mrs. Armstrong's hand crept toward hers, and Miss Armstrong grasped the other with vigor, as though she were being introduced at a school board meeting.

"Let us pray together," Cassie said, and she began to recite, in a low, sonorous voice, the prayer she had learned from a New Orleans spiritualist who called on the Catholic saints as well as the spirits.

"Eternal Father, bring us together to find the truth, and light our souls with love and charity. Let the spirits of peace and light guide us and drive away the darkness. Let the light of the spirits open our minds and console our hearts. Let them show us the brilliant path that leads to the eternal home on the other shore, where we will be received with glory."

"Amen," Mrs. Armstrong murmured.

TJ snuffed the candles, and the air stirred slightly, like the faintest breath from a spirit.

Cassie said, "Titus Armstrong, your mother and your sister are here, with me, and they are eager to speak to you. Will you come to us?"

She felt the young man's spirit fill her. She felt the contours of his body inside hers, the broad shoulders, the muscular arms and legs, the big, powerful hands. She felt his mind inhabit her own, full of pride and hope and eagerness. Then his voice came to her, a deeper version of Miss Armstrong's resonant tones, in the Shelby County accent that Cassie herself had heard, in fact had spoken in, until she left Memphis five years before. "I'm right here."

Mrs. Armstrong started. "Titus? Is that really you?"

"Mama! Of course it's me! It's so good to hear your voice!"

"I've missed you so," Mrs. Armstrong said, her voice thick, and if she hadn't been holding Cassie's hand in a tight grip, she would have put it to her face to catch the tears.

"I've missed you too, Mama."

Miss Armstrong spoke. She sounded surprised. "Titus?"

"Oh, Cissy! Are you here, too?"

Miss Armstrong started at the nickname. "How do you know to call me that?"

"Oh, Cissy, I've missed you so much, too."

Miss Armstrong was unable to reply.

Mrs. Armstrong's voice recovered a little. "How are you, Titus? Where are you?"

"I can't say where I am, Mama. But I'm all right. I'm not in pain. I'm not in trouble."

"Is it like they say? Heaven? A beautiful place, where you wear a starry crown?"

Titus laughed in Cassie's throat. "No, Mama, it's not like that. But it's good. Believe me."

Miss Armstrong loosened her grasp on Cassie's hand. "Titus, do you know what happened to you?"

"Oh, Cissy, don't ask. It's nothing I want to remember."

"But you do remember."

"It's so bad."

Miss Armstrong whispered, "I want to know."

Titus's voice softened and became a plea. "Are you sure?"

"Yes. I won't be at peace unless I know."

Titus said, "I'm not at peace, either."

"Then tell me. Tell us. What happened to you?"

"I remember being in a crowd on Main Street. I

remember the sound of screaming and gunfire." The voice faltered. "Oh, Cissy, it's so hard to remember—"

Narcissa's voice was hard. "Tell us."

"I remember being shot. And that I fell. And that's all."

"Nothing more?"

Titus began to moan, a terrible sound, like a man mortally wounded.

Cassie felt him slip away. She tried to summon her personal voice, Cassie's voice, to reassure the living Armstrongs.

What happened next had never happened before.

The voice of the spirit that spoke to her, that guided her, that had never arisen in a séance before, now rushed through her and demanded to be heard. She had never heard that voice speak aloud, much less in anger, but now her spirit's voice thundered in the room.

The familiar voice, made so strange with anger, cried out, "Your ancestors knew me, but you have forgotten me. In Africa, I was the goddess of truth. I divined the truth. My words were oaths and those who swore oaths called on me. I swear I know the truth, and I will tell it."

Mrs. Armstrong gasped.

The voice was as resonant as a preacher's. "I have come back, and you will know me again. I am the goddess of justice. I am the goddess of punishment. I reserve my harshest punishment for those who take lives."

Mrs. Armstrong's voice was so soft that Cassie could barely hear her. "My son—"

"Your son's blood calls to me from the spot where he died. His blood calls for justice! His blood calls for vengeance!"

Miss Armstrong let go of Cassie's hand and put her hand

to her stomach as though she'd taken a blow there. Mrs. Armstrong screamed and sobbed uncontrollably.

Cassie struggled to speak in her own voice. "We have heard you," she said.

"Heed me!"

"We will heed you," Cassie said. "We promise."

"Keep that promise!"

Cassie summoned every scrap of strength to say, "We will."

And the African goddess melted away, as though she'd never been there.

Afterward, a gray-faced Narcissa said to Cassie, "That was quite a performance."

Cassie, who was shaken as she'd never been shaken before, said, "It wasn't a performance."

After they left, Cassie let TJ lead her into the front room, where she collapsed onto the sofa. He didn't bother to bring her a glass of water. He found her a glass of whiskey.

Her head aching, her limbs sore, she took a gulp and asked the voice aloud, "What was that?"

TJ stroked her forehead.

But the voice was silent.

THE EYEWITNESSES

NARCISSA KNOCKED ON LYDIA'S OFFICE DOOR. HER FACE HAD the grayish tone of too much emotion, and there were dark circles of fatigue under her eyes.

Lydia said, "Come in and sit down. And close the door behind you."

Narcissa sat as though her back ached.

"What's the matter, Narcissa?" This was no moment for the politeness of "Miss Armstrong." Narcissa looked as though she needed kindness.

Narcissa's voice was hoarse. "We visited the spiritualist yesterday."

"I'd guess it didn't go well."

She raised her eyes to Lydia's. "Mama is in a state. Hysterical. I tried to get her to take some laudanum. She wouldn't. She's still bedridden, shaking and sobbing."

"What happened?"

Narcissa said, "The spiritualist wanted to call up Titus. Well, she did. Whoever was talking, it sounded just like him. It was as though he was in the room with us."

"What did this voice say?"

"It called me 'Cissy,'" she said. "That was always my brother's nickname for me."

Lydia made her voice gentle. "Narcissa, don't you think it might have been a lucky guess?"

"It was uncanny."

"What else did you hear? What upset you so much?"

Narcissa said, "Well, it wasn't enough to bring Titus back from the dead. We all heard another voice. That was even more uncanny."

"Whose voice?"

"It called itself the African goddess of truth and justice." She shook her head. "And it called for vengeance."

Lydia thought, *Why prey on the grieving like that?* She reached out. "Give me your hand, Narcissa."

Narcissa obliged, and Lydia clasped Narcissa's hand. "My dear friend, who do you think was speaking?" Lydia asked.

Narcissa said, "I don't really know. Well, if I weren't so upset, I would admit I do."

"The spiritualist," Lydia said softly.

Narcissa shook her head. "But why? Why would a spiritualist want vengeance for a stranger who lost his life in the massacre?"

"I wonder who she is," Lydia said. "If she ever lived in Memphis, or if she's related to someone who does."

"If she wants justice, that's a mighty roundabout way of getting it."

"What about you?" Lydia laid her hand on Narcissa's arm. "What do you want?"

"In a better world than this, I'd want justice for Titus, too. But we don't live in that world."

"Have you thought of trying to make a case? Trying to see if the matter could go to court?"

Narcissa's eyes rested on Lydia's face. "Your husband is a

lawyer. I'd think you'd know, better than anyone, that justice for a Black man who died in the massacre is a dream," she said.

Lydia met Narcissa's gaze. "No one has tried," she said.

"Because we despaired of it," Narcissa.

"What if someone did?"

Narcissa was silent.

"What if you did?"

Narcissa shook her head.

Lydia said, "My husband is fond of saying that he likes to fight battles he can win. But I've seen him fight for the right thing, even when he knows it's hopeless."

Narcissa hesitated. "In my mind, I struggle," she said. "I think of what's right, and I think of what's possible. I worry that I don't have the strength to try. But when the spiritualist spoke—when the African goddess spoke through her—"

Lydia waited.

"The thought of vengeance was sweet, for a moment. But that's not what Titus's memory cries for." She looked up at Lydia, and she had the grim face of unresolved grief. "He would want justice. He would want to fight for it."

"As you do."

"Yes." Suddenly Narcissa's eyes were clear. "For that, we don't need to go back to the spiritualist," she said. "We need to go to a lawyer. Would your husband help us?"

"I'm sure of it."

THAT NIGHT, when Lydia asked Elias for help, he sighed. "It's going to be difficult."

She twined her fingers in his. "She knows that."

"By all means, tell her I'll talk to her. And I'll ask James Dorsey to join us."

Narcissa came to Elias's law office, situated in a modest brick building on Main Street, built since the war. Inside, the place was comfortable rather than luxurious. The Yankees who consulted him didn't care for show, and the furnishings reassured Black people that he cared more about justice than money.

Narcissa knew James Dorsey, and she asked after his wife, as they were fellow church members and persons of consequence in the Black community. Dorsey said, "It's a pleasure to see you, Miss Armstrong."

She nodded. "It may not be such a pleasure after I speak my piece today."

Elias said, "We're both prepared for that. Before we start, would you like any refreshment?"

Narcissa shook her head. "No, I want to get to the business at hand."

"Please do."

"How much do you know?"

"A bit, but I haven't told Mr. Dorsey much. Fill us in."

She drew in her breath. "It's about my brother, Titus Armstrong, who lost his life in the massacre," she said. "We've always known he was murdered, but we never pursued the matter, since the police were so indifferent to investigation afterwards."

Dorsey said, "That's a polite way to put it."

"We've always thought that he was murdered by a policeman."

"It's been two years," Elias said. "Why now?"

She looked a little abashed. "Did Mrs. Aronson tell you about the spiritualist?"

"Yes, but Mr. Dorsey hasn't heard the story."

"My mother insisted on visiting a spiritualist, and I went with her."

Dorsey asked, "Who is this spiritualist?"

"Her name is Mrs. Auburn. A Black woman, recently moved to Memphis."

Dorsey nodded.

"She promised to help us talk to Titus. She told us she'd summon him."

Dorsey nodded again.

"Well, we heard a voice. I don't know who was talking, but it rattled both of us, because it sounded so much like Titus. As though he'd taken possession of her and he was using her to talk to us. I know spiritualists say they do that, but I'd never seen it happen before. And I have to tell you, it was eerie."

"What did she say?" Elias prompted her.

"She didn't tell us anything we didn't know. It was so vague I have trouble remembering what she actually said, but she certainly stirred us up. My mother was so upset that it made her ill, but I was angry. The more I thought about Titus's death, the angrier I felt." She looked at Dorsey, then at Elias. "Angry on my family's behalf, because we miss him so much. But angry on behalf of all of us, the community that never had justice for anyone murdered in the massacre." She took a deep breath. "That's why I want to know who murdered Titus," she said. "Whoever it was, I want him arrested. I want him charged. I want him tried. I want him punished. For myself. For my mother. And for all of us."

Elias exchanged a look with Dorsey. He steepled his fingers together. "There are a number of obstacles you should know about, Miss Armstrong," he said.

"I'm no stranger to obstacles, as you well know," Narcissa said.

"Even if this were the most straightforward kind of legal complaint, there's the fact it happened two years ago. Witnesses may be hard to find. Those we can find may have hazy memories of what happened. That's one obstacle, and it's the lesser difficulty."

"And the greater one?"

Elias sighed. "It's very difficult for a Black plaintiff to bring a criminal case to court at all," he said. "And the likelihood of a fair hearing, of a fair trial, is very low."

Narcissa leaned forward. "I've heard that all my life," she said. "Freedom? An impossibility. Education? Too difficult to attain. Fair treatment? An uphill battle. Isn't it time to insist? To fight?"

Elias said, "We lawyers like to pick the fights we can win."

She said, "Mr. Aronson, your wife has assured me that you feel some battles are worth fighting, whether we win or not." She gazed at Dorsey. "Isn't that so, Mr. Dorsey?"

Dorsey said, "I would be overjoyed if you could have a fair day in court. I would be overjoyed if you could win such a case. I would be overjoyed if you could see justice done." He sighed. "As much as I long for it, I'd be fooling you to say it's likely."

Elias said, "I'd be remiss if I didn't warn you that there are dangers as well as obstacles."

"Yes, I know." She lifted her chin. "To myself. To my family. To the school. To all of us. I know."

Elias said, "We would do what we can to protect you."

Narcissa was momentarily silent. Then she nodded. "If you decided to represent me, where would you start?"

Elias said, "Typically, a criminal case begins with an arrest by the police, and an investigation into the circumstances of the crime. Since they won't do that, we should start with an investigation of our own."

She nodded again.

Elias said, "We'd look for likely witnesses. People who were at the scene. People who knew your brother well."

"I wasn't there, so I can't tell you what happened. He was at the fort, but he'd come into town, because he was so worried about us. Mother and I were at home, doing our best to stay safe." She closed her eyes, momentarily overcome by her memories. She straightened herself in her chair, opened her eyes, and said, "We know where he was shot, because we retrieved his body when it was over." She said grimly, "We were lucky to find his body to bury it."

Elias spoke very gently. "Miss Armstrong, I know this is difficult for you."

"It's dreadful, but I feel obliged," she said.

"Would you like us to call on you? To allow your mother to be there, as well?"

"My mother can't even bear to admit he's dead," she said.

Elias looked away.

She said, "There are people who lived on the block where he died—people who may have seen it—" She knotted her hands in her lap. "Witnesses. I can consult my memory. And ask others who might remember."

"And his friends?" Elias asked. "Do any of them remain in town?"

She said, "He was close to the men of his company in the 3rd Artillery. I don't know what happened to all of them. But I may know someone who does."

"That will help," Elias said.

Dorsey nodded in agreement.

She reached for her reticule. "Do you need any money from me?"

"Have you heard the expression *pro bono*?"

"Yes, since I studied Latin at college. For good."

"Short for *pro bono publico*. For the common good. Lawyers routinely argue cases like yours, and for that, we don't charge a fee."

"You'll do this as a favor? That seems wrong."

"I do it as a matter of justice. As I fought in the war. I don't charge for cases like that."

She inclined her head, and despite her composure, her face was drawn and shadowed. She took a deep breath and straightened herself in the chair. "Let me make some inquiries for you," she said. She rose. "As soon as I have something for you, I'll let you know."

After she left, Elias said, "I feel wrong asking her to make the inquiries. I wish we could find an inquiry agent that members of the Black community would talk to."

Dorsey hesitated.

"What is it, James? You don't need to keep it from me."

"It's never easy to make an inquiry. But I'd think these people know you well enough by now, and trust you well enough, to talk to you."

"How did you put it for Miss Armstrong? That you would be overjoyed if we lived in a different world from the one we find ourselves in?"

Dorsey shook his head.

"Battles we can win, James."

Dorsey said, "I was approached last week by an inquiry agent who's new in town and trying to drum up business by calling on lawyers. He told me he'd been a scout in Georgia, in advance of Sherman's march."

Elias said, "I'm not sure that recommends him, since we're hardly planning to set fire to Memphis."

"There was something about him that struck me. He might be useful to you, if you have other criminal cases."

Elias said, "I hope not. I hope for the tedium of civil suit after civil suit."

"Would you agree to meet him?"

"Meet him, yes. Employ him, probably not."

WHEN ELIAS TOLD Lydia that he was meeting an inquiry agent at James Dorsey's request, she actually laughed. "God help him," she said. "Does James think that he'll have any better luck talking to the tight-lipped Black people of Memphis than we did?"

"Your luck was always better than mine."

"No luck involved. I wasn't wearing a blue army coat." She was still laughing. "I wish I could be there when you meet him."

"Don't worry, I'll fill you in."

MR. RANDOLPH, the inquiry agent, was tall and lean, with a melancholy face made fairer in appearance by dark hair and darker eyes. Those eyes were marked by crow's-feet and their gaze was as keen in a lawyer's office as it had been when he was a scout. His voice was low and pleasant, as if he'd gotten some experience in elocution, and his speech was an educated man's. He wore an ordinary black frock coat and a black cravat. Elias wondered if it was a disguise meant to reassure lawyers, or his natural dress.

When Elias asked about his experience as an agent, he explained that he'd begun his career in New York City as a photographer, and had accompanied an Ohio regiment in the war, selling the photographs to newspapers back in Ohio.

The regiment's commander, appreciating his powers of observation, had asked him if he'd like to muster in as a scout. He'd been with General Sherman in Georgia on the March to the Sea.

When the war ended, he'd decided to use his powers of observation as an inquiry agent.

"What brought you to Memphis?" Elias asked.

He smiled. "It seems to be a place where many things go missing," he said. "A good place for an inquiry agent to do business."

Elias nodded. "Did my esteemed colleague, Mr. Dorsey, explain that I work on civil cases? Business contracts, primarily? I rarely have a need to look for missing persons, or missing information, as is common in criminal cases."

His eyes gleamed. "Information is always useful," he said. "Even in the most sedate of civil matters."

"Mr. Randolph has a nose for information," James said.

Randolph laughed. His teeth were white, and his canines were sharp. "Thank you for saying so, Mr. Dorsey."

"That's very interesting," Elias said. He was thinking, *He's selling, but I have no reason to buy.*

Randolph looked at Elias. "Mr. Aronson, you're a native of New York City yourself, are you not?"

"Yes, that's true," Elias said. "It's no secret."

"And an Israelite?"

"That's no secret, either."

Randolph's eyes gleamed again. "Mr. Aronson, I understand that you achieved the Jewish passage to manhood, the bar mitzvah rite, at Temple Emanuel-El in New York?"

Elias looked at him in surprise. "Again, no secret, but not generally known."

James laughed. "You won't believe what he learned about me," he said.

"That you're really an Israelite?"

"That I organized a baseball team at Oberlin College," James said, smiling. "And played on it, to some acclaim."

Elias said, "Mr. Randolph, these revelations put me in mind of a parlor trick. Clever and amusing, if not serious. I don't care that someone knows I attended Emanuel-El as a boy, even though I'm a little perturbed that anyone would try to scout that out. I'm afraid I don't have anything more serious for you."

Randolph said, "But you're looking into a murder, are you not? One with a very cold trail, from the disturbance here two years ago."

Elias thought, *It's common gossip in every Black church in town. But how did he hear?* "James, did you tell him?"

"Of course not."

"Mr. Randolph, that isn't common knowledge. And it is a secret. How did you know?"

He smiled.

James said, "Mr. Randolph, would you mind waiting in the anteroom for a moment? I'd like to talk to my colleague in private."

"Certainly," Randolph said, and removed himself there.

James shut the office door.

"Why all the secrecy on your part?" Elias asked.

James lowered his voice. "He has African ancestry and he's passing for white."

Elias asked, "How do you know?"

The fair-skinned Mr. Dorsey met Elias's eyes. "Believe me, I know."

Elias said, "We know the people here," he said. "We know the circumstances. We know exactly how to tread carefully. This man worries me." He looked at Dorsey. "What do we know about him, aside from what he's so carefully told us?"

Dorsey said, "Maybe we should make an inquiry."

Elias felt annoyed with Dorsey. "Don't you go to church every Sunday? And doesn't your wife call on her friends every Tuesday afternoon? That's our line of inquiry."

LYDIA WAS glad of her spacious parlor as she and Elias seated Narcissa and welcomed the three witnesses Narcissa had found. The Montgomerys, husband and wife, were Narcissa's age, but they were marked by toil and care, and looked much older. Narcissa had also invited Mrs. Harding, a widow in her fifties, slight and bright-eyed, whose dark dress was slightly dusted with flour. She excused herself as she sat. "I have a bakery and I always have flour on me somewhere. No matter how hard I try to brush it off."

Elias, having gotten the names beforehand, had checked the report from the extensive Congressional hearing held in Memphis in August of 1866, at which a surprising number of Black Memphians had testified to the violence that had left almost fifty people dead.

Lydia had chided him for it.

"No, it's only in the spirit of inquiry," he said. "If they testified, their memories were fresher then."

"Trust them to tell you what they remember," she said, "and trust yourself to know what to make of it."

But Narcissa's witnesses had not spoken to the committee; there was no record of their names in the report.

Lydia served refreshments, which no one took. Elias thanked them for coming here. "I know that none of this is pleasant for you to remember."

Mrs. Harding said, "It ain't, but I'd do just about anything for Miss Narcissa. My grandchildren go to her school."

Elias said, "I understand you lived on South Street two years ago."

"Yes," she said. "I ran a business. Baked bread and pies and sold them. Started in the last year of the war and I was doing all right."

Elias nodded and asked the Montgomerys about themselves. Mrs. Montgomery said, "We came to Memphis when the Yankees captured the town. I stayed at Camp Shiloh and my husband mustered into the army."

Mr. Montgomery said, "Joined the 5th Heavy Artillery." That had been a sister regiment to the 3rd.

Elias asked, "Do you remember Colonel Horvath?"

"I do. He did what he could for us." Mr. Montgomery shook his head, as though Colonel Horvath could never have done enough. "I mustered out in 1865, just after the war ended, and we moved into town. When it happened, we were living on South Street."

"What do you remember?"

Mr. Montgomery said, "The night before it happened, we heard gunshots. Wasn't unusual. People who'd been drinking fired their guns into the air. Heard more of it just before people mustered out."

"That was April 30, wasn't it?" Elias asked.

Mr. Montgomery nodded. Mrs. Montgomery said, "And then we heard about the dustup. The first one." She added, "On May 1. That wasn't unusual, either. The police hated the sight of a Union coat. Beat up soldiers for no reason." But she pulled into herself as though she felt cold, even though the room was full of the warmth of a spring afternoon.

Mrs. Harding's face was set into tight lines.

"Mrs. Harding?" Elias asked. "What do you recall?"

"I recall how it got worse. The police came. Supposed to

carry clubs, that was bad enough, but they all had pistols. Some of them never bothered to hide them." She took a deep breath, as though bracing herself. "Irishmen, all of them. Dear Lord, they hated us. Wished we were all dead." She stared at Elias with hard eyes. "Oh, they got their chance. They fired at anyone wearing a blue coat. Nearly killed a little boy who happened to be wearing a blue jacket." She sat up as though her back hurt. "Went up to innocent men, minding their own business, and beat them until they fell down. Then they shot them. Shot men who were running away. Shot them in the back."

Mrs. Montgomery looked as though she wanted to sob. She said, her voice very low, "I saw a woman in the street, cradling her husband in her lap. His face shot to pieces. Her dress all over blood. He was hurt so bad she thought he was dying. Couldn't find anyone to move him to get him help. She had to leave him there because she was afraid they'd shoot her too. He died in the gutter that night."

Mrs. Harding said, "Police broke into a house down the street and raped a woman there. Pregnant woman! Raped her over and over. She was never all right after that." She continued, "There were policemen everywhere, shooting people. Women and men. People running away, trying to get safe. People shot. Oh, they went after those blue coats. And what they said! That they wanted to kill us all."

Lydia tried not to dwell on her own memories of the massacre. Elias, who knew what had happened and how she still felt about it, shot her a sympathetic look. *Courage.* She nodded.

Mr. Montgomery said, "Weren't you in town then, Mr. Aronson? You and your wife? You must have some bad things to recall yourself."

Elias looked at Narcissa, whose skin was taking on the

grayish tinge of distress. "This isn't about us. Please, may I ask you a few questions about Titus Armstrong?"

All three of them nodded.

"Did you know Titus Armstrong by sight?"

Mrs. Harding said, "Yes, I knew him. He bought pies from me when he came into town."

"Mrs. Harding, did you see him that night?"

"Yes, I did. I was standing in my shop, looking out the window, as long as I dared to. I saw him running down the street."

"Was he alone?"

"He was with some other soldiers. Wearing blue coats. I didn't know who they were."

"Did you see who was pursuing them?"

"Policemen, all of them. In their uniforms. Carrying pistols."

"And did you recognize any of them?"

She nodded. "They walked our beat. South Street." She added, "The worst of them was a man named Dailey. Hated us well before May 1st. Beat people for no reason. Standing on the street, peaceable as could be, and he'd beat them. Shot a man once. Killed him. Never punished. Said it was self-defense. Self-defense!" She would have spat if not for respecting Lydia's Turkish carpet.

"And you saw this man running after Titus Armstrong?"

"He was running after a group of Black men."

"Did you see him shoot?"

Mrs. Harding's face was grim. "He shot at every man on the street in a Union coat. I saw him shoot a man who fell, and I saw him bend over to shoot a man who was down. Shot him in the head to make sure he was dead."

Elias's voice was more than polite. It was soft. "Mrs.

Harding, did you see Mr. Dailey shoot Titus Armstrong? Did you see him give Titus Armstrong a mortal wound?"

Mrs. Harding said, "I saw Titus Armstrong run by. And I saw that man Dailey shoot every man he saw wearing a blue coat."

Elias was silent. Lydia saw the lawyer struggle with the man whose heart ached for the victims of the massacre. Finally she spoke, in a quiet voice. "Mrs. Harding, are you sure? In the darkness, in all the confusion?"

"I'm sure that policeman, and the men with him, shot at every Black soldier on South Street that night."

Elias rubbed his chin. He said, "Mrs. Harding, you've been very helpful."

She was still bitter. "Have I?"

Elias said, "Every bit of information helps us."

Lydia thought, *That's the lawyer talking.*

She said, "The next night, they came back. And they set fire to my shop and my house. They burned me out, and I lost everything I had. I was lucky to escape with my life."

Now the silence was thick and painful.

Mrs. Montgomery clenched her hands in her lap. She said, "We should go." Her husband nodded, and they both rose to leave.

Elias said, "Thank you, all of you, for coming to talk to us. I know how difficult it was for you."

As Mrs. Harding rose to go, she shook her head. "Won't do any good," she said.

Lydia said, "We'll keep trying."

Elias said, "Miss Armstrong, do you have a moment?" Narcissa nodded and stayed seated.

When the visitors had been ushered out, Narcissa said to Elias, "They didn't help much, did they?" She had folded her hands tightly together. Her face was grayer than ever.

Elias sighed. "They told the truth about what they remembered. I have no doubt of that. But if I brought them into court, and the opposing attorney asked them to swear that they'd seen Mr. Dailey shoot your brother, they couldn't."

Narcissa said, "They didn't see it."

"Miss Armstrong, we're not finished yet. Far from it. But we need to find someone who saw it happen."

Lydia asked, "Was there someone in his regiment who might have been with him that night? Or a friend? Someone who was in a position to witness what happened?"

She raised her head. "I've been asking," she said. "I've been looking. I haven't found him yet." She stared at her hands, twisted together in her lap. "I'll keep trying."

After Narcissa left, Elias remained in the parlor with Lydia. They stared at the coffeepot and the untouched tray of refreshments.

Lydia asked, "Elias, my love, what are you thinking? You have that look of fierce concentration."

He raised his head. In the afternoon sunlight, the wrinkles around his eyes were more pronounced than ever. "I think it may be time to call on the spiritualist," he said. "Who is she? And why would she care about Titus Armstrong's murder?"

THE SURPRISE

Cassie took her seat at the breakfast table as her aunt stared pointedly at the empty chair and asked, "Where is that boy? He knows when we eat."

Will said softly, "Last I knew, still washing his face upstairs."

Sam rushed into the room. His face was dry. He dropped into his chair. "I'm hungry," he said.

"We pray first," her aunt Matilda said, and she firmly grasped Sam by the hand. She bowed her head and said, "Bless the Lord for this good food."

The voice whispered to Cassie: *They should be thanking me, too.*

Cassie thought, *You hush.*

Sam held out his plate. "Manners," Matilda Hayes said.

"Please?" he said, with reluctance.

The days of dry cornbread for breakfast were gone. This morning, as every morning, the family ate bacon with their eggs, and spread jam and butter on the white bread from Mrs. Harding's bakery. The adults drank coffee with sugar and cream. The boys had grown taller. Her aunt had stopped coughing. Her uncle, now standing straight, had put on flesh. Matilda and Moses Hayes looked ten years younger than they had when Cassie first arrived.

But Will was still polite and distant with her, and Sam was still angry.

There was little conversation, aside from her aunt's admonition to Sam not to eat so fast, to use his fork, and to wipe his mouth when he was done. After Moses and the boys left the table, Matilda said, "I try and try, and still that boy has the manners of an animal."

Cassie suddenly thought of the Mason plantation, which she'd been taken to when she was a little enslaved girl. The Masons had fed the children on the place from a trough. Like animals.

Matilda asked, "What is it?"

She shook her head and smiled, willing the past away. "It's nothing," she said.

"Spirit visit you?"

"You know it doesn't work like that," Cassie reminded her aunt.

As they cleared the table, her aunt said, "Well, however it works, those spirits have been good to us. And I never thought I'd say so."

Cassie heard the low chuckle as she nodded.

Once the washing up was finished Cassie went downstairs, where she surveyed the front room. Satisfied with its order and cleanliness, she unlocked the door. She didn't expect much business so early in the day, but she'd have time to enter the newest appointments and the newest *gifts* in the ledger. Between her séances and TJ's inquiries, there was plenty of money to buy what the grateful customers didn't give her. She gladly took the eggs and the vegetables along with the cash *donations*, she reminded the voice.

The door opened and a man in a blue coat entered the shop. No, not that kind of coat. The policemen in Memphis also wore blue coats, along with the billy clubs they kept slung around their hips, and the pistols they concealed under their uniforms. He was one of the Beale Street policemen who patrolled during the day. He'd never introduced himself, but she knew his name was McMahon.

He was about thirty, she judged, with black hair and vivid blue eyes, coloring called "black Irish." If he hadn't been a policeman, someone she was predisposed to dislike, she would have admitted he was a handsome man. Like most of the Irish policemen, and most of the Irish in general in Memphis, he had no love for Black people.

She said pleasantly, "Mr. McMahon, is there something I can do for you?"

He walked up to her, a little too close. He wasn't interested in her that way. She knew he was married and had three little children. He was here for something else, and it wasn't hard to guess what it was.

He said, "As a matter of fact, there is."

"Please, whatever it is, I'll do my best to oblige." She knew the ladylike demeanor and the courtesy were a waste of her time. Nonetheless, she played her part.

"I heard you're set up as a medium who says she can talk to the dead."

"I'm a spiritualist, yes."

"And that you charge people for whatever it is you do."

"Well, not exactly. I give them my services freely. Some of them give me things, out of gratitude."

"Sums of money?"

"Sometimes. Many of my customers are people of modest means. If they want to give me a few eggs from the henhouse, I don't refuse."

"I hear different. That you bilk them."

Slavery's over, she thought. She met his eyes and smiled in the most disarming way she knew. "Mr. McMahon, I keep very careful records. I could show you what I receive, if you'd care to take a look."

He rested his hand on the billy club at his hip. "I should take you down to the station," he said.

She said, "I'm sure that won't be necessary." Smiling again, she said, "Just let me reach into my pocket." She withdrew two dollar bills. "I'd be glad to make a contribution to the Police Fund," she said.

He didn't hold out his hand.

She'd enacted this scene in New York, and she knew how it went. She folded the bills up small. "For the widows and orphans," she said.

His expression didn't soften.

She extended her hand, the bills small between her fingers.

He took them.

"Will that do?" she asked him.

He looked her up and down, as though committing her to memory. "For the time being," he said.

Once he left, she felt shaky. *So it's started*, she thought. He'd be back, perhaps once a month, perhaps every week. She hoped it would stop with the financial contribution. She had no desire to pay in other ways.

She sat down at the table where she settled those who wanted to consult her. She struggled to compose herself. Ida had warned her, and she'd told Ida she could handle herself. She was sure she could. But she didn't like it.

She spread her hands on the tabletop and stared at them. When the door opened, she looked up, telling herself that there was no reason for alarm. McMahon wouldn't be back, at least for a week.

It was TJ, who joined her at the table. "You look a little pale. Is there trouble?"

She told him about McMahon's visit.

TJ said, "The man on the beat stopped by every week in New York."

"It was all business with that one," she said. "He used to joke with me as he tucked the money away. This one bothers me. It isn't about the money for him. He doesn't like me, and he wants me to know it."

TJ said, "I'm surprised you're surprised. You grew up here."

She laughed, a bitter, strangled sound. "Before the war, we enslaved people thought we were better than the Irish," she said.

TJ sighed. "Pay the bribe and keep your head down."

She raised her head in defiance. "Yes," she said. "As I well know." She took a deep breath. "How goes it with you?"

He said, "I came by to ask if you have anything for me."

That was easy. She righted herself. "Yes, another ghost from the massacre."

"So the word has spread. Is it someone who wants an inquiry?"

"No, just a talk with someone on the other shore." She tried hard not to shiver with the recollection of the tale she'd heard.

"Ah, you're holding out on me," he said. "What's the story?"

"She saw her husband shot," Cassie said. "She saw who did it. She told me she never even considered going to the police about it."

"Was it the police?"

She nodded.

"Is the family in the Report?" He meant the congressional report on the riot, more useful to them than the police blotter or the newspaper social pages. They had each ordered a copy from the government printing office in Washington, DC.

"Yes."

"I'll start there and see what else I can find." When she wrapped her arms around herself, he asked, "Do you want me to get your shawl?" His voice was suddenly soft.

"No, it's not that kind of cold," she said. "I feel them, all of them. The victims of the massacre. And other victims, from the days of slavery."

His voice still soft, he asked, "How long are you planning to do this? How long are you planning to stay?"

She looked up. "I still have some unfinished business here," she said.

"On the other shore, or in the courtroom?"

She shook her head.

SHE HAD a sole visitor that morning. The woman who came to see her was young and worried. "No one's dead," she said. "But I can't have a baby, even though God knows we try. I thought you might help."

Cassie said, "Have you seen a doctor?"

"Can't afford a doctor. Saw a root doctor and she gave me something horrible tasting to drink. That didn't do any good, either."

"I've never asked the spirits for that kind of help," Cassie said. "I hate to promise something I can't provide."

The woman looked up. She was so young that the events

of her life—slavery, escape, war, massacre—hadn't marked her. She had only her private sorrow, her longing for a child. "Why can't you try? If it doesn't work, there's no harm. But if it does—" Yearning suffused her face.

"Well, in that spirit—"

The low chuckle. *That isn't my province. But I know whose it is.*

She took the young woman's hand. "I'll do what I can," she said.

THAT AFTERNOON, once school ended, the door opened, and her son Will walked in. He always entered at the side and used the stairs to the second floor. He had rarely been on the first floor, and the only time he had come into the back parlor, the séance room, was to admire it politely, as he'd admired the new carpet on the floor upstairs.

Cassie rose from the table where she sat, writing about her newest consultation in the ledger. "Will!" she said. "What brings you here?"

"I'm not interrupting you?"

"No, not at all. It's quiet. Would you like to sit down?"

He sat tentatively at the table.

"What is it, Will?"

He rubbed his upper lip, still the smooth hairless skin of a boy. "I don't know if I should ask you," he said.

Oh, she knew that look. Everyone who came to consult her looked like that. *Why am I here? I don't know how I can even talk about it. Oh, how it troubles me. Can you help me?* "Is there something worrying you?" she asked.

"I heard about that policeman," he said. "The one who visited you."

"How did you hear about that?"

"People talk." He asked, "Was he angry because you talk to the spirits?"

She sighed. "Oh, Will. That's not about the spirits. That's just a mean way to bother people. I bet that policeman bothers every Black person in business on Beale Street the same way. The grocer and the pie lady don't have anything to do with the spirits."

He looked serious and sad. "Do you think the spirits are real?"

She owed him the truth as she understood it. "I know they come to me. It's not something you choose. I've been told it's a gift. Sometimes I wonder."

"Has my father ever come to you?"

That gave her a chill. She'd heard his voice once. "I don't summon him," she said.

"But could you?"

"I could try. But I don't really want to."

"If I asked—"

She shook her head.

"For a séance?"

"No, Will. This is not for children."

"I'm not a child," he said, his voice quiet.

She was ashamed, because he was right. "Is there something you want to know? Perhaps I can tell you outright, without bringing the spirits into it."

He met her eyes, and she was disconcerted at how knowing they were. He nodded.

"Please, ask me, and I'll do my best to tell you what I know."

"Ma'am—"

She said, "Will, you know you can call me 'Mama,'" she said.

He hesitated. When he spoke, he asked, "How did my father die?"

"Have your aunt and uncle told you anything about it?" she asked. She tensed, waiting for the answer.

"Uncle Moses said he drowned. That it was an accident. That he slipped and fell into the river."

Holding his gaze, she said, "That's true."

He didn't falter. He met her eyes as though he expected her to tell him something more.

She said, "Your father wasn't kind to me, and he wasn't good to you. I'm sorry for all of that, Will."

He looked away. Was he blinking? Were his eyes wet?

How she wished she could take him in her arms and hold him close and murmur, "It's all right, sugar."

He looked up. He nodded. Then he rose and walked away, his head down.

THAT NIGHT, as she nestled into the comfort of her bed, she let her mind drift. She thought of the young woman who wanted a baby. The voice said, *It's her husband who can't make a baby.*

She asked the voice, *How are we going to manage it?*

You'll see.

A few days later, the young woman came into the storefront, with a peculiar expression on her face.

"How are you?" Cassie asked.

"I don't quite know," she said.

"Sit down and tell me," Cassie said.

She sat, smoothing her skirt beneath her. "I don't dare feel happy yet," she said. "Because it came about from something sad."

Cassie raised her brows.

"We have a neighbor. Her husband died not long ago. He had a wasting disease, and he was never well. He left her with a little one, just six months old. And then she got fever and now she's gone, too."

"I'm sorry to hear it."

"She was all alone in the world. No one to care for that little boy." She took a deep breath. "So my husband and I went to our minister and offered to take that baby in. He told us he could help us adopt him and do it right, so he belongs to us. And we agreed we'd do it."

Cassie nodded. *You rattle me,* she thought. The voice didn't reply.

The woman asked, "Is it all right? To have a baby because his mother is in her grave?"

The voice said, *Did what you asked.* Cassie said, "Love him and bring him up right." She thought of her own sons, whom she had struggled to love, and had failed. "What's his name?"

"Theodore. We're going to call him Teddy."

The voice said, *That's Greek for "God's gift."*

Cassie thought, *Which God? Our Father in Heaven? Or you? Or someone I haven't met yet?*

Silence.

CASSIE ROSE as she watched the couple approach her front door. Despite the heat, they'd walked here. They were white, and they were well-dressed. She wondered if they were here to consult her. She'd never solicited anyone white. Perhaps they had other business on Beale Street. Hers wasn't the only storefront on the block.

But they stopped before her door and hesitated.

She got a good look, and she was glad that she would have a moment to control her astonishment.

The man was Elias Aronson, who held the hand of the woman Cassie had known as Lydia Owens.

She hovered by the door, but she let them open it and walk in.

When they caught sight of her, they were stunned. Elias recovered first. He said, "Mrs. Aronson mentioned that you'd enrolled your children in her school, but I had no idea you were the noted spiritualist we'd been hearing about."

"Well, it appears that I am," she said. "I hope you're not offended."

Elias said, "No, of course not. Why would I be?"

She gave him a long, appraising look, letting the wartime past shimmer in the air between them.

He ignored it and said politely, "I was just surprised. Weren't you?"

"I had a little warning," she said. "I spied you out the window."

He was silent.

She asked, "What brings you here?"

Lydia said, "Miss Armstrong told us about her visit to you. It encouraged her to think about legal redress, and she called on Mr. Aronson to discuss it."

"For her brother's murder?" Cassie asked.

Lydia nodded.

Cassie hadn't heard about Narcissa Armstrong's intention to find her brother's murderer, and what was certain to be a fool's errand to try to bring him to justice. It was news, but it didn't surprise her. "I don't encourage anyone to seek out legal advice," she said. "That's not what the spirits tell me."

Elias said, "I've found that people are litigious all on their own."

The door opened again. It was TJ. "Oh, excuse me, Mrs. Auburn," he said. "If you're busy, I can come back later."

Elias turned at the sound of his voice. TJ, skilled at curbing his surprise, greeted him politely. "Mr. Aronson."

Cassie asked, "You've met?"

Elias said, "Mr. Randolph called on me to offer his services as an inquiry agent. Mr. Randolph, I don't believe you've met my wife, Mrs. Lydia Aronson?"

"Pleased to make your acquaintance," TJ said to Lydia.

Elias asked Cassie, "And how are you acquainted with Mr. Randolph?"

"He's made several inquiries for me."

Elias said, "I thought the spirits would tell you what you needed to know."

Cassie said, "They tell me a great many things. But as Mr. Randolph is fond of saying, it never hurts to share your own knowledge with them. It encourages them and lightens their task."

"I see," Elias said.

"You're a skeptic, Mr. Aronson."

"I believe in what I can see and hear and prove. Does that make me a skeptic?"

Lydia said, "Perhaps, but it's a good quality in a lawyer." She looked at Cassie. Her voice was light, suitable for the parlor. "He's very much the lawyer these days."

Cassie thought, *Unlike the days of the war, when he was an inquiry agent himself, and hot on my heels.* "Is there something I can do for you, Mr. Aronson? Mrs. Aronson?"

Elias said, "I came here out of professional curiosity, since you talked to the Armstrongs about Titus Armstrong's death. I hoped to ask you what you knew."

"What the spirits told me?"

He said, "Oh, not at all. I'm sure that's all in confidence.

But if you've made an earthly inquiry, that might be a different matter."

Cassie remembered everything that Elias had done to get her to talk when he was inquiring into her fiancé's murder. "It depends on your intentions," she said.

Lydia said, "We have no intention of going to the police, if that worries you."

In his wartime inquiry, Elias had prodded her and tried to provoke her to talk. Lydia had always taken a gentler approach. But Lydia was as ruthless for the truth as her husband. Cassie said, "An earthly inquiry is a private matter, too."

"Miss Armstrong wants to see justice done," Elias said. "So do I. I'd hope that you would, too."

"Justice is a very slippery business," Cassie said. "Particularly in a Memphis station house, a Memphis jail, or a Memphis courtroom."

Lydia put her hand on Elias's arm. Cassie remembered that from the inquiry in 1863. It was Lydia's gesture of restraint and appeasement. "As we're well aware," Lydia said.

THE BROTHER IN ARMS

LYDIA OPENED HER FRONT DOOR TO FIND NARCISSA accompanied by a tall young man. He stood straight, like the soldier he had once been, even though he was now wearing his Sunday best, a new black wool suit. But his forehead was beaded with sweat, as though with fever, and his face had the faint grayish cast of distress.

Narcissa introduced him as Marcus Whittaker, Titus's comrade-in-arms in the 3rd Heavy Artillery, United States Colored Troops. Lydia held out her hand, saying, "Thank you for coming here."

After a moment's hesitation, he took her hand. His palm was wet and clammy. Lydia thought, *Now I'm worried.* But she ushered them both into the parlor, where Elias rose to greet them.

Everyone sat. Lydia offered coffee, but Narcissa declined politely and Whittaker shook his head.

Elias said, "Mr. Whittaker, thank you for coming to talk to us."

Whittaker looked at Narcissa, who clasped her hands tightly in her lap. He pulled out his handkerchief and wiped the sweat from his brow. He didn't look refreshed by it. "I felt I owed it to Titus," he said. "I'd do anything to help Cissy."

Elias spoke politely. "Miss Armstrong mentioned that you live on President's Island. I trust you had an easy trip into town."

He nodded. "It wasn't any trouble," he said.

President's Island was the third and the last contraband camp established after the Union army took Memphis. It was far enough from the city that the people who stayed there farmed the land, using it for free during the war, and afterward, renting or buying it for themselves. Once a temporary settlement, President's Island had become a Black community.

Elias said, "Miss Armstrong mentioned that you have some land out there."

Whittaker looked puzzled, as though he didn't see why it mattered, but he replied with a courtesy to match Elias's. "We own a little plot there. Not forty acres and a mule, but a few acres and a henhouse. We sell vegetables and eggs in town and we make a good living by it."

"I'm glad you're prospering," Elias said.

Whittaker looked surprised at Elias's good wishes, but he said, "So are we."

There was a silence, thick and humid like the afternoon air. Whittaker knotted his hands in his lap. He said, "Narcissa told me that you wanted to hear about Titus."

Elias looked at Lydia, who said gently, "Whatever you can tell us."

He looked down at his hands and wiped his palms on his trousers. He took a breath, looked up, and nodded.

Lydia was the one to ask, "How did you meet him?"

"We were in the 3rd together." He paused. "I mustered in later than he did, but we bunked together and drilled together. Got to be good friends, even though I came from Mississippi and never met him before the war. Those Shelby County men all mustered in together and they were tight as ticks. But they let me in and we got along fine."

He looked at Narcissa and his tone began to falter. "He was my best friend in the regiment."

Narcissa nodded at him, encouraging him to go on.

He took another deep breath. "We knew we were mustering out at the end of April in 1866. We were glad of it, but we hadn't been paid yet. Colonel Horvath was mad about that. The army didn't treat us right. Gave us old hardtack and spoiled meat and took God's own time paying us. He was always complaining to someone about it. Good man, even if he couldn't fix it for us."

Elias said, "I was his aide-de-camp until I mustered out. He was a good man."

Whittaker sat up straight, at attention suddenly, bracing himself. "Even though we were free to go, we decided to stay at the fort until we got our money. Some of the men went into town to celebrate. Went to Mary Grady's and any other saloon that would let them in. I didn't go into town much. Never did, when I was a soldier. Too many people hated the sight of a blue coat and I didn't want trouble."

The thought of trouble clouded his face. "I remember the first of May. We began to hear what was happening in town. Heard about the scuffle, but that didn't bother us too much. Then we heard about the police marching on South Street. A whole troop of police, bent on hurting people. We heard they started by beating up soldiers and turned their hand to hurting any Black person walking down the street."

Then he stopped.

Elias asked gently, "What happened then?"

He hesitated.

Elias said, "If this is too difficult—"

Whittaker looked at Narcissa, whose face was still. It wasn't composure. It was a way to conceal her own emotion. She nodded at him, and he spoke.

"Colonel Horvath gathered us together and told us he didn't command us anymore, but he was worried about our safety, and he wanted us to stay put at the fort. But Titus was worried sick about his family. They were living on Beale, not far from South, where the worst trouble was, and he decided he had to go into town. And I told him I'd go with him."

He faltered again and stopped.

Narcissa's expression softened. "There's no hurry, Marcus."

He took a breath and nodded. "We went into town, dressed in our uniforms. We'd both turned in our rifles when we mustered out, but we had pistols of our own, and we brought them with us. Hoped not to use them. But it wasn't safe to go into Memphis unarmed."

Then he stopped. He stared at his hands, splayed on the thick black wool of his trousers.

"What did you see?" Narcissa asked, her voice very gentle.

He bent his head, unable to reply. His shoulders began to shake, and when he looked up, his face was as gray as ash. His voice thick, he said, "Excuse me," and he rose, hurried to the door, and let himself out to stand on the veranda.

Through the window, they could all see how he buried his face in his hands.

Narcissa didn't bother to excuse herself. She rose and ran outside. Lydia and Elias watched as she pulled him into her arms, and even though he was a head taller than she, how she let him rest his cheek on her shoulder and stroke his hair.

Lydia looked away. "Elias, I think we've done something terribly wrong."

Elias said, "It's even worse than losing a friend in battle. There's a good reason for a battle. This was worse because it was so senseless."

They waited as Whittaker wept. Lydia drank a cup of coffee she didn't want. She said to Elias, "When they come back in, I'm going to apologize."

Elias nodded.

When they returned, he clutched Narcissa's hand tightly in his own.

Lydia said, "We are so sorry. We had no intention to cause you such pain."

His voice was thick and pitched low. Still holding on to Narcissa's hand, he said, "I can't. I thought I could talk about it, but I can't." He looked at Narcissa with a face swollen with tears. "I'm so sorry, Cissy."

Narcissa held her hand to her eyes. When she looked up, her voice also thick, she said, "It's all right, Marcus."

"No," he said, his gaze fixed on her. "It will never be all right. I'm still here, but he's gone."

LYDIA SLIT OPEN the unaddressed envelope that Mr. Jasper had found when he unlocked the door this morning. The page, without salutation or signature, said, *Didn't you get the message? Leave now, you Yankee bitches, or we'll make sure that you do.*

She'd saved the earlier message, and she could compare the handwriting. Not that it mattered much. No one needed to sign a message like this.

She'd have to ask Miss Kidder, head of the Lincoln School, if she, too, had gotten a message. She hadn't last time.

Sue Kinsley poked her head in the door. "You look like thunder," she said.

"We've received another threatening message."

Sue strode to the desk, hand outstretched. "Let me see it."

Lydia gave it to her. She read it and tossed it on Lydia's desk. "As though we'd pack up and leave because of a few nasty words," she said. "Does Narcissa know?"

"I just opened it. I haven't talked to her yet."

"I'll tell her," Sue said, her eyes flashing.

Lydia didn't answer.

Sue said, "I'm not afraid."

"I am," Lydia replied.

ELIAS SAT in his office with Dorsey, his heart heavy. Lydia's second threatening message had worried him, even as he'd tried to reassure her. But he hadn't asked Dorsey to his office to talk about the Phoenix School's difficulties. Instead, he told Dorsey about the unsuccessful meeting with Marcus Whittaker. "He couldn't even talk about it," Elias said.

Dorsey nodded. "Soldier's heart," he said, even though he had spent the war behind the lines on garrison duty in Virginia.

"Worse after the battle. And sometimes worse months or years after the battle." Elias shook his head. "I've been racking my brains on how to proceed next. I wish we could talk to the police. I can't see how anyone who was on the police force in 1866 would talk to us."

Dorsey said, "There's something we might try."

"What?"

"There are two Black men on the police force now. They

were appointed last year." He smiled a little. "One of them is John Harris."

"Our John Harris?"

"The very one."

John Harris was a Republican stalwart in Memphis, an organizer with a fiery talent for oration. Elias didn't know him well, but all the men active in the Black ward, Ward 7, were acquainted with each other, and all who hoped to attend the county convention, and beyond it, the state convention, were connected.

"I heard that he got appointed to a position. What is he doing for the police?"

"He's a turnkey." Dorsey laughed. "A jailer. He locks the men in at night and keeps watch over the jail at the First District Station."

"Appointed last year." Elias frowned. "Not in a spot to know what happened in 1866."

"Who knows? He may have connections. He may know someone who would talk to us."

Elias said, "Why not?"

WHEN ELIAS TOLD her that he was going to meet with John Harris, Lydia asked, "Another political meeting?"

"No, we're hoping to talk to him in his new capacity. As a member of the police force."

Lydia said, "When did that happen?"

"Recently."

"Is he walking a beat? How did I miss this?"

"No, he's a turnkey."

She snorted. "A jailer? He locks the criminals in for the night? How do the white drunks and thieves feel about that?"

"I doubt they have any choice," Elias said.

"What can he possibly do for you?"

"He's a member of the police force. Presumably he knows other members of the police force." At her puzzled expression, "No, not on our behalf. On Narcissa's behalf. That is, Titus's."

"Oh," she said in surprise. "When you mentioned the police, I thought you might have been thinking about the letter."

He sighed. "It should be a police matter."

She said, "Perhaps we should take it up with Mr. Harris."

"Oh, Lydia. We should go down to the local station and lodge a complaint."

"For all the good it will do. When are you meeting with Mr. Harris?"

"I don't know yet."

"Bring him here. I want to meet him. We'll bribe him—"

"Lydia—"

"With our housekeeper's lemon cake."

He groaned.

"Elias, why do you think I make light of this? Because otherwise I would be too—" She faltered.

He put his arms around her and pulled her close. She pressed her cheek to his and said, "Too upset to go on."

Mr. Harris agreed to call at the Aronsons' on Sunday afternoon. Evidently turnkeys were allowed to briefly leave their posts. He greeted Elias and Dorsey with warmth, as brothers in politics, but he was surprised to see Lydia. He apologized, saying that he was here to talk about politics and crime, subjects not fit for a lady.

Lydia said, "I'm a Yankee schoolteacher, not a lady. Before I married Elias, I helped him investigate a murder. I can listen to anything."

Even more surprised, Harris asked, "Ma'am, did you make this lemon cake? It's delicious."

"No, I can't take the credit for that. It's my housekeeper's doing."

John Harris, like many of the party activists she'd met, had a mellifluous voice and an orator's cadence, even though the subject was only cake. He'd educated himself while still enslaved and had parlayed a natural talent for public speaking into public life in politics since the war's end. He owed his position on the police force to a political appointment.

When she asked him how white criminals felt about him when he turned the lock on them, he said ruefully, "They don't care much for me. And it's unfortunate that as a member of the police force, I wear a blue coat."

After his second piece of cake, he sighed with satisfaction and put down his fork. He looked from Elias to Dorsey to Lydia. "You must have a situation on your hands," he said. "What is it?"

Elias said, "It arose from something that happened during the massacre back in 1866." He explained about Titus Armstrong's death and Narcissa's desire to pursue the matter, two years after the fact.

Harris said, "I take it you've tried to find witnesses in the Black community."

Elias nodded. "We've made some initial inquiries. We could keep trying, but I suspect that finding someone who saw what happened and who's willing to talk will be diffi-cult." He gave Lydia a knowing glance. "We thought we'd try to come at the situation from a different direction. We'd like to find a member of the police force who might talk to us."

Harris looked somber. "That's a different set of difficulties, as you must be aware."

Lydia said, "To find a policeman who might act as a witness to a murder? Yes, we're well aware."

"We hoped"—Elias gestured toward the three of them, emphasizing their common purpose—"that you might know of someone who could steer us in the right direction."

Harris sighed. "The men on the beat, and the men who command them, keep things very close," he said. "Being on the police force is its own closed society, and being an Irishman on the police force is more closed still."

"They appointed you," Dorsey said.

"To stay in the station house and lock the door. Not to walk the beat, or to arrest anyone, or to investigate crimes."

Elias asked, "Is there no one you're close to? No one you trust?"

"There's another Black turnkey at the north station. Mr. Cook. A loyal party man, appointed at the same time I was. The rest of the police force doesn't like or trust him, either."

Lydia leaned forward. "Mr. Harris, we're all used to hindrance. The last time my husband and I made an inquiry, we were frustrated at every turn. No one wanted to talk. No one wanted to give up a secret. The truth suffered because of it. Justice suffered, too. I would hope, with all my heart, that things have changed, at least a little, since 1863."

Harris said, "How I wish that were true." He sighed. "And how I wish I had the power to help you. But if I inquired, as you ask, I'd suffer worse than frustration. I'd be thought a troublemaker. I would lose my appointment, and with it any ability to advance the rights of Black people in Memphis."

Dorsey said, "I'll say this, because I'm a Black man and

you can't accuse me of hiding behind the safety of my race. When will it be time to make trouble, Mr. Harris? We're willing to trouble the waters at the ballot box. We'll march in the streets, dressed in our army coats, to vote for General Grant. Why shouldn't we cause some trouble in the courts, too? In the matter of a man who may have been murdered by a member of the Memphis police?"

Harris said, "If you're hoping that the police will look into the murder of a Black man by a policeman, you're hoping for something that won't happen. All of you know that."

Elias said, "We don't know yet who murdered Titus Armstrong. He died during the massacre. Perhaps a member of the police witnessed it. Perhaps the testimony of a policeman might point us toward the real murderer."

"No policeman would tolerate an interview with you," Harris said. "The chief of police himself would deny you. What makes you think they would entertain any request from me?"

Lydia thought, *He's self-seeking and ambitious, but he isn't a fool. He's right.*

As Harris left, he said, "Dorsey, Aronson, don't look so downcast. There's a battle we can win at the ballot box." He bowed a little to Lydia. "A pleasure to meet you, ma'am, and the cake was delicious."

Once he was gone, Elias stared at the empty cake plates. "Damn the cake," he said.

Dorsey looked at Lydia and raised his eyebrows. Lydia shook her head.

Elias asked, "Well, what do we do now?"

～

ON MONDAY, Narcissa knocked on Lydia's door first thing in the morning. "How did things go with Mr. Harris?" she asked. At the sight of Lydia's expression, she said, "He wasn't persuaded."

"No, he insisted that his own position is too tenuous. He can't be the one who prods the police into investigating themselves."

"The lemon cake didn't help?"

"Oh, he liked the lemon cake. He ate two pieces, and he would have had a third if he didn't feel he had to depart after he delivered his bad news."

Narcissa began to laugh. She put her hand over her mouth. "I don't know why—none of this is funny—"

Lydia said, "Sometimes, when you don't know whether to laugh or cry, it's easier to laugh."

Narcissa caught hold of herself. She wiped her eyes. When she was calm enough, she said, "I need to talk to Marcus again."

Now Lydia didn't know whether she should laugh or cry. "Don't promise to marry him if he'll talk to us."

Narcissa laughed so hard the tears ran from her eyes, and neither of them knew whether mirth or sorrow had the upper hand.

WHEN MARCUS WHITTAKER returned to the Aronsons' parlor, Narcissa led him to the settee and sat beside him. "You're sure you can do this?" she asked.

He took a deep breath. "I'll do my best."

She reached for his hand and clasped it tightly.

Lydia said, "We're more aware than ever that this is diffi-cult for you."

"May I ask you some questions?" Elias asked. "To estab-lish what happened? I'll be as careful as I can."

"What kind of questions?"

"What you saw and what you heard."

He braced himself. "All right."

Elias said, "If anything troubles you too much, tell me, and we'll stop."

He nodded.

"About what time did you come to South Street?"

"After sunset. Don't remember the exact time. I remember how dark it was."

"What did you see? Even though it was dark?"

"People running." He took a deep breath. "Black people running. Men and women, all trying to get to safety."

"Did you see the police?"

"Yes. They were chasing after people. Had their arms stretched out, clubs in their hands."

"Were they armed?"

"Someone was, because I heard shooting. Pistols. That worried me, and I had my hand on my own pistol."

"What were you doing, you and Titus?"

"We wanted to get to Beale Street, where his family lived. He wanted to make sure they were safe. To protect them, if he could. But we got caught up in the crowd and we ran along with them. Couldn't do much else."

"Did anyone shoot at you?"

"Not right at us, but someone was shooting all around us." He pressed his hands on his knees, so hard that the tendons strained. "Titus was hit. His leg. He screamed and fell down. He was clutching his leg and crying out. 'I'm shot, I'm shot.'"

"And what happened then?" When Elias spoke in sympa-thy, two lines appeared between his brows. His face was furrowed now.

"I went down on my knees to help him. I thought I could get him away, get to safety. 'Let me hoist you up,' I said, but he was bleeding bad and he just moaned and grabbed at his leg." He looked down at his hands.

Lydia said, "Don't let us go on if this is too hard for you."

He shook his head. "I can go on."

Elias asked, "Did you get him to his feet?"

"No, he couldn't stand. I was still trying when someone grabbed me by the shoulder." He shuddered. "And when I didn't get up, he pushed a pistol into my back. I didn't move. He said to me, 'This isn't about you. Get away.'"

His voice shook. He was as gray as the grave. "I never saw his face, but I heard his voice. He wasn't an Irishman. Didn't know him, but he sounded just like my old massa back in Mississippi."

AFTER HE LEFT, Narcissa remained in the parlor with Lydia and Elias. She had that still expression again, her mask over pain, and her cheeks were tinged with gray.

"Narcissa?" Lydia asked gently.

"If he stops at a saloon on the way home, I will never forgive myself for it."

Elias shook his head.

She took out her handkerchief and held it to her face. When she took it away, she said, "After Titus died, he drank so much we were afraid he'd die of it."

Elias said, "He carries a terrible burden. Even though it's not his fault."

"I hoped—oh, I hoped that thinking about justice might help him. That telling the truth of what happened might be some balm for his heart and his soul. I am so, so sorry to have been wrong."

Lydia reached for Narcissa's hand. "It's bad enough that he blames himself for something he shouldn't. It's even worse that you do the same."

Narcissa wiped her face again. When she set the handkerchief aside, a little color had returned to her face. "I need to remind myself why I went down this path. Why I want to stir up the pain it causes." She looked at Elias. "Because the spiritualist was right. Titus's blood cries out for justice." She took a deep breath and crumpled the handkerchief in her fist. Then she thrust it into her pocket. "Marcus said something I can't get out of my mind," she said. "That the man who put a gun to him said, 'This isn't about you.'" She looked from Lydia to Elias. "I think he meant that it was about Titus."

Elias said, "You have a suspicion."

"A white man with a planter's accent. Someone who knew Titus well enough to bear a grudge against him."

Elias was about to speak, but Lydia laid her hand on his arm. *Let her say it.*

Narcissa raised her eyes to Elias's. "Old massa is right." Anger glittered in her eyes. "Marse and young marse. The Beardsleys, father and son. William and John."

There was a long silence. Elias said, "It's a slender reed, Miss Armstrong."

Lydia said, "One worth grasping, I think."

Narcissa looked up.

"It's not as though we can call on them, either of them, to ask where they might have been on the night of May 1st," Elias said.

Narcissa's eyes were still bright with anger. "There is something you can ask, and something you can know," she

said. "Who served them? And who escaped their enslave-
ment, to be able to tell you?"

91

THE MAN ON THE BEAT

WHEN CASSIE FIRST TOLD TJ THAT SHE PLANNED TO RETURN to Memphis, he advised her to disguise herself with a new name and a new past, along with new bearing and her new accent. She'd told him it didn't matter. The people who remembered her as Cassie Andrews were Black, and they would keep her secret. The white people who remembered her best—the Union army officers and the provost marshal, the army's wartime chief of police—were gone. She was unlikely to come to the attention of her former enslavers, the Beardsley family, and their friends or relations in Memphis. Now that she was free, William Beardsley had no reason to care about her. Since she had been gone, she was sure that the Mason family had forgotten about her.

TJ thought she was a fool for believing that she could hide in plain sight because she was Black. She'd told him, "People see what they expect to see. It doesn't matter who they are. None of them expect to see that a slave turned into a lady." And so far, she had been right.

A fair number of the people who walked into her storefront were merely curious. In the retail parlance, they were lookers, not buyers. Very few of them had recognized her. Evidently the reinvented self was camouflage enough. Her aunt and uncle hadn't hidden her identity, but most Black people who remembered her trouble from 1863 had no desire to stir up the past. Mahaley Smith had helped with that, too. Anyone who said, "Ain't she the one who got tangled up in that mess with the Mason family?" got a resounding reply from Miss Mahaley. "She's come up in the world since, and that should be all you need to know."

It was summer, and the air was dense with the wet heat that came from the river. Cassie ran her finger over a chair back and sighed. The streets were dried mud in this weather, and the dust came in through the smallest cracks in the windows to cover every surface. Every morning, she filled a vase with cut flowers, the most fragrant she could find in the backyard, but the scent didn't cover the smell of manure from the street or settle the dust any.

A woman opened the door and stood in the doorway, surveying the space as though it surprised her. She was stout, with a servant's apron over her cotton dress, and a kerchief wrapped around her hair.

Cassie said, "Ma'am, please come in." *And shut the door*, she thought. *You're letting the dust in.*

"I come here when this was a dressmaker's," she said, in the accent common to the enslaved in western Tennessee. She looked around again. "Now it ain't."

Cassie said, "No, it's not."

She looked hard at Cassie, and Cassie recognized her. It was Dolly, who had been a house servant on the Beardsley place before the war. Her position in the kitchen had made her officious. She'd felt as free to punish Cassie, the youngest of the housemaids, as missus did. She'd always been stout and plain, and missus had never wanted her for anything but the kitchen. But Dolly had her own ambition, which was to become a housekeeper someday.

Now she said, "Cassie Andrews! Is that really you?"

"I'm called Mrs. Auburn now."

She peered at Cassie. "You can call yourself whatever you like. Cassie Andrews! Back in Memphis!" She looked around the room again. "You do business here? What kind of business?"

"Haven't you heard? I'm a spiritualist. I help people speak to their dead."

Dolly snorted.

Cassie asked, "May I help you in any way?"

"Oh, there's no one dead I want to talk to," Dolly said. "Can't believe you came back, not after the way you had to leave."

Cassie said, "I don't know what you heard. I left because I wanted to look for work up north."

Dolly looked her up and down. "Did a dead man pay for that dress? Or a live one?"

"Miss Dolly, is there any reason you've come to see me?"

Dolly laughed, an unpleasant sound.

Cassie said, "Do you live in Memphis?"

"Yes, I do. Still work for Marse William, but in town. I'm his housekeeper now."

Cassie thought unkindly, *Now that all of the others ran to freedom.* She nodded.

Dolly said, "Do Marse William know that you're back in Memphis?"

"I haven't called on him," Cassie said.

"He might like to know."

Cassie held herself still. "I don't think he remembers who I am," she said.

Dolly looked her up and down. It was the appraising stare

of a dealer in livestock or a madam in a whorehouse. "Oh, I think he do," she said.

CASSIE LEFT the storefront to walk down the street to Mahaley Smith's boardinghouse. Its fresh paint and cheerful front garden seemed to mock her today. Sighing, she knocked on the door. When Mahaley answered, Cassie said, "Can you spare a moment?"

Mahaley ushered her in and sat her down in the kitchen at the well-used pine table. Before the war, many enslaved women had kneaded bread and chopped vegetables at this table. Mahaley offered her coffee, but she declined it. "No, I've come for advice," she said.

"Is it that policeman? McMahon?"

"No, that's in order. Does he bother you, too?"

Mahaley said, "He doesn't bother me as long as I give the Police Fund a dollar every week."

Cassie reflected that her business cost her more, in every way. "Do you remember Dolly, from the Beardsley place?"

"That sorry old thing? Yes, I do. Still working for Marse William, last I heard."

"His housekeeper, now."

Mahaley snickered. "He must be desperate for help, if he's hired her as a housekeeper."

"Or she might be lying."

Mahaley said, "Wouldn't be the first time. Did she call on you?"

"Just now."

"And she worried you."

"She'll make sure that William Beardsley knows I'm back in Memphis."

"As though he'd listen to her! I bet he doesn't even know her name."

"He knows my name," Cassie said.

"Only because you made so much trouble for him. Back in slavery days he didn't know you from the kitchen table." She rested her hand on the scarred wood. For a woman who worked with her hands, she had smooth skin and well-shaped fingers.

"He certainly knows me now."

Mahaley thought for a long moment before she spoke. "He doesn't like trouble," she said. "He never has. He likes making money. And since the army came to Memphis, he's made a lot of money selling cotton. Now he needs the planters who are growing cotton again, and he needs the people who buy it from him—those factories up north. Do you think he wants to dig up your old trouble from the war? He'd be glad to live the rest of his life not remembering who you are."

Cassie stared at her fingernails, which she had cut and buffed that morning. She now had the hands of a lady. She looked up. "What about the Mason family? Before I left, they wanted the police to prove Everett Mason was murdered."

Mahaley snorted. "They don't even show their faces in town these days because they've been brought so low," she said. "They haven't grown a crop of cotton since the Yankees came, and I don't know how they manage. They don't have two nickels to rub together. Do you think they can get the police to do anything?"

Cassie considered this. Mahaley Smith didn't have a scrap of sentiment. She had never bothered to spare anyone the truth. She wasn't offering comfort. She was offering hard common sense.

Mahaley said, "I don't know why you're still in Memphis.

You could go back to New York and send your family money. You don't need to be here for that."

She said, "I worry about the boys."

Mahaley sighed. "You lost them a long time ago," she said. "You should leave them to Moses and Matilda."

No, Cassie thought. With defiance in her voice, she said, "I'm not ready to give them up, not yet."

A FEW DAYS LATER, a white woman walked into Cassie's storefront. She was short and slight, her face and figure marked by deprivation during the war and since. She wore a black silk dress, the height of fashion in 1861, now faded with age. The fabric gave off a sour smell, as though it had been worn so often that washing no longer freshened it. She wore no jewelry of any kind, not even a wedding ring. She must have sold it long ago.

It gave Cassie a malicious pleasure to extend her hand. "I'm Mrs. Auburn," she said.

"Do you really expect me to call you that?"

"Most people do, these days."

The woman gave her a hard, appraising stare. Cassie knew that look. It was missus, getting ready to take out the strap.

"Can I help you, ma'am?" Cassie asked, the courtesy like the heft of a pearl-handled revolver in her hand.

"You speak to the dead, don't you?"

"I'm privileged that the spirits speak to me, yes."

"I want to speak to my dead son."

Cassie said, "Why don't we sit down? I'd like to know a little about you and the son you hope to speak to."

She sat at the table as though it offended her.

Cassie asked, "Who am I addressing, ma'am?"

That hard stare again. "Don't you know?"

Cassie smiled. It was delicious to talk like this to the wife of a ruined planter. "Everyone is so changed by the war."

"Stop that. You knew me before the war. As I knew you."

"Ma'am, if that's true, you'll have to refresh my memory."

"My son was Everett Mason. I'm his mother."

That's trouble brewing, she thought. The voice, capricious as ever, wasn't helping her. She'd have to handle this on her own.

She pretended to become thoughtful. "Ma'am, the people who consult me are—from the neighborhood. They are people of color, of modest circumstances. A lady like yourself—"

Mrs. Mason snorted.

"Another spiritualist might serve you better," Cassie said.

"I want you," Mrs. Mason said.

"Ma'am—"

"Did you not hear me?"

Cassie said, "Ma'am, what concerns me is that the spirits may not hear you. Not if you ask for them through me."

"Can you talk to the dead or can't you?"

"The spirits are mercurial," Cassie said. "It's important not to put anything in their way."

"That's your worry, isn't it? Not mine."

"Ma'am, I never promise that the spirits will come, or what they will say," Cassie said. "And under these circumstances, I fear that they will refuse to come at all."

The woman rested her palms on the table and leaned forward, a remarkably aggressive gesture for a person who was barely five feet tall. "I can go to the police, you know. I can tell them you're Cassie Andrews, who ran away after my son was murdered."

Cassie said, "Would you?"

"Do you really want to find out?"

Cassie was silent for a moment. "How do I know you won't go to the police in any case?"

She drew herself up in heated indignation. "I am a lady. What do you take me for?"

A lying, mean, hateful woman. "Ma'am, I won't make you a promise. I can't. But if you insist—"

"I insist."

The vile old tone of command. *I could sell you.*

As mildly as she could, Cassie said, "I'll see what I can do."

Mrs. Mason said, "You'll do better than that."

More sharply, Cassie said, "I will do what I can."

As though she hadn't heard, Mrs. Mason said, "I'll come back tonight. I don't want to stay in town any longer than I have to."

THAT AFTERNOON, when TJ walked in, she took him into the back room for a private talk. "We have some business we don't want." She told him that Mrs. Mason had insisted on a séance and had brought up the subject of the police when Cassie tried to demur.

TJ asked her, "Have you told me everything about Everett Mason, Cassie? Or is there something more I should know?"

Cassie shook her head.

He put his hands on her shoulders. "I mean it," he said. "I can't help you if you're keeping anything from me."

She covered his hands with her own. "I'm not. I swear it."

He pulled her close and embraced her. *Courage,* that embrace said.

She stepped back to look into his eyes, so dark they

seemed to be all pupil. "How in God's name do we handle this?"

TJ said, "I have an idea, and I hope your spirit is listening."

❧

THAT NIGHT, when Mrs. Mason arrived, the room was as eerie as they could manage to make it, the curtains drawn, the candles lit, the air smoky with burning sage. TJ stood beside her to welcome Mrs. Mason to the séance.

Mrs. Mason said sharply, "Who is this? You order a white man to do your bidding?"

TJ bowed and introduced himself. "I'm also a spiritualist. I sometimes aid Mrs. Auburn at our sessions to reach the dead."

Mrs. Mason's eyes glittered with distaste. "Well, I'm here. We should get on with this." She sat at the table and waited.

TJ snuffed the candles. Cassie said, "Take my hand, Mrs. Mason."

"Take your hand? I will not."

Cassie sighed. TJ said, "It helps to create a bond between us. That bond attracts the spirits."

She said, "You'll have to make do without. Touch her hand!"

Cassie said softly, "Ma'am, please try to be as calm and quiet as you can. A peaceful atmosphere encourages the spirits."

Mrs. Mason snorted.

Cassie felt lightheaded and distracted. She breathed deeply, trying to calm herself despite the currents of anger and disgust emanating from the woman who had come to ask for her help. *Help me,* she reminded her own voice.

In the silence, a sweet, high tone reverberated in her ear. It rose to the back of her throat.

It was the voice of a little boy. "Mama!" he said.

She'd heard that voice before. It belonged to the son of a planter, still young enough to love his enslaved nurse and play happily with the enslaved children of the place.

"Mama!"

Startled, Mrs. Mason said, "Who is that?"

"Mama, don't you know me?"

"What is this?"

"Oh, Mama, it's me! It's Everett!"

Mrs. Mason spluttered but said nothing.

The little boy said, "Oh, Mama, it's so lovely here. Old Ben is here with me." Old Ben had been an enslaved stable hand on the Mason place before the war. "And my pony Dapple is here too. I ride him every day, Mama! And Ben takes care of him for me."

Mrs. Mason found her voice and it was furious. "My son was a grown man when he died."

"Mama?" the sweet little voice piped up. "Don't you want to talk to me? I'm right here."

"I want to talk to a grown man, not a child!"

"Oh, Mama," the little voice said, fading.

Cassie waited, and her own spirit, who called on the African goddesses when it suited her, was the one to speak. "He's gone," it said.

Mrs. Mason was so upset she could barely get the words out. "I want to talk to Everett as he was when he died. I need to talk to him!"

The voice was weary, an old Black woman at the end of a long day. "The spirits don't come as we wish. They come as they wish."

And there was silence.

"Is that all?" Mrs. Mason demanded.

"I'm afraid so," Cassie said. "Mr. Randolph, the lights?"

TJ lit the candles.

Mrs. Mason said, "You're nothing but a fraud. You deceived me and you cheated me."

Cassie said, "No money has changed hands."

"It doesn't matter. I'll go to the police tomorrow. You're a cheat and a fraud, Cassie Andrews, and you know who murdered my son. That's what I'll tell the police."

TJ said, "Ma'am, I don't think there's any reason to talk to the police."

Mrs. Mason snapped, "And I'll tell them about you, too. Her conspirator in fraud and deception!"

After she left, Cassie asked, "Should we worry?"

"No."

"Should we prepare to flee?"

"Do you want to?" TJ said.

"No."

That night, TJ remained, trying to comfort her, but afterward, as he slipped into slumber, Cassie was unable to sleep.

Everett Mason's voice came to her. A spirit? A memory? A fear? It was thick with malice. *I told you I wasn't done with you yet.*

She rolled over and put her hand on TJ's back, wishing that his steady breathing could reassure her. She thought, *I'm not done with you yet, either.*

BUT THE POLICE didn't arrive on her doorstep the next morning, nor the morning after that. Cassie breathed a little easier. It was one thing to make a threat. It was quite another to carry it out.

McMahon, the beat policeman, stopped by on his usual day. When she handed him the money, he waved it away. Puzzled, she didn't put it back in her pocket.

He dropped his voice and said, "You should be nice to me."

She pretended to misunderstand. "Do you need another dollar for the Police Fund?"

"I'm not talking about that." He moved closer, much too close. "You know what I mean."

She stepped away. "I'm afraid I don't."

He moved close again, close enough to touch her.

Not this again. Not ever again.

"In back," he said.

She couldn't stop the memory of being pressed against the pantry wall while Everett Mason fumbled with his trousers. She hadn't been able to struggle. But now?

If she struck a policeman, she'd be arrested. Charged. Jailed. She took a deep breath.

Ask him about the child, the voice said.

The child. She caught the faintest disturbance in the air. The tiniest cry. She struggled against her disgust for this man to let it speak to her. She moved away again and asked, "You suffered a loss recently, did you not? A child?"

His voice came out in a growl. "What's that to you?"

"Such a heart-wrenching loss. A little girl, wasn't it?"

He stared at her. "What?"

The voice said, *Ask him about his wife. That's why he's here, bothering you.*

"It must have been very hard for your wife."

He stared at her. "Why would you care?" he asked.

She backed away a little more. "Would it help her to hear that her babe is happy in heaven?"

He blinked, unable to look at her.

"I would be glad to help her," she said. "As my gift to both of you."

He stepped away. He looked dazed. When he spoke, his voice was thick with emotion. "You watch yourself," he said.

"Oh, I will."

He tried to recover. "You stay out of trouble, or I'll take you down to the station."

She reached into her pocket and pulled out three dollar bills. She folded them up small to hand to him.

He waved the money away and flushed a deep, angry red. "To find out what Cassie Andrews knows about the death of Everett Mason."

THE REST of the day was uneventful. People came to consult her on lost objects and lost affections, and inside her head, the spirit's voice whispered advice. The last visitor of the day was a woman who said, "My man and I are going to the horse races on Saturday. We need advice on what horse is going to win."

Cassie's head ached. "I'm afraid the spirits have never been much help in that way," she said. "If they were, I'd be a rich woman."

The woman drew her brows together. "Why not?"

"I don't think the spirits care that much about money."

The woman asked, "What do they care about?"

The words slipped out. "Love. And justice."

"No advice, then."

Cassie said, "Go to the races and enjoy yourself. And if you lay a bet, only risk what you can afford to lose."

At that the woman laughed. "You sound just like my mama."

And at that the spirit chortled.

When the woman left, Cassie remained seated at the table in the front room. She let herself slump, and in the late afternoon quiet, she rested her face in her hands. Alongside the fatigue, she felt fear, and she felt anger, too.

When the door opened, she looked up. It was TJ, who read her face as easily as he read a hostile landscape. "You look weary," he said.

She rose. "Let's go in back," she said.

He followed her into the back room, where the curtains were always drawn. She sat heavily at the table and waited as he lit the candles. Outside, it was summer daytime, fully light. Here, in the artificial gloom, she told him about Mr. McMahon's visit.

TJ grasped her wrist, a more insistent gesture than taking her hand. "I know I said we shouldn't worry," he told her. "And that we shouldn't run. But this bothers me, Cassie. Someone knows about your past, and someone has told the police."

"Do you think I like it?"

"Why would you stay, after this?"

She said, "Let go my wrist, please."

He looked abashed. He was much more worried than he'd like to admit. He let her go.

She said, "Five years ago I ran away. I turned myself into a fugitive, out of fear. I'm not a fool, TJ. I know I still have reason to feel afraid. But this time I don't want to run away."

"There are times to make a stand, and times to retreat," he said.

"Don't give me the officer's lecture. I didn't even think about taking care of my family when I left last time. I abandoned them. And now that I'm back, I carry the remorse of my cowardice and my neglect. I don't want to do that again, either."

"Has it occurred to you that Moses and Matilda might be safer if you were gone?"

"Perhaps. And perhaps not."

"You could certainly send them money from New York."

She said, "I can't repair the damage I've done to my boys by mail from New York."

He said, "If you want them with you—"

"What are you thinking?"

"We could go back to New York and take them with us."

She said, "I've thought of that. And I've lost sleep, wondering whether my aunt and uncle are better for them than I would be. Can love them better than I can." She put her hands to her face.

He covered her hands with his own and drew them away. He looked into her eyes, and sadness suffused his expression. He had never known his father, and his mother had died when he was a boy. He knew all about being abandoned. He put his arms around her and drew her close. "Oh, Cassie."

She said, "I can't leave yet when I have so much unfinished business here."

He rested his hands on her back as though they were dancing. He sighed. "I don't want to watch the police investigate you," he said. "And I'd never forgive myself if you went to jail."

She said, "No one is going to accuse me of a murder I didn't commit."

He nodded.

"I want to find out who's doing this. It isn't coming from the Masons. Someone else is behind it. Who? And why?"

At that, he grinned. "I think you need an inquiry agent."

She leaned close and kissed him. "How lucky that I know one," she said.

THE NIGHT IN QUESTION

THE DAY AFTER THE CONVERSATION WITH MARCUS Whittaker, at the noon break, Narcissa tapped on the door of Lydia's office. There were dark circles under her eyes. "Do you have a moment?"

Lydia nodded. "Do you want to shut the door?"

Narcissa shut the door and sat in the guest chair. "I didn't sleep well last night. I was too upset."

"I'm sorry," Lydia said.

"I didn't go down this path for my pleasure," she said. "I thought a lot about whether the Beardsleys, Mr. William or Mr. John, might have murdered my brother."

"Elias and I thought a lot about that, too."

"What did he say?"

"He had the lawyer's question. He wondered whether your brother had made any enemies as a free man in Camp Shiloh or Fort Pickering."

She shook her head. "If he'd had trouble with a white man, we would have heard about it," she said.

"And another lawyer's question. Was there any ill feeling between either of the Beardsleys and anyone in your family?"

She snorted. "We all lived on the Shelby County place for years until we left for Camp Shiloh. But we were only the hands who worked in the cotton fields, and the Beardsley family was as far away as God. No, farther, since we spoke to God once a week, in church." She added, "None of the Beardsleys knew us enough to call us by name, let alone to be angry with any of us."

Lydia said, "If there's a connection between William Beardsley, or John Beardsley, and your brother, we need to find it."

Narcissa said, "We can hardly call on them, either of them, to ask them." Then she looked up, and her eyes were clearer. "But we can go sideways."

Lydia waited.

"I should have thought of this sooner. The people who worked in the house. On the country place, and in the house in Memphis. They would know."

"Would they talk to us?"

Narcissa looked up. Her eyes were suddenly clear. "There's someone who knows the Beardsley family very well," she said. "Back in slavery and during the war, at least until he left the place after Emancipation. Moses Hayes."

Lydia thought of the investigation that she and Elias had made during the war, and all the difficulty they'd had with Moses Hayes. "If he'll talk to us."

Narcissa said, "He'll talk to me. Let me go with you."

THEY MET Narcissa on the sidewalk outside the building on Beale Street. She looked puzzled. "Isn't this where Mrs. Auburn, the spiritualist, holds her séances?"

"Yes," Lydia said.

"Why are we here?"

"Because the Hayeses live upstairs," Lydia said.

"They rent from her?"

Lydia said, "I thought you knew."

"What am I missing?" Narcissa asked, truly puzzled.

"Mrs. Auburn is their niece," Elias said. "Before the war, she was called Cassie Andrews."

Narcissa stared at Lydia and Elias in astonishment. "I looked her full in the face, I heard her voice, and I had no idea," she said. "Cassie Andrews! I barely knew her on the Beardsley place. I never went into the kitchen. And once we escaped to Camp Shiloh, I never saw her there, either. But I should have known her. I feel a fool."

Elias said, "I believe it's been her aim to fool people."

Narcissa shook her head. "Cassie Andrews," she said.

They opened the door of the storefront. The front room was empty. Lydia tapped on the door to the back room, where the séances were held. Cassie emerged and even though she looked surprised, she greeted them politely. "Ah, Miss Armstrong, I remember you," she said. "From your mother's séance."

With equal politeness, Narcissa said, "Mrs. Auburn, when we first met, I didn't realize we'd known each other before the war. I hope you aren't offended that I once knew you as Cassie Andrews."

Cassie said, "It's not a secret."

"I can remain discreet, if you'd like."

"Thank you. I don't mind if you tell your mother. Just don't tell the police." Cassie looked pointedly at Elias.

Elias said, "No, this isn't a police matter. Miss Armstrong has asked me to look into the circumstances of her brother's death."

"That I know. But it might become a police matter."

"We're here to talk to your uncle," Narcissa said.

"About what?"

Narcissa looked at Elias. "May I explain?"

Elias said, "Please do."

Narcissa told Cassie about Marcus's hint and their guess.

Cassie was silent for a long moment. "The Beardsley family," she said slowly.

Impulsively, Narcissa asked, "Is there anything you might be able to tell us about the Beardsley family?"

Cassie was silent.

"Nothing incriminating," Elias said, risking a smile.

Cassie gave him a sharp look. "Before a lawyer, anything might be incriminating," she said.

"Ah, Mrs. Auburn, you have such a low opinion of me," Elias said.

"Which I believe is justified, sir."

Narcissa said softly, "It would be a great help."

Cassie's luminous eyes gleamed. "I can't risk it," she said. She looked toward the staircase that led to the second floor. "I can't stop you from talking to my aunt and uncle. But I can insist that you don't trouble them."

THEY ASCENDED the stairs to the second floor, where Matilda Hayes let them in. She greeted them all with a cautious look. "Come in."

Lydia said, "The house looks lovely."

Matilda said, "Yes, that's Cassie's doing."

"The carpet! Is it the one from your place in Camp Shiloh?"

Matilda Hayes said bitterly, "No, we lost that in the massacre. This one turned up later."

Moses Hayes rose from his chair. "Miss Narcissa," he said, taking her hands. He nodded to Lydia and Elias. Everyone sat.

"It's another inquiry, isn't it?" Moses asked, looking at Elias.

But Narcissa was the one to speak. "I trust you've heard that I've been talking to Mr. Aronson about my brother's death." She paused. "About his murder. As a matter for the courtroom."

Moses set his mouth in a tight line.

"You know that's not why I'm here," she said. "I'm here because I loved my brother. None of us, none of his family, will be able to rest until we know what truly happened to him."

"We all know that Titus Armstrong was shot. And that he was murdered. That isn't news to any of us," Moses said.

Narcissa said, "We talked to a good friend of his from the regiment. Marcus Whittaker. He was with Titus that night."

Matilda said, "What did he tell you?"

Narcissa said, "He knows that someone shot Titus. And when Marcus bent down to help him, someone put a gun to his back and said, 'This isn't about you.' A white man with a planter's accent." Narcissa looked from Moses to Matilda.

Both Moses and Matilda were silent.

Narcissa added, "We thought it might have been someone from his days in slavery."

The silence was very thick.

She leaned forward. "We thought of the Beardsleys."

Moses raised his arm, hand up, palm out. *Stop.* "I want no part of that," he said. "I did my duty during the war, keeping things in order," he said. "That's over for me. There are things I can't even bear to remember, let alone talk about."

Narcissa leaned forward, her face imploring. "And we thought you might be able to help us."

Moses said, "We've been down this road before, back in 1863. And I'll be damned if I go into a courtroom on your behalf, Mr. Elias Aronson."

Lydia said, "We aren't asking you to go to court, Mr. Hayes."

"I remember your last inquiry a little too well," Hayes said.

Puzzled, Narcissa said, "The only reason we're here is that you know the Beardsleys better than anyone. Whatever you can tell us might help."

Moses shook his head. "I don't want to say anything that would make me into a witness." At her stricken look, he said, "Not even for you, Cissy. I'm sorry. I can't." He looked at Matilda, who nodded.

Outside the door, on the landing, the three of them exchanged rueful looks. "Now I have to say that I'm sorry, Mr. Aronson," Narcissa said.

Elias said, "Well, I hoped for better, but I'm not surprised. It's not your fault, Miss Armstrong."

"What happened in 1863?"

Elias looked at Lydia, then at Narcissa. "I thought you knew."

"Knew about what?"

"We investigated the murder of a captain in the 3rd Heavy Artillery," Elias said. "We talked to Mr. Hayes more than once."

Narcissa said, "He knew more than he wanted to tell you."

"And we pushed him to tell us everything he knew," Lydia said.

Narcissa said, "And he's still angry at you."

Both Lydia and Elias nodded.

"Did he ever tell you what you wanted to know?" Narcissa asked.

Lydia said, "No, he did not."

~

LYDIA AND ELIAS walked home that afternoon, arm in arm, looking like an affectionate married couple. But their conversation, in low, intimate tones, was that of fellow investigators.

"We've been here before," Elias said.

Lydia sighed. "Yes, talking to people who know something, and who all have their reasons for keeping it to themselves."

He was silent. The touch of his hand on her arm was tender, even though his face was furrowed with a lawyer's thoughts.

"We're not looking for eyewitnesses," she reminded him. "We're looking for information on the Beardsleys that will let us approach them. We need someone who can fill us in on their history." She put her hand over his. "Before the war, during the war, and during the massacre."

He looked at her and nodded. "You're right. We don't need a witness. We need a storyteller."

"Which is a much nicer term than 'gossip.'"

He laughed. "We both know someone like that."

"Mrs. Mahaley Smith," Lydia said.

Mahaley Smith had been the housekeeper in the house where Lydia boarded when she first lived in Memphis and taught at Camp Shiloh. Mrs. Smith had served the planters who used to own the house on Beale Street. She had returned there to work for General Grant when the Union army vanquished Memphis, and she remained there when the Sanitary Commission turned it into a boardinghouse for teachers and missionaries. She knew everyone in pre-war Memphis, Black and white, and every scrap of information came to her.

Elias said, "Would she talk to us?"

"We'll ask until she stops talking," Lydia said.

Mrs. Smith now ran a boardinghouse on Beale Street, not far from Cassie's storefront. They went to see her early in the evening, just after she'd cleared her boarders' dinner dishes away. She didn't settle Elias and Lydia in the parlor. "That's for my boarders," she said. She took them into a smaller, less elegant back room, obviously her office, furnished with a desk and several chairs. She arranged the chairs for conversation, and they sat.

Elias complimented her on the boardinghouse, and she acknowledged that she'd been fortunate to make a success of it.

They'd both talked to her during their wartime inquiry, and she knew from their expressions that they were full of difficult questions. She folded her hands in her lap. "I hear you're making another inquiry," she said.

Neither of them asked how she knew.

"It's about the Beardsley family, isn't it? You're creeping up on them, aren't you?"

They both nodded. "Since we can hardly go straightaway," Elias said.

"How can I help you, the two of you?"

Elias said, "We're looking for a bit of history."

She smiled. "How far back do you want to go?"

"As far as you can remember," Elias said.

She rested her hands on her knees, the storyteller's stance, and began. "Before the war, the Beardsleys were the richest family in Shelby County," she said. "William Beardsley made a fortune in cotton in those years. He owned over a hundred slaves. And it's a curious thing, but he was never hot for secession like the smaller planters were. He liked selling his cotton up north. He liked the money he made. He didn't want to lose that.

"John Beardsley was his eldest son, and he expected to inherit the place and the cotton business one day. But his father didn't let him do much besides watch. It chafed young Marse John. It looked like his father didn't think much of him." She paused. "And he didn't.

"They both went off to war, father and son. John mustered in first, as soon as he could. His father waited a few months. They both ended up fighting in Tennessee, and they both got wounded and invalided out in 1862. Mr. William wasn't hurt much. He recovered right away, and once he took stock of what had happened to his place while he was gone, he decided to sell cotton instead of growing it. He took the loyalty oath, he bought a cotton license, and he sold cotton to the Union army. He moved to Memphis and stayed in his town house and made even more money than before the war."

Both Lydia and Elias listened quietly. Little of this was news to them. But they would let her tell them whatever she wished.

"Things were different for young Mr. John. He got wounded bad at the battle of Shiloh, and he came home with a bad leg and a bad disposition. His father told him to stay on the place and run it. Well, it was a mess, with all the people gone off to Memphis to work for the army. The '62 crop never was picked or ginned or baled, and the '63 crop never went into the ground.

"Young Mr. John came back from the war a bitter man. He was bitter about being wounded and he was bitter about what had happened to the place. His father was in Memphis, making money, and he was in the countryside, busted up because all of us had gone to Camp Shiloh to work for the army. He'd never been kindly disposed to Black people, even before the war, but after he came home, he was angry all the time. When he visited Memphis and saw some of the people who'd freed themselves, he was especially mad. And the sight of his old slaves in Union coats made him madder still. When he was drunk he swore he'd be glad to shoot any slave of his who ran away to muster in as a bluebelly."

Elias asked, "Was there someone in particular who told you that, Mrs. Smith?"

"It's all gossip," she said.

"Yes, hearsay, as we lawyers call it. But sometimes it leads to a truth that can stand in a courtroom."

She thought for a moment, then said, "The woman who used to be the cook at the Beardsley house in town," she said. "She heard all kinds of things when she worked for Mr. William Beardsley."

"Where is she now?" Lydia asked. "Is she still in Memphis?"

"Yes, she works for some Yankees now. She says they pay her better, and they don't act like they own her."

"Might she talk to us?"

"I can ask, but that's up to her," Mrs. Smith said.

Mrs. Maggie Rice was pleased to usher them into the front room of the little house in South Memphis. "It's plain, but it's ours," she said, smiling.

The furniture was well-used and worn, but the muslin

curtains were fresh, giving the room a golden glow in the early evening sun. "It must be pleasant to sit here," Lydia said.

Her smile broadened. "I don't live in. Can't tell you how glad I am of that." She arranged her skirt.

Lydia said, "Thank you for talking to us."

"I didn't talk to that commission from Congress that came to Memphis after the massacre, but I knew people who did," she said. "I hoped it would bring some justice for us. I was bitter when it didn't." As she spoke, the intelligence that she kept banked for white people began to glow brighter and brighter. "Now I want to do what I can. How can I help you?"

Bless you, Lydia thought.

Elias asked, "How long did you work for the Beardsley family?"

"I was born into slavery on the place in Shelby County. I always worked in the house, in the kitchen. Came with the family when they went into town. When Mr. William moved into town for good, just after he came back from the war, he brought me along to run the kitchen."

Lydia asked, "You were there during the war?"

"Yes, and for a while after. I stayed there until last year. Then I left and went to work for a Yankee family."

Elias asked, "Did Mrs. Smith explain why we wanted to talk to you?"

"Oh, Miss Mahaley made it plain. You're looking into the murder of that poor Armstrong boy, and you think the Beardsleys might have had a hand in it."

Lydia nodded.

Elias said, "We were wondering if you knew if the Beardsleys were interested in the Armstrongs in any way."

"Besides owning them, before Emancipation?"

Lydia asked, "Why? Was there a connection that you know about?"

She said, "When they were out on the Beardsley place, they were all in the fields, and I know for sure that William Beardsley didn't even know their names."

"We were wondering if the Beardsleys bore the Armstrongs any ill will," Elias asked.

"Ill will? How could they, when they didn't know who they were? Mr. William and Mr. John never even spoke to the folks who worked in the fields. They left that to the overseer and to the driver. Moses Hayes. Have you spoken to him?"

Elias said, "Yes. As far as he's concerned, that's all in the past. He doesn't want to talk about it."

She sighed. "As though we could ever forget," she said.

Elias asked, "So there was no history with Titus. No bad blood."

She looked pensive again. "Not with him personally," she said. "But there was a lot of bad feeling about the people who left, starting when the Yankees came."

Elias said, "Mrs. Smith mentioned that you heard William and John Beardsley arguing about that."

"They argued every time Mr. John came into town. I couldn't help overhearing, they were so loud. Mr. William didn't think Mr. John was running the place right, and Mr. John told him he was doing his best."

"Mrs. Smith told us you once heard John Beardsley say he'd like to shoot his former slaves who joined the Union army. Is that true?"

She looked at Elias, then at Lydia, and her face was somber. She nodded. "I remember that fight, because it was the ugliest. It was in 1866, before the massacre, about the time to start getting ready to plant cotton, if you were going to put in a crop. Mr. William told Mr. John he'd better make a crop this year, and Mr. John got mad and told him he didn't have the hands to put in a crop. Mr. William got mad, too, and told him he had to try harder to enforce the labor contracts and to keep people working on the place. Mr. John was yelling at the top of his lungs, saying that he hadn't been able to keep them on the place since 1863, because they ran to Camp Shiloh and to Fort Pickering. Mr. William told him he wasn't doing enough to keep them from running off. Mr. John said that if he saw any of their people in Memphis in their Union army coats, he'd shoot them to let the others know the consequences of running off."

Lydia asked, "Was he serious? Or just angry?"

Mrs. Rice considered this. "Mr. John had always had a temper," she said. "It was worse when he got back from the war. He was in pain from his leg all the time, and he drank a lot for it. When he was drunk and angry—well, people knew to keep out of his way."

Elias asked, "Did he ever shoot anyone on the place?"

"Before the war? When they were still enslaved? Lord, no. His father would have had his hide for damaging his property." She paused. "But after the war, once they were free and they weren't property anymore—" She looked down. "Well, we saw how that worked out in 1866."

Elias said, "Did you hear that he shot anyone after the war?"

She shook her head. "If I talked to the commission, and they asked me, 'Did you see that happen?' I'd have to say no."

Lydia asked, "Can we ask you about the massacre itself? Would you tell us what you remember?"

"I was all right. That's why I didn't talk to the commission. Mr. William shut up the house, even though the trouble was far away from us, and forbade anyone to leave. We waited it out like you'd wait out a storm. No one got hurt."

"Was John Beardsley in town during the massacre?"

"He wasn't at the house. But sometimes he'd come into town and stay at a hotel. He liked the Gayoso on Main Street. He'd drink and play cards in the back room." She looked thoughtful. "The man who would know is Charlie Southall, who was his coachman then. He doesn't work for the Beardsleys anymore. He lives in Memphis, not far from here."

CHARLIE SOUTHALL, John Beardsley's former coachman, was bursting with energy and good cheer. He told them, "I drive a wagon for a lumber company now, but with that and my wife's wages as a washerwoman, we're saving money so I can buy my own horse and cart."

"How long did you work for the Beardsleys?" Elias asked.

"I was born on the Beardsley place. All my life, before the war. And after Mr. John Beardsley came home from the war, I was his coachman." He looked at both of them and said, "Mrs. Maggie Rice explained to me about the Armstrongs and your investigation. And so did Mrs. Mahaley Smith. What do you want to know?"

He, too, remembered the night of May 1st with painful clarity. "Yes, I drove Mr. John into town that day," he said. "Tried to talk him out of it, because we'd been hearing about disturbances on the streets. He said he didn't employ me to argue with him, but to do as he asked. So I did."

Elias asked, "Where did he stay that night?"

"Not at his daddy's house. He stayed at the Gayoso. He liked to play cards there."

Elias asked, "Did he go out that night?"

"Well, that was an odd thing. He'd been in the hotel for a while, at the card table. He came out to the stable—he was lit up—and told me he was going out, but he didn't need me to drive him. I told him we were hearing about how bad things were on the streets, and it was dangerous. And he reminded me it wasn't my place to talk to him like that. He looked like he might strike me. I shut up and let him go."

Elias asked, "Do you have any idea where he went?"

Southall shook his head.

Lydia asked, "Had you ever heard him say he'd like to shoot any former slave of his who left to put on a blue coat?"

He looked grave. "That wasn't any secret," he said.

"Did he ever mention Titus Armstrong?"

"No, he didn't," Southall said.

Elias asked, "Where were you on that night?"

"I was in the stables. I knew the stablemen at the hotel. We all heard about the trouble on South Street, and the other men were worried sick about their families. But they couldn't leave to see how they were doing."

Elias looked disappointed. "So you don't know where he went, and you didn't see what happened on South and Beale that night."

"I ain't finished yet," Southall said. "He came back late that night. After midnight. Found me in the stables. He was holding his pistol, looking wild-eyed, shaky on his feet. He wanted me to drive him back to his place in the countryside. I said, 'Marse John, why don't we stay put tonight? At the hotel, or at the house in town?'"

He hesitated. Then he said, "He pointed the pistol at me. I told him, as gentle as I could, that he should put his pistol away. He told me he needed it. 'Not here,' I said, 'It's quiet here.' And he said, 'Not over on South Street. The n—s are rioting on South Street. Men in blue coats.' I tell you, my blood ran cold.

"Then the other stablemen came to help me. We took hold of him, as gentle as we could, and took the pistol away.

He crumpled up and I said, 'Let me help you into the carriage and take you to your daddy's house.' He looked up. There was no more fight in him. I got him into the carriage, and that's when I noticed I had blood on my hands. I said to him, 'You're bleeding. Are you all right?' And he said, 'That isn't my blood.' And that froze me."

Elias started forward and Lydia laid a restraining hand on his arm. *Let him tell it.*

Southall continued, "I took him to his daddy's house and I woke up the butler. He saw the blood on Mr. John's clothes. I gave him the gun. He sniffed it. 'Fired recently,' he said. And he told me he'd take care of things." He fell silent.

Elias asked, "What happened to the gun? And the blood-stained clothes?"

"The butler took them away. I don't know what he did with them."

"Whose blood was it?" Elias asked.

Southall said, "I wasn't there and I didn't see it. But I believe in my heart that he shot a Black Union soldier on South Street that night."

THE BEARDSLEYS

CASSIE SAT IN HER FRONT ROOM. THIS EARLY IN THE MORNING, it was already hot. The dust from the street wafted under the sills and the door and danced in the sunlight. It would be pretty, Cassie thought, if it weren't such a misery. The door opened, and Dolly walked into the storefront, smoothing her apron, looking smug.

Does her employer know she gads about? Cassie thought. She said, "You look well."

"I do fine," Dolly said, smirking.

"I had quite a visit recently from the policeman on my beat," Cassie said. "Might you know anything about that?"

"Policeman? What does that have to do with me? I don't know a thing," Dolly said, but her expression said otherwise.

"I wonder," Cassie said.

"Wonder all you like."

"Is there something that you want from me?" Cassie asked, her voice sharp. "Because I already spent all my bribe money."

Dolly pretended to look hurt. "What a how do you do," she said. "I came to ask you a question for the spirits."

"Really? What do you want to know?"

She drew up her short, lumpy body. "I want to know if my man will marry me," she said.

Cassie wondered how a woman as disagreeable as Dolly had found a man to consider marriage with her. She was mildly curious to discover what the spirits might tell her. "All right. But there's a condition."

"You ain't in a circumstance to make conditions."

"Is that a threat?"

Dolly snickered. "What condition, then?"

"I won't ask you for payment. But you need to answer a question for me."

She snorted. "Depends on the question."

"Do you want an answer from the spirits, or not?"

"Shouldn't we go in back? Where you call them spirits up?"

"This won't require a séance, believe me. Just hold out your hand, palm up."

Dolly gave her a scornful look, but she held out her hand.

"What is his name?" Cassie asked.

"Don't the spirits know?"

"The spirits don't consult the city directory," Cassie said.

"Called Joe. Joe Morgan."

Cassie didn't really need to look at the palm, but she scrutinized it anyway. She didn't even have to hear the voice. Her mind drew the image of a man with a mild demeanor. "Not tall? A little bowed in the legs?"

Dolly stared at her in surprise. "How do you know?"

Cassie thought, *I just described half the overworked, underfed men in Memphis who used to be enslaved.* She said, "I can see him clearly."

"Will he ask me?"

"He does love you. And his intentions are true." *God help him.*

"When? I want to get ready."

"Soon," Cassie said. At Dolly's look, she said, "The spirits don't keep a calendar, either."

Dolly waited, then asked, "Is that all?"

"That's all the spirits tell me right now." She let go of Dolly's hand. "Now you owe me."

Dolly's grin was mean. "Said you wouldn't charge me," she said.

"Not in money. But you do owe me the answer to a question."

"What kind of answer?"

Cassie looked directly into Dolly's dark, squinting eyes. After a moment Dolly turned her face away.

Cassie asked, "Did you tell Mr. William Beardsley about me?"

Dolly rubbed her eyes as though they hurt. "No. Why would he listen to me?"

"You must have told someone."

Dolly blinked.

"Who did you tell?"

Dolly's voice was a little sullen. "Don't stare at me like that. I told my cousin, who works for Marse John Beardsley."

"And did she tell Mr. John Beardsley?"

"I suppose she did."

She made a leap. "And did someone tell Mrs. Mason, Everett Mason's mother?"

Dolly shrugged. "I don't know that."

Cassie said, "Is that the truth?"

"Don't stare at me again, it bothers me."

Cassie stared at her.

"If I tell you, will you stop that?"

Cassie waited.

Dolly cried out, "Yes! Mrs. Mason knows!"

Cassie broke her gaze.

Dolly rubbed her eyes again. They were red and watering. "Are we even?"

Cassie nodded. "As even as we'll ever be," she said.

As Dolly left, the voice spoke to Cassie. *She has a hole in her heart.* Cassie thought, *That's for sure.*

The voice said, *No, she has a sickness. She'll drop dead without any warning. Don't know when. Could be anytime.*

Cassie had no satisfaction in knowing that. She was furious.

HER FURY DIDN'T ABATE as the day progressed, bringing a woman who wanted to arrange to talk to her lost husband and a man who'd lost his cat. She took the woman's name and the husband's for TJ to look into. As for the cat, she said, "He went to the house around the corner. He's all right. The children are making a fuss over him."

The man was old and grizzled. "Don't see why he'd do that," he said, looking hurt. "I dote on him."

"Just wanted a change. Cats do that sometimes."

"How do I get him home?"

"Fish," Cassie said.

When the man left, she was angry again. Her secret was out, and it wasn't safe with the Beardsleys or the Masons. And neither she nor her family were safe because of it. The threat from the police was the least of it. She wondered, with a feeling of weariness, how else she might be in danger, and from whom.

That evening, at the supper table, she was short with

Moses when he asked her for the biscuits and even sharper when Matilda prodded her to help clear the dishes. "What's gotten into you?" her aunt asked, as they picked up the dirty plates.

She told her aunt about Dolly's visit. Matilda snickered. "Can't believe she found a man fool enough to want to marry her," she said.

"She was fool enough to make sure that Mr. John Beardsley and Mrs. Mason know I'm back in Memphis. I'm sure that Mrs. Mason complained to the police about me. The police came by to let me know about it."

"About the spirits?"

Cassie set the dishes on the kitchen table. "About Everett Mason."

Matilda said, "That's over and settled. How can they bother you about him?"

"Aunt Matilda, you know full well the police can bother me for walking around breathing while Black. And they will, if they feel like it. And all the more so if they're doing it at the Beardsleys' bidding."

Matilda shook her head.

Cassie said, "Did you say anything to Miss Narcissa when she came asking about the Beardsleys?"

Matilda grew indignant. "You know we didn't," she said. "Your uncle just about threw them out, Mr. and Mrs. Aronson. We don't want anything to do with the Armstrongs' trouble."

"The last thing I need is for the Beardsleys to know the Armstrongs are turning up the past, too. And looking for Beardsleys under the rocks."

Matilda said, "No one is telling the Beardsleys anything."

Will lurked in the doorway between the dining room and the kitchen.

Matilda said, "Will, what are you doing there? What did I tell you about listening to conversations that don't concern you?"

"No, Aunt Matilda, just bringing in the biscuit dish." He set it on the kitchen table.

Cassie said, "Will, you were listening in. Why? Have you heard anything?"

He hesitated. "Ma'am—"

She sighed, but he still wasn't ready to call her anything else.

"Miss Armstrong talks to Mrs. Aronson about her brother's—" He hesitated and didn't finish. "She frets over it."

"Really?" Cassie asked. "What does Mrs. Aronson say?"

"Tells her not to worry." He hesitated again. "Because she and Mr. Aronson will keep inquiring."

Cassie looked at her self-possessed son, who was now as tall as she was. "Does she talk about what they're looking for?"

Will ducked his head. "No, ma'am," he said, his voice very soft.

Matilda said, "Leave the boy alone, Cassie. He's not an inquiry agent. Ask that Mr. Randolph of yours."

Cassie said, "I just might."

"Ma'am, is Mr. Randolph a Black man?" Will asked.

Cassie looked afresh at her fair-skinned son whose resemblance to his father still caused her pain. "He's as Black as you are," she said, a little too sharply.

Will gave her a long, searching look. "Why does Mr. Randolph come here at night sometimes?"

"His business is irregular. Sometimes we confer at night."

Will didn't reply, but Cassie could read his expression. The voice helped her, just a little. *Don't admit that Mr.*

Randolph sometimes visits all night. Cassie thought, *Does Will know?* She heard the familiar chuckle.

THAT NIGHT, as she lay in bed with TJ, she raised herself on her elbow. He looked very pale in the darkness. He touched her cheek, and she said, "My son Will knows too much."

"Yes, he does, but what in particular are you thinking of?"

"He knows about us."

He let his fingers trail down her face to rest on her bare shoulder. "He's old enough."

"I don't like it."

TJ sighed. "I doubt he was ever innocent," he said.

She sighed.

He asked, "What else weighs on you?"

She met his eyes. "Too much," she said.

"Just the heaviest thing," he said.

She told him about Dolly's visit. "The Beardsleys, father and son, know that I'm in Memphis," she said. "As do the Masons. Now I know who went to the police."

He nodded. "Who talked, and who encouraged," he said.

"I'm going to talk to Elias Aronson."

"Why?"

"I want to know what the Memphis police can arrest me for. And what they can't." She curled her free hand into a fist. "I am unspeakably angry," she said.

He curled his free hand over it. "Use it carefully," he said.

CASSIE STOOD outside Elias Aronson's office on Main Street, trying to compose herself. She was angry that she had come here at all, and angrier still to speak to Elias Aronson, whom she remembered too well from his inquiry during the war. She smoothed her skirt and touched her bonnet. She opened the door and was startled at the way the hinges creaked. Did he leave them like that to warn himself of a visitor?

She opened the door, letting the familiar smell of lawyering—leather-bound law tomes, fresh paper, and ink—come to her. She wished that it didn't remind her so much of the office of her lawyer in New York, who had set up her business and, several times after that, defended her right to ply it.

Elias Aronson looked up, rose, and extended his hand to her. "Mrs. Auburn," he said. "Please sit."

She sat in his guest chair, carefully arranging her skirt, making him wait a moment. She said abruptly, "I need legal advice."

"I can do my best to help you, but I'm surprised you didn't go to see Mr. Dorsey."

She says, "There's an advantage to having a white lawyer."

He felt her barb, but he didn't respond to it. "I see your point. Mrs. Auburn, how can I assist you?" He reached for a piece of paper and a pen.

She said, "I'd like to know what the police can arrest me for."

He said, "There's what you've done, and what they suspect."

"How much suspicion allows them to make an arrest?"

"Have they threatened you with arrest?"

"Yes. It was harassment as well as intimidation."

He poised the pen over the paper. "What happened?"

She let her disgust show on her face as she told him about McMahon's latest visit.

He listened and nodded as she spoke, then made notes. "Do you want to make a complaint?"

"Of course not. We know it's useless to try. But I'd feel better knowing if they have any grounds to arrest me."

He said, "We'll take the accusations one at a time." He ticked them off on his fingers. "Can they charge you and arrest you for changing your name? No, they can't. For fraud? They don't have anything to go on, since you don't charge for your services. Have you ever refused a donation or a gift?"

"Yes, I have, and I've made a record of it." She leaned forward. "Can they arrest me on suspicion of the murder of Everett Mason?"

"Not unless they have evidence."

"You know that never stopped the Memphis police before."

"Can they railroad you into jail? Sadly, yes. Can they railroad you into a trial? That would be considerably more difficult."

She wasn't reassured, and she didn't reply.

Elias said, "Why are they trying to revive an inquiry into a death that is five years old and that was acknowledged at the time to be an accident?"

"The Mason family was very angry at the time. Don't you remember?"

"Yes, very well."

"Could they insist that the police revisit Mason's death?"

"They could." He gave her a searching look. "Do you have reason to think they might?"

She told him about Dolly's news.

He said, "Whether the police would consider it worth their time to look at Everett Mason's death again—well, that's another question. They have all the usual crimes and vices to handle. And they now have scrutiny of a mayor and a governor with strong feelings about belonging to the party of General Grant."

"Mr. Aronson, you know as well as I do that the Memphis police are still holding out their hands for bribes. Whoever pays them enough gets their attention."

"Do you think someone bribed them?"

She leaned forward. "The Masons don't have a dime," she said. "I'd look to the Beardsley family."

He started. "Have you asked Mr. Randolph to do that?"

"Not yet," she said. "Should I?"

He looked at her with curiosity. "I wonder what he would find," he said.

She met his eyes. "Mr. Aronson, I know that Narcissa Armstrong has asked you to look into her brother's murder," she said. "With an eye to discovering the culprit."

He laid his fingers on his blotter. "Mrs. Auburn, as I'm sure you're aware, I can't talk about the affairs of one client with another. My promise of confidentiality forbids it."

"Ah, so she's your client," Cassie said.

He didn't reply.

She nodded. She knew enough.

CASSIE CALLED on the Armstrongs that evening, when Narcissa was likely to be home. At the sight of her, the younger children clustered around Narcissa, wide-eyed. "Who is that?" one of Narcissa's little sisters whispered.

Mrs. Armstrong said, "This is Mrs. Auburn, who can talk to the spirits, and who helped us talk to Titus."

The little girl asked, "Can we talk to him, too?"

Cassie inclined her head as Narcissa frowned.

Mrs. Armstrong said, "Oh, I would give anything to hear from him again. Just to hear his voice!"

Cassie said, "That can be arranged, if you wish it."

Narcissa said, "My mother was so upset after our last séance that she was ill."

The little girl's face tightened. She pulled on Narcissa's sleeve. "I don't want Mama to be sick," she said, her voice tiny.

"I'm sorry to hear that," Cassie said. "I'll do my best to prevent that from happening again, but the spirits are mercurial."

Narcissa said, "I'm not interested in their excuses. Or yours. Why have you come to see us?"

"We may have common cause."

"Do we?"

"Not in a spiritual matter. In an earthly one."

"I doubt it," Narcissa says.

"In the business of looking into the Beardsley family," Cassie said.

"Who told you about that?"

"It's common knowledge in every Black church in Memphis," Cassie said.

"It may be common knowledge that we're pursuing justice for my brother," Narcissa said. "But it's not common knowledge that the Beardsleys may be involved. Who told you that?"

Cassie inclined her head.

"If it was Mr. Aronson—"

"It was not. Mr. Aronson is too high-minded for that."

"I doubt it was a spirit," Narcissa said.

"There's no reason to consult the spirits when common sense will do."

"Someone spies for you, no doubt."

"Someone makes inquiries for me. And he can do the same for you, if you wish. Do you?"

Narcissa was silent.

Cassie said, "Mrs. Armstrong, if you want peace for your son—"

"Oh, of course I do," she said. Her voice held a plea. "Cissy, don't you?"

"I want justice," Narcissa said.

Cassie said, "We can accomplish both."

"I don't trust you," Narcissa said.

"Let me try," Cassie said. "Let my inquiry agent try."

"For a fee, no doubt."

"No, there's no fee." Cassie looked at Narcissa with her luminous eyes.

Narcissa looked away. After a long moment of reflection, she said, "Tell your inquiry agent to be careful."

THE COTTON PLANTER

TJ walked into the storefront, looking pale and drawn. "It's hot in New York in the summer," he said, "but not like this. This is like wading through a swamp."

"Let's go in back," Cassie said. "It feels cooler there with the curtains drawn, and you can take off your coat and loosen your cravat."

She led and he followed. He shrugged off his coat. His shirt was wrinkled, and he smelled of sweat. He wiped his face with his handkerchief as he sat. "Do you have something for me?"

"Yes," she said.

"Lost ring? Straying husband? Deceitful servant?"

She smiled.

"That's your villainess look," he said.

She let her canines show. "The Beardsley family."

He was quiet for so long that she asked, "What are you thinking?"

"Why pursue this, Cassie? I thought the man who hurt you so badly is dead, and he wasn't a Beardsley."

"William Beardsley allowed it," she said. "I want my

revenge on the Beardsleys, too." She dropped her voice. "And if I can help Narcissa—"

He was sharp. "Miss Armstrong's trouble is hers, not yours," he said.

"I want to hurt them worse than they hurt me," she said.

"At what cost?"

She fell silent.

"Revenge is a fool's game," TJ said.

"What else can I do? I can't take them to court!"

He said, "You can walk away. You can leave. You can take the boys with you—"

"I want to do this." She laid her hand on his arm. "I need you, TJ." When he hesitated again. "Not as a soldier. As a scout. As an inquiry agent." She curled her fingers around his arm. "As my friend."

He shook his head. "I like you a great deal, you know that. But I don't like this."

"I'll do it, with you or without you," she said.

"You can't do it without me."

She leaned close. "Then help me."

"God help me. God help both of us."

"He will. And she will, too."

His face was shadowed. "What do you want me to do?"

"Get as close to them as you can. And learn whatever you can." She added, "We want to trouble the water. Find out what you can about their connection to Titus Armstrong's murder."

"Let me think about the part I should play."

She said, "Mr. William Beardsley is a cotton broker. And his son John runs the family's cotton plantation."

He said slowly, "Might they talk to a Yankee who wants to go into the cotton growing business?" he said. "Encourage him, even?"

"I believe they would."

"Then that's the mask I'll wear." He leaned back in his chair, resting as he contemplated the labor before him. Then he sat up straight again. "Where do you suggest I start?"

"With William Beardsley. He's in town, and he's easier to approach."

"What does he care about?"

She laughed, a bitter sound. "Money," she said. "He's always cared about money. Whatever can make him money will get his attention."

He nodded. "I'll keep that in mind when I call on him."

She pressed her hands together. "How I wish I could go with you."

"Don't even suggest it," he warned her.

TJ RETURNED from his visit to William Beardsley looking surprised. Even a little pleased.

"It went well?" she asked.

"It was even easier than I thought."

"You fooled him?"

"He took me at face value." He gestured toward his skin. "And as soon as he heard that I was looking for land to work, he suggested that I talk to his son John, who has land in Shelby County that's standing idle."

"Which bothers him, no doubt, since there's no profit in it."

"He's not happy that John Beardsley is standing idle, either. He made it clear that he thinks his son is lazy."

Cassie snorted. "Yes, he's not half the man his daddy is," she said. "And it's made him crazy since he was a boy."

TJ nodded. "Good to know."

"Don't go out there to meet him."

"Oh, I have no desire to go into the countryside," he said. "They still think they're fighting the war, and it isn't safe yet. And isn't Mrs. Mason, who's seen me, a neighbor of theirs?"

Cassie nodded.

"The good news is that I didn't even have to object to a meeting on the plantation. William Beardsley insisted on asking his son to meet me in town. I'm invited to speak with John Beardsley at their town house the day after tomorrow."

Cassie said, "I'd bet Mr. William thinks—rightfully so—that you'd turn tail if you saw what a shambles the place is."

Now TJ snorted. "The Union army's doing, no doubt," he said. "Glad to have been of service."

"Does Mr. William Beardsley know you were a Union officer?"

"He didn't ask, and I didn't tell him. I'll do the same with Mr. John Beardsley. I'll let him draw his own conclusions."

As TJ WENT to call on John Beardsley, Cassie remained in her storefront. She couldn't sit still. She got up from the table, stared out the plate glass window, paced the length of the room, and sat down again. She fidgeted at the table. She thought, *I know I can't be there, but I wish with all my heart I could manage it.*

The voice said, *Sit and be quiet.*

Cassie thought, *That's easy for you to say.*

The voice was sharp. *We'll know soon enough.*

And then? Cassie thought.

We'll know that too.

She got up again to stride to the window and stare down

the street. She was looking in the wrong direction, and when the door opened, she was surprised to see Lydia Aronson.

She hurried to compose herself. "What brings you here, Mrs. Aronson?"

Mrs. Aronson gestured to the table. She didn't remove her gloves or her bonnet, the signs of politeness in a social call. "May we sit?"

"Yes, of course."

Cassie smiled at her. "Is there some way I can help you, Mrs. Aronson?"

She said, "I understand that you know that Miss Armstrong has been looking into the circumstances of her brother's death. She's asked my husband for his help."

Cassie inclined her head in acknowledgment. "Yes, I'm well aware of it."

Mrs. Aronson said, "But I hadn't known that you were looking into the matter on her behalf."

Cassie said, "I hope I can help her."

Mrs. Aronson said, "She told me that you were investigating the Beardsley family." She added, "With an eye to making a connection to Titus Armstrong."

Cassie said, "That's true."

Mrs. Aronson gave her an odd look. "Given your history with them, I don't know whether to thank you for your help or caution you for your safety," she said.

"I'd take either," Cassie said. "But you shouldn't be concerned on my behalf. I'm not approaching them myself. I've asked Mr. Randolph to do so." She felt a shiver and folded her hands together to control any shaking.

Mrs. Aronson gave her a long, appraising look. "May I ask you a favor?"

"Perhaps," Cassie said, smiling a little to acknowledge the history she had with Lydia Owens Aronson.

"Would you share what you find with Mr. Aronson and myself?"

"With Miss Armstrong's permission, certainly."

"Of course. Thank you." She didn't rise to go. She looked drawn and tired. Something troubled her. Cassie thought idly, *What is it?* But the spirit's voice was silent.

Cassie asked, "Mrs. Aronson, do you ever hear the voices of your dead? Your husband, who fell in the war?"

She looked up in surprise. "Yes, I do. The memory of my former husband is always with me. He abides in my mind and my heart."

"Does Mr. Aronson know?"

"Yes, he knows that I remember Dan."

"Does it bother him?"

"No, of course not. Elias knows I had a life before I met him. I didn't cast it away to marry him."

Cassie said, "Have you ever attended a séance, Mrs. Aronson?"

She tugged on the fingers of her gloves. "I have, with more than one friend. But I've never attended as a believer."

Cassie leaned forward. "Would you like to hear your former husband's voice again? Not just in your mind?"

Mrs. Aronson's tone held a familiar irony. "Are you offering that to me?"

"If you wish."

Mrs. Aronson's eyes met hers. That forthright Yankee gaze was powerful in its own right. "I might like to attend. Not as a believer. But to see how you do it."

Cassie laughed softly. "That I can offer you," she said.

∼

WHEN TJ RETURNED from his visit to John Beardsley, Cassie wrinkled her nose. "You smell like you've been in a saloon," she said.

"I have been. But let me tell you the story from the beginning."

They went into the back, where Cassie opened the curtains enough to let in the still-vibrant day. They sat at the séance table, side by side. She said, "From the beginning, then."

He nodded. "When I arrived at the Beardsley family's house, the butler showed me into the study. Mr. John Beardsley was there, smoking, slouched in his chair. The first thing I noticed was how difficult it was for him to rise to greet me. He limps very noticeably, and he seems to be in pain all the time."

"He was wounded at the battle of Shiloh," Cassie said.

TJ nodded.

Cassie asked, "How did he strike you?"

"Diminished," TJ said. "Defeated. Mr. William Beardsley is a very handsome and vigorous man. His son is not."

"Not half the man his daddy was," Cassie murmured.

"He told me that his father had described my purpose, to go into the cotton business, and that he had also reminded him, John Beardsley, that he had land standing idle that he could rent to someone who wanted to use it. He didn't look happy to tell me that. I told him that I was looking for the right opportunity, and if he presented it to me, I'd be glad of it, but if not, I wouldn't trouble him further."

"And he didn't doubt you? He took you at face value, a Yankee who wanted to go into the cotton business?"

"Evidently. He looked at me and then he looked past me, at the wall behind my head, and he said that he was damned if he was going to let his father run his business for him, or his life for him, and he needed a drink. I expected him to pour the whiskey from the decanter, but he said that he would take me to a saloon where he could talk freely."

"Where did you go?"

"It was on Main Street. No, not the Gayoso. Down the street, toward the river. A much seedier place."

"The address?"

He told her and she said, "That's where the Rebs used to drink during the war."

"Do you know it?"

"Too well," she said.

"It seems that the former Rebs still haunt the place," TJ said. "Mr. Beardsley greeted someone when we walked in and called him 'Colonel.' He had a Tennessee accent. I don't think he wore a blue coat in the late conflict."

"I think you're right."

"When we sat down, he asked me if I'd ever managed Black people before. He didn't use a polite term."

Cassie said, "Before the war, planters thought that word was vulgar and mean."

"He used it freely," TJ said. "When I told him I hadn't, he said he had some advice for me. Black people needed a firm hand. They needed to sign labor contracts for the entire year, and they needed to agree to take shares of the crop. He leaned forward and told me that there were all kinds of ways to ensure that they never got properly paid for their share. If they stayed in debt, he told me, they could be arrested and jailed for leaving and reneging on their debt."

Cassie shook her head.

"After the second round—he drank, I poured mine discreetly on the floor—he told me that he didn't let them work their own plots. He kept them in gangs and insisted that they live in the old slave cabins, as before the war. He was happy to punish anyone who shirked, or malingered, or objected. When I mentioned that his methods seemed extreme to me, he told me that he wanted to ensure that they were afraid to cross him."

"Does he whip them, as in the days of slavery?"

"He was on his third glass by then, and I suspect he'd started drinking at home, well before we walked into the saloon. He told me that he threatened them with bodily harm, and if anyone had it in mind to run away, as he put it, he'd come after them."

Cassie said, "It hardly seems like a way to encourage anyone to stay, much less to work."

"Oh, he hates anyone who runs away. He boasted to me that he shot a man. I said to him, 'We all did, if we fought in the war.' He told me that it wasn't in the war, but after the war, in Memphis. I asked him if it was a barroom disagreement. And his eyes gleamed. 'No, it was during that disturbance two years ago. A bluecoat. Probably a runaway.'"

Cassie leaned forward. "He didn't say more?"

"No, and I didn't press him."

Cassie knotted her hands on the table in frustration.

TJ continued, "He told me that he was by no means the only one who felt that way about Black people who should be working the cotton fields. He mentioned that he was part of a band of men who made sure to frighten these people and keep them in their proper place."

Cassie said, "White hoods? Fear at night? Forrest's men?"

TJ nodded. "He made it clear that if I rented land from him, I was free to join their ranks."

"My goodness. How drunk was he? Or is he unhinged, even when he's sober? He doesn't know you or your loyalties!"

"That tells us something," TJ said. "That he'd tell such a thing to a stranger."

"What is he, then? A useless, foolish drunk, or a Klansman?"

"A useless drunk with a rifle is a very dangerous man," TJ said.

She looked at him. "You aren't going to take him up on his offer."

"No, I'm not planning to join Mr. Nathan Bedford Forrest's merry band. My ability to dissemble doesn't extend that far."

She was momentarily silent.

He asked, "What is it? You're stuck on something."

"We have a man unhinged by rage and drink, who hates runaways and boasts of having shot at least one," she said.

TJ nodded.

"This is a man perfectly capable of murdering a Black Union soldier," Cassie said.

TJ said, "That thought crossed my mind as well."

Cassie shook her head. "I can hear Mr. Aronson talking to me, as clear as if he was sitting here," she said. He would say, 'Yes, but we don't know which Black Union soldier he shot.'"

"There may be enough here for Narcissa to take to Mr. Aronson. And for Mr. Aronson to use to pursue the matter."

"I wonder," Cassie said. She fell silent again.

"You're still bothered by something, I can tell."

"I know that the Beardsleys remember me," she said. "I wonder if John Beardsley remembers me as a runaway."

TJ said, "I hope to God not."

She didn't reply, and TJ was silent for a while. "I'm staying close by," he said. "I can shoot, and I plan to remain sober." He sighed. "You can rely on that."

~

AFTER TJ LEFT, Will knocked on the door to the back room. His face was grave. "Ma'am?" he asked. "May I come in?"

"Of course, Will," she said. She thought that her son would make a good inquiry agent. Or a good spiritualist. He was able to enter a room without a sound. He was also well-versed at listening outside closed doors.

He came in and stood beside the table but didn't sit.

She reached out her hands to him, but he didn't take them. "Oh, Will. I wish you wouldn't call me 'ma'am.' I'm your mother. You could call me that if 'mama' sounds too childish to you."

He didn't reply and his face was very still.

"What is it, Will?" she asked, putting a plea into her voice.

In the half-light of the room, with its partially open curtains, he looked much older than his age. He had a gravitas that made him look very different from his father. She could imagine this serious boy, grown up, as a minister or a lawyer. "Are you in trouble?" he asked her, and he put a plea into his voice to match hers.

"Why would you think that?"

He looked unhappy, as though she was pressing him to betray a confidence.

"Did Uncle Moses say something? Or Aunt Matilda?"

He didn't speak. He didn't nod. He gazed at her, and even though his eyes were lighter than her own, they had a weighty gaze she knew very well. He had inherited that from her.

"You're a brave boy," she said to him. "If something upsets you or frightens you, you wouldn't run away from it."

At that he inclined his head, as though he wasn't used to praise. "Thank you, ma'am," he said softly.

She wished he would let her take his hand. "Will, it's all right," she said, her voice also soft. "Look at me."

He obeyed her.

"I'm not in trouble," she said. "And even if I were, I wouldn't run away." She smiled. "I think you can understand that."

He didn't smile in return. "Yes, ma'am," he said.

SEVERAL DAYS LATER, when Mr. McMahon opened the door, he was accompanied by another policeman, stockier and younger. She thought, *Do I have to pay them both?* She sighed and reached into her pocket. "Good morning, Mr. McMahon."

"You can put that away," he said.

"Really?" she asked.

He reached for her arm. Puzzled, she pulled it away. Then he grabbed her by the hand.

"Let go of me!" she cried out. Surely he wasn't planning to assault her while his fellow policeman watched.

"You're under arrest," he said.

"For what? Fraud? You can't arrest me for that. I haven't defrauded anyone."

The second policeman asked, "Fraud?"

McMahon said roughly, "You're under arrest for the murder of Everett Mason."

She struggled against the rough hand that held her arm.

"If you go quietly, there's no need for these," he said, and in his free hand, a pair of handcuffs dangled.

"I'm not going anywhere with you," she said. She struggled, and the second policeman pulled her hands together across her middle and locked the handcuffs around her wrists. They were so tight they chafed her skin.

Then she saw the windowless wagon outside.

As they dragged her out the door and into the wagon, she asked the voice, *How do I get out of this?*

McMahon slammed the door shut and she heard the key turn in the lock. Without a trace of humor, the voice said, *You'll see.*

THE ARREST

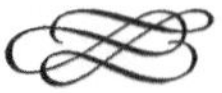

ELIAS READ OVER A CONTRACT, MAKING SURE HE'D COPIED IT properly, as the door to his office burst open. His visitor was a little boy in short pants, whose cap perched precariously on his curly hair. Breathless, he gasped, "Got a message for you from Mrs. Auburn."

Elias looked up. "What is it?"

"No note," he said, still struggling to catch his breath. "She said, 'You were right.'"

"Right about what?"

"She's at South Station. Wants you to come right away."

Elias felt a wave of fury. *They arrested her.* He fumbled in his pocket and found a dime for the messenger. The boy grinned as he pocketed the money.

Elias locked the door behind him and ran down the street to find a hansom cab to take him to South Station on Causey Street. The driver was a Black man with a no-nonsense air. He'd probably been a sergeant in a Black regiment, although Elias didn't recognize him from Fort Pickering. Elias sat in the cab, his hands on his knees, thinking through his approach toward the police. It hadn't been easier during the war, when the Memphis police worked side by side—much to their chagrin—with the Union army's police force. The provost marshal, as the military chief of police was called, hadn't been his ally, either.

At the station, he cooled his heels on a hard wooden bench near the front desk. He watched as the beat cops brought in the drunks and the soiled doves for tomorrow's Municipal Court. He waited.

A Black man in uniform stopped before him. "Mr. Aronson!" It was John Harris, politician and jail warden. "What brings you here?"

Elias said, "A client of mine has been arrested. I'm waiting to see her."

"Who is it?"

"Mrs. Auburn."

Harris said, "The spiritualist?"

Elias nodded. "I'm here to find out what's happened," he said. "I don't think she should be here at all."

Harris gave him a rueful look. "Let me see what I can do."

Ten minutes later, a constable summoned Elias. He looked too young for his blue uniform and billy club. The constable took him down the hall and opened the door to a small, windowless room, scarcely big enough for a table and two chairs. The table was badly scarred and burned, as though it had been through the war and hadn't come out the better for it. The room smelled of dirt and sweat and a distillate of misery and despair, as all police stations did. Elias sat and waited.

She came in the grip of a different policeman, this one older and grizzled. She was handcuffed, and the man held her arm so tightly that she winced. He pushed her down into the empty chair. Her head was bare, her hair was untidy, and her dress was rumpled. She looked ashen and drawn. But she didn't look as though she'd been physically abused.

Elias said, "Are those cuffs necessary?"

The policeman said, "It's on my head if she bolts."

Cassie rolled her eyes.

The policeman said, "She ain't the least bit cooperative. She wouldn't say a thing to us."

Cassie said, "I was waiting for my lawyer."

"Well, he's here. Fifteen minutes, then I'll be back."

Elias said, "After I talk to my client, I want to talk to the man who's in charge of her case."

"The detective?"

"Yes, if he's the one in charge."

The policeman shrugged and locked them in.

Elias said, "I am so sorry that you're here."

"It's not your fault."

"Tell me what happened."

She said, "They made good on their threat. They arrested me on suspicion of Everett Mason's murder."

"On what grounds?"

She snorted. "What do you think? Mrs. Mason's complaint and a Beardsley bribe to encourage them, no doubt."

"I doubt they have a shred of evidence," he said.

"Does it matter?"

He asked, "Have they mistreated you?"

"Aside from arresting me and cuffing me? No. I'm in a cell with a lot of soiled doves. We have water to drink and a necessary in the corner." She laughed bitterly. "A few of them asked me to read their palms. They were disappointed when I told them the spirits couldn't predict how their court appearances would go."

"The police have no reason to hold you here."

"What will free me? Will it be bail? Or a bribe?"

"Neither, if there's no evidence." He curled his hand into a fist. "They need probable cause, a suspicion grounded by evidence. And I can't imagine they've found any."

She regarded him with those luminous eyes. "Then this is nothing more than harassment," she said.

"Absolutely." He was still clenching his hand into a fist. "But we can fight this," he said. "I have a few ideas as to how."

She said bitterly, "Fifty dollars should do it."

He shook his head.

It hadn't been fifteen minutes, but they heard the key turn in the lock. It was the young policeman who'd brought her into the room. "Back to your cell," he said roughly. He stared at Elias.

Elias said, "I'm waiting to talk to the detective who's in charge of Mrs. Auburn's case."

The young man grabbed Cassie's arm and hustled her through the open door. He didn't look at Elias, let alone speak to him.

He waited. The room was so hot that the air was difficult to breathe. He rose and opened the door to look down the hall toward the front of the building. He thought, *They want to harass me, too.*

When no one came, he left the room and walked down the corridor to ask again at the desk. Mercifully, no one stopped him. But he had to wait his turn at the desk, and once he explained who he wanted to see, the policeman behind the desk, who looked as bored as a man dragged to church by a nagging wife, told him to sit on the bench to wait.

After half an hour, a man he hadn't seen before stopped before him to say, "Mr. Aronson?"

He was surprisingly slender. He wore a suit instead of a

uniform, and he was dressed with care. His frock coat was well-cut, and his silk cravat was fresh. He was pale and dark-eyed, and he introduced himself as Detective Doherty in a voice with the accent of Tennessee rather than Eire.

He led Elias back to the same little room where Elias had talked to Cassie. He said, "Not the nicest place, but it's private."

Elias thought, *He must be the good policeman. The polite one.*

They sat, and Doherty folded his hands on the table, a gesture very like a lawyer's, and said, "I understand you wanted to see me."

"Yes, in the matter of Mrs. Auburn's case. You're the detective, are you not?"

He nodded.

"I understand you suspect her in the murder of Everett Mason. On what grounds?"

"Sir, you know we can't talk to you about evidence."

"I do know. I'm curious as to the basis for your suspicions. You must have some, since you plan to take this case to court."

"Someone has come forward," he said. "Someone whose word we can trust."

Elias said, "I know something about this case. I know a great deal, in fact, since I investigated it on behalf of the Union army back in 1863. I know that two surgeons examined the body and decided that Everett Mason's death was a case of accidental drowning. At that time, police matters in Memphis were in the hands of the Union army's provost marshal. I met with him and he told me that the police had no desire to pursue an investigation. That they were satisfied with the surgeons' conclusions." He rested his hands on the edge of the battered table and said, "There was no evidence, there were no statements, and there were no witnesses back in 1863. I can't believe you've found something new."

"Well, we have," Doherty said, his tone affable.

"I'd be careful, if I were you. I've argued cases before Judge Woodley in Criminal Court. He has plenty of valid cases to try and he doesn't take kindly to cases where there's no evidence. There's no way to make him angrier than to present him with a case he'll dismiss."

With just a hint of irritation, Doherty said, "We know how to bring a case to Criminal Court."

Elias said, "You don't have evidence. You don't have probable cause. What you have is a beat policeman who's demanded bribes of Mrs. Auburn on a regular basis. The last time he visited her, he tried to force his attentions on her. And when she refused him, he threatened her with arrest on suspicion of Everett Mason's murder. This arrest is intimidation and harassment and nothing more."

The detective's face remained unruffled. "She's been arrested for a reason, and we won't allow bail," he said. "She has no reason to stay in Memphis, and if we release her, she'll leave like a shot."

Elias said, "Bail is for arrests that have probable cause. This doesn't." He gave Doherty a hard look. "And don't hint about my giving the police department a financial consideration. I don't pay bribes to the police. I never have, and I never will."

Doherty rose. "I think we're done here," he said, and he opened the door and ushered Elias from the stuffy little room.

～

AFTER ELIAS LEFT the police station, he didn't hail a hansom. Instead, he walked back to Main Street to James Dorsey's office. Dorsey's space was on the second floor of a brick building, smaller and more cramped than Elias's. After squeezing in a lawyer's desk and chair and a bookcase full of legal references, Dorsey barely had room for a visitor to sit.

Elias dropped into Settle's chair and wiped his face. Without asking, Dorsey poured him a glass of water. It was lukewarm, but Elias drank it with gratitude.

Dorsey said, "You look like the Furies are after you."

Elias said, "They're within. I just came from the Second District Station, where Mrs. Auburn is being held."

"On what grounds?"

"She's been arrested on suspicion of Everett Mason's murder."

"Ah, I recall you mentioned that to me," Dorsey said. "It's an old case, isn't it? From the years of the war?"

Elias felt a flash of the fury that had compelled him to visit Dorsey. "An old, cold case," he said. "The police didn't bother to pursue it at the time, even though they suspected Mrs. Auburn, who was called Cassie Andrews then, of having blood on her hands."

"Why dig it up now?" Dorsey asked.

"Do you really have to ask?"

"As the lawyer, yes."

"She's made the Beardsleys angry," Elias said.

Dorsey said, "Ill will, then. Is there evidence?"

"I talked to the detective who's looking into the case. He wouldn't tell me."

"Of course not, even if they had something," Dorsey said.

"They don't." He looked at Dorsey, hoping for reassurance more than useful information. "How do we get her out?"

"Second Station? That's Harris's spot, isn't it?"

"He locks them in and looks over them while they're in there," Elias said. "He doesn't decide to release them."

"Send him a message," Dorsey said. When Elias shook his head, Dorsey added, "Ask him to keep an eye on her. He can do that."

"I want to talk to the chief of police," Elias said.

"Why? Do you think he'll be any happier to hear you lecture him on the law than the detective was?"

Elias said bitterly, "This reminds me of talking to the police during the war. And they were ours. The Union army's. But all they wanted to know was how much you'd take from your pocket for a bribe."

Dorsey frowned. "That's no good," he said. "They'll just expect more next time. And they won't bother to do anything in the interim."

A man named Woodley was the judge of the Criminal Court, and he'd been a Union man during the war. But he was Governor Brownlow's appointee, and Brownlow, even though he'd been a Union man, had never been strong in opposition to slavery. After the massacre, Woodley had never heard a case naming a white man as the murderer of a Black one.

Dorsey sighed. "Don't you know his clerk?"

"Yes, we're acquainted."

"That might come in handy. But not yet."

"I can scarcely contain myself," Elias said. "I'm still furious."

"Yes, I know," Dorsey said. "I understand. But we have a bigger battle to fight, and a better chance to win it."

"The Armstrongs," Elias said.

Dorsey nodded.

"I can't help wishing we could do more for Mrs. Auburn," Elias said.

"You know better than to fight just to fight," Dorsey said. "You've been a soldier as well as a lawyer. We want to fight to win."

Elias mopped his face again with his handkerchief.

Dorsey poured him another glass of water. "Drink this," he said. "I trust you have whiskey at home. Shall we draft a message for Mr. Harris?"

ELIAS CAME into the parlor in his shirtsleeves, tugging on his cravat as though he wanted to tear it from his neck. Lydia, who had been reclining on the settee, sat up with an expression of concern on her face. "Let me pour the claret," she said.

"No, don't get up, I'll pour some for both of us."

He handed her the glass and sat down, too heavily. The settee was small enough so they had to be *companionable*, as Lydia put it. On happier days they both enjoyed it more.

She took a sip and put her glass on the doily on the lamp table. "It was a bad day, I can tell that much," she said. "How so?"

Elias said, "Cassie's in jail."

She gasped. "For what?"

"For reminding the Beardsleys how much they hate her."

"As though they needed a reminder," Lydia said. "No, be serious. Nobody gets arrested for—"

"Lydia, who gets arrested for no reason at all?"

At that she picked up her glass and fortified herself with a most unladylike gulp. She stared at the glass and asked, "Should I be worried for Narcissa?"

"No, this has nothing to do with Narcissa." He reached for her free hand. "Or you."

She raised her eyes to his.

"It's about Everett Mason's death," he said.

"I thought no one cared how that was settled."

He shook his head. "It isn't even about Everett Mason," he said.

She took another gulp and set down her glass. She didn't reply. She looked at nothing in particular on the wall behind his head. "All that anger," she said, "All that hatred." And then she fell silent and looked down at her hands.

He put his arm around her. "You're shivering. Are you cold?"

"In my soul, yes."

He pulled her close and she embraced him, laying her cheek on his shoulder. She held him like that for a long moment. When she let him go, she looked into his eyes.

He asked, "Are you afraid?"

She said, "I keep telling myself to be a good soldier."

"You aren't a soldier."

"Soldiers of light and love, the Missionary Association called us during the war, and we were in as much danger as any man with a rifle. Only we didn't have rifles." She felt a stab of guilt for the pearl-handled revolver she always carried now.

"There's no shame in feeling afraid."

"Yes, there is, because it leads to acting afraid. And as weary as I am of fear, I can't afford it."

"Have you had another one of those awful messages? Have you not told me?"

She shook her head. "If I had, I would tell you right away," she said. "I haven't kept that from you."

He said, "What is it? Let me help you."

She shivered again. "I worry about you all the time," she

said. "Even more than I worry about myself. Violence is in the air here."

"It's not like it was just before the massacre. You know that as much as I do."

"The threat never goes away. It just goes quiet. Or worse still, into hiding." She drew in her breath. "I can't help feeling afraid, even in town, where we're safe. Safer." She shook her head again. "Not safe enough."

He asked, "Do you want to leave Memphis?"

Her shoulders sagged. "I can't," she said. "I still have a mission here." She looked up. "As do you. Why? Would you go?"

His voice was hoarse. "I'm not afraid for myself," he said. "But I don't just think of myself anymore."

THE NEXT DAY, early in the morning, Cassie appeared in Elias's office. She looked disheveled and tired. "I was released this morning," she said. "I haven't been home. I wanted you to see me as I am."

"How are you?"

"Dirty and tired, but we all were, since we slept on the floor. Eight of us, in a tiny holding cell. My companions were all women of the streets, and they were kind to me, in their way, and good-natured. One of them bribed the guard so she could send out for dinner for all of us. As soon as I got my reticule back, I gave her some money to thank her."

"The guards? How did they treat you?"

"They didn't mistreat me."

"Did Mr. Harris speak to you?"

She looked surprised that he knew. "He did," she said. "Was that your doing?"

Elias was glad to hear that the message to Harris had done some good. "Did they ever tell you why they arrested you?"

Her laugh was humorless. "They arrested me for no reason," she said. "Why shouldn't they release me for no reason? We both know the reason." She lifted her chin in defiance. "Should I be afraid?"

"If I were in your position, I might be."

Rebellion gleamed in her eyes. "And would you leave town? Run away?"

He thought of Lydia, shivering with worry, and his reply was stark. "If anyone I loved was in danger, I might."

She shook her head.

"Mrs. Auburn, is there anything I can do for you? As your lawyer?"

She rose, smoothing her wrinkled, stained skirt. "Next time, make sure they have some evidence," she said.

WHEN NARCISSA HEARD about Cassie's arrest, she was standing in Lydia's office at the school, and she began to shake, as Lydia herself had, the day before. Lydia shut her office door, settled Narcissa in a chair, and put a maternal arm around her shoulders. Narcissa held her handkerchief to her face and breathed deeply to calm herself. Finally, she removed the handkerchief from her eyes, folded it into a square, and put it back in her pocket. "Excuse me, Mrs. Aronson," she said, her voice still shaky.

"You're on edge, as we all are," Lydia said.

"That the police could accuse her of murder—on a whim—"

Lydia sighed. "No, I understand all too well. This isn't a matter for me. It's for my husband, the lawyer."

That Sunday afternoon, Elias and Lydia welcomed Narcissa into their parlor. Elias had asked James to join them. Lydia had asked their housekeeper to make lemon cake, and it was served and eaten. Narcissa said, "You're distracting me, but the cake is delicious."

"No, Miss Armstrong, we hoped to give you a little sweetness before we got down to business," Elias said.

Narcissa put down her plate. "Mrs. Aronson told me about Mrs. Auburn's arrest," she said.

Elias nodded.

"If the police are willing to arrest someone for no reason, they should certainly be able to arrest someone for good reason," she said.

James steepled his fingers, the lawyer's gesture, and Elias suppressed a sigh.

She said, "Don't we have enough to ask them to charge John Beardsley with the murder of my brother?"

Elias and Dorsey looked at each other. Elias said, "I'll let you speak."

"As a lawyer, or as a Black man?"

"You have the advantage of both, as I do not," Elias said.

Narcissa said, "I feel an admonition coming in."

Dorsey said, "No, Miss Armstrong, not that. But a caution about the reality of justice in Memphis."

Narcissa said, "Do you think I don't know? That Cassie was arrested because a white planter accused her, even though there wasn't a shred of evidence, and that a white planter won't be arrested on the say-so of a Black family, even if they have good reason—how do the lawyers say it? Probable cause?"

Elias sighed again, and Dorsey said, "You've put it better than I have."

Narcissa leaned forward. "I know it won't be easy," she said. "I know it may not even be successful. But isn't it time to try?"

Now Dorsey looked at Elias, who spoke. "If we want to try, we need more than circumstance," he said. "We need undeniable evidence." He looked from Narcissa's resolute face to Lydia's worried expression to Dorsey's dignified, weary look, his lawyer's gesture, as though they were the jury he needed to persuade. "We need a witness. And not just any witness. A witness whose testimony will stand, no matter how unreasonable and unfair the challenge to it." He looked at each of them again. "And I don't know how we'll find someone who can do that."

ELIAS SAT IN HIS OFFICE. The air was hot and full of dust, and as often as he wiped his face with his handkerchief, he didn't feel any cooler. He thought of Narcissa's case. He felt a familiar despair. Once again, in the face of the most obvious wrong, there was no one who could—or who dared—to step forward.

No witness. No proof. No charge. No arrest. No trial.

He didn't like to remember how justice had been served the last time he'd found himself with a case like this.

He mopped his face again as the door to his office opened.

Will Andrews stepped inside. He shut the door quietly and winced as it creaked.

Elias said, "I'd been meaning to find someone to fix that.

But I find I don't mind. It lets me know when I have a visitor."

Will took a few steps within and waited.

"Young Mr. Andrews, it's a pleasure to see you. Have you come with a message from your mother?"

"No," he said shyly.

"Or the Hayeses?"

"No, sir. I've come on my own account. Is that all right?"

"Quite all right. Would you like to sit down?"

Cautiously, he edged forward. Elias made an expansive gesture toward the guest's chair. "Please."

He sat. Elias recalled his father's homely admonition. "It's all right, you can sit with more than one buttock." Will needed that kind of encouragement. "What is this about, Mr. Andrews?" Elias asked.

Will looked at Elias with big, frightened eyes. He swallowed. "Is it true that you have to keep what I tell you in confidence?"

Elias said, "It's true that what my clients tell me is privileged, as a lawyer says it. That means it's in confidence."

"Does that include me?"

Elias said, "You didn't turn twenty-one when no one was looking, did you?"

The boy looked puzzled. "No, sir, I'm only thirteen."

"That means you're a minor, in legal terms. And minors, young people under twenty-one, can't sign a binding contract and become legal clients."

His face fell.

"But I still have an obligation to keep things in confidence. When I was called to the bar, I swore an oath to uphold the law."

He asked, "Is that like the loyalty oath?"

"I swore that oath, too, when I became an officer in the Union army."

He nodded. He understood the loyalty oath well, since he knew Black men who had sworn it when they mustered in, and when they registered to vote for the first time.

Elias said, "As a practicing lawyer, I became an officer of the court. And I swear on my honor as an officer, of the court as well as of the Union army, that whatever you tell me will stay in confidence, unless you tell me differently."

He took a deep breath. He wasn't ready to talk yet.

Elias asked, "Does your mother know you've come to see me?"

"No, sir."

"Does she know anything about the matter you've brought to me?"

He shook his head.

"What about Mr. and Mrs. Hayes? Do they know?"

His voice was very soft. "I didn't tell them, Mr. Aronson. I can swear to that."

Elias said, "Then it is between the two of us."

The boy nodded. He hesitated, gathering his courage.

Elias said softly, "Take your time, young Mr. Andrews. There's no hurry here."

Will said, "It's about Miss Narcissa's brother."

Elias was quiet.

Will looked as though he was about to take a dive into the Mississippi River from a high bluff.

Elias said, very softly, "This is difficult, I understand. You're very brave to talk to me."

The words came out in a rush. "I was there. I saw what happened. I know who murdered Titus Armstrong."

THE TRUTH COMES OUT

WHEN THE HANSOM DRIVER SHUT THE DOOR, CASSIE PULLED open the curtain to catch the breeze from the open window. She also fanned herself against the heat. Elias Aronson's office was only a short walk away, but she wanted to arrive as composed and unwilted as she could manage. Nonetheless, she sweated in her new dress, finery from New York, as she worried about the reason for her lawyer's summons.

Am I in trouble? she mentally asked the voice, which never seemed to illuminate her own future when she most needed it.

Despite her bravado with TJ, she had thought constantly about leaving Memphis since she'd been arrested. What vengeance could she wreak on the Beardsley family? And if she wanted to teach her sons to love her, shouldn't she take them with her back to New York and rely on TJ's good humor to help raise them?

She let the fan rest in her lap as she leaned back against the cushion of the hansom, which felt hard and lumpy, even though all the ladylike layers of cloth she wore. She didn't have to close her eyes to recall how she had felt five years ago, when she had run and gone into hiding, terrified for her life. She hated the memory of that self, sick with fear and grief. It lingered inside the hansom like the smell of tobacco smoke and cheap hair pomade.

She mentally implored the spirit, *Remind me that the past is over.*

The spirit said dryly, *Remind yourself.*

Why does my lawyer want to see me? Don't tell me "You'll see."

Silence.

When the hansom stopped she put down the fan and pinched the skin on the underside of her wrist, making it hard enough to hurt and to leave a mark under her lace-trimmed sleeve. That would be her reminder.

Elias Aronson sat behind his desk, his frock coat buttoned up but his hair already fighting its pomade and curling in the heat. There were dark circles under his eyes, as though the heat disturbed his sleep at night, too.

When she saw the guest who already sat in the chair before the desk, the fear in her chest tightened like a fist.

It was her son Will.

In her panic, she didn't watch what she said. "Whatever are you doing here?"

Will looked at Elias, who nodded at him to encourage him. Will said, "Ma'am, I have something important to tell you, and Mr. Aronson has agreed help me."

Hearing him say *ma'am* hurt her more than the worry of whatever had brought him to a lawyer's office. "If you're in trouble—"

"No, ma'am, I'm not."

"Mr. Aronson, why is my son here?"

"Because he is my client, and he's disclosed something to me that he wants to keep in confidence. But he wants to tell you."

Her heart pounded. The office felt as hot as the street, and the dust in the air chafed her throat. "Stop foxing me, both of you, and tell me what this is about."

Will suddenly turned pale, his light complexion going even lighter, and looked down at his hands. When he looked up, it was at Elias, not at her, and he struggled to find the words.

"May I?" Elias asked.

Will nodded.

"Will spoke to me in confidence, as a client to a lawyer," Elias said. "As you yourself did, Mrs. Auburn."

"Then what are you telling me? And why?"

"His admission to me has legal implications, but by law, he's a child," Elias said. "Your child. And it only seemed right, to both of us, to tell you what he said to me."

Cassie looked at her son. He struggled again to speak but could not.

Elias said, "He saw what happened to Titus Armstrong."

Cassie asked, "Is this true, Will?"

He nodded.

Elias said, "He saw that Titus Armstrong was shot. Fatally shot."

In the hot, humid room, where the leather-bound law books seemed to sweat, Cassie began to feel a chill. She threw her son an imploring look.

He nodded again.

Elias said, "He knows who murdered Titus Armstrong."

Cassie put her hand to her mouth to stifle her desire to moan. Her eyes traveled from her son, who clenched his hands in his lap, to her lawyer, whose gaze was unwavering and full of sadness. She took away her hand and let it fall into her lap. "He's your witness," she said, her voice catching in her throat.

Elias spoke softly. That had always been his habit whenever he had bad news to impart, or to pry out. "Yes," he said.

She wanted to argue, but she faltered when she said, "You want to drag him into court—you want to use him to force the police—"

"No," Elias said. "Not without his permission. And yours."

"Will?" she asked. "Do you want to do this?"

In a very small voice, he said, "I think so, ma'am."

"This isn't about Miss Narcissa, is it? I know how much you think of her."

Will blushed, but he said, "No, ma'am, it isn't."

"Do you understand what you're doing?" Cassie asked her son.

At that he dropped his eyes again and fell silent.

Elias said, "As far as I know, your son understands that his knowledge will let the Armstrongs make a case and take it to court. And believe me, he also understands it puts a great many people in danger. Himself and you, as well as the Armstrongs."

Cassie felt anger rise in her. After all the fear, it was a good feeling. She thought of the African goddess of vengeance who had spoken through her. "Does he?" she asked Elias.

Will raised his head and spoke to her directly. "Yes, ma'am, I do."

The anger was an invigorating warmth, not at all like the draining humidity in this very room. "And what happens now?"

"Nothing, unless we have young Mr. Andrews's assent, and yours."

She gave Elias Aronson the penetrating gaze that usually worked to discomfit anyone who kept the truth from her. "And who shot Titus Armstrong?" she asked.

Elias returned her stare with the look of a man at ease in a courtroom, where the judge, the jury, the newspapermen, and the public were all staring at him at the same time. "I should ask my client if he wants to share that confidence," he said.

Will took a deep breath and spoke to his mother directly. "It was John Beardsley," he said.

She was so surprised that she was temporarily stricken into silence. And in that silence, the voice spoke. *Kill two birds with one stone*, it said. *Hurt them worse than they can hurt you.*

CASSIE ORDERED another hansom to take Will to school, but he was silent during the drive. He didn't speak as he dismounted from the cab. She watched as he walked, with an adult's gravity, up to the school's front door.

She sighed and told the driver to take her back to the storefront.

That night, at supper, Will was so quiet that Matilda asked him, "You feeling all right, sugar?"

Her aunt hadn't noticed Cassie's silence, or hadn't bothered to inquire about it.

"I'm fine," he said in a soft voice. But he didn't eat much, and after he'd pushed the food around his plate long enough, he asked to be excused. Sam said, "I'm excused too!" and he ran down the stairs, stomping on the treads, to join his friends in the street. Matilda, not convinced about Will's health, put her hand on his forehead. He pulled away. "I'm fine, Auntie," and he rose to leave the table. All three of them, Matilda, Moses, and Cassie, heard him go into the bedroom he shared with Sam and shut the door.

Matilda rose to clear the table and Cassie followed suit. In the kitchen, Matilda asked Cassie, "You know what's wrong with Will?"

Cassie spoke to her aunt in a low voice. "Come downstairs when we're finished here, you and Uncle Moses."

Matilda's eyebrows rose.

Cassie gestured with her chin. "I don't want him to hear."

Once the dishes were done, Cassie ushered both her aunt and uncle downstairs and into the back room. She opened the curtains a little to let in the summer evening's light. The ray of sun showed off the dust, which eddied in the air in a ghostly way. The corner of her mind that wasn't distracted thought, *I wonder if we can do that on purpose.* The room still smelled faintly of the sage that she had burned for the last séance.

Puzzled, Matilda asked, "Are we going to talk to the spirits?"

"No, you're going to talk to me," she said, her voice firm.

Moses looked from his niece to his wife. "Is this about Will?"

"Yes," Cassie said.

"What's he done?" Matilda asked.

"He went to see my lawyer, Mr. Aronson. Did he tell either of you?"

"No," Matilda said, alarm creeping onto her face. "Why?"

She looked from one careworn face to the other. "Mr. Aronson needed a witness to Titus Armstrong's murder." Her gaze was as probing as she could make it. "Now he has one."

Matilda put her hand to her mouth and Moses said, "Will?"

She set her mouth in a hard line. "Yes, Will."

They were silent.

Their silence infuriated her. "Did you know anything about this?" she asked.

There was another silence, thick and uncomfortable, and finally her uncle met her eyes. His face was as sorrowful as she'd ever seen. "Yes," he said.

"And how long have you known?"

Matilda reached for his arm, as though she could stop him, but he put his hand over hers and gently took it away. He sighed deeply. "Since it happened."

"Did you see it yourself?"

"No. Only Will did."

"When did he tell you?"

"Right away. He came into the back room and told us right away." Then he fell silent.

"Uncle Moses, I know that look of yours," she says. "Your 'can't say' look. What aren't you telling me?"

He hesitated. "I'd never seen that boy so upset," he said.

The air stirred in the room. She had long since stopped wondering why she felt the occasional draft. She waited for the rest.

Her uncle looked as though he was dragging a burden he wished he didn't have to carry. "He wanted to know if we should tell the police."

"And what did you say to him?" She was too agitated to be gentle.

"I told him it was an awful thing he'd seen. An evil thing. But it wouldn't do any good to go to the police. They were evil, too. I told him that he should put it away and forget he'd seen it. And never talk about it anymore."

You let him carry that burden, she thought. *And that memory.* She had to breathe deeply to contain her anger. "You knew? You've known all along?"

Moses nodded.

"And you never said a word!"

Her uncle roused himself like a man coming out of a bad dream. "I had a reason," he said. "I'd think you'd know what it was. Maybe you forgot."

The memory of her own trouble rose in her and she was flooded with shame. Her uncle had hidden the truth back then to save her. The secret he'd kept for Will was just as dangerous as the one he'd kept for her. "No, I didn't forget," she said. She let her voice rise. "All the more reason to bring the Beardsleys to justice now."

Moses sat up straight in his chair. "If you really think that, you're a fool," he said. "And a selfish one at that. I've kept quiet for Will's sake. And for ours. Do you really want to risk all of us for revenge?"

The voice was suddenly clear in her ears. *Damned whatever you do*, it said.

She thought, *Can't you do better than that?*

All I can do is show you the way. You're the one to travel it.

She splayed her hands flat on the table, as if she were running a séance and summoning the spirits. But the only spirit in her was despair. "Of course not," she said, her voice hoarse.

Someone opened the door without knocking and she thought, *Is that TJ? He knows better than to come in here without warning me.*

But it was Will, whose face was very pale, except for the two red blotches of anger on his cheeks. "It was supposed to be a secret!" he cried out. "You were supposed to keep it a secret!"

She looked from her uncle's face to her son's. "It was no secret here," she said.

"You promised!"

She said, "Mr. Aronson made a promise to you. He'll keep

it." She looked at her uncle again. "But between all of us, the secret is now out." She wondered why he wasn't angry at his great-uncle.

"You promised me! You lied to me!" He looked as angry, and as young, as his little brother. "I'll never tell you anything again!" And at that, he ran out the side door and let it slam behind him.

A breath of wind gusted into the room, re-creating the ghostlike eddy of the dust from the street. Neither Matilda nor Moses spoke. She sat with them in silence, thinking of the voice's counsel. *I'll show you the path but you'll have to walk it.*

Where did that path lead? She didn't know. Every fork in that path was full of peril. The police station. The courtroom. She let herself remember the worst things from her trouble five years before. The dark alley, where someone she cared for had been fatally shot. The river bluff, where a man she hated had fallen to his death. She closed her eyes, and when she opened them, her aunt and uncle were gone.

IT WAS late in the afternoon, the hottest moment of the day, and the busiest time on Beale Street. Cassie sat in her storefront, listening to carriages and wagons clatter past as drivers shouted and horses neighed. Dogs barked and yelped, and from the backyard, where her aunt Matilda did her wash, the women of the neighborhood called to her at a volume of people used to hollering at one another across a cotton field.

Cassie's head ached. She put her hand to her forehead, thinking of the remedies her root doctor gave her. She'd been busy all day. She'd seen the location of a lost brooch, delighting a young woman who said, "It's the one thing I had to remember my mama by, even though it isn't worth much." Another young woman, her face creased with worry, had come to her about a baby she hadn't expected. Cassie referred her to the root doctor, who had darker remedies than those for headaches. She'd talked to a woman whose son had died bravely in battle in the war, but who said, "I still miss him like it was yesterday." Despite her aching head, Cassie had put a consoling hand on her arm. "Tell me about him, and I'll do my best to bring him to you."

Nothing had lightened the grief she felt about Will, and the anger she felt at herself.

The door opened. It was Narcissa Armstrong, finished with her day of teaching, a smear of chalk dust forgotten on the front of her skirt. She looked tired, and Cassie suddenly saw—no help from the spirits, only her powers of observation—how Narcissa would age, her full cheeks hollowing, her pretty mouth turning thin and firmly set. Cassie thought, *Today I feel decades older than I am, too.* Cassie looked at Narcissa and she knew. "It's about Will, isn't it?"

Narcissa sighed as she sat. "Yes."

"Did he tell you?"

Narcissa didn't ask, "What?" She said, "He told me that he was a witness to my brother's death." She took a deep breath. "To my brother's murder." She shook her head. "Mr. Aronson now has the witness he yearned for so much."

Cassie nodded.

Narcissa's gaze was troubled. "At such a cost," she said. "When I started this, I knew I'd be in danger. But I never dreamed—" She faltered. "He's such a serious boy. Old beyond his years. It's hard to remember that he's just a child."

Cassie couldn't help it. She had to claim him. "My child," she said, not caring if it stung.

"Ours, too," Narcissa said softly. "The school's. A responsibility that I feel, very heavily."

She loves him, too, Cassie thought. The thought hurt, and she didn't reply.

Narcissa said, "I'm so torn. I want to go to court. I want justice for my brother. But if it hurts Will—" She shook her head. "I don't know what to do."

Narcissa's admission unsettled her. It was too much like her own, and it startled her into the truth. "I don't either," she says. "Even though I'm not as high-minded as you. I want my revenge on the Beardsleys, and I don't think Will loves me much."

"I'd believe that he's very angry at you. But you're still his mother."

Cassie felt a pang in her chest. "Did you know he calls me 'ma'am'? Even though I've begged him to call me 'mama'?"

Narcissa said, "He won't be angry with you forever."

Cassie shook her head. "I wonder."

"Can't you see the future?" Narcissa's tone had the slightest teasing note.

"In this, no better than anyone else," Cassie admitted.

Narcissa met her eyes. "I don't believe in what you do," she said. "But I recall clearly that you once told me that we have common cause. It seems that's still true."

Cassie said, very slowly, "To punish the Beardsleys. But not to hurt Will."

"Yes," Narcissa agreed.

Cassie was silent. *This is my path to travel,* she thought. She had never assumed that anyone could travel it with her. "But how to do it?" she asked. "That's the trouble, isn't it?"

THE VISIT TO THE POLICE

Elias walked into the Second District Police station
and took in the now-familiar odor of sweat, tobacco, and
misery. He was deeply uneasy about being here. It didn't help
that he was there for Narcissa Armstrong to report a murder,
and he didn't feel better because James Dorsey accompanied
them.

The previous evening, he told Lydia that they were now
equipped to pursue a criminal suit for Titus's murder. He
admitted, "I'm worried." She had put her arms around him
and said, "I'm worried too." Then she pulled back to look him
in the eye. "But I won't tell you not to."

He wished that he could say, "I won't." But he had made a
lawyer's promise to Narcissa, to pursue the truth despite the
danger, and for her sake, he would keep it.

Now, this morning, they waited in line at the station to
talk to the policeman at the front desk.

In a room full of streetwalkers in soiled silk, and poor
women, Black and white, in ragged dresses, Narcissa stood
out. She wore her Sunday best, a severe dress in dark blue,
with only a white lace collar to relieve it. Under her bonnet,

its strings firmly tied, she held her head up. Her back was very straight.

Elias thought, *Genteel as a schoolteacher and brave as a soldier.*

One of the soiled doves said to her, "What in God's name did you do?" She was pretty except for a missing tooth that showed when she grinned.

Startled, Narcissa said, "I'm here to make a complaint."

The soiled dove snickered. "You can complain all you like," she said. "It won't do you any good."

Narcissa gave her a pitying look. "That's why I've brought my lawyers with me," she said.

When their turn at the desk came, the policeman looked them over. He asked Elias, "What is it?"

Narcissa stepped forward. "I'm here to report a crime," she said.

"Why didn't you send for us?"

Elias eased himself beside her. "It wasn't recent."

"When did it happen?"

Narcissa said firmly, "On May 1, 1866."

The policeman began to write down the date, then looked up. "During the riot?"

"May 1, 1866," Narcissa repeated.

"What was the crime?"

Narcissa leaned forward, not touching the counter, which looked as though it had accumulated years of dirt. "My brother was murdered."

The policeman said, "I'll let you talk to a detective, but I don't know what good it will do you." He gestured toward a hard wooden bench near the door. "Wait over there."

The bench was already crowded with supplicants. One of them, an old Black man, unshaven and gummy, looked up at Narcissa. "We make room for you, miss," he said.

Elias said, "We may be waiting for a while. Please sit, Miss Armstrong."

She thanked them both, her lawyer and the stranger, and gathered her skirt close to her as she sat on the edge of the bench.

From the other end of the bench came a plaint: "Don't ask us to move down! We're already squeezed like bugs in here!"

They waited. Narcissa asked Elias, "Is it always like this?"

The old man said, "They don't want you comfortable. Make you wait, even if you got a good reason to be here." He shifted on the bench, wincing. "My leg ain't all right," he said.

They continued to wait.

Elias looked at his watch. Dorsey, who shifted from foot to foot, whispered to him, "It won't go faster if you know what time it is."

Elias sighed.

The door to the station opened and an awful shriek billowed into the room. "I ain't done nothing! You can't arrest me for nothing!" It belonged to a ragged Black woman, whom a policeman dragged by the arm. "Let go of me, you bastard!" she yelled. "You're hurting me!" He ignored her and yanked her past the desk and down the hall. They could all hear her as she disappeared: "Goddamn bastard Irish police!"

Dorsey said, "Well, that's one way to get quick service around here. Come in resisting arrest."

Neither Elias nor Narcissa laughed.

When the detective arrived, Elias recognized him right away. He was Detective Doherty, the well-spoken, dapper man who had refused to let Cassie go. He said to Elias, "I recall you. You're a lawyer. You're here to report a murder?"

"I am," Narcissa said, her voice firm.

They followed him down the hall, into one of the small, cramped rooms the police used for interrogations, and they sat elbow to elbow around the small rectangular table, with the detective at its head, like the father at a Sunday dinner. It smelled even more powerfully of sweat and tobacco than the front room.

"Who are you?" he asked.

Elias said, "This is Miss Narcissa Armstrong, who has come to make a complaint. I'm Elias Aronson, whom the Armstrong family has retained to pursue a criminal suit. This is my colleague, James Dorsey, also a lawyer."

Doherty nodded. "Who was the victim?" he asked.

Narcissa said, "My brother, Titus Armstrong."

"And where did the murder occur?"

"On South Street." She paused. "We collected his body on the street." She gave the address.

"And when did the murder occur?"

Narcissa said, "As we told the man at the desk, on May 1, 1866."

"During the disturbance."

Elias knew that Narcissa was thinking "massacre," but she inclined her head politely and said, "Yes."

He rested his hands on the table. "Those cases have all been investigated, and now they're closed," he said.

Elias said, "I don't recall a thorough investigation."

He said, "We didn't share it with the public. We made our investigations, and we cooperated with the Congressional commission, too. Those cases were closed."

Dorsey said, "Sir, I realize it's difficult to look at a case of murder that's two years in the past. My colleague and I recently made an investigation of our own, and we're happy to share any evidence we found with you."

Doherty stared at Dorsey, as though he was having difficulty seeing him as a lawyer. "That isn't necessary," the detective said.

Elias said, "I don't understand why an unsolved murder from two years ago presents the police with such a problem. I was here, not a month ago, in the matter of a client of mine who was arrested on suspicion of a murder committed five years ago, during the war."

Doherty's voice took on an edge. "I couldn't talk to you about it at the time, and I can't say any more now," he said.

Elias said, "Perhaps your captain might be more helpful."

Doherty rose from his chair. "I don't think so," he said. He cast a warning look at Elias. "Don't try to get around me."

They weren't dragged out the door, but they were hustled down the hall without a word.

In the crowded, noisome front room, Dorsey bent to speak softly to Elias. "Would Mr. Harris be able to help us? Get us in to see the captain?"

Elias tugged on the lapels of his coat. "No, we're done here," he said.

Narcissa's face was set with disappointment. "I hoped for better than this," she said, her voice pitched low.

Elias met Narcissa's unhappy gaze. "This is just round one. We aren't done yet, not by a long shot."

ELIAS WALKED BACK to his office on Main Street, his head down as he dodged the crowd. On Main Street, people bound for honest work were outnumbered by men intent on dissipation. He bumped into a man drunk at ten in the morning, who swore at him. Elias ignored the insult.

Elias unlocked his office door and went inside. He sighed at the sight of the dust, which defeated every effort at cleaning, no matter how frequent. He sat at his desk heavily, just like his father, thirty-five years his senior. Memphis and its problems were aging him, he thought. His head ached and his joints ached.

At ten in the morning, he wished he were in bed with his wife, with his head on her shoulder and her strong fingers tangled in his hair. He didn't need the assurance she could give him in the parlor or at the dinner table. He wanted a more primal comfort.

The frustration he felt about Narcissa's suit was all too familiar. Five years before, he'd suffered the same obstruction from the police. The wartime provost marshal had been a lazy man. These policemen were worse. They had plenty of energy to ignore a complaint from the Black community. And even more energy to do the bidding of a wealthy white planter with money to bribe them.

During the war, as a soldier, he'd been issued a pistol, and he'd carried it everywhere. In his role as aide-de-camp to the fort's commander, he never used it. But he liked knowing that he might. As an officer of an occupying army, he had the authority to shoot, if necessary.

He remembered how he'd felt five years ago, so badly thwarted by the police that he wanted to charge in with the wrongful force of military might. Sometimes justice was served by going outside the law. He rubbed his eyes. As an officer of the court, he was forbidden to serve that kind of justice. But he wished he could.

He knew where they should go next. They should visit the superintendent of police. Samuel Beaumont was one of General Brownlow's appointments. He had been a Union man during the war, but like all the Tennessee Republicans, he'd been tepid in his opposition to slavery. Did he know how corrupt the men on the police beat were? Did he share their greed? Elias had never met him. He didn't know.

He and Dorsey would accompany Narcissa to see Beaumont, and they would all find out.

The door opened, the creaking hinge warning him. He looked up. His visitor was the aptly named Mr. Goldman, the jeweler down the street whom he knew from Temple Israel. He'd handled Goldman's business affairs since he gone into private practice after the war ended.

"How are you, Mr. Goldman?"

"I'm fine, thank you, and business is also fine," said Mr. Goldman, in the German accent so familiar from Elias's childhood, just like his father's.

"What can I do for you?"

He waved his hand as though he were brushing away a fly. "Nothing for me," he said. "I've come because I'm a little worried about you."

He joked, "My health is fine. My wife's, also fine. Why would you worry?"

Mr. Goldman sat heavily in the desk chair. "It's not good to get mixed up so much with the Black people," he said.

"Excuse me?"

"To do a favor every so often, that I understand. Only decent. But getting involved in murders—that's different. Not so wise."

Elias said stiffly, "My clients, and their legal business, are confidential," he said.

"Nothing stays a secret here. You know that."

Why was gossip so easy to come by, and testimony so difficult? he wondered. "Legal privilege is more than a secret," he said.

Mr. Goldman inclined his head very slightly. "There are people I know, men from the Temple, who think you have too much interest in the troubles of Black people," he said.

"And what do you think, Mr. Goldman?"

Mr. Goldman evaded the question. "I'm just telling you what I hear," he said. "I thought you should know."

Elias suddenly heard his father's voice, with its German and Yiddish inflection. *Business like that, I don't need.* New York was big enough to let some business go. Memphis, especially Jewish Memphis, was not. As pleasantly as he could, Elias said, "Well, now I do. Is there anything else, Mr. Goldman?"

The man rose. "A good day to you, Mr. Aronson."

As the door closed, Elias thought, *Thank you for spoiling it.* He reached for pen and paper to write a note to Narcissa about meeting with the superintendent of police.

THE BUILDING that housed the city's police headquarters spoke of neglect. Evidently the post-war boom in the cotton trade had not extended its largesse to maintaining the police department. Elias thought of Fort Pickering, the Union army outpost, swiftly built after the victory in 1862. Everything at the fort had been fresh and new, shining with authority and efficiency. By comparison, Superintendent Beaumont's head office seemed to say: *We don't have enough, and we can barely manage.*

The building was dim inside, with warped wooden floors that complained with every step. The interior of the building was windowless and dark at midday. The smell was the same as the district station, sweat and tobacco, mingled with manure from the street outside.

Of course, they had to wait, as policemen, miscreants, complainants, and the occasional lawyer walked into the front room and joined the queue.

After thirty minutes, a tired-looking policeman, his hat

askew on his head, his coat too tight across his middle, ushered them into Superintendent Beaumont's office.

Beaumont had a look familiar to Elias from the war. His eyes were pouchy and tired, and he had a wartime mustache, bushy and unkempt. He smoothed it as he looked them over. "Who are all of you?" he asked, his tone direct but not impolite.

Elias introduced everyone. Beaumont gave Dorsey and Narcissa quizzical looks, as though he was unused to meeting genteel, educated Black people. They sat and Beaumont asked, "What brings you here?"

"Sir, we've tried to ask the police at the Second District Station to look into a murder, and they've refused us," Elias said.

"Refused you? Why?"

Narcissa leaned forward. "It happened during the—" She paused. "The disturbance two years ago, sir."

He said, "Well, we don't typically look into cases that are so old."

Now Elias leaned forward, too. "Yes, sir, the detective explained that to us. But are you aware that they recently arrested a woman on suspicion of a murder committed five years ago, during the war?"

He inclined his head. "I heard about that," he said. "I insisted that they release her, since there was no evidence. I told my men that we have plenty of current trouble to handle." He looked at Narcissa. "Why come forward now?"

Elias said, "We've done some investigating, Mr. Dorsey and I, with Miss Armstrong's assistance. We've found evidence that points to a suspect, which we'd be glad to share with the police."

Samuel Beaumont's mouth pulled downward, taking his mustache with it. "I wish I could help you," he said.

Elias thought, *Tell us why you won't.*

Beaumont's shoulders slumped under his gold-braided blue coat. "Memphis is a tinderbox, as all of you must know. We still have former rebels going after Yankees, just because they're Yankees. Last year a local man murdered an Ohio man out in Germantown, just because he was from Ohio. Do you think we could manage to arrest him and prosecute him?" He shook his head.

Narcissa sat up very straight. "Sir, murder is always vile, however it happens. But in the case of my brother, it was a very great wrong. He was a good, upright man. And he was murdered on the day after he mustered out of the Union army as a member of the 3rd Heavy Artillery Regiment of the United States Colored Troops. His blue coat made him a victim, sir. He deserves justice."

Elias was proud of her composure. She'd do very well in the courtroom.

Beaumont shook his head again. "If I resurrected a case from the disturbance, the consequences would be disastrous." He regarded each of them in turn. "Do you want to cause another race riot?"

"That isn't our intention," Elias said.

"I can't create such a hazard to public safety," he said. "I can't risk it."

Elias said, "We have solid evidence, sir. We have an eyewitness."

Beaumont shook his head for a final time. "I can't help you," he said.

DORSEY ASKED if he could accompany Elias back to his office, and as they walked, Elias said, "No help from the police."

Dorsey dodged a man in a loud plaid suit, who gave him a nasty look and mouthed an insult. Dorsey ignored him. He said to Elias, "Didn't you tell me you knew Judge Woodley's clerk?"

"I did."

"What might he say?" Dorsey asked.

"I don't know. But I can ask."

Elias met Henry Copeland at his office, which was located on the second floor of the police headquarters. Elias had gotten used to discussing matters of justice in dilapidated surroundings. Courts-martial had rarely been held in courthouses that were palaces of justice. Nonetheless, the police station odor of sweat and tobacco oppressed him.

Copeland was young for an experienced clerk, but he was dressed better than his surroundings merited. In the corner of his office sat a tall, glossy hat, the height of fashion for an ambitious man, in the South as well as in the North. Like Judge Woodley, he was a Brownlow appointee, and he shared the judge's Union sympathies. Elias didn't know where Copeland stood on the matter of fairness for those who had been enslaved. He was here to find out.

After the niceties, Elias was blunt with Judge Woodley's clerk. "Has Judge Woodley ever heard a case of murder committed during the disturbance in 1866?"

Copeland shook his head. "Not that I know of."

"Has no one brought one forth for prosecution?"

"No, I've never seen one brought to court," he said.

"Where is the obstruction? Is it with the police, or with the court?"

Copeland winced. "The police never arrested anyone for murder during the disturbance, or charged anyone."

"Because so many of their numbers were complicit?"

"Do you need to ask?"

"I'm a lawyer, just as you are. I always need to ask."

"Is this a hypothetical question, Mr. Aronson? Or do you have a situation in mind?"

Elias said, "A young woman whose brother was murdered in 1866 wants to see justice done," he said. "I've been looking into the circumstances of the case, and there's enough evidence to charge a suspect."

"A member of the police force?"

"The planter who owned him, in the days of slavery," Elias said.

Copeland drew in his breath. "The police won't touch that."

"I know. I wondered if there might be any way to persuade the court to—well, encourage them to bring the case forward."

Copeland was silent.

"This isn't about public order," Elias said. "It's about justice. Aren't the Black victims of the massacre owed justice?"

Copeland sighed. "I don't see how that can happen."

Elias said, "They were very badly wronged. And as I recall, I fought a war to right that wrong." He put his hands on Copeland's desk, trespassing. "They now know how badly they were wronged, and they want to claim their place as citizens who deserve justice. We owe them a great deal, but that's one of the least things we owe them."

Copeland was silent for a while. "Memphis isn't ready," he said. "The South isn't ready. The formerly enslaved aren't ready, either. Give it time, Mr. Aronson. This isn't the moment."

"As these people say in church, 'How long, O Lord?' When will it be time?"

Copeland didn't reply.

Elias said, "The time will never be right. Why wait? Why not cause the trouble now, to begin to give these people what they're owed?"

"The case will never come to court," Copeland said. "I won't lie to you about that."

ELIAS LEFT the office and building to plunge into the smell of the street, where the stink of horse manure was an honest one. Head down, he walked back to his office. As he walked, his hand went to his hip, the spot where his army-issued pistol used to rest.

He thought, *If all I can do is shoot, I'm no better than the worst of my enemies.*

He realized he was a few doors from Dorsey's office, and when he arrived there, he opened the door, tapping lightly on it to forewarn Dorsey. Dorsey was at his desk, writing. He looked up.

Elias said, "I've talked to Judge Woodley's clerk."

"And I can read the answer in your face."

Elias sighed. "No help from the prosecution, either," he said.

"Sit down," Dorsey said.

Elias sat.

"The newly free have told me, more than once, that they have become used to making a way from no way," Dorsey said. "I have an idea or two. Would you like to hear me out?"

THE HIDING PLACE

CASSIE COULDN'T SLEEP, AND SHE ROSE QUIETLY TO PUT ON her dressing gown and creep down the stairs. She opened the door to her séance room and sat alone in the dark to wait for TJ.

She knew that he was drinking at the saloon the former Rebs favored. He went there several times a week. "They know me and they trust me," he'd told her one afternoon, as they readied the séance room for a consultation. "Which means they tell me useful things when they're drunk."

They're always drunk, she thought. "What do they say?"

He sighed. "What they plan to do in the countryside," he said. "And whether they plan to try anything in town."

She'd picked up a box of matches, intending to light the candles that sat on the table. Suddenly her hand trembled so badly she didn't trust herself. She set the matchbox down. "Do they dare?"

He drew her close. "I worry about you all the time," he said. "And now I worry about Will and Sam, too."

Will. She had a bad conscience about everything to do with Will. Narcissa's affection for him had cut her to the heart, and she was still bleeding in her jealousy. A good mother didn't resent her own son for finding a grown woman he could trust and who wanted to take care of him. And a good mother didn't spend her time brooding about revenge instead of assuring the safety of her children.

She knew how much Will wanted to help Narcissa, but the Armstrongs' desire to see justice done for Titus was a fool's effort. Will would never serve as a witness because the case would never go to court. She knew that as well as she knew the sound of the voice. If she had any sense herself—not to mention the milk of maternal kindness—she'd pack up both boys, over their objections, for the sanctuary of New York.

But she hadn't.

Now, in the darkness, the side door opened, with the stealth of someone who didn't want to wake anyone asleep upstairs. It was probably futile. She knew that Will slept as fitfully as she did. She hoped he hadn't risen to sit on the back stairs so he could eavesdrop, knowing that TJ had arrived.

TJ shut the door and joined her at the table. "Why are you sitting in the dark?"

"No reason to bother lighting a candle."

"You couldn't sleep," he said.

"I was worried about you."

In the dark, he looked like a phantom, his face gleaming ever so faintly in the dusk. "No reason to worry about me," he said. "They take me for someone like themselves. They don't suspect a thing."

She shuddered.

He reached for her hand. "Cassie, we can't stay here."

"I know, you've told me again and again."

"No, I mean it. I heard something tonight—"

Her voice rose. "What?"

"Hush, don't wake the boys."

She took a deep breath. "What did you hear?"

"I drank with John Beardsley," he said. "He was drunk when he said it. But you need to know what he said."

She whispered fiercely, "Is he coming for me? Does he want to lure me into a dark alley and shoot me?"

TJ winced. He knew the story of the death of the white Union officer, a romantic idealist who had loved her. "No," he said. "He knows a better way to harm you. He boasted that he's going to have you arrested again and charged with murder."

"He can boast all he likes."

His hand tightened over hers. "Cassie. He told me that this time he has a witness."

"Witness!" she hissed. "There's no witness. Who has he bought? Who has he intimidated?"

"That, he wouldn't tell me, drunk as he was," TJ said. "It doesn't matter. If the police believe him, that's all that matters." He grimaced. "And you can be sure that William Beardsley's influence will do its work."

She looked away, sickened with rage. When she looked up, her voice was hoarse. "We have to fight back," she said.

"We have to go," he said. "We need to leave Memphis. I wouldn't even wait for tomorrow morning. We need to go tonight."

She yanked her hand away. "I can't leave Will."

"Of course not. We take the boys with us."

"You know he doesn't want to go. He's a witness himself, a real one."

"He'll never give testimony if he stays. There will never be a trial. If the Beardsleys find out about him—"

She muffled her cry.

"Rouse the boys. Don't bother packing much. I'll find us a horse and carriage. We shouldn't take the train or the steamer from Memphis."

"You're crazy!" she said.

"I'm not."

She began to think furiously. "What if we hid here?"

"What if they found you?"

The memory of running and hiding, five years ago, returned to her, and she felt sick again. "I know how to hide so they won't," she said.

"Now you're the one who sounds crazy. We can be safe in New York. Why would you try to hide here?"

She heard a loud, commanding voice in her head, not the familiar one. The vengeful goddess's voice. Her head began to ache. "Because I have unfinished business here," she said. "You know what it is. You know why it matters so much. I can swear to you that I'll keep myself safe. I'll take the boys with me. They'll be safe. The Beardsleys will never find us."

He stared at her. "I hate it," he said.

"You don't have to like it."

"Because I love you."

He'd never said it before, and this was an odd time for it to slip out. She nodded, too tired to give him the proper answer.

"At least let me help you," he said. "I know how to hide, too."

She said, "I'll go tonight. Tomorrow I'll make provision for the boys. There's no reason to wake them and terrify them now." Before he could object, she said, "Give me a few minutes to gather my things. Then walk me over to Ida Simmons's place."

Bag in hand, she hesitated on the landing. The door to the

boys' room was open, and moonlight slanted over the quilt that covered them both. Sammy was curled into a ball, his face pressed into the pillow. Will lay on his side, his face touched by moonlight. He stirred a little in his sleep but didn't wake. He looked young and innocent, as he never did when awake.

She felt a pang of regret so profound that she had to press her hand to her chest. Once again, she was leaving them, without a word of goodbye, to keep them safe.

She slipped quietly down the stairs to meet TJ by the side door.

They walked to Ida Simmons's bordello in the dark, in silence. They took the side streets, but she didn't feel safer there. She started at the sound of the leaves rustling in the night breeze. When she saw a shadow, she grabbed TJ's hand. "It's only a stray dog," he whispered.

Once there, she guided him to the side door, where the light from the kitchen spilled into the yard. TJ hung back and waited as she knocked softly on the door. The cook, a woman she didn't know, opened it. Behind her, someone familiar sat at the kitchen table. It was Izzy, who had been Ida's business partner during the war. It seemed she still was. Izzy, dressed for her work in a low-cut evening dress, rose from her chair. Laughing, she extended her hands. "Cassie Andrews, are you in trouble again?"

THE NEXT MORNING, Cassie sat in the kitchen with Ida. The day started late in a bordello, and at nearly noon, they were eating breakfast. Ida finished her eggs and bacon and delicately wiped her mouth. "Just like old times," she said.

Through the open window came air scented with the

magnolia that bloomed in the backyard. Cassie hadn't eaten much, but she pushed away her plate. "Don't remind me."

"You can't stay here," Ida said.

"I know, you have enough trouble with the police."

"I'm not worried for myself," Ida said. "I'm worried for you. Let me think about the best place to hide you."

As they rose from the table, there was a discreet knock on the back door. Ida opened it. She turned to Cassie. "It's Mr. Randolph," she said.

An angry voice added, "And it's your aunt Matilda, too."

Cassie sighed. "I'll talk to them both," she said.

Matilda Hayes strode past TJ into the kitchen and sat heavily in the chair that Ida had just vacated. "Don't say a thing," she said to Cassie. "I know what's going on. Mr. Randolph explained it to us." She glared at Cassie. "Explained it to your boys, too."

Ida said, "Mrs. Hayes, would you like a cup of coffee?"

Matilda glared at Ida. "No, don't bother. I'll say my piece and I'll go." She laid her work-worn hands on the table. "If you had a grain of sense, you'd go back to New York." She threw a venomous look at TJ. "And take him with you."

Cassie didn't reply.

"But you don't have a grain of sense, do you?"

Ida said, "She wants to stay in Memphis to keep an eye on her sons."

"They're in danger too," Matilda said. "Thanks to you."

TJ said, "I told her I'd be glad to take them with us when we leave for New York."

"I'm not leaving," Cassie said.

Ida said, "I can help her find a place to lie low. And I'd be glad to help you hide the children, if it comes to that."

Matilda rose. She said bitterly to Cassie, "You run, like you're good at. And we'll keep them safe, like we're good at."

She swept from the house. TJ remained. He rarely looked abashed, but he did so now. Cassie suddenly wondered if his mother had been a forceful woman. "I did my best to persuade her."

"As you persuaded me," Cassie said, making him the target of her anger.

He sighed and shook his head. "I'll keep an eye on your boys," he said. "I'll do whatever I can to keep them safe."

Ida said, "Let me help."

He sighed again, and this time he nodded.

A FEW HOURS LATER, Ida said, "I have a place for you. I don't think you'll like it much, but you'll be safe there."

"Is it in the Second District Station jail?"

Ida snorted. "South Memphis," she said. She looked at Cassie. "You shouldn't go there dressed like that."

"In my New York finery?"

Ida led Cassie into her bedroom and told her to wait. She returned with some clothes in her arms and laid them on the bed. She'd brought an old, worn cotton dress, a ragged kerchief, and a chemise and petticoat that were thin and threadbare with age. She laid a pair of battered old boots on the floor.

Cassie said, "My disguise."

Ida nodded. "Do you need me to unlace you?"

"No, I'll manage."

Alone, Cassie took off her dress and her underthings, laying them neatly on the bed, and dressed in the clothing that would make her unremarkable on the street in South Memphis. When she was dressed, she looked at herself in

Ida's ornate cheval mirror. *I look ten years older*, she thought. She rounded her shoulders and dropped her head.

Her spiritualist friends in New York had taught her how to look imposing and beautiful, which they called "the glamor." Now she worked to un-glamor herself. It wasn't a spiritual talent. All good actors knew it, and she had a natural talent herself, which she had honed by going to the theater.

She retrieved the speech she had heard as an enslaved child in the Tennessee countryside. "Yas'm," she whispered. *I look like I don't know I'm free.*

She opened the door to Ida, who drew in a breath. "If I didn't know you well, I wouldn't have recognized you," she said.

Cassie nodded.

Half an hour later, she clambered into a cart that smelled of decomposing greens. The driver wasn't a drayman, but a farmer who delivered produce and butter to Ida's house. He pulled a canvas tarpaulin over the wagon bed, and she rode to South Memphis that way, as uncomfortable as a cabbage rolling around in the back of the cart.

They stopped and he pulled open the canvas to help her jump from the wagon. The street was unpaved, the ruts permanent in the dust, and it smelled like garbage and sewage. The houses were tiny and rickety, most of them haphazardly patched with whatever had come to hand, bits of wood or tin. The house where they stopped was whole, but it looked as though a summer storm might topple it. Once painted, it was now bare, splintered, weather-beaten wood. The wooden steps had rotted. There was a burn scar under the front window—a memento of the massacre? Did the smell of charred wood really linger? The farmer waited while she knocked on the door.

The hinges whined and a shadowy face peered out. "Ida sent you?" asked a raspy, uncertain voice.

"Yes, ma'am," Cassie said in her country accent.

The door opened all the way, the hinges groaning like an old woman in pain. "Then come in," she said.

She was bent with age, and she stood as though every joint was racked with rheumatism. Her hair, completely white, wisped around her wrinkled forehead. One of her eyes was completely clouded. The other was big, dark, and beautifully lashed, a disturbing reminder of the young woman she'd once been.

As the farmer drove away, Cassie entered the house. The front room was so small that the settee and wing chairs filled it. The furniture, like the house, looked too shaky for use. The cushion on the settee had split and the horsehair stuffing protruded from it. The room smelled of dust, sweat, and bacon grease.

The woman said, "Ida helped me once. I owe her, and that's why you're here. But let me tell you, I don't want to know what kind of trouble you're in. If you bring me trouble while you're here, I don't care what Ida said. You're gone."

Cassie's throat was too dry for speech. She nodded.

Her room was filled by a narrow bed, a little pine wash table, and a kitchen chair, scorched like the exterior of the house. On the bed was a sheet, dingy with age, and a threadbare blanket. The landlady gestured toward the wash table. "If you want water, it's extra," she said.

When the landlady left, Cassie sat heavily on the edge of the bed. The mattress was thin and hard. The air in the room was hot and unbearably close. She walked to the window, pulled aside the stained muslin curtain, and took in the view of the midden in the alley. If she opened the window, the room would smell like rotting garbage.

She thought of the pleasant rooms in the house she had rented on Beale Street. She thought of the comfort of her lodgings back in New York. She fell onto the bed and buried her face in her hands. *I hate this*, she thought. *But I deserve it, too.*

AT NIGHT, South Memphis was completely dark, since the city didn't bother with streetlights in this poor Black neighborhood, and the sounds were disconcerting. The clop of hooves and the rattle of wheels. A curse when the wheels stuck in a rut. Soft hooting noises. Owls. She hadn't heard owls on Beale Street. The laughter of men getting drunk a few houses down. A snatch of fiddle music. And as she drifted off to sleep, a woman's wordless scream. She bolted upright, wondering if she could go downstairs to see what was wrong. But the house around her, the landlady sleeping on the first floor near the kitchen, her other boarders asleep on the second floor and in the attic, didn't wake. They didn't even stir.

In the morning, she asked the landlady if there was a book in the house.

The unclouded eye stared at her. "We ain't a lending library."

"Not even a Bible?"

"We ain't a church, either."

"Can I do something in the house? Help you?"

"Don't need no help."

This was a lie, since the rooms were dirty with neglect. "Just sweep out the parlor a little," Cassie said, wheedling as she had not since she was an enslaved girl.

The gaze from the good eye was uncanny. "It ain't too dirty, but all right."

Cassie swept, and when the landlady left to buy a few provisions, she went looking for a rag and a bucket. She gave the parlor a scrub. When she emptied the bucket, the water was filthy. She shook her head and sighed. *She won't even notice*, Cassie thought.

She didn't go out. She tried to sit in the parlor, now that it was cleaner, but she ached for something to occupy her mind. She'd brought her cards, but she left them in her room. She was in enough trouble without telling fortunes. If Ida or TJ came to see her, she'd ask for a book. Several books. Long ones, like the books Will liked to read.

But no one came that day. She worried about her aunt and uncle, and even more about her sons.

She wondered who the witness could possibly be.

At dinner that night, she met her fellow boarders as they all spooned up black-eyed peas with rice. *Too much grease*, she thought. The landlady couldn't see to cook, either. They were a woman and a man, both of whom worked downtown, the woman as a maid and the man as a day laborer. The woman looked tired enough to fall into her plate, and when she finished eating, she rose without speaking and went into her room.

The man looked at her with a spark of interest. He had a rough, seamed, pitted face that made it impossible to guess his age. He asked, "Sugar, are you in trouble?"

She bristled at the word "sugar." She remembered to talk in her slave's accent. "Why ask me that?"

"You're here, ain't you?" He gestured around the mean little room.

"I aim to keep my trouble to myself. Not to bother anyone else with it."

"Can I help?"

The voice, which had been silent so far, said to her, *It's all right. He's no danger to you. Just lonesome.*

You know that?

The familiar low chuckle.

She said to him, "Keep your eye out for the police, if they come around."

At that he laughed. "Police? They don't bother coming here. They don't care what we do to each other here."

She sighed and looked down at the table.

"Where you from?" he asked.

She raised her eyes. "Grew up in Shelby County," she said. "Came to Memphis during the war."

He said, "You ain't what you seem."

Startled, she asked, "Why would you say that?"

"I know all about hiding. And keeping a secret." He dropped his voice. "Ran away before the war." But there was no suspicion in his voice, only sympathy.

She thought of the cards in her bedroom. "Do you want to know your fortune?"

He laughed. "You tell me a story, don't you?"

Her accent slipped a little. "No, the spirits speak to me, and I can see a little bit into the future."

He said, "Why not?"

"Let me get my cards." She ran upstairs and returned with the cards in her hand. Before she could sit at the table to lay them out, she knew. "I can see it, as clear as daylight," she said. "You're standing behind a chair, with your hands on the back, and there's a woman sitting in it. Like you're having your portrait taken."

"Is she pretty?"

"Pretty. Round-faced. Smiling. She has a baby on her lap,

a little girl in a long white dress, and there's a little boy standing by her knee." She looked up.

His irises were so dark that his eyes seemed to be all pupil. "How am I supposed to meet a woman like that?"

She knew that, too. "Go to church this Sunday," she said.

He snorted. "Haven't been to church in years."

"Go to church this Sunday," she repeated, her voice soft.

"You ain't angling for yourself?"

She laughed. "I've never had round cheeks, and I haven't been to church for a while, either." She tapped the tabletop. "Go."

This small act of charity was like a candle in the darkness of South Memphis. But it didn't last. She woke to a furious voice floating down the street, a woman's voice: "If you come back here, if you show your face here again, I cut you."

As she shut her eyes, she heard someone running away.

THE NEXT DAY, Cassie sat in the front room while her landlady puttered in the kitchen. When TJ arrived, she was so glad to see him that she nearly forgot her disguise and flew into his arms. She caught herself in time. *That won't look right*, she thought. Instead, she motioned to him to sit on the torn settee. He didn't say a word. His look around the room said everything he needed to say.

"It's not for long, I hope," she said.

He didn't reply to that.

"How are the boys?" she asked, leaning forward in her eagerness.

"They're safe."

"Are they happy?"

He snorted. "They're mad, both of them. Sammy is loud

about it. He told me, 'She ran off again and didn't tell us. I hate her.'"

"And Will?"

"Will is very quiet."

Cassie frowned.

TJ said, "He goes into his room, and he stays there to read. I brought him a copy of *Ivanhoe*. He asked me if I could get him *David Copperfield* next."

"That's how he gets mad," she said. "Even though he won't say." She looked up. "Please, bring me something to read. A long book, like Dickens."

He looked around the room. "Read?"

"Yes, because I have nothing else to occupy myself."

He shook his head.

She took a deep breath. "How are my aunt and uncle? Have the police been back?"

"Fortunately not. But your lawyer wasn't so lucky."

"Mr. Aronson?"

"The police visited him too."

"What happened to him?"

"They roughed him up while they asked him where you were. They thought he'd abetted your escape."

"Is he all right?"

"He looks like hell, but he isn't badly hurt. A black eye and a split lip. He's well enough to be furious. He went down to the Second District to file a complaint. He gave me quite an earful."

Cassie didn't have the energy to worry about Elias Aronson. "Well, I can't help that, or help him," she said. She raised her eyes to TJ's face. "Any progress in finding out who the witness might be?"

"Not yet."

After TJ left, the landlady emerged from the kitchen. She was grinning.

Cassie said, "You're wrong. He isn't my fancy man."

"I didn't say a word."

"You were thinking it so loud I could hear it."

"What is he, then? Part of your trouble?"

Cassie said firmly, "He's an inquiry agent. I've hired him to help me with my trouble. The one you're not supposed to ask me about."

THAT NIGHT, as she struggled to fall asleep in her stuffy, smelly room, she heard a shot. She sat up, her heart pounding, stifling a scream. But no one screamed, either in pain or in rage, and she lay down again, her eyes gritty but her mind racing.

She must have fallen asleep, because the dream came to her again, the one she hated and feared most. She was in a familiar dark alley, which smelled of whiskey and vomit. She saw the gun barrel glinting ever so faintly in the darkness, aimed at her. She heard the shot—

And she woke, more frightened by the gun in the dream than the gun in the street, and she had no more rest that night.

TJ KNOCKED on the door late that afternoon. He carried a battered book with a cloth cover. "It's Dickens," he said, as he handed it to her. "But all I could find was *A Tale of Two Cities*."

"I'd read the Memphis City Directory. Thank you."

The landlady called from the kitchen, "Do the inquiry man want refreshment?"

"No, thank you," Cassie called back.

"She knows I'm an inquiry agent?"

"I thought it was better than letting her think that you keep me," she said.

He sighed.

"Is there any news?"

"Your family is fine," he said.

She leaned forward and dropped her voice to a whisper. "You know what I mean."

He whispered, too. "Is there somewhere more private where we can talk?"

She sighed. "Out in the yard."

"Into the yard, then."

"It's nasty."

"I'm sure I've been in worse places."

Cassie called, "We're going in back for a breath of air."

The landlady snorted.

The yard was bare dirt where it wasn't badly overgrown with weeds, and in the corner nearest the alley, flies buzzed around the midden, which emitted a rank smell. She held her hand to her nose, thinking with longing of the scented handkerchiefs in her dresser drawer back on Beale Street. She took her hand away. "What's the news?"

"It's not good."

"Just tell me."

"There really is a witness," he said.

"Who told you?" Cassie asked.

"John Beardsley."

"How drunk was he when he told you?"

TJ snorted.

"Who is it? Did he tell you that?"

"When I asked, he said, 'Why would you care?'"

"Suspicious?"

He nodded. "He wasn't drunk enough."

Anger surged in her. "Who could they have found? Do you want to guess?"

"No. I'll only tell you what I know."

"Tell me that."

"John Beardsley said he's told the police," TJ said. "He boasted about it. He said that they'd be willing to arrest you."

The air suddenly seemed too hot and too noxious for breath. "But it wouldn't last a moment in court. You know that."

He curled his hands around her wrists. "It doesn't matter, and you know that."

She thought of the way the police had handcuffed her, and she shook free. "Help me. Find out who this witness is."

He dropped his voice. "Cassie, we have to go," he said. "All of us. I can find us passage on a steamer. Down to New Orleans, to confuse the trail. From there to New York, and safety."

"No."

"Cassie—"

"I'm not going anywhere." She balled her hands into fists. "Find out."

He covered her fists with his hands. "I hate that you ask me to do this." His voice was hoarse, but his touch was soft.

"If you truly love me—"

"You know I do."

They stood very close together. Anyone watching from afar would think they were lovers quarreling. "Then find out."

THE DEMONSTRATION

Elias sat in Dorsey's office, shifting in the chair. "You need a better chair for your clients," he said.

Dorsey sighed. "More than that."

"Perhaps we should take up a collection for it," Elias teased him.

Dorsey laughed. "If Mrs. Aronson is in charge, I'll feel confident," he said. He sobered a little. "She does well? The school hasn't received any more of those nasty notes?"

"Not lately, thank God," Elias said. He shifted again in the chair, but it was only to annoy Dorsey. "I'm curious about your plan to make bricks without straw in Miss Armstrong's case."

Dorsey smiled. "We won't get satisfaction from the police or the courts, so we'll go to the court of public opinion instead," he said.

Elias flashed a smile. "Our friend General Eaton at the *Post*," he said.

"We'll start there. Would you like to join me in calling on him?"

The *Post* took its place alongside the *Appeal*, the local

paper with the greatest longevity, and the *Avalanche*, the paper with the loudest Conservative—that meant Confederate—voice. The *Appeal* ignored the Black community, but the *Avalanche* hated it. The *Avalanche* had whipped white residents into a frenzy in the days before the 1866 massacre.

The *Post*'s office was on Union Street, an irony Elias relished, a stone's throw from the riverfront, on the commercial thoroughfare near downtown. The location spoke to the paper's seriousness of purpose. Housed in a new brick building of two stories, the paper's name was prominent on the window, in gleaming gold lettering.

Eaton had a serious face, and he wore the long, unkempt beard common to New England teachers and ministers. Like many men who had seen too much grief in the war, his smile was melancholy. He'd become a brevet general by the end of the war, but he'd begun as a chaplain. Before that, he'd been a teacher, both in his native New Hampshire and later in Memphis for the Freedmen's Bureau, and now he combined his editorial work at the *Post* with an appointment as Tennessee's superintendent for public instruction. That meant the state-funded schools for white children. He was a Republican, but he was considered a moderate, even by the local Conservatives he opposed. He reported fairly on the party of General Grant and addressed the Black community with common courtesy. Whether he was Radical enough to support Narcissa's cause remained to be seen.

He welcomed them into his office, cluttered with past issues and the paste-up of today's paper. He knew them both, as they were all active in the local Republican party. "How can I help you, gentlemen?" he asked.

Dorsey nodded at Elias, who said, "We have a situation you'll want to keep an eye on." Elias explained about the

Armstrong family's effort to bring Titus Armstrong's murder to the police and their refusal to consider it.

Eaton nodded. "I have to tread carefully."

Elias and Dorsey exchanged a rueful look.

Eaton said, "Of course it's wrong," he said. "But I want to inform public opinion, not to inflame it."

Dorsey said, "The audience is not just in Memphis or in Tennessee. It's elsewhere, in the North, where it isn't as risky to arouse public opinion."

"Yes, I know," Eaton said.

Elias shifted in his chair, irritated by Eaton's caution. He had lived in Memphis long enough to understand why a white man with moderate views would want to be cautious about matters of race. But the party of Grant liked to remind his supporters to "vote the way you shot." Elias was inclined to agree with Dorsey. The time for moderation was past.

Dorsey said, "We'll keep you apprised." He looked at Eaton with the gaze he brought into the courtroom. "And we'd hope you'll be fair in letting the world know what is happening."

"That I can promise," Eaton said.

AFTER TALKING TO EATON, Elias and Dorsey, along with Narcissa, decided to visit City Hall. They planned to call on Mayor McDavitt. Whether he'd receive them was another story.

In Memphis, City Hall was housed in the Cotton Exchange building, which said a great deal about who ran the city and what mattered to it. Narcissa paused on the sidewalk to look at the imposing entrance. Elias asked softly, "Are you ready, Miss Armstrong?" She looked from

Elias to Dorsey, unable to smile. "As ready as I'll ever be," she said.

Inside, the Exchange building was equally impressive, with marble floors and ceilings ornamented with gilded friezes. The war had left this building untouched. The anteroom to the mayor's office was similarly ornate, and at a desk sat a small man who had removed his frock coat. He was writing, and as they approached, he made a blot and frowned. He looked up at them. Narcissa approached the desk with a teacher's perfect posture. In a firm voice, she said, "We're here to see Mayor McDavitt."

The man looked down at the blot and frowned again. Then he stared at Narcissa. "Who are you?"

"My name is Miss Armstrong, Miss Narcissa Armstrong, and I'm accompanied by my lawyer, Mr. Elias Aronson, and his colleague, Mr. James Dorsey, who is also a lawyer."

The man squinted. "Two lawyers? What's this about?"

She said, "We would like to talk to him about a matter the police have refused to investigate."

"Police? We don't handle police matters here. Go back to the station. What is it, the Second District?"

Elias stepped forward. "We've been there. And to the main headquarters."

Narcissa said, "My brother was murdered, and the police refuse to investigate his death."

The man said, "They would know." He returned to the paper.

Narcissa said, "My lawyer and his colleague have evidence. They refuse to consider it."

He stared at Narcissa again.

Narcissa said, in her firmest teacher's voice, "We would like to see the mayor, please."

The man said, "He's a very busy man."

"I'm sure he is," Elias said.

The man stared at Elias. "I know you," he said. "You're that Radical lawyer who gets the colored people all stirred up."

Elias said, "I support the party of General Grant, who was my commander during the war, and I know many others who do the same."

"Radical," he repeated. "Aren't you married to that woman who gads about teaching at the colored school?"

Elias said, "I fail to see what that has to do—"

"The mayor won't see you," the man said. "Get out, before I have you shown out."

"Sir," Narcissa said.

"Thrown out," the man said.

THE THREE OF THEM, Elias, Dorsey, and Narcissa, didn't linger outside City Hall. Dorsey took Narcissa's arm, shielding her from the dirt of the street and from the insult of the crowd, and Elias followed them as they walked back to Dorsey's office. Dorsey offered Narcissa the guest's chair and Elias stood next to her, leaning against Dorsey's desk.

Elias said, "That's not what we hoped for."

Narcissa smiled. He marveled at her composure. "The only person he insulted was you," she said. "He didn't call us anything worse than 'colored.' That's better than I expected."

Elias looked at Dorsey, who was smiling like a cat looking at a dish of cream. "What are you thinking?" he asked his colleague.

Dorsey said, "I think it's time to give Mr. Eaton something to write about."

~

THE FOLLOWING SUNDAY, Elias and Lydia stood across the street from the Second District Station. It was noon, just after the churches had finished their services, and the heat on the unshaded sidewalk was fierce. Elias mopped his face with his handkerchief, and Lydia dabbed at hers.

Since it was Sunday, the street was relatively quiet, unchoked by the carts and wagons that thronged the thoroughfares on weekdays. The occasional carriage rattled down the street. A few stragglers, too unkempt or unsteady to be churchgoers, wandered down the sidewalk.

Lydia peered down the street and Elias laid his hand on her arm. "I know it will be hard not to intervene," he said. "But if everything goes as we expect, we'll play our part later."

"I worry for Narcissa."

"So do I. But she has four very good men along, all of them former soldiers, one a former master sergeant. If things go badly, they'll protect her."

Lydia shivered despite the heat. "As much as they can."

Eaton hurried toward them, his head bare, his frock coat unbuttoned in the heat. He waved a notebook in the air, and when he halted, he pulled a pencil from his pocket. "I hope I'm not late," he said. "My church's service ran over."

Elias shook his head. "No, they aren't here yet," he said.

Outside the station, two policemen patrolled the sidewalk, watching the street in both directions. One was taller and the other was stockier. The taller one rested his hand on the billy club at his hip.

Lydia whispered, "Do they always look for trouble at the station house door?"

Elias said, "They look for trouble everywhere."

They waited. Now Eaton pulled out his handkerchief and mopped his forehead. He said to Lydia, "I envy you ladies, with the shade provided by your bonnets and parasols."

Lydia said, "I wish I'd remembered my parasol. It has a sharp point. It might come in handy."

Elias hushed her, and Lydia peered down the street as if expecting a parade.

Then they came into sight, from about ten feet away. They numbered a dozen, walking slowly down the sidewalk, two abreast like schoolchildren in line. Eaton poised his pencil over his notebook.

Lydia whispered, "I thought there would be more of them."

"Dorsey assured me that there would be enough," Elias whispered back.

Two men, dressed in their Sunday best, who held themselves in a stance familiar to anyone who had served in the army, led the group. Just behind them walked two women, also in their Sunday best, each clasping a child by the hand. The children were wide-eyed and quiet, all old enough to understand what they were doing. The men held up a hand-painted banner that read "Let us have peace."

Elias said, "General Grant's other campaign slogan."

Lydia knew "Vote as you shot." "I wasn't aware he had another one."

Elias said, "The other is a little too inflammatory for the occasion, I think."

Eaton looked up. "It's a fitting sentiment, though."

Elias stifled a snort.

The two policemen watched as the orderly column approached. The man with the club pulled it from his belt and began to tap his palm with it.

Lydia's breath caught in her throat at the sight of the

children, whom she recognized as students at the Phoenix School. Their leaders were a serious girl in a starched white pinafore, and Will Andrews. The two of them bore a banner with their school's motto: "We have risen from the ashes."

Lydia pressed her hand to her stomach. She whispered, "If there's trouble—if they arrest him—"

Elias knew what she meant. Will, their witness. Elias returned his gaze to the former soldiers at the front of the group. "They won't."

Both policemen watched the children with an expression of disgust. During the massacre, Black children had not been spared, as every child at the Phoenix School knew. But the police let them pass.

Behind the children walked a dignified man in a frock coat, the minister at Beale Street Baptist Church, and Narcissa. Between them, prominently displayed, they held a banner, the words bright and carefully painted: "Justice for Titus Armstrong."

Lydia shivered again and Elias put his arm around her shoulders.

The two policemen let the children pass, but they blocked the sidewalk to stop Narcissa and the minister. One of them said, "Did you get a permit?"

Narcissa stood very still. Calmly, she said, "I wasn't aware that we needed a permit to walk down the street."

"You need a permit if you're going to have a procession."

The minister said, "Sir, we're just walking to the park for a church picnic."

The men with the political banner and the children with the school banner stopped on the sidewalk. The men turned around to keep an eye on the policemen.

The other police officer said, "This sure looks like a political procession to me." He gestured at the banner with his billy club. "What in hell is that?"

Narcissa remained calm. "We're expressing an opinion," she said. "I believe we're within our rights to do that, as long as we're peaceful about it."

The first policeman said, "You're obstructing the sidewalk, and you're creating a disturbance."

Narcissa stood very still and didn't reply.

The second policeman reached for the banner. "We'll take that," he said.

Neither Narcissa nor the minister gave up their grasp on it.

"Hand it over," the first policeman said.

Neither Narcissa nor the minister moved.

Both policemen snatched at the banner and the cloth tore. Neither Narcissa nor the minister let go of the remnants. One of the policemen grabbed the minister by the arms and the other grabbed Narcissa. The first policeman raised his club. "We can add resisting arrest to obstruction and disturbance," he said. Narcissa didn't flinch. She didn't even move.

One of the men who had been carrying the political banner turned to walk toward the policemen. "Sirs," he said. "Please. Just a peaceful walk to the park for the church picnic. This young lady is a Sunday school teacher."

The policeman ignored him. He pulled Narcissa's hands behind her back. She offered no resistance. "You're under arrest," he said, cuffing her.

"Sir!" the political man said. "This ain't right!"

"We can arrest you, too," the policeman said.

The minister said calmly, "No, please leave him alone." He held out his hands in a gesture that offered no resistance. The second policeman said, "If that's the way you want it." He cuffed the minister. "You're under arrest, too." He glared at the man who'd tried to intervene.

The minister said, "You have both of us. Please leave him be."

The rest of the group, the women and children, watched in silence. Not even the littlest child made a sound.

The minister said, "Let's do this quietly. Don't frighten the children."

Lydia thought, *Every one of those children remembers the massacre.*

The second policeman said, "Resisting arrest," and he yanked the minister toward the door of the station. The first policeman pulled on Narcissa's upper arm, and he was unhappy that she came without a struggle.

Lydia leaned toward Elias and whispered, "Resisting arrest, indeed."

Narcissa and the minister disappeared into the station. The man who had tried to intervene picked up the torn banner with Titus Armstrong's name on it.

ELIAS INSISTED that Lydia go home. "I need to look after Narcissa," he said. He touched her cheek. "Take a hansom, dearest."

She nodded and he walked into the station house.

At home, she took off her sweat-soaked dress and exchanged it for a clean one. She went into the kitchen to see what their housekeeper, who had Sunday afternoons for herself, had left for dinner. She wasn't hungry. She wandered back into the parlor to wait for Elias.

She picked up the latest edition of the *Post*, but she didn't have time to read it. Elias came in, calling to her from the foyer, where he hung up his hat and coat. He was sweaty and rumpled when he came into the parlor, but she didn't care. She rose from her chair to hold him close.

He kissed her and said, "It's all right. All I did was argue with the man at the desk."

"Is Narcissa all right?"

"I talked to John Harris, too. He's furious that she was arrested. He'll make sure she's safe and that she's properly fed. He was furious about the reverend, too, but I think he figures a man can take care of himself."

"What happens now?"

He stepped back and rested his hands on her shoulders. "They'll go to Municipal Court. Maybe tomorrow, maybe the day after. I need to get some character references. It's a bit of a problem. Usually a minister is a good reference. But her minister was arrested along with her."

"What can I do?"

"Give me a statement. As her employer."

She nodded. "Will Mr. Eaton report on the arrests?"

"I believe so. We'll know tomorrow morning when the new edition comes out."

There was a knock on the door and Elias released Lydia to answer it. He returned to the parlor, ushering Dorsey into the room.

Dorsey sat down without ceremony and said, "I talked to Harris. He told me they were arrested and they're in jail." His eyes gleamed. "As we foresaw."

"Have they been scheduled to appear in court?"

"Yes, the day after tomorrow."

"Good, that gives us time to prepare our case."

Dorsey said, "The presiding judge is George Waldran." His face was alight. "There's no love lost between Waldran and the police."

"I know about the effort to unseat him last year. Is there something else I haven't heard?"

Dorsey looked at Lydia, then at Elias. "There are indictments against three of the police commissioners and the captain of the police for failure to report, and worse still, an indictment against Beaumont for corruption. The police department hates him, and he has an eagle eye on them for misconduct."

Elias said, "Then we make a case for wrongful arrest."

"Even more than that," Dorsey said.

Elias brightened. "We explain the reason behind the protest," he said.

"We tell him about the murder. And the police department's indifference."

Elias said slowly, "There may be grounds for a civil suit." He looked at Dorsey. "For police misconduct."

Dorsey said, "One thing at a time. Let's see if we can get the reverend and Miss Narcissa out of the room with a dismissal."

Elias said, "We'll need a witness or two. The men who led the procession had a good view of the proceedings."

"I'll get them there," Dorsey said.

THE MUNICIPAL COURT was always full of people—the accused, their families, the reporters who hovered there, looking for juicy stories for the *Appeal* and the *Avalanche*, and a roomful of spectators, because the proceedings were more interesting than a variety show, and free. Elias had lost the expectation of a dignified setting for justice during the war. But the Municipal Court reminded him of a circus.

Elias sat on the lawyers' bench with Dorsey and one of

the men who had led the procession. He was dark and calm; he'd been a master sergeant in the 3rd Heavy Artillery during the war. They waited for the prisoners to be brought in.

Both Narcissa and the reverend looked rumpled and tired, but neither were limping or visibly bruised. Jailkeeper John Harris had kept his promise. They'd likely been upset and frightened, but they hadn't been abused.

Judge Waldran was a Michigan man who had fought for the Union and settled in Tennessee just after the war. He wore thick dark whiskers that obscured his face, and his natural look was fierce. Elias hoped that he would insist on pursuing justice instead of punishing the lesser crime that had come to the Municipal Court.

As was customary in these cases, the police acted as prosecutors, describing the offense and offering evidence of the crime. The information must have been taken directly from the police report, because it echoed the accusations the police had made on the sidewalk: obstructing the road, creating a disturbance, and resisting arrest.

The judge listened with an air of weariness. When the police officer finished, the judge said, "I'd like to hear from the defense. Mr. Aronson, is it?"

Elias rose. "Yes, Judge Waldran."

"Go ahead, Mr. Aronson."

"I'd like to call a witness."

The police officer said, "This is a waste of our time, Your Honor."

"You had your say," Judge Waldran said. "They'll have theirs."

Their companion was sworn in as a witness and Elias quickly established his character, emphasizing that he had been a soldier and was a regular churchgoer. He asked the man what he had seen.

"We were walking down the street, lined up, but we were quiet and orderly. I was carrying a banner about peace and there were children behind me, carrying a banner with their school motto on it. They stopped Miss Narcissa and the reverend, grabbed their banner away and ripped it up. Then they began to accuse them of obstructing the street and disturbing the peace. When they said quietly that they weren't, the police took out their clubs and said they were resisting arrest."

Elias asked, "What did Miss Armstrong's banner say?"

"Justice for Titus Armstrong."

"Who is Titus Armstrong?"

"Was. He was her brother, murdered back in 1866 during the disturbance."

"And why was Miss Armstrong insisting on justice for her murdered brother?"

"Because she'd gone to the police and asked them to look into it. Told them she had evidence. And they turned her away."

Elias thought, *If the judge is going to disallow this, it will be now.* But Judge Waldran continued to listen with the same weary air. Elias said, "What reason did the police give her?"

"Said it was too long ago and not worth the trouble."

"Even though she had found evidence that pointed to a suspect?"

"They wouldn't touch it," the man said.

The judge said, "Mr. Aronson, we are going far afield here."

Elias braced himself. "Your Honor, this is not a case about disturbing the peace. It is about the misconduct of the police, not only in arresting these people without cause but in neglecting to respond to their legitimate complaint about a man's murder."

The judge's mouth quirked in something that might have been a smile. "Mr. Aronson, that might be the subject of a very different suit. But I agree with you. There are no grounds for arrest here."

The policeman said, "Your Honor—"

The judge gave him a piercing look. "The next time you arrest someone, make sure they're doing something illegal." He said, "I'm going to dismiss the charges. These people are free to go."

Elias and Dorsey led Narcissa and the reverend from the bench. As they walked toward the door, a young man in a checked suit followed their progress. Once they were in the hallway, he joined them.

He held out his hand to Elias and introduced himself as a reporter with the *Appeal*.

There was no love lost between Judge Waldran and the *Appeal*, either. The *Appeal* called him "the carpetbagger judge."

The reporter asked Elias, "If there's enough evidence to point to a suspect, why wouldn't the police investigate? Why wouldn't they make an arrest?"

Elias said, "I can't speak to that."

"Is the suspect a member of the police force?"

Elias said, "I can't say."

Narcissa said, "I can."

"Please, Miss Armstrong," Elias said.

"What is the suspect's name?" the reporter asked eagerly.

Narcissa's face was as calm as the winter ice on a lake in upstate New York. "John Beardsley," she said. "He's William Beardsley's son."

THE FALSE WITNESS

They have a witness, Cassie thought. *The Beardsleys have a witness against me.*

She turned the thought over in her mind until it was hard to eat or to sleep. Who could it be? She felt cold with dread that the Beardsleys might have pressed her uncle Moses into agreeing to testify against her in court. She let her worry go even farther afield. What if the Beardsleys had gotten to Will? In her room in the boardinghouse, from which she could do nothing for her sons, she buried her head in her hands. What if they knew that he was Narcissa's witness? What would they do to him if they found out?

She felt trapped in the mean little house with its tattered furniture and greasy walls and the noisome odor that never diminished. When she wasn't holed up in her room, she paced through the living room until the landlady said, "Stop that. It make me crazy to watch you."

She nearly turned on the old woman to say something bitter. Or worse yet, cruel. She stopped herself. "I'll go into the yard," she said.

She stood there for a long time, unable to calm her

thoughts. TJ found her there, staring at the midden, which had attracted a cloud of flies. At his approach, she recalled how angry she'd been when they parted. "Have you found out?" she asked.

"Yes," he said.

"Who is it?"

He dropped his voice. "It's Dolly."

The relief hit first. Not her uncle. Not her son. And then she was flooded with rage. She lowered her voice to match his. "William Beardsley's housekeeper?"

"Yes."

"She's a liar," she said. "She always has been. And she'll say or do anything the Beardsleys tell her to. Who told you? Was it John Beardsley?"

His face was suddenly haggard. "No. It was the detective."

"McMahon?"

He nodded.

"What did he say?"

"They're ready to charge you and arrest you." He reached for her hand. "We really have to go. All of us. Right away."

She pulled her hand away. "No."

"Cassie—"

"Don't bother to buy a steamer ticket."

"Do you really want to stay?" he asked.

She didn't speak, but she gave him a long, searching gaze.

"To do what?"

"She can't be a witness," she said.

He looked into her eyes. His voice dropped to a hoarse whisper. "And how do you intend to stop her?"

She shook her head. "You know how I feel about her. But do you really think I'd—"

His expression reminded her: *I know you. I know what you've done.*

"No," she said. "Not that."

"Then what?"

"I need a witness of my own," she said slowly. "I need you to find a witness who will speak for me. And against her." In her ragged disguise, she put on the glamor she used when she called the spirits. "Do you love me enough for that?"

He laid his hand on her arm and his voice was a warning. "Yes. Enough to remind you to be very careful."

Bitterness overwhelmed her. "Don't worry, I won't lay a hand on her, much as I'd wish to."

He said, "Stay here, lay low, and you can wish as much as you want."

THAT NIGHT she had the dream again. She was in a dark alley. She knew it was behind a saloon on Main Street, the one where the Rebs gathered during the war to get drunk and talk treason in occupied Memphis. In the street, carriages rattled and drunken men shouted. The alley was so dark that she couldn't see her hand when she held it out to look.

Then she heard the gunshot, and she knew a man had fallen dead at her feet, even though she could not see his face.

TJ DIDN'T VISIT, but he sent a note. "When I have something for you, I'll be there to tell you."

Not soon enough, she thought, crumpling up the note and stuffing it into her pocket.

Her landlady asked, "What is it? Bad news from your friend?"

"He's my man of business, not my friend," Cassie said.

"Hah!" the landlady said.

Another note came from TJ, telling her that he would call and bring Mr. Aronson with him. Just before the appointed time, Cassie gave her landlady a dollar and told her to buy some shrimps for dinner. "Take your time," she said. The landlady's eyes lit up. "A dollar!" she said. "Buy a lot of shrimps and have money left over." Cassie was surprised she could see well enough to discern the denomination.

She was alone in the house when Mr. Aronson arrived, escorted by TJ. She invited them both into the unpleasant little parlor. Mr. Aronson looked around the room and said, "I'm sorry that you're staying here."

She couldn't help the bitterness. "It's better than the jail at the Second District Station."

He said, "You won't go there."

"Are you in the business of foretelling the future?"

"I wouldn't dream of trying to best you in that, Mrs. Auburn." He glanced at TJ. "But we do know something."

"What did you find?" she asked.

TJ said, "We found two people who knew where Dolly was in the summer of 1863. Mrs. Maggie Rice—"

"Miss Maggie? She was the cook on the place when I was a girl."

"In the summer of 1863 she was the cook for the Beardsleys in their house in Memphis. She told us that Dolly was out in the countryside. She remembered it well, because Dolly wanted to go to Memphis. But she was on the country place."

Cassie said, "And unhappy about it, no doubt."

"Mrs. Rice didn't say. There's something better. I talked to Mr. Southall, who was John Beardsley's coachman, and who lived out on the country plantation. He saw Dolly all the time."

Cassie wasn't reassured. "Could she have made her way to town, just for one night? Found her way to the river bluffs, where it happened?"

TJ said, "I asked him that, since I knew that people left the place, especially by stealth at night. He told me that if she'd tried, he would have known." TJ hesitated. "By then, John Beardsley was so angry about runaways that he kept a pack of dogs that he let loose at night. If anyone tried to slip away, the dogs came after them." He looked down. He kept a little notebook in his coat pocket, but he wasn't consulting it. He couldn't meet her eyes. She touched his arm and he looked up. "He said that those dogs kept everyone on the country place a prisoner."

Elias said, "I've spoken to both Mrs. Rice and Mr. Southall. They're credible witnesses—intelligent and well-spoken. And it doesn't hurt that Mr. Dorsey knows Mrs. Rice as a fellow member of his church."

Cassie said, "Would they speak against the Beardsleys? Go to court to do it?"

Both men were silent.

Cassie said, "As though it would make any difference in the courtroom."

Elias sat up straight. "Mrs. Auburn, I assure you, we aren't planning on going to court."

"Ah, you're foretelling the future again."

"No, it's a lot simpler than that. We're going to force the Beardsleys to think very hard about taking a hopeless case to court."

"We're going to blackmail them to shut them up?" Cassie asked, her eyes glinting.

Elias rubbed his face. "Not to put too fine a point on it," he said. He shook his head. "What kind of a lawyer have I become?"

Cassie ignored this. "What happens then? If their witness is useless to them?"

Elias said, "In a reasonable world they'd drop the effort to get you charged."

"But we don't live in a reasonable world."

Elias fell silent.

Cassie said, "They'll come after me, won't they? To shut me up? And they won't bother with the police or the courts to do it." She looked at TJ. Her voice cracked. "Just like last time," she said. "In hiding, and in fear all the time."

Elias said, "They could try to send you to the gallows. But they'd send their own reputation there, too. They might think about that."

After they left, Cassie remained on the shabby settee, remembering all too well the feeling of being imprisoned on the Beardsley place, even before the dogs had become police and judge and jury. She thought of Dolly, too terrified to risk a run to Memphis, as badly as she yearned to be there. She looked around the small, squalid room and thought, *This is a prison, too.*

SHE HAD TOO little to do and too much time to think. Despite the weight of Dickens's book in her lap, she found it impossible to read. She sat upstairs until the heat drove her out. She sat in the parlor until its misery oppressed her too much to remain. She stood in the yard until the smell and the flies drove her back indoors.

She had just returned to the house when the landlady said, "Someone here to see you. Colored girl, but dressed nice. Another friend?"

It was Narcissa, her back straight on the butt-sprung chair by the settee.

Cassie said, "I believe so."

The landlady cocked her head to look at Narcissa with her good eye. "She help you?"

"Maybe."

The landlady said, "I go next door. Need to get an egg for our dinner."

"Thank you," Cassie said. She sat on the settee, smoothing the skirt of her worn, faded dress. "How did you find me?" she asked Narcissa.

"I asked Mr. Aronson. I hope you don't mind—either that I asked or that he told me."

"It depends on why you've come here," Cassie said.

Narcissa's eyes gleamed. "I'll get right to the point," she said. "We have common cause again."

Cassie leaned forward. "Tell me how."

"Did Mr. Aronson explain to you about my arrest?"

"You? What in heaven's name were you arrested for?"

"For expressing an opinion while Black," she said. She told Cassie how the congregants of her church processed past the police station and described the offending banner.

Despite herself, Cassie laughed. "That's a fool's courage," she said.

Narcissa smiled. "No, it was all planned. I knew they'd arrest us. The whole point was to get into Municipal Court to tell the judge that the police had refused to investigate Titus's murder."

"And what did the judge say?"

"He let Mr. Aronson explain the situation, and he threw my case out of his courtroom. I went free."

Cassie said, "I don't yet see why we have common cause."

"Because I did something we didn't plan." She looked into

Cassie's eyes. Her own face was limpid as clear water. "I told a reporter from the *Appeal* that we have enough evidence to suspect John Beardsley of murdering my brother."

"What possessed you?"

Narcissa didn't falter. "The spirit moved me." On her face was a faint and familiar glow.

Cassie heard the softest chuckle in her head. She asked, "Did they print what you said?"

"No. They didn't. But Mr. Aronson thinks that someone told the Beardsleys, John and William both, what I said, and I tend to agree with him." She inclined her head. "So they have reason to be very angry with both of us."

She felt a chill. Evidence. A witness. "Do they know about Will?"

"No. No one knows." She reached for Cassie's hand. "He's safe, I swear it."

"Did Mr. Aronson tell you about my case?"

"He hardly needed to, since the news is all over town. You're talking about the false witness against you?"

She nodded. "They've forced their servant Dolly to swear she saw Everett Mason's murder. They want the police to arrest and charge me, and they want the Criminal Court to hear the case against me." She took a deep breath. "They want me dead, one way or another."

Narcissa said, "I don't doubt it."

"You should be afraid for yourself."

"I am," she said, and for a moment the fear showed in her face. Then she composed herself again. "I'm not sure whether they want to hurt me or to damage the school."

Cassie winced. "Or both."

Narcissa said, "You don't need to remind me."

"I'm sorry. I wasn't here two years ago."

"The Phoenix, Mrs. Auburn. Literally risen from the ashes."

"I'm very sorry."

They looked at each other, two women in trouble, and they both shook their heads. "I don't know what to do, Mrs. Auburn," Narcissa said. "Do you?"

"Besides leave town, as Mr. Randolph has been advising me for weeks? No."

"I can't leave," Narcissa said. "My duty is here. Not just to the school. To my family. And to my brother's memory."

Cassie said, slowly, "Mine is to my sons, even though they don't love me."

Narcissa looked at her. "Do you really believe that?"

"Yes, I do."

"Do you think they would be so angry if they didn't love you?"

Cassie was silent for a long moment. Finally she said, "Do we want justice, or revenge?"

Narcissa leaned forward. "I'm tired of being long-suffering. I want both. The question is how."

WHEN CASSIE WAS ALONE AGAIN, she began to think about what she might do. She hadn't told TJ the truth. She wished Dolly very ill. She wished her dead.

TJ was far removed from the world of root doctors and wise women, and the people who consulted them, who believed that a curse had power. But he knew that she had never left that world, and that it had come to her anew in the voice and the spirits the voice brought to her. He knew what it meant to wish for someone's death.

But it was one thing to wish someone dead in a moment

of anger. It was another to summon the power to make it happen.

She knew how to do both.

That's dangerous, the voice said.

I know.

That night, in her stifling little room, she sat in the darkness and called up the goddess of vengeance. Even in the silence of her mind, the goddess's voice was powerful enough to make her temples ache.

She whispered, "I'm sorry I can't do this properly."

You're my daughter, as all the people of Africa are. Wherever they are.

"Can you help me?"

Talk to me, daughter.

"I want to wish someone ill."

Who?

"Her name is Dolly. She has a hole in her heart. It could kill her at any moment."

Let nature take its course.

"No. She has the power to speak against me in court. To send me to my death." She shuddered. She hesitated. "Let it happen soon."

It will be heavy on your conscience.

"I know."

You'll carry it to your grave.

"I know." She hesitated again. "Do it."

THREE DAYS LATER, TJ was on her doorstep. He pulled her into the yard. His eyes blazed and his light-skinned cheeks showed a spot of angry red. But when he spoke, his level voice was worse than a burst of fury. "What have you done?"

Her own anger relit like a fire that had never been properly extinguished. Her conscience fed the flame. "What do you mean? I've been here, minding my own business. Why? What's happened?"

"Dolly is dead."

She felt both triumph and terror. "How? When?"

"Yesterday afternoon. She was standing in the kitchen and suddenly she clutched her chest. Then she fell over, dead on the spot." He said, "You haven't been talking to one of your root doctors, have you?"

At his accusation, fury coursed through her. "Do you think I'd be stupid enough to poison her?"

He grabbed her wrists. "I think you're desperate enough to do something stupid."

"Let go of me," she said, panting with anger.

"What did you do?" His eyes were blazing.

"Let go of me! I'll tell you!"

"If you've put yourself in jeopardy—and the boys in jeopardy—"

"Let go of me and let me talk!"

He released his grip. Still furious, she retreated across the room. Glaring at him, she said, "Perhaps it was stupid. But I swear to God—to every divine being I know—that I never touched her."

He waited, as angry as she was.

"I wished her ill."

"You cursed her."

"Yes, I did. I asked the spirits for help. I didn't stab her, or poison her, or even creep up behind her to startle the living daylights out of her. I wished her ill."

He stared at her. "Do you realize there's a hell of a mess to clean up now? There's going to be a thorough investigation into her death. And the Beardsleys and the police will be looking right at you."

"Bring Mr. Aronson here," she said. "This is his kind of mess, isn't it?"

~

THAT AFTERNOON, Mr. Aronson showed up at her boardinghouse, with TJ at his elbow. She could see them at the door as her landlady opened it. "Your friends are back," she called to Cassie.

Cassie said, "If I give you another dollar, would you go out to buy something good for dinner tonight?"

She nodded. "You got secrets?"

"Haven't we all? I just want to be private."

"Shrimps?" The shrimps, which had gone into a stew, had been much appreciated last time.

"Whatever strikes you."

She laughed, sounding decades younger. "Strikes my fancy!" she said. As the two men settled into the parlor, she said, "I go out. You all talk private as you like."

After she left, Mr. Aronson said, "What does she know?"

"As much as she can glean. She can barely see, but she has an uncanny way of hearing what she shouldn't." She said, "Even if she talked, who would she tell? And who would believe her? She's no more credible than I am."

Aronson said, "Don't say that."

"It's true, isn't it?"

She couldn't hide her fear. Tears rose to her eyes. "They'll blame me for Dolly's death. If they find me, they'll try me for it, too." The tears trickled down her face.

TJ said, "Tell her."

She looked up. "Tell me what? That there's a warrant out for my arrest?"

"No," Mr. Aronson said. "The police aren't convinced it's suspicious. It looks like to them she died of natural causes. They don't understand why the Beardsleys are so worked up about the death of their servant."

Surprised, she said, "Do the police think the Beardsleys had anything to do with it?"

"I doubt it. But the Beardsleys want a surgeon to examine her thoroughly. And the police have agreed to oblige them."

"Will that do any good?" She looked at TJ, too.

"It should prove how she died."

"Does it matter?"

Mr. Aronson leaned forward. He looked as though he wanted to take her hands. "Mrs. Auburn," he said.

"Call me Cassie. My slave's name. That's what they'll call me in court."

"Listen to me. I swore an oath to your son on my honor as a Union man and a lawyer. I swear it to you as well. I'll do everything I can do to protect your rights as a free woman. I fought for that during the war, and I'm ready to do it now."

She shook her head.

"I'm going to vote the way I shot, as General Grant has reminded me," he said. "I'll fight for you the same way."

His face was still bruised. They'd hurt him, too. He'd put himself—and his wife, too—at risk in helping her.

She said, "Give me your hand."

He extended it as though she was going to shake it.

"No, palm up."

He gave her a quizzical look, but he did so.

She looked at his palm, which had never been roughened much by battle, and she traced the deepest line that creased it. She looked at his face.

"What do you see?" he asked.

She said, "That you're better at wielding a pen than a gun, Mr. Aronson. And much more likely to be successful."

He let her fingers rest on his palm. "Will you trust me on that?"

She tapped her fingertips on his skin. "It's all I can do," she said.

∼

AFTER THE TWO MEN LEFT, Cassie went upstairs to her room, shut the door, and sat on the bed. She hadn't seen anything in Elias Aronson's palm. She had given him a show, as much for herself as for him. His future was as unreadable as her own.

She succumbed to despair. She thought, *I'm done for.*

The voice came to her. *It's not over yet.*

She spoke aloud, as though the spirit was in the room with her and could hear as well as any living thing. "Does that mean I'll go back to New York and live a happy life? Or that I'll die at the end of a rope?"

You don't know that.

"Do you? Why don't you tell me?"

Wait.

Her landlady called up the stairs. "Who you talking to up there?"

Cassie opened the door and called back, "No one."

∼

THAT NIGHT she dreamed again about the alley. The darkness. The shot. The dead man at her feet, whose face she couldn't see.

When she woke it was the middle of the night. She put her hand to her chest, trying to calm her heart, which beat so hard that she couldn't take a breath. She couldn't stay in this house, in this prison, for another moment. Shaking, she packed up her little bag and crept down the stairs as quietly as she could. When she stepped into the parlor, the floor creaked. Her landlady was instantly awake. She came into the parlor in her shabby nightdress. "Where you going at this hour?" Then, with her good eye, she saw the bag. Her voice was surprisingly gentle. "You running away again," she said.

"It's better that you don't know where."

She nodded. "You go," she said. "Quick and quiet."

As Cassie edged toward the door, the landlady said softly, "If anyone ask, I don't know who you are. You were never here."

On the street, she started at every sound and every shadow. When she came to Ida's house, she stood on the back steps like a stray dog, panting, looking with longing at the brightness within. She rapped softly on the door, a signal of the days of slavery. Ida opened the door and, without a word, drew her inside.

The next morning, she slept as late as the ladies of the evening did. When she woke, she found that Ida had left her a decent dress and the undergarments to go with it. She washed and dressed, feeling strange without her ragged disguise. She walked softly down the back stairs into the kitchen, where Ida already sat at the table. As Cassie sat, she poured her a cup of coffee. "You look presentable again," Ida said.

"I don't feel it." She pushed the coffee away.

The cook said, "Fresh biscuit? Can't tempt you?"

Cassie shook her head. She felt too sick to eat. "I know I shouldn't stay. I'll figure out where—I'll ask TJ to help me—"

Ida put down her coffee cup. Her eyes were bright. "You haven't heard the news about Miss Dolly?"

"I heard that she was dead."

"You didn't hear about the surgeon? And what the Beardsleys asked him to do?"

"To examine her," Cassie said, puzzled.

"They ordered him to perform an autopsy."

"What?"

"To cut her open to find out what killed her."

"That's awful!"

"Her family was furious, but it wasn't their say. The Beardsleys told the police to make the surgeon do it. And he did."

Cassie felt sick again. "What did the surgeon find?"

"I know the woman who cleans for the surgeon," Ida said. "She was there while he was looking. It was awful, she said. Like watching someone gut a dead animal."

"How can they bury her like that?"

Ida shook her head. "My friend told me what the surgeon said. She wasn't shot or stabbed or poisoned. She had a hole in her heart. It could have killed her at any time. He said it was a tragedy, but it was natural."

Cassie turned ashen.

"What's wrong with you? I didn't think you were squeamish."

Cassie felt thoroughly sick to her stomach. She hadn't realized her conscience would bother her that way. Ida brought her a basin just in time, and afterward, gave her a cloth to wipe her mouth. "Don't tell me you're carrying, on top of everything else."

She groaned at the thought. "I'm not."

Ida gave her a long, appraising look. "Now they can't arrest you."

Cassie looked up. Feeling sick again, she pressed her hand

to her stomach. "Now all I have to do is watch for the surprise in the dark alley. Or the fall into the river."

SHE WENT BACK TO BED, and as she slept in the daylight, she had a dream that began like the others. She stood in the darkness in the alley behind the Rebs' saloon. The war was over, but she knew the place was still full of former Rebs. She could hear them shouting. A man crept into the alley. She froze. He raised the gun. She couldn't move. Suddenly there was enough light to see his face.

It was John Beardsley. He said, "You're done for."

When he fired, the bullet went straight to her heart. She fell to her knees, and as she pressed her fingers helplessly to her chest, her life bled away into the dirt.

THE FIRE NEXT TIME

Dolly's death was received with little sadness in the Black community, but the news of the surgical examination she'd undergone was the subject of a great deal of discussion. It had been disrespectful and defiling, and the Black schools and churches seethed with fury about it. In the Aronson household, Dolly's demise, and her autopsy, were the subject of discussion as well, but from a lawyer's perspective. Now that the Beardsleys' best witness—false or not—was dead, they had no case against Cassie. At least Elias hoped so, as he told Lydia over their before-dinner glass of claret a few days after Dolly's autopsy.

Lydia had been calming the fears of the children and listening to the outrage of her teachers all day. Now, tonight, she took a sip of claret and closed her eyes as she savored it. She sighed and opened them again. "Will they let it go?" she asked, looking at Elias. The bruises from his beating at the hands of the police had faded, but they were still visible. She was reminded of how vulnerable they both were. It still gave her a shiver of pain to see the reminders of the police's brutality toward her husband.

"I've written to William Beardsley, asking to meet with him. He wrote back and told me he'd talked to his lawyer and told him to contact me. I haven't heard a word. I doubt that either of them will speak to me."

"Would you insist?"

"No." He touched the fading bruise around his right eye. "I don't need to tell them what we plan to do."

She felt a stab of worry. "Elias, be careful," she said.

"We're going to file a civil suit that can be heard in Municipal Court. It will be about the way the police mishandled the investigation into Titus Armstrong's death." He added, "Since we can't get the police to start a criminal proceeding."

She reached for his hand. "But a civil suit is just an excuse to mention what the Beardsleys already know," she said. "That you have evidence to point to John Beardsley as the murderer."

He didn't reply.

She said, "Prosecuting a civil suit puts you at as much risk as a criminal one."

He was still silent.

"And it puts Narcissa and her family at risk, too. And Will Andrews."

He met her eyes, and she saw something that bothered her. It was the long stare of the soldier, looking toward the horizon at a horror that no civilian knew. "Yes, it does," he said.

LYDIA HADN'T TOLD Elias what Narcissa had told her—that a white man had tried to follow her when she walked home from the school a few days ago. Narcissa was so bothered by his attention that she returned to the school and asked Mr. Jasper if he could walk her home. Now Mr. Jasper, their watchman and guardian, escorted Narcissa in both directions.

Lydia asked Narcissa if she'd gotten a good look at the man.

Narcissa said, "Yes, but it's not as though we can ask the police for help."

"Did you recognize him?"

"No, he was a stranger. But if I saw him again, I'd remember him." She said, "He was unpleasant to me."

"Did he touch you? Or try to?"

She shook her head. "He didn't have to," she said. "His expression was bad enough."

MR. JASPER TAPPED on the door of Lydia's office. For a big man, he had a soft touch. He proffered the envelope.

Lydia blanched. "I think I know what that is," she said.

"It was under the door when I unlocked. I didn't open it, ma'am."

She took the unmarked envelope and ripped it open with the letter opener, which was sharp enough to stab a man. She pulled out the sheet to read it.

We'll burn your school to the ground. Haven't you learned your lesson?

She laid the letter on her desk.

Mr. Jasper asked softly, "Like the others, Mrs. Aronson?"

"Worse than the others." She read it to him.

He shook his head. "I worry about the children," he said. "And you teachers." He looked around the room, a proxy for the building he guarded.

"I'll tell Miss Kinsley and Miss Armstrong," Lydia said. "I think it's time to talk to Superintendent Barnum." She shook her head. "I hate to think of closing the school. But I can't risk the safety of the children."

"Their mothers and fathers might want a say, too," Mr. Jasper said.

Lydia felt no better as she nodded.

WHEN LYDIA ARRIVED HOME, Elias was already there, sitting in the parlor in his shirtsleeves. He looked disheveled and tired. There was a glass of claret at his elbow. His cheeks were flushed, a sign that it was not his first.

He looked as though he needed comfort, and she wasn't sure how much she had in her. It had been a difficult day, telling Sue and Narcissa about the letter and sharing the plan to guard the school. She hadn't bothered to tamp down their fears. They had both been in Memphis when the Black schools burned to the ground.

But she said, "You're home early."

He lifted the glass. "There was little to do today," he said.

"A moment of respite?" she said, sitting on the settee without bothering to smooth her skirt beneath her.

He drank deeply and set the glass down. "I had a number of letters from my coreligionists at Temple Israel," he said.

"And not to ask you to contribute to the building fund."

"Clients. They were clients, at any rate." He picked up the glass again. "No longer." He drank some more. "None of them wants a lawyer associated with trouble." He looked at her over the edge of the glass. "And Black people are trouble."

She said, "Pour me a glass, would you?"

His eyes settled on her face. He wasn't drunk, only tipsy,

and he could read her expression perfectly well. "What's wrong?"

She pulled the letter from her pocket. "This came to the school today." She handed it to him.

He read it and held on to it, his hand shaking a little. "Lydia, this is—"

"I know how serious it is." She rubbed her face. "Mr. Jasper has offered to set up a watch at the school."

"That's not enough," he said.

She said wearily, "It's time to talk about closing the school. If it were only my peril, I wouldn't flinch. But to put fifty innocent children in danger? I can't have that on my conscience."

He didn't rise to join her on the settee and to take her in his arms. Evidently, he was too drained to comfort her. She said, "I'll talk to Superintendent Barnum. I think the children should go to the other schools, and my teachers and I should stay home for a while. Mr. Jasper thinks the parents will want a say, and Narcissa has offered to organize a meeting at her church."

He stared at her, then he rested his hands on his knees, and his head in his hands. His voice low and indistinct, he said, "I've brought you to this—I've brought us to this—"

She'd seen him in despair before, and she had no desire to lift him from it. She said, "Don't blame yourself. There's more than enough blame to go around about who's put who in danger."

He raised his head. "I don't know if I can live like this." He looked at her. "I'm not afraid for myself." His bruises were very faintly visible on his eye and his cheek. "But for you—"

She shook her head, and it felt as heavy as a stone on her neck. "I've told you, again and again, how I fear for you," she said. "I can't say it again. I'm too tired."

He looked at her and didn't answer.

"Elias, I can't help you right now. I can't cajole you out of this. Or argue you out of it. Or love you out of it." She meant the consolation that came in the marriage bed, but it sounded worse than that.

He got up. He poured himself another glass, and he poured her one, as well. He handed her the glass and sat beside her on the settee. After she'd taken a sip, he said, "Lydia, don't tell me you've stopped loving me."

She raised the glass again and this time she gulped down the wine. She hadn't eaten all day, and the alcohol made her lightheaded. "I'll love you forever," she said. "But I don't know if I can live like this anymore." She raised her eyes to his. "Can you?"

"Are we fighting?" he said softly.

She set her glass down. She had rarely felt faint in her life, but she did now. "I don't want to fight with you," she said.

He reached for her hand, and she let him take it. "What do you want to do?" he asked softly.

She didn't reply for a moment. Then she said, "Every Black woman who's taught in the South since 1863 has broken down at least once," she said. "My friend Edmonia went home in a terrible state, crying and raving on the train. And everyone she knows suffered the same way." She put her glass on the sofa table and leaned back against the settee. She closed her eyes against the dizziness.

"Do you want to leave Memphis? Go to New York?" he asked.

She opened her eyes. "Would you go?"

He didn't reply. She knew he wanted to stay. She knew he felt it was his duty to Cassie and Narcissa, and all the other Black people who needed his help.

She said, "If I told you I needed to go—would you go with me?"

He was silent. He drank his glass down instead of speaking.

That was her answer. It was no answer.

LYDIA HAD PROMISED Sue Ann and Narcissa that she would talk to Mr. Barnum, the superintendent for Memphis's Black schools, about the letter and its threat. She found him shoehorned into a tiny office, where he had managed to organize boxes of books and slates neatly in a corner. His desk was covered with paper, but it was neatly piled, with room on the blotter to read and answer correspondence.

When she came in, he looked up from his reading. He smiled at her. "The most recent monthly reports," he said. He liked the detailed reports that told him that attendance rose every month while expenses held steady. He also liked to preside over the public exhibitions the Black schools held, proving the students' proficiency in oration and singing. He had led the mayor through the Lincoln School, showing off the reading ability of a well-dressed little boy and praising the speech of a pretty little girl.

As she sat, he said, "I've seen your reports from the Phoenix School. Very good," he said, as he would praise a schoolchild.

Lydia had worked for more than one superintendent in her teaching career, and she had always known how to manage them. "It's not difficult when I have such dedicated teachers and such diligent pupils," she said.

"Miss Armstrong works for you, doesn't she?"

"Yes, she does."

"I hear she's received quite a lot of attention because of her effort to look into her brother's death."

"That's true," Lydia said.

"I've also heard that your husband has had his own difficulty supporting her."

Lydia had no desire to talk about the trouble stirred up by Elias's investigation into Titus Armstrong's murder. She said, "Yes, that's also true. But that's not why I wanted to talk to you."

Barnum steepled his fingers. "I've heard that you've received some unpleasant anonymous letters."

Lydia said, "Yes, there have been threats, as many teachers in Black schools have received."

"Why didn't you bring them to my attention?"

In her earliest years as a teacher, she had managed her superintendent by being deferential. Now, she chose to be blunt. "Mr. Barnum, as you well know, every woman who teaches Black children, whether she is white or Black, has received threat and insult, if not in writing, then on the street. It wasn't worth bringing it to your attention."

He frowned. "We might have made the effort to go to the police."

"No, Mr. Barnum, the police are no friends to the Black people of Memphis, and I never even considered it."

"Then how did you respond?"

"We have a man who guards our building and looks after our safety, the children's as well as the teachers'. He was a sergeant in the Union army, and he's well prepared to take care of threats to us."

"What exactly brings you here today, Mrs. Aronson?"

"There's been another threat." She removed the letter from her reticule. "This came to us a few days ago. Slipped under our door at night, as the others were. It's not about us, the teachers. It's about the school and the children."

He read it and set it on the desk. Among the other papers that covered the surface, the sheet seemed to have its own malevolent glow. "That's quite troubling," he said. "If I were you, I would consider taking the matter to the police."

"Mr. Barnum, if I thought the police would look into it, if I thought the police would even bother to listen to a complaint, I would." She felt thoroughly exasperated. "I know better." She thought, *As should you.*

He picked up the letter again and reread it.

"Mr. Barnum, I'm here to tell you that I think we should close the school."

He put the paper down and looked up. "I would be very unhappy to disrupt the education of these children," he said.

"I've given that problem a great deal of thought. I'd propose we ask the other Black schools to temporarily take in the children. I've talked to Miss Kinsley, and she's glad to go wherever she's needed to help."

"And Miss Armstrong?"

"I'm very worried about her," Lydia said. "I'd prefer for her to stay home, again temporarily. I'd want to continue to pay her, since her family depends on her wages."

"Closing the school is a matter of last resort," he said.

"We are in a position of last resort, Mr. Barnum."

He held up the letter. "Are you sure of this, Mrs. Aronson?"

She said, "I understand that you weren't here in 1866."

"No, I arrived in Memphis in 1867," he said.

"I was here in 1866," she said. "I was a witness to the events of the first, the second, and the third of May."

He crossed his arms over his black-coated chest. "I'm quite familiar with the events of 1866," he said.

"Please, let me remind you," she said. She thought, *I'm being rude, but I'm too angry and tired to be polite.* "Do you know why the school where I teach was named the Phoenix?"

"Of course. I know of the fires," he said stiffly.

"Every Black church and every Black school burned, as the fire department and the police did nothing."

"Yes, I know," he said, and to his credit, his voice was tinged with sadness.

"But not as I do. I witnessed it," she said. "I stood in the street and I watched as the Lincoln School burned to the ground."

He softened further. "It was a terrible thing," he said.

"I don't really fear for the building. It can be replaced once more. Another phoenix. But I fear for the children."

"As we all should."

She stared at him, another rudeness. "Do you know how the mob murdered Black children during the massacre?"

"Is that germane?"

She leaned forward, anger coursing through her. "They set houses on fire. Houses with children inside. And they shot any mother or father or brother or sister who went back to rescue them. I don't know how many people died that way." She put her hands on his desk and rose from her chair. "That's how they used fire back in 1866," she said.

He was silent. Finally, he spoke, in a low, unsteady voice. "Would they really try such a thing again?"

"Yes," she said, and she had to lean heavily on her palms, because she was feeling faint again. She sat down and looked at him.

Suddenly he looked pale. "Have you spoken to the families of the children?"

"I plan to. I want to explain the situation to them. And to take their feelings and suggestions into consideration." She gave him a hard look. "But I want your assent to close the school if they agree to it."

He regained control of his voice. "Yes, I'll agree to that."

THE MEETING with the parents was quickly arranged. Narcissa asked her minister—the man who had been arrested along with her for carrying a banner asking for justice for Titus Armstrong—for help. With Lydia's blessing, word quickly spread about the letter and the trouble it portended. Only a day after the letter arrived, the meeting was called, and when Lydia entered the building on Elias's arm, the church was full.

The church had been rebuilt at the same time as the schools, and the congregants were proud of the brick exterior and the newly painted interior, with the big glass windows that let in light. Lydia, used to the plain churches of the Methodists and Congregationalists, felt at home there. Elias had told her he didn't feel right unless there was plenty of stained glass, and after attending Temple Emanuel-El, she understood why. It had been inspired by the elaborate architecture of the Episcopal Church.

Elias escorted her down the aisle, which gave her a pang, because it reminded her of their marriage ceremony at Temple Emanuel-El. They were still irritated with each other, but Elias was worried about her, and she didn't refuse the comfort of the carriage ride or the support of his arm. At the pulpit, he let her go, and Mrs. Armstrong, who sat in the front row, gestured to him. Narcissa sat next to her. All the rest of the Armstrong children squeezed together in the pew to make room for him.

Lydia took the stairs to the pulpit to stand beside the

minister. He looked tired. In a soft voice, she said, "I hate to add to your burdens."

Also softly, he said, "Don't worry, Mrs. Aronson, you haven't."

The church buzzed with talk. These people knew why they were meeting, but they also knew each other, and as at every church gathering, this was a way to share news and gossip. The minister smiled and raised his arms, and they quieted. "Brothers and sisters," he said. "Thank you for being here. We have some serious matters to discuss, relating to the Phoenix School. Mrs. Aronson, the school's principal, has joined us. She will tell you about the circumstances that have brought us here, and we will all talk about the best way to respond to them."

Lydia faced the crowd. She saw the worried, expectant looks. "I wish this were a happier occasion and that I had happier news for you. I know that many of you have heard about the letter received at the school yesterday."

People nodded and murmured in assent.

"I didn't want you to hear by rumor. I want you to know exactly what happened." She told them about the letter. She read it to them.

There was a moment of silence as they listened to the threat and took it in. And then there was an angry outburst from a man a few rows back. "Why didn't you tell us sooner?"

Lydia said, "This was as soon as we could tell you, all of you, and at the same time answer your questions and propose a plan of action." She hesitated. "I'm alarmed enough to consider closing the school."

A woman asked, "Close the school? How are the children going to get their schooling?"

"I feel the same way. I don't want them to miss a day of

schooling. I've spoken to the principals of the other Black schools, and they've agreed to take in our children for as long as we need them to."

Another woman asked, "Will they be safe there? Plenty of white people hate that our children go to school at all."

Lydia said, "As I well know. But I can reassure you that none of the other schools have received a threat like ours. Your children should be safe elsewhere."

Several people shook their heads, and they muttered in tones too low for her to hear.

Lydia said, "I've spoken to the superintendent, Mr. Barnum, and he agrees that temporarily closing the school and sending the children elsewhere is a good idea."

A man asked, "Why ain't he here to talk to us?"

"He has confidence in us," Lydia said.

The man snorted.

Lydia said, "Miss Kinsley will continue to teach. She has told me she will go wherever she is needed most. Miss Armstrong will take a leave of absence, since I believe she is at risk herself."

A woman said, "Miss Narcissa, you brought this on yourself with that legal complaint of yours!"

Narcissa turned in her pew where she sat. Elias caught Lydia's eye. Narcissa rose and faced the congregation. "If I had never made any complaint, would we be any safer? All of us? Would our enemies leave us alone?" She looked around the room, meeting worried eyes and angry eyes. "When it comes to the children—oh, our precious, precious children— I say we should close the school to keep them safe. But when it comes to justice for an innocent man brutally murdered— then I say we should stand tall and refuse to back down, even if it costs us. Because we're not just fighting for ourselves. We're fighting for our children and our children's children.

And they will never be free and equal unless we accept the danger of trying to change the world we live in."

The minister broke the silence. "Those are lofty words, Miss Armstrong, and thankfully we don't have to make that decision now. Today our only decision is about the safety of our children. Shall we close the school temporarily or not?"

The room burst into a loud, unruly argument. Lydia heard a woman cry out, "Keep the children safe. Close the school!" And she heard a man shout, "They want us to be afraid and act afraid. Keep the school open! Guard it every moment, but keep it open!"

Mr. Jasper, who was sitting in the second row, raised his hand as though he were at school. The minister raised his arms for quiet. "Yes, Brother Jasper?"

He stood, a big, reassuring presence in the church as he was every day in the school. "I work at the school, keeping an eye on things," he said. "Like I used to when I was a sergeant in the 3rd Heavy Artillery. I have an idea about how we can do both. Keep the children safe and stand up for the school."

They waited to hear. He said, "Once the children go to the other schools, I want to put together a watch for our school," he said. "Day and night. I'll need good men with me. How many of you served at Fort Pickering?" Several men nodded assent. "Even if you weren't a soldier, you can be one now. You can join me." His eyes swept over the congregation. "Our children safe, and our people on guard. Standing up for all of us."

A man stood. He said, "I'll join you, Brother Jasper."

Another man stood. "So will I." And another. And another, until twenty men stood, their faces somber.

One of the men said, "If it comes to the worst, we can always build another school. But if one of those precious children is harmed—"

The memory of the massacre hung in the air like smoke.

The minister asked, "Shall we send the children elsewhere? And guard the school?"

Mr. Jasper said, "When we go to our ward meetings, we vote. Reverend, should we take a vote here, too?"

But before the minister could reply, people began to rise to their feet. In a moment everyone stood, and agreement swelled in the room.

THE IDLE HANDS

Lydia walked past Mr. Jasper's guards and pulled open the door of the school. The building, usually so crowded and noisy, was now empty. As she walked to her office, the heels of her boots echoed on the wooden floor.

Mr. Jasper, who patrolled the interior, stopped to greet her.

"Was there any trouble last night?" she asked.

"No. But that doesn't mean there won't be."

She gazed down the hallway and sighed. "I hope this is over soon," she said.

"We don't know when."

She nodded. "I'll be in my office," she said.

"Mrs. Aronson, you don't need to be here."

She looked up and down the hallway, then at him. "None of us should have to be here," she said, and she squared her shoulders to walk past the empty classrooms.

Once there, she found she couldn't settle down to anything. She should draft a report for Superintendent Barnum, letting him know that the building was closed and the students had been accepted at the other schools. She'd noted where each child had gone. She could figure out how the school fees should be re-allocated. The superintendent would be glad to see that. She picked up the pen and poised it over a sheet of paper. When she tried to write she spoiled the sheet with a blot.

She put the pen back in its holder by the inkwell.

She could hear Mr. Jasper talking to the men out front. The masculine voices sounded odd in a place that had always been full of the tones of women and children. She wondered how Sue Ann was getting on. She'd gone to the Causey Street school, the smallest Black school in Memphis, which was likely to need the most help with an influx of a dozen new children. She worried about Narcissa, who was idled and at home. She'd stop to see Narcissa when the day was over.

She would, if she had the patience to sit here all day and feel so useless. She wished she could offer her services at another school. But like Narcissa, she was a target, and her presence would only bring attention, and very likely danger, to another school.

She thought of the school in Manlius, New York, where she had taught before the war. There, the worst misfortune she had faced was the bad behavior of the oldest boys, taller than she was. No one had ever brought a gun into the schoolroom. No one had ever tried to burn down the schoolhouse. Nothing had ever happened to bring her close to a nervous collapse like her friend Edmonia's, who had been in New Orleans in 1866, caught up in a massacre as bad as Memphis's.

She stood to walk down the hall to a classroom. She hoped to tidy a little, but it was Narcissa's room, and despite all the worry of the past few days, she had left it neat. Sue Ann had done the same for hers.

She returned to her office and decided to write a letter.

She knew that sympathetic Northern papers often published letters from people living in the South. Elias might have a connection with a paper in New York and could advise her where to send it.

She picked up her pen and sighed again. She didn't feel any more comfortable at home than at the school. She and Elias "weren't right," as Matilda Hayes might say. He was so worried for her, and she was so irritable about it, that they couldn't sit in the same room without bickering. For the first time since they'd married, they'd been too unhappy with each other to fall asleep in each other's arms. They slept side by side, alone in their mutual unhappiness.

Mr. Jasper rapped on her door. "Ma'am?" His expression was grim.

"Is something wrong?" Of course there was.

"We just found this." He held out the envelope.

She knew before she touched it. "No one saw who left it?"

He shook his head. "I asked. No one knows."

"You opened it."

"Wanted to see what it was. One of my men can read. He read it."

"Let me see."

We'll burn the place with you in it.

She blanched and dropped the letter onto her desk. "They know," she said. "That the children aren't here, and I am." She looked up. "Are they watching us?"

"We'll watch for them, if they are," Mr. Jasper said.

She nodded.

"Mrs. Aronson, I know you want to be here, but I'd feel better if you went home," he said.

Her hand went to her pocket. "Did you know I have a pistol?"

He said, "Ma'am, I want you to be safe, too."

She buried her head in her hands. She should tell Elias about the letter. She knew what he'd say: *"Mr. Jasper is right."*

"Ma'am?" Mr. Jasper said. His voice was soft. "The children are precious to us, but so are you."

Tears stung her eyes, and she blinked against them. She touched the gun in her pocket. Then she raised her head. "Thank you," she said. She thought of the burden her presence would lay on the guards. It was one thing to watch the building. It was quite another to assure her safety. "I'll go home for the rest of the day. But I'll be back tomorrow to see how things are going."

Mr. Jasper insisted on putting her into a hansom cab. But she didn't tell the driver to take her home. She told him to drive to Elias's office on Main Street.

As SOON AS she walked into his office, he rose from his desk. "What's wrong?" he asked.

Despite her fear, she was short-tempered. "Why do you start with that? Why not wish me a good morning?"

"Because you would never leave the school to see me unless something is wrong. What happened?"

She sat in the guest chair and fought the impulse to slump. "We got another letter."

"When?"

"Just now. This morning."

"Do you have it?"

She nodded and handed it to him. He pulled it from the envelope and read it. His fingers trembled as he tossed it onto his desk.

"Mr. Jasper insisted I go home," she said.

"And so do I."

She rose. She felt dizzy suddenly, and she had to rest her hands on his desk to steady herself. "I'm a coward," she said bleakly. "I'm a deserter."

Abashed, he said, "Lydia, no one would say so."

"Soldiers of light and love, they called us during the war. Soldiers don't run from the battlefield."

He was suddenly caustic. "Did they issue you a firearm?"

She touched her pocket. "You know I carry a pistol. It's the one you gave me."

"Lydia, don't talk or act like a fool. Go home and take your gun with you." He sighed and brought his fingers to his temples. "We should arrange for a guard at home, as you have at the school."

"Am I to sit at home as though I'm in prison? Not to go out, except under escort?"

He stood, and for the first time since they'd known one another, he shouted at her. "Do you know how much danger you're in?"

And for only the second time since they'd known one another, she lost her temper. "Of course I do!"

"Then act like it!" As she turned to leave, he bellowed, "Don't walk home, damn it! Let me find a hansom cab for you!"

Her hand on the doorknob, she bellowed back, "I'll find my own cab, thank you!"

WHEN LYDIA DESCENDED from the cab, she slammed the door. She went inside the house and slammed that door, too. She sat in the parlor, her hands knotted in her lap, too angry to do anything but think dark thoughts and blame herself.

Once home, she stayed home.

Her mood persisted, and on the next morning she was still angry at Elias, as he was with her. She had said, "I want to stop by the school to talk to Mr. Jasper." He had said, "Only if I escort you." And she had said, "I won't stand for it."

She paced through the parlor. She had to do something. She couldn't find out who had sent the letters. She had a good idea what kind of people they were—unreconstructed Rebs who were likely members of the Klan. But exactly who?

She stood at the window, staring into the street. She realized who might be able to find out. The inquiry man, Mr. Randolph.

Randolph had worked for Elias, but Lydia had never sought him out. She knew he often worked for Cassie. After Dolly's death was proven a sad medical accident and not a murder, Cassie had emerged from hiding and returned to the building on Beale Street. She had moved back in with her family and reopened her business. Cassie could tell her how to reach him. Lydia jumped up and put on her bonnet.

Elias wouldn't like it, but it seemed senseless to call a hansom to take her a few blocks. Certainly she was safe on the street in broad daylight. As she walked over to Beale Street, she regarded the crowd on the street. Were any of these ordinary-looking people hostile to her? Had any of them been watching her?

I'll make myself crazy, she thought, as she walked the familiar route.

At Cassie's front door stood a burly Black man whom Lydia didn't know. He asked, "Ma'am, what's your business with Mrs. Auburn?"

So Cassie had a guard, too. "You can tell her that Mrs. Aronson is here to call on her," she said. "She knows who I am."

The man went inside. Lydia waited. When he came back

out, Cassie stood behind him, at the open door. "Come in," she said. "I'm sorry for the inconvenience."

"Have you had trouble?"

"No, but Mr. Jasper's suggestion inspired me," she said.

Lydia came in and sat at Cassie's consultation table.

"I'm surprised to see you at this hour," Cassie said. Cassie was well-dressed again—the color was plain dark blue, but the cut was stylish in New York manner—and the expression on her face was unruffled.

"The school is closed, as you know." Lydia hadn't seen Cassie at the meeting at the church, but she must have been there. Hiding in plain sight, as she was good at.

"Yes, I do. I sent my boys off to the Lincoln School." She smiled. "They protested, both of them. Sam, because he thought he should be able to stay home, and Will, because he doesn't like being parted from Miss Narcissa." She looked at Lydia. "How is Miss Armstrong?"

"Well, as far as I know," Lydia said. "I think I might want to persuade her to rely on a guard, too."

Cassie sighed. "Mrs. Aronson, how can I help you?"

"I came because I'm hoping to employ Mr. Randolph," she said. "I thought you could contact him for me."

"I can do better than that," she said. "He's in back. I can ask him to join us—unless you'd prefer to meet in back in more privacy."

"No, it doesn't have that kind of delicacy. I can show him the reason why, and right here is quite all right."

"Has there been another threat?"

Startled, Lydia said, "How would you know?"

"It's not hard to guess. I'll summon Mr. Randolph and you can tell us both about it." She disappeared, and in a moment, she emerged from the back room with Mr. Randolph at her elbow.

They both sat at the table, and he said to Lydia, "I hear that you may want to make an inquiry."

She nodded and drew the envelope from her pocket. "I've gotten another threatening letter," she said. "I assume you heard about the previous one."

"The arson threat," he said, nodding. "And there's been another? When?"

"Yes, now that the school is closed. Just yesterday."

She handed it to him, and he took it, opened it, and read the letter. Cassie read over his shoulder. He laid the letter on the table. "A threat for you this time."

"Someone knew I would be there, even though the school was closed."

"Watching you? Or the school?"

"I don't know. Both, I would think."

"Did your guards see anyone?"

She shook her head. "I hope to discover who sent it to me. If it's possible to find out."

"If it's possible," he said. "Do you have any idea who?"

She laughed bitterly. "I have a very good idea," she said. "Former Confederates. Members of the Klan. That narrows it down, doesn't it, in Memphis?"

"The Beardsleys come to mind," he said.

"Yes, but there's no way to know for sure. I doubt they'd answer if anyone asked them."

Cassie said, "TJ drinks with John Beardsley. In the bar the Rebs used to frequent during the war."

Lydia said, "I don't know whether that's brave or foolish."

"He believes I agree with him," TJ said.

Lydia shook her head.

"I can make an inquiry," TJ said.

Lydia said, "Please be careful. There are already too many

people in peril here. I wouldn't feel right if I endangered you, too."

"Don't worry about me," TJ said.

"Don't tell me the spirits protect you."

His eyes gleamed. "That won't hurt, if they do," he said. "But I was a sharpshooter during the war, and I'm still an excellent shot."

WHEN SHE LEFT Cassie's office she thought, *I should tell Elias I've hired Randolph.* She felt a chill as she left and she took a hansom to his office.

There, she found Elias alone. He wasn't reading a document or writing up a contract. He sat idly at his desk, and on his face was a look of worry, which didn't diminish when he saw her. "Is there something wrong today?" he asked, the worry deepening.

"No, not more than there was this morning when you left," she said. She gestured around the empty office. "What about you? How are you?"

"You're sure there's nothing—"

"There isn't," she said. "I take it you aren't busy?"

At that, he looked so unhappy she was ashamed of herself. "I've just lost a few more clients," he said. "The letters came this morning."

"More coreligionists?"

"No, carpetbaggers like ourselves."

"The same reason? They think you're too close to trouble?"

He nodded. "I thought better of them," he said.

She didn't reply.

He said, "I don't like losing the business, especially since we don't have your wages right now."

She knew that he drew a comfortable sum from his inheritance every month, and it had always funded their life in Memphis. She was sharp with him. "We can always live on my rent money," she said. She still owned her late husband's farm, and she rented it to her brother-in-law.

He was sharp in return. "That won't be necessary, and you know it."

She shifted her weight on his guest chair, as though her crinoline was bothering her.

He said, "I know, I need a better chair."

"I didn't come here to complain about your chair," she said. "But I'm not sure I want to stay here to tell you, if you're going to be disagreeable to me."

He sighed. "I feel as though my head aches all the time," he said.

Despite herself, she felt a stab of sympathy. "I know."

"What is it, Lydia? I should apply myself to the business of finding some new clients. Paying clients."

The odor of manure drifted into the office from the street. Did every building in Memphis smell so bad? Did their own house stink, too? "I wanted to let you know that I called on Mr. Randolph. I thought he might look into the letters we've been receiving at the school. Throw some light on who's sending them."

His tone was sharp again. "Why? Even if he can learn something—which I doubt—what good will it do? We can hardly take it to the police."

She leaned forward. Her back ached and her corset seemed too tight. "We can do something," she said. "I suspect the Beardsleys, and I know you do, too."

"And even if you're right—which again I doubt—what can we do about it?"

She put her hand to her side. She must have broken a stay. "How can you say that?" she cried out. "Take them to court, for God's sake, and if that doesn't work, return the favor. Threaten them. Do you think I want to sit at home and let them terrorize us and everyone we care about in Memphis?"

He looked haggard. "We can go," he said. "Go to New York, where we can live a life free of terror."

She rose. "I've never known you to run from a fight, Elias Aronson."

He shook his head and didn't take the bait. "I've never been a coward for myself, Lydia. You know that. But I find that I've become a coward when it's on your behalf." He sighed. "I'd run back to New York in a moment to keep you safe."

She said, "What about Narcissa? And Will? And all the children at the school? How can you be a coward when you think of them?"

"Go home, Lydia," he said, weariness thick in his voice. "Please don't stay here to make things worse between us."

She suddenly thought, *Where is home?* Not Manlius. Not New York. And perhaps not with Elias in Memphis, either.

He turned away, and she stared at him, incredulous. Shaking, she made her way to the door, and they both heard the hinges cry when she shut it.

AT HOME IN THE PARLOR, Lydia was too upset to turn to anything useful, even if she had something useful to do. She had never been idle before. She'd taught for a living in

Manlius, and after she'd married, she'd run the farm along with her husband. After his death, she'd begun to teach again, and she had never been idle during the day, which she had always thought of as time to work. Having the time to read or write letters or to do nothing bothered her more than she could stand. There was no one to call on, as most ladies did to pass the time. All her friends were teachers, and they were working.

Except for Narcissa, idled like herself. She should call on Narcissa to find out how she was. She should tell her about engaging Mr. Randolph. But she didn't move. She sat on the settee as though rooted there, knotting her hands and thinking about her anger at Elias and her fear for her teachers and her school.

It seemed that terror had done worse than idle her. It had paralyzed her.

When the knock on the door came, she jumped up in alarm. She peeked out the window to see Narcissa on her doorstep. She opened the door, and her relief came out as scolding. "I hope you didn't walk here! Or come by yourself!" She pulled Narcissa inside.

Narcissa untied her bonnet strings. "No to both, Mrs. Aronson. Our neighbor is a drayman, and I came in his wagon. He insisted on waiting to take me home."

"Have you had any trouble?"

"No one has tried to set fire to the house, no." She didn't have her usual calm. There were dark circles under her eyes, the sign of sleepless nights, and even though she was trying to joke, the corner of her mouth twitched. She raised her hand to her face as though she could rub the tic away.

"Don't talk like that. Sit down. Do you want refreshment?"

Narcissa shook her head.

Lydia worked to calm herself. "How are you faring?"

Narcissa sighed. "My mother keeps me busy with the house and the little ones." She looked up at Lydia. "And I'm so bored I could scream. I want to be back in the classroom. How are you?"

Lydia struggled with herself. She wanted to tell Narcissa the truth, and she wanted to remain the principal, calm and in charge. "I'm the same. I want to be at the school. I'm so snappish that my husband despairs of me."

"You don't have a guard here, I see," Narcissa said.

"We haven't felt the need. Do you?"

"No, but all the neighbors keep an eye out. The drayman was in the 3rd Heavy Artillery. And his wife, who stays at home, has a sharp eye for an intruder and a stout arm to handle one."

"You weren't honest with me. You have had trouble."

"There's a man who's been loitering around the house," she said. "A white man. We don't know who he is, but we all recognize him."

Lydia was suddenly bitter. "If the police would do anything—"

"Don't waste your breath," Narcissa replied.

"I feel so useless," Lydia said. "As does Elias." She looked up at Narcissa. "It may be the only thing we agree on these days."

Narcissa looked away. She took a deep breath. "It won't last forever," she said. "When it dies down—once we can go back to the school—I'll come to consult your husband about the suit."

"He's lost most of his clients because of the suit," Lydia said, and as soon as the words were out, she regretted them.

Narcissa sighed again. "Are you still with us? Now that you're being treated—"

"I know how we're being treated! The n— teacher and the n— lawyer! That's what we are now!"

Narcissa's voice was very calm and her face was still. "You can turn away whenever you choose," she said. "You can go away, if you choose."

As we cannot. Full of shame, Lydia put her hands to her face. It didn't stop the tears. She sobbed. When she could talk again, she raised her head and said, "It's finally happened to me. It happens to every Northern woman who comes South to teach Black children, Black or white. We all break down. I'm breaking down, just like my friend Edmonia." She looked up. "She was teaching in New Orleans in 1866. They had a massacre, too."

Narcissa didn't speak. She handed Lydia her hand-kerchief.

At this small kindness, Lydia's eyes filled again.

Narcissa said, "Oh, Miss Lydia." She put her arms around Lydia and held her as she'd comfort a crying child. "I am so sorry it's come to this."

Lydia leaned against her shoulder. "Don't be," she whispered.

Narcissa let her go and waited until Lydia had wiped her face and blown her nose. Lydia said, "I've made a mess of your handkerchief."

"As though I care about the handkerchief."

"What a sight, your principal having a nervous collapse in front of you."

"Don't even mention it," Narcissa said.

Lydia sat up straight. She wiped her face once more and struggled to pull herself together. "What about you? Are you all right, Narcissa?"

Narcissa took a deep breath. "For the moment," she said. "But I may break down yet."

Lydia crumpled the sodden handkerchief in her fist. "Don't hold back on my account."

Narcissa smiled ruefully. "Don't worry, I won't."

A DAY LATER, Lydia received a message from Mr. Randolph. That evening, she told Elias that Randolph wanted to make a report. "He wants you to be there, too."

Elias said, "How bad is the news, I wonder?"

What could she say? Nothing that would make him any happier with their circumstances or with her. "I reckon we'll find out," she said.

Mr. Randolph came to visit Elias and Lydia in their parlor a few days later. It was early evening, still too light for candles or the kerosene lamps. Randolph looked composed and as well-dressed as a man bound for the opera. Lydia wondered if his next appointment was a séance. He doffed his tall hat and refused refreshment, sitting easily in their guest chair.

Once they were seated, Lydia asked, "How is Mrs. Auburn?"

Randolph's face clouded. "She's well. She has a séance tonight."

Lydia asked, "Has she had any trouble?"

"No," Randolph said.

Elias asked, "No spirits for us tonight?"

"No," Randolph said. "No spirits."

Elias's tone was sharp. "The truth?"

"What little I know of it."

"Then go ahead."

"Mr. Aronson, I understand this is a difficult time for you—"

"Just tell us."

Lydia threw Randolph a look meant to mollify. "It has been a difficult time," she said.

Randolph nodded. "It's not hard to find men who don't mind entertaining the thought of setting fire to a Black school," he said. "But it's not easy to find anyone who admits to planning to do it."

Elias curled his hand into a fist on his knee. "Everyone knows, but no one will say," he said. He looked up at Lydia. "As in every inquiry we try."

In irritation, it seemed, she and her husband were equal.

"What did John Beardsley say?" Elias asked. "I assume you talked to him. Or tried to."

He said, "It was indelicate."

"We're very low on delicacy here," Lydia said. "Just tell us."

"He asked me if I was a n— lover," Randolph said.

Elias asked, "Does he suspect the truth about you? That the blood of Africa runs through your veins?"

Randolph gave Elias a piercing look that probably worked to great advantage in the séance room. Lydia saw Elias shrug it off. "They see what they want to see," Randolph said.

Elias said, "We're in danger, aren't we? And the culprits are hidden and faceless, even though they're likely to cause us a lot of harm." He raised his eyes to Randolph's. "We all know men like that, who hide their evil intent behind a white hood. And don't tell me they don't do their work in town. Evidently they do, without taking the hoods out of the clothes press."

"Mr. Aronson, do you go about armed?"

"Yes, I do."

"Mrs. Aronson, do you?"

Lydia drew her derringer from her pocket. "Always."

Randolph said, "Mrs. Aronson, you need a better pistol than that."

Lydia laid the pistol on the table beside the settee. "It's quite lethal at a short distance."

Red spots appeared on Randolph's cheeks. Lydia doubted he felt embarrassed. He was angry, and too polite to let it sound in his voice. "I'd recommend that you provide yourself with more firepower," he said. "Mr. Aronson, would you advise your wife?"

Like Randolph, Elias was skilled at controlling his anger. "I'd advise my wife to get on the next packet that would take her to New York," he said.

Lydia saw no reason to pretend she wasn't angry. She didn't bother to tamp down her ire. "You know I will not."

LYDIA HADN'T SLEPT WELL since she had stopped teaching. She woke in the middle of the night and lay awake, not trying to move. Elias slept uneasily, and if she tossed and turned, she woke him.

She lay on her back, feeling hot even in her thinnest cotton nightdress. Elias slept on his side, facing her, his head propped on his arm. He would feel the pain of that position when he woke, she knew. In sleep, she saw his real face, the lines that the war had etched at the corners of his eyes and his mouth. As he slept, it was easy to remember the sympathy that came so easily to that face. She wanted to touch his cheek. But she would wake him, and he was unlikely to look at her with sympathy.

Do you really want me gone? she wondered.

She put her hand beneath her, touching the tight, sore spot on her back. She rubbed it a little and sighed.

Then she heard it. She knew exactly what it was: the sound of shattering glass.

Elias stirred in his sleep. She sat upright, her heart pounding, and without caring what he would say, she shook him from sleep.

"What?" he asked, his voice groggy.

"Did you hear that?"

"What?"

"Glass breaking. Downstairs."

He was instantly awake. He threw off the covers and so did she. "No," he whispered.

She reached for the derringer. "Don't tell me no."

He crept toward the landing, his bare feet silent on the wooden floor, and she followed him. At the top of the stairs, they both hesitated.

There was no sound from below.

They advanced downstairs, hesitating to look around the room. Elias's eyes darted around the dimness. But they heard nothing.

She pointed. "Look," she whispered.

The curtain around the front window had been drawn aside. How had that happened? She closed the curtains every night. And they billowed around a star-shaped hole in the glass as big as a man's head.

He put her hand to her mouth to stifle her shock. "The window," she said.

He inched forward.

"Careful," she said.

The brick lay in a sparkling mess of glass under the sill.

She dropped to her knees. "What are you doing?" he asked. "Being careful," she said. She reached out for the brick and retrieved it. She stood.

It was the most ordinary kind of brown brick, the kind

that filled draymen's carts every day in construction-mad post-war Memphis. But around it was wrapped a piece of paper, secured with string.

She untied the string to read the note, which read: *Next time it will be a bullet. For you both.* She handed him the note.

"I need to sit down," she said, and he took her arm to guide her to the stairs, far from the shards of glass. They both sat, Lydia holding the brick in her lap as Elias stared at the note.

They both looked up at the same time, and Lydia saw the battle weariness on her husband's face. She thought, *We have real enemies, and we're fighting with each other.* "What are we going to do?" She struggled to keep the fear from her voice.

He laid his hand on her arm and she let it rest there. They sat like that, connected by the lightest touch, until he rose. "Don't get up. Wait here."

"Where are you going?"

He mounted the stairs, gripping the railing as though he needed the support, and disappeared into the bedroom. He came downstairs in slippered feet, and he held her slippers in his hands. He wasn't smiling, but he looked better.

"What on earth?" she asked.

"There's a lot of broken glass to clean up," he said. "Shall we do it together?"

THE LOST BOY

HER CUSTOMER REACHED INTO HER RETICULE. AS ALWAYS, Cassie said, "There's no obligation, you know."

She smiled. "I do know. Just want you to know how grateful I am." She pulled out the money and left it delicately on the table. As Cassie thanked her, the side door was thrown open and feet pounded on the stairs to the second floor. The upstairs door was also flung open, and her aunt's voice was perfectly audible. "Sammy, what's the matter with you?"

Loud gulping sobs followed.

"Someone ain't at all happy," the customer said.

"My youngest."

The sobs grew louder.

The customer rose, and Cassie did too, sighing. "I'll see to him," she said.

When she entered the parlor upstairs, Sammy was buried in Matilda's arms. He was still sobbing.

"What's the matter?" Cassie asked. Sammy was given to outbursts. He'd probably skinned his knee or his elbow.

Her aunt's expression was much too grim for a skinned knee.

He pulled away from Matilda's embrace and managed to choke out, "A man—a bad man—"

She stifled a gasp. "What happened, Sammy?"

Sammy's sobs began to diminish. "He followed me."

She bent and put her arms on his shoulders. "Did he talk to you?"

"He grabbed me. And then he said—"

Cassie suddenly felt dizzy. "What, Sammy?"

"He asked me where Will was. And he said he'd hurt me unless I told." He cried harder.

What do they know? "What did you tell him?"

"I didn't know! I told him I didn't know!"

"Did he hurt you?"

Sammy held out his arm and pushed up his sleeve. She felt sick at the sight of the bruises on his upper arm. When the policeman had grabbed her, to arrest her, he'd left a similar bruise.

"Why did he want to find Will?"

"I don't know." He sobbed afresh and she folded him into her arms. She pressed her cheek to his. "Do you know where Will is now?" she asked, her voice soft.

"He's not home yet," Matilda said.

Cassie rose and looked at her aunt. "Do you know something?"

"No more than you do."

Cassie felt the full weight of her aunt's blame. If bad men were following her sons, her aunt was sure it was entirely Cassie's fault.

The door opened and TJ stepped in. Sammy was still sniffling. TJ took in the angry aunt, the worried mother, and the crying child. "What happened to him?" TJ asked.

With bitterness, Matilda said, "Ask him."

Sammy liked being the center of attention. "A bad man hurt me," he said, wiping his face.

"Some stranger grabbed his arm hard enough to leave a bruise," Cassie said.

TJ stared at Cassie. "Why?"

"He wanted to find Will."

"And did he say why?"

Sammy shook his head.

Now TJ knelt so that he could be face-to-face with the boy. He put his hands on his arms, being careful of the bruised spot. "Sammy, can you tell me what this man was like? Had you ever seen him before?"

Sammy nodded. "He was following me."

"Besides today?"

Sammy nodded again and Cassie felt sick to her stomach.

"Do you know who he was?"

Sammy shook his head.

"What did he look like?"

"A white man."

"Was he tall or short?"

"Shorter than you."

"How was he dressed?"

"A coat. Black. Not like yours. Not new."

"What color was his hair?"

"He wore a hat. I didn't see."

"What kind of hat?"

"Like a bowl."

"Did you see his eyes?"

Sammy shook his head. "I was too afraid to look," he said.

TJ rose and patted Sammy on both shoulders. "That's good," he said.

Sammy asked, "I bet you can find him."

TJ's expression was grim. "I believe I'll try." He looked at Sammy again and laid his hand gently on the top of his head. "You really don't know where Will is? Please, if you do, say so."

Sammy burst into tears again.

Now the door opened, and Will walked into the house. Three pairs of eyes turned to him.

Cassie cried out, "Where have you been?"

Surprised, he said, "With my friend Luke." Luke was a classmate from the Phoenix School who lived in South Memphis, a ten-minute walk from Beale Street. He stared at his upset mother. "What's the matter?"

TJ put a hand on Will's shoulder. It hurt Cassie that Will accepted TJ's caresses, while he refused hers. "Sammy said there was a man looking for you."

Will snorted. "You know he'd say anything to get your attention."

Sammy raised his arm and pushed up his sleeve. "He grabbed me! He hurt me!"

"Were you stealing apples from him?" Will said scornfully.

Sammy burst out, "You're a liar! You weren't with Luke! You were visiting Miss Narcissa!"

Cassie put her hands over her mouth, but TJ signaled her to be quiet. "Is that true, Will?"

Will shook off TJ's hand and glared at his mother. "What if it was?"

Cassie recovered enough to remove her hands from her mouth. She scolded, "Because it's not safe! There are men loitering outside Miss Narcissa's house to bother her and her family, and you shouldn't be going there. It's not safe for you either!"

Will raised his voice. "What do you want me to do? Stay locked up in the house? I won't do it!" His face began to quiver. "I hate it, all of it. I want to go back to school. I want to see Miss Narcissa. This is all your fault! I hate it!"

He turned, ready to flee to his room, but TJ grasped his arm, gently.

"Let me go! I'm not a prisoner and I won't act like one!" Will squirmed in TJ's grasp.

TJ said, "Will, quiet. Listen to me, please."

Will stopped squirming.

"I know how worried your mother is, but you're right, we can't lock you in the house. I'm worried about you, too. Will you let me walk you to and from school? And if you want to visit Miss Narcissa, will you let me escort you there and back?"

Will blushed, the red spots obvious on his fair-skinned face. It was clear to everyone that he had a schoolboy's crush on Miss Narcissa, and he was embarrassed that they knew. "I'm not a baby, like Sammy is. I can walk around by myself—"

TJ said, "No one is saying you're a baby. You're a young man. But I don't like that a white stranger is looking for you. Let me help you. Miss Narcissa lets Mr. Jasper help her. Can I help you like that? Make sure no harm comes to you?"

"You'll let me see Miss Narcissa?"

"I'll walk you to her door."

Will tugged on his sleeves, which had ridden up in his effort to shake free of TJ. "She gives me books to read," he said. "She asks me how I like them."

"I know she does," TJ said. "She's a fine teacher, and she cares about your education. The next time you plan to visit her, will you let me take you there?"

Will glanced at his mother. Cassie sighed and nodded at TJ.

"All right," Will said.

~

TJ HAD ESCORTED Will to see Miss Narcissa and brought him home safely. He joined Cassie in the séance room, where the curtains were drawn against the afternoon light and heat. The air was close and smelled powerfully of sage from the last séance.

He sat heavily at the table. "He shouldn't be going there at all," he said.

"Why? Did something happen?"

"The Armstrongs are in danger, and they all know it. Her neighbors have put together a guard, and someone is watching the house all the time. I asked her about the man Sammy described, and she said she'd seen him."

"Recently?"

"Yes, she knows he's been looking for Will."

"Does she know why?"

He looked away. Cassie grabbed his hand. "Don't hide the truth from me," she said, her voice hoarse and fierce. "Tell me what she knows."

"She told me that he'd accosted a neighbor as she walked down the street. Gave her a message. 'You have a witness, don't you? We know what can happen to a witness. No witness, no case, no suit.'"

Cassie leaned back in her chair. She felt faint. "How would he know?"

TJ curled his hand into a fist and pressed it on the table-top. "Does it matter?"

"If it's the Beardsleys—"

He opened his fist and pressed his hand against the table-top. "Of course it's the Beardsleys," he said in a tone of tightly controlled anger. "And since we can't arrest them, sue them, try them, or shoot them in a dark alley, what should we do?"

She pressed her hand atop his, hard enough to remind him of her strength. "Keep him close," she said. "It isn't safe for him to visit Narcissa Armstrong."

"He'll hate it. He'll buck at it."

Cassie removed her hand. She wanted to slap him. She growled, "Can you make it clear to him? That someone is looking for him to hurt him, perhaps to kill him, to make sure he never tells the truth about Titus Armstrong's murder?"

TJ grabbed her hand, not in affection, but to restrain her. In a low rumble to match her own, he said, "I'll make it as clear as I possibly can."

TJ TALKED TO WILL. There was no outburst. Will went quiet and shut himself in the room he shared with Sammy. When Cassie tapped on the closed door, he said, "Go away." She opened the door, and he didn't raise his voice. He didn't put down the book he held in his lap. "I'm reading," he said in the voice of self-control he'd used when she first returned to Memphis, more ominous than shouting or sobbing.

"TJ talked to you?"

He looked down at the book and didn't reply. She waited but he remained silent. She said, "It's to keep you safe." Her voice sounded weak and plaintive to her ears.

He began to read again.

What was she going to do? Insist to him, "Look at me when I'm talking to you"? He was lost to her again. She closed the door.

That night, Cassie lay in bed with TJ. He rested his hand on her hip, but she took it away. "Will has gone quiet again. He's furious."

TJ rolled over on his back. "He didn't mince words with me. He told me he feels like a prisoner now."

Cassie thought of her own weeks in the boardinghouse, and her days in hiding five years ago. She let herself sound as upset as she felt. "As though I want to keep him cooped up! It's not some trivial punishment. There's a man out there who wants him dead. Doesn't he understand that?"

TJ sighed. "I think he's reached his limit for understanding," he said. "He wants this to be over. He wants life to be as it was before. I can't persuade him that it will never be like that again."

Cassie was quiet.

TJ turned to look at her. "Why do we stay here? We can—"

"I know. Be in New York in a week."

"Will would like New York," TJ said. "It's full of bookstores. We could find him a good school there. One with a pretty teacher—"

Cassie felt a wave of anger. "Will doesn't want to leave Memphis, any more than I do. For his own reasons."

TJ groaned. "Fools, both of you," he said.

"You're free to go to New York whenever you like."

He put his hand on her hip again and said, "No, don't pull away. Listen to me."

She stared at him, seeing both affection and worry in his expression.

"I'm not getting on a packet for New York without you and yours."

"Then you're a fool, too," she said, but she was weakening, and he knew it.

He stroked her hip, and this time she let him do it. "It will send me to an early grave, protecting you and yours, Cassie Andrews," he said.

~

CASSIE KNEW when school let out, and she began to expect Will, escorted by TJ, shortly afterward. When he didn't arrive, she took a deep breath and told herself that he might have wanted to visit Narcissa. TJ would take him there and wait for him. They'd be home before suppertime.

Cassie could hear Matilda in the kitchen, the floor creaking under her weight. She heard the sound of plates going on the table. Sammy must be helping. He rattled the plates too much.

TJ and Will didn't appear.

Matilda descended the back stairs and walked into the storefront, where Cassie waited at the table. "Will hasn't come home yet?' she asked.

"He must be with TJ."

"Doing what?"

Cassie wanted to wring her hands, but instead she splayed out her fingers on the table. She took another deep breath. "Staying out of trouble, I'd hope."

Matilda shook her head. "I hope so too." She added, "Supper in a few minutes."

Cassie nodded. She had no appetite. Her worry propelled her into the worst possible thoughts. She took another deep breath. "I'll wait a bit," she said.

As Matilda ascended the stairs, the door opened, and TJ walked in.

He was alone.

Cassie rose to her feet. "Where's Will?" she demanded.

TJ looked tired. "He left school early," he said. "Gave me the slip. I've been looking for him."

"Did someone take him?"

TJ said, "No one saw anything like that. I suspect he's just hiding somewhere. Showing us he can."

"Where did you look?"

"I tried his friends from school. And I stopped by the Armstrongs. No one's seen him."

Cassie didn't hold back. "He's been kidnapped," she said." She looked at TJ with desperation. "I can feel it. He's in danger!"

He caught her by both arms. "Is that the spirit speaking? Or just a mother's fear?"

She tried to shake him off. "Does it matter? We have to find him."

He held her fast. "Cassie. Listen to me. Let me look. I can go places you can't." He loosened his grip. "Stay here. I'll keep looking."

He left her standing in the middle of the storefront, her hands bunched on her hips, her heart pounding, her mind working on the thought of Will stolen. Held somewhere. Worse. She closed her eyes.

Matilda's voice floated down the stairs. "Cassie?"

She locked the front door and ran up the stairs. Moses and Sammy sat at the table, and Matilda stood beside it, a serving dish in her hands. Matilda asked, "Where's Will?"

Cassie leaned against her chair at the table. "Missing," she said.

Moses rose. "Missing? We'll look for him."

"No, TJ's looking." She took another deep breath. "He'll scout for him."

Matilda said, "If any harm comes to that boy—"

Cassie's fear came out as anger. "TJ will find him."

Unusually silent, Sammy stared at his plate.

Cassie said, "I can't eat." She ran down the stairs again and shut herself in the séance room, where the dark and the faded scent of sage folded around her like a blanket.

She thought of the man who had frightened Sammy. The worst thoughts came, and she didn't push them away.

Will was hidden somewhere. He was hurt.

He was dead.

"Help me," she whispered to her spirit, yearning to hear its voice.

You're doing the right thing. Sending out a scout for him.

"Is he all right?"

There was no answer.

"Is he alive?"

Still no answer.

She buried her face in her hands. She had never loved Will well enough, and he had always known it. If she lost him again, she deserved it.

There was a tap on the door, and she started upright. But it was Matilda, who held a plate in her hands. "You sure you aren't hungry?" she asked.

"Did he come home? Did he run up the stairs without my hearing it?"

Matilda set the plate on the séance table. "No," she said. "But you should eat something."

"Why?" she cried out. "If he's dead, what difference does it make? I deserve to be dead, too!"

Matilda sat in the chair next to her. She sighed. "We're all worried," she said. "But it doesn't help to think the worst." She reached a tentative hand toward Cassie's arm. "Not until we know for sure."

"Leave me alone," Cassie said.

Matilda rose. "Eat something," she said. "Whatever happens, you'll need your strength."

After Matilda left, Cassie laid her cheek on the table,

letting the hard surface cause her pain. The smell of the food nauseated her. She reached out to push the dish away. She closed her eyes.

She must have fallen asleep, because the sound of a tap on the doorframe woke her. She sat up with a start, her neck aching.

It was TJ, and he was alone.

"You didn't find him?" she asked.

He shook his head.

There was a sound of footsteps on the back stairs, surprisingly soft. The same footsteps crept into the séance room. It was Sammy, who looked as though he'd been crying.

He asked, "Is Will home?"

"No," Cassie said abruptly.

His lower lip quivered.

"What is it?" Cassie demanded.

His eyes filled. He rubbed them with his fists, like a much smaller child.

TJ said, "Sammy, what's the matter?"

The tears came in earnest. "He told me—"

"Will?"

Sammy nodded.

"He told you what?"

"He told me he was going to run away."

Cassie grabbed Sammy roughly by both arms. "When?"

"Yesterday."

Cassie gripped her son hard enough to bruise his skin. "You knew? And you didn't tell us?"

Sammy sobbed.

Cassie let him go and slapped him hard across the face. "You knew! You didn't say so!"

He put his hand to his wounded cheek and wept harder.

TJ grabbed her and pulled her away from the boy. "Sit

down," he said, the voice of command, a battlefield tone. "Calm down." He knelt in front of Sammy and touched the sore arms with gentleness. "What did your brother say?"

"Just that he was going to run away. Because he was causing so much trouble for everyone. He said it would be better if he ran away."

Cassie, already nauseated with anger and guilt, remembered how she had felt five years ago when she ran away.

TJ's voice was also gentle. "Did he say anything about where he planned to go?"

The sobs slowed. Sammy shook his head. "No."

"Think hard, Sammy. Is there anything he said or did that might have given you a hint as to where he'd gone?"

Sammy shook his head again. "No," he whispered. He looked at his mother, who sat at the table, her shoulders slumped, her head propped on her hand. "Will she hit me again?"

TJ said, "No." He put his arms around Sammy and hugged him. "Why don't you go upstairs?"

In a very small voice, Sammy said, "What if the bad man gets him?"

Cassie raised her head, but TJ said firmly, "He won't. Because we'll get him first." He released the boy. "Go on upstairs."

Sammy ascended the stairs, his tread now heavy with fear. When he was gone, Cassie looked at TJ. "What good does that do us?"

TJ raised himself to his full height. In the dark, he seemed to have the glamor that made him look even taller. "I know where a boy goes when he runs away."

"Where is that?"

"Let me go looking."

~

AFTER TJ LEFT, Cassie went upstairs to her room, shutting the door to lie on her bed, not even bothering to take off her shoes. Her corset pinched her. She lay still as the sun set and the room darkened. The parlor, ordinarily the spot for conversation and laughter, was silent tonight. Cassie put her hand over her eyes and wished that her aunt allowed liquor in the house. Matilda permitted laudanum, but Cassie had taken the last drop from her little bottle last week for a headache. She was alone with the pain in her head, and worse still, the pain in her mind.

This was her fault. She had put him in danger. She had made him a target for the people who wished her so ill. She had allowed him to become a witness, at the risk of his own life.

And he had reacted in terror, just as she had five years ago, by running away.

She spoke aloud to the voice. "Damn you, why can't you just tell me where he is and how he is!"

Don't disrespect me, the voice said, and she was too angry and too tired to apologize.

She fell into an uneasy, sweaty sleep, and she dreamed of the dark alley where John Beardsley waited for her. When the footsteps woke her, she sat bolt upright and had to stifle a scream.

It was TJ, who carried a candlestick, which cast a shadow that made him look deathly tired and a decade older.

Her hand on her heart, she gasped, "You startled me."

He set the candlestick on the nightstand and sat heavily on the bed.

"You didn't find him," she said.

He sighed. "But I know where he went."

"Oh God!" she cried. "Where?"

"Hush. Let me talk."

"Tell me!" she said, her voice still too loud.

"I went down to the docks. And I found a man who works as a stevedore," he said. "He saw Will earlier today. Said he wanted to get on a packet for Cairo, but he didn't have any money. The stevedore knows the steward on the boat. He told Will he could travel to Cairo if he went to work in the galley."

"He got on the boat? You know that for sure?"

"The stevedore took him to the steward, and the steward hired him."

Cassie put her hand to her mouth. Five years ago, she had escaped the same way—in the scullery on a steamer to Cairo. "Has the boat left?"

"Yes, late this afternoon." He turned to her. "I'm going to Cairo. I'll find out if he went any farther or not."

"Cincinnati."

He nodded.

"I'm going with you."

He said, "No, it won't help. I'm going as a white man, and you'd be a complication."

"A veil—a heavy coat of paint—an illusion—"

"No," he said, hoarse with fatigue. "Stay home. I'll find him."

She was too tired to sit upright anymore. She slumped back on the bed, her hands crossed over her chest, staring into the darkness.

AFTER TJ LEFT, Cassie thought of everything she had done wrong with her sons. Sammy was afraid of her again. He didn't even summon the energy to say, "I hate you," with its undertone of disappointment. He shrank from her.

She sat in the séance room and let Sammy's fear and Will's absence trouble her soul to its very depths. Late at night, she sat at the table, her head in her hands. It was a day since TJ had left.

The voice said, *Don't do this to yourself.*

"Go away," she said.

Her head ached and her back ached and her soul ached. She didn't eat and she didn't replenish the laudanum. She wanted to suffer.

The root doctor she knew best came to see her. She walked into the séance room and said, "Bright day outside."

Cassie shook her head.

The root doctor said, "I heard your boy's missing. Heard he might have run off."

"Or he might be dead," Cassie said.

"May I sit?"

"Suit yourself."

"If he's run off, he's probably all right," the root doctor said.

Cassie raised her head. "Do the spirits talk to you?"

The root doctor smiled. "Someone does," she said. "Used to hear those voices back in slavery days. Used to whisper how to get away. Steal away."

Cassie didn't reply.

The root doctor reached for her hand, and when Cassie tried to pull away, she grasped it and laced her fingers through Cassie's.

"Don't tell me to have faith," Cassie said, her voice bitter.

The root doctor laughed. "Not in God," she said. "But in Mr. Randolph, who could find a needle in a haystack if he set his mind to it."

"Go away," Cassie said.

~

THE NEXT MORNING, a boy came to her front door, and for a moment she thought it was Will. But it was a stranger, shorter and stockier and darker than Will. "Is it a letter?" she asked.

"No, ma'am. A telegram."

Fear shot through her. During the war, telegrams had always announced death. Her fingers shaking, she tore open the envelope to read: *I've found him. He was working in a hotel kitchen in Cairo. He was very dirty and very hungry. He isn't hurt, but we'll see what happens to his spirit once he's home. We'll be on tomorrow's packet for Memphis.*

She stared at the messenger in a relief so profound that she didn't realize why he held out his hand. She shook her head and reached into her reticule. Her fingers were still shaking. She pulled out the first coin she touched. It was a quarter.

He grinned. "Thank you, ma'am."

"You brought me good news! God bless!"

He went away laughing.

~

WHEN WILL CAME HOME, ushered into the parlor by TJ, Matilda held out her arms to him and he let her hug him. "You're all right?" she asked. She didn't wait for his reply. She smoothed the hair from his forehead. "Looks like Mr. Randolph cleaned you up. Did he feed you, too?"

He nodded. Then he extricated himself from her embrace, as gently as he could. He approached his mother, slowly, and Cassie rose from her chair. He had the abashed look of a much younger boy. He came closer. He swallowed hard, his Adam's apple showing in his throat. He met her eyes, and he said, "Mama, I'm so sorry."

Without hesitation, she opened her arms, and he nestled into them. Despite his small voice and little-boy's demeanor, he was taller than she was, and he had the long bones and the toughening muscles of a young man. He laid his cheek on her shoulder.

She stroked his hair and whispered to him, "Will, sugar, so am I."

THE STORM

ELIAS WALKED INTO DORSEY'S OFFICE, HAMPERED BY THE object he carried. He let it down on Dorsey's desk with a thud and sat heavily in his guest chair.

Dorsey said mildly, "I see what that is, but why have you brought it with you?"

Elias pushed the hair from his sweating forehead. He leaned forward. "It came through my parlor window a few nights ago." He pulled the paper from his pocket. "This was wrapped around it."

Dorsey read the note. He looked up. "That's nasty," he said. "Any idea who was responsible?"

Elias snorted. "A very good idea," he said. "Even though he's too much the coward to sign his name to it."

Dorsey leaned back in his chair and steepled his fingers. "You should protect yourselves," he said.

"Mr. Jasper, whose men guard the school, has sent someone over to stand watch over us at night."

"How is Mrs. Aronson?"

"Not hurt. But shaken and angry, as I am."

Dorsey sighed.

Elias let his voice rise. "It's one thing to go after me on the street. I was a soldier, and I go about armed. But to threaten my wife—in our house—as she sleeps—" He curled his hand into a fist and pressed it into his thigh. "Worse yet, that it's happened before."

Alarmed, Dorsey asked, "When?"

"Years ago. During the war. But the memory lingers."

Dorsey rubbed his eyes. "What would you like to do?"

"Like to do?" Elias asked. "I'd like to beat John Beardsley to a jelly."

Dorsey didn't reply.

"But I'd have to go into the countryside to find him, and I'd need an armed guard for that," Elias said. "Preferably a white one."

Dorsey sighed again. "And would it do any good?"

Elias tamped down his anger and his reply came out as a snarl. "I don't know."

Dorsey said, "I wasn't in the army, but I know plenty of soldiers. Not just you. And I know something about fighting to win instead of to fight."

Elias looked up. "I served under General Grant," he said. He calmed down a little. "He never fought a battle he knew he couldn't win."

"Think of that," Dorsey said.

"I still want to file Miss Armstrong's civil suit," Elias said. He uncurled his fist, but he stared at his fingers, splayed on the cloth of his trousers. He took a deep breath and looked up at Dorsey. "I want to call on William Beardsley."

"About the suit?"

Elias picked up the heavy object that he had dropped on Settle's desk. "About the brick," he said.

Dorsey said, "God help you."

Wʜᴇɴ Eʟɪᴀs ᴇɴᴛᴇʀᴇᴅ ʜɪs ᴏꜰꜰɪᴄᴇ, William Beardsley looked up from the letter he was reading. He set it down. His desk was so neat that the wood gleamed around the edges of the blotter. It looked as though he had servants to tidy it for him every evening when he left the office. "Mr. Aronson," he said, his tone a little wary. "What brings you to see me?"

Elias sat without being invited and dropped the brick on the desk. It landed on the blotter, but he wouldn't have cared if he'd marred the wood.

Beardsley looked at the brick in surprise. "What is this, Mr. Aronson?"

Elias tossed the note beside the brick. "Read that," he said, his voice curt.

Beardsley looked puzzled, but he picked up the note and read it. He set it down carefully. "That's deplorable," he said.

"There are other words for a threatening note wrapped around a brick thrown through a man's parlor window in the dead of night," Elias said.

Beardsley said, "I certainly don't condone such a thing. Why have you brought this to me?"

Elias leaned forward and didn't hide the emotion in his voice. "You know full well," he said.

Beardsley looked puzzled again. "I'm afraid I don't."

Elias's voice rose. "Your son, John Beardsley, has been harassing and intimidating my wife, her teachers, and her school. He has threatened the safety of Mrs. Auburn and her son Will. And he is behind this."

"I don't think—"

"If not by his own hand, at his insistence," Elias said. "His friends, and the ruffians they hire to dirty their hands with this."

Beardsley's voice was mild. "Mr. Aronson, as a lawyer, I believe you care a great deal for proof," he said.

Elias said, "We're past that. You know who did this. You can put a stop to it. A few words with your son—with his confederates—"

Beardsley remained mild. "Mr. Aronson, even if I knew what you were talking about, you're greatly overestimating my influence," he said. "I regret that there are ruffians in Memphis, just as you do. But I have no sway with them."

Elias put his hand on the brick. For a fleeting moment, he thought of the satisfaction of bringing it down on Beardsley's well-barbered skull. Shaken, he pulled his hand away. *Not even for Lydia*, he thought. He forced himself to speak with more composure. "No, sir, you underestimate yourself. Especially in the matter of your influence over your son." He took a deep breath. "I want the threats to stop. The threats against the school. And the threats against my wife. How can you call yourself a man of honor, when your son and his friends threaten women and children?"

Beardsley said, "Mr. Aronson, I can understand why you're distraught. But you are talking to the wrong man. I'm sorry this is happening, but I have no idea why. And there's nothing I can do to help you."

Elias waited.

"Good day, Mr. Aronson," Beardsley said.

Elias rose. He was too angry to speak. He reached for the note and crumpled it into his pocket. Then he grasped the brick. He weighed it in his hand for a moment. Then he looked at Beardsley. "Good day, Mr. Beardsley," he said.

SINCE THE BRICK had come through the window, Lydia stayed at home, too shaken to do much. Every so often, she found a shard of glass they had missed as they swept. Her fingers were full of shallow, painful cuts. At every splinter, her lethargy was punctured along with her skin. As her blood welled, so did her fury.

Elias came home to discover her staring at the tip of her finger. She said, "It's nothing. Just another bit of glass."

"I called on William Beardsley," he said. He still carried the brick in his hand.

The blood beaded and she put her finger in her mouth to catch it. "How did it go?"

"I nearly hit him in the head with this," he said.

She removed her finger. "I need a sticking plaster."

He sighed. He put the brick down and pulled his handkerchief from his pocket. "Give me your hand," he said.

"It's nothing. It's already stopped bleeding."

"Let me do something useful. And kind."

She extended her hand, and he gently bound up her finger. As he held her hand, she said, "You really thought about beating his brains out?"

"Yes, God help me," he said.

She began to laugh. She didn't like the wild edge in it. "We can't live like this."

"I'm going to talk to Narcissa about filing the civil suit." He cradled her hand in his. "Don't tell me to wait. Wait for what?"

She shook her head.

THE KNOCK on the door worried Lydia, but when she opened it, she was relieved. It was Mr. Jasper. Through the open door, she felt the stare of a neighbor on the sidewalk, a well-dressed matron with a servant in tow. Lydia had long since dispensed with insisting that her Black colleagues and friends use the back door. As the neighbor pursed her mouth in distaste, she welcomed Mr. Jasper inside and shut the door.

He said, "Ma'am, I can go in back next time, if that would help you."

"It won't. Please, sit down. Would you like any refreshment?"

"No, I'm all right." He sat and mopped his face with his handkerchief. "Sorry, Mrs. Aronson. It's mighty hot out this morning."

"I know." She felt the heat indoors, too, even though she kept the curtains closed at the hottest and brightest time of day. She ran her hand over her damp neck. "Is there trouble at the school, Mr. Jasper?"

"Nothing this minute," he said. "But the night watch saw something they wanted me to know about. And I thought you should know too, ma'am."

She nodded.

"Men loitering around the school," he said. "White men, even though they pull their hats low so we can't see them well in the dark. Just looking at the building. Smoking, sometimes. It bothers me that they smoke."

"The danger of fire," she said slowly.

"I believe that if they're firebugs, they'll do the same as during the massacre. They won't set a fire by dropping a smoldering cigar. They'll throw a torch or a brand. They haven't done anything yet. But the watchmen are wary."

"You can't identify them? Any of them?"

He shook his head.

"When will this be over, Mr. Jasper?"

He said, "We all felt like this during the war. Didn't know when that would be over, either. And waiting for a fight was worse than having one."

"What precautions are you taking?"

"Added a few more men to the watch," he said. "And we tested the mains, in case we need the water."

Because the fire department wouldn't help. She thought of the massacre, when the fire department had declined to put out any of the conflagrations at the Black schools or churches. She said, "So we watch. And we wait." She looked down at her fingers, where the tiny cuts hadn't yet healed. She looked up. "And we hope for—what?"

He sighed. "I don't know," he said. "Whatever it is, we'll do our best to be ready for it."

SUMMER IN MEMPHIS was always hot and humid, but after Mr. Jasper's visit, Lydia sensed the weather in her body, a headache and a backache that never went away. She felt so caged in the house that she risked a walk down to the river, accompanied by one of Mr. Jasper's men. She tried to joke a little with him, telling him that she looked forward to the day when she could walk freely down the street by herself, but he was somber.

He reassured her that there had been no trouble at the school, even if strangers were often loitering. "They haven't tried anything, because we're watching," he said.

She sighed.

They walked toward the site of Fort Pickering, which had been demolished in 1866. Nothing remained of the encampment or the fort she remembered. New construction had grown up around it, and it was now difficult to find the riverfront that used to be easily accessible from the fort and from its neighboring contraband camps, which were also completely gone.

They halted at a spot where the riverfront sloped gradually into the water. She knew the view from the bluffs, where the water was many feet below the shore, but this was a gentler vantage point. The water was brown and silty, and the breeze that rose from it was as hot and humid as the air in her parlor. The sky was a soupy gray. Clouds of insects hovered over the water—gnats and mosquitoes at this time of year. She waved them away from her face.

Her guide and guard said, "Feels like it might storm."

"It's felt like that for days," she said. "Do you think it might feel any cooler if it rains?"

He looked over the water. They didn't know each other well, and he didn't have Mr. Jasper's ease with her. "Hope so, ma'am," he said. "But I don't know."

She sighed. It wasn't pleasant to watch the murky water under the hazy gray sky. She put her hand to the ache in her lower back. "I've seen enough," she said.

SHE HADN'T BEEN SLEEPING WELL, between the heat and her own unease. Tonight, it was too hot to get under the coverlet. She lay atop it, pulling up her nightdress to cool her legs. Beside her, Elias slept a shallow sleep. He hadn't bothered to wear a nightshirt. He said it was too hot to bother. He snored softly and started in his sleep.

She closed her eyes, and she must have nodded off, because the knock on the front door made her sit bolt upright. Dazed and groggy, she rose. Then her head cleared enough to reach for her pistol, which she now kept within reach, even when she slept at night.

Elias stirred and woke. "What is it?" he asked, his voice thick with sleep.

"Someone at the door."

"Trying to get in?"

"Knocking."

He threw on his dressing gown and they ran down the stairs together. She gripped the pistol in her hand as she peeked through the parlor window. The window that had been replaced.

Even in the darkness, she could see that her visitor was Mr. Jasper.

Elias opened the door.

Lydia's heart began to pound. She opened the door and at his grim expression, she asked, "The school?"

He nodded.

"Fire?" Elias asked.

Mr. Jasper nodded. "Hurry."

Elias said, "Give us a moment to get dressed and we'll go there with you."

They threw on their clothes. Lydia picked up her derringer. Elias had talked about getting her a bigger gun, but she liked being able to carry her pistol in her pocket. Elias had taken to wearing a holster, and he buckled it around his waist and tucked his pistol into it.

They locked up the house. As they left, the man on night watch asked Mr. Jasper, "You need me?"

"I need you to stay here," Mr. Jasper said.

Three abreast, they left to go into the darkness.

As they ran down the steps, Lydia felt the water on her face. At first, she thought it was sweat, since the humidity hadn't abated with sunset. But it was the finest droplets of rain.

Somewhere far away, thunder rumbled, a low, slow sound.

Mr. Jasper set the pace, a soldier's stride. Lydia clutched her skirts to pull them up as she hurried with the men who flanked her. She lengthened her step to match theirs, and the pistol in her pocket banged against her thigh.

The droplets became drizzle. Lydia wiped her face with her sleeve, trying not to slow down.

The streets were dark and empty. She heard the thunder again, louder this time, and in a few seconds, the distant sky lit up with a sheet of lightning.

She thought of the night of the massacre, when fire bloomed from the roof of the school, wild and bright, too hot and angry to control. The memory filled her whole body with fear.

But when they arrived, she didn't see flames anywhere, only a cloud of smoke. "Where is the fire?" she asked.

"It was in back. It's not out yet."

Elias asked, "Do you have a bucket brigade?"

"We're using the water main."

"I'll help," he said.

The rain began to come down in earnest, the kind of gentle soaking that farmers prayed for. It streamed down her face and wetted her dress. Lydia found her voice. "So will I," she said.

Mr. Jasper turned to talk to the men who were holding the hose they'd attached to the main. And at that moment, they all saw the torch fly through the air and land at the side of the building, where the flames licked at the wood.

Whoever had thrown it was long gone as the building began to catch.

The sight paralyzed her. She couldn't move.

The rain began to fall more thickly, and the thunder was suddenly very close by. It sounded like a crack of cannon fire, as though Fort Pickering had miraculously risen from its foundations and the men of the 3rd Heavy Artillery were at their riverside post, firing to repel a Rebel attack. Lightning struck the water in a brilliant, jagged stream of electricity.

She was suddenly terrified that lightning would strike the building. She stared at the fire, but she was no longer in the present. She was lost in her worst memory from two years before, when she watched fire engulf the Lincoln School, standing by helplessly as the roof burned in an awful bonfire. The blaze spoke. It said: *This is how much we hate you and what you do.*

Without thinking, her hand crept to the pistol in her pocket, and for the first time since the massacre, she let herself think of the memory she wanted to push away forever. The day she had closed her hand around this very pistol and taken it from her pocket. The day she had used it.

Thunder boomed overhead and she looked up. Very close by, lightning hit the ground. She closed her eyes, the school's fate and her guilt intertwined in her mind. *I will never forgive myself*, she thought. Did tears trickle down her face, or was it wet with rain?

Suddenly the rain became a deluge, plastering her hair to her head and drenching her down to her skin, chemise and petticoat as wet as her dress. The water streamed into her eyes. She drew in her breath and wiped her face with her sodden sleeve. Thunder resounded once more, followed by a terrifying strike of lightning. She cried out as the deluge continued.

The rain came down in a sheet, completely obscuring her vision. What had happened to the bucket brigade? She couldn't see a foot from her face. The water stung her eyes, and she blinked against it. It didn't help. She was still blind.

In the darkness, drenched by the ferocity of the rain, she listened to the thunder. Even through the rain, she saw lightning strike again, and didn't know where it had hit.

She thought, *I will die here.* Did she weep? Or was it the rain that hit her in the face like a fist? Someone grabbed her hand, and she screamed, too terrified to reach for her pistol.

He shouted, "Lydia! Lydia!"

It was Elias. She looked up and he reached to pull her close. As the rain pelted down, as the thunder roared again, as the lightning struck once more, he held her tightly, now murmuring her name. "Lydia."

Sobbing, she said, "Elias."

They stood like that, his heart beating hard and fast against hers, as the deluge continued, drenching them both to the skin.

Still holding her tightly, he said, "Lydia. Look."

She raised her head. Without any help from the hose, or the brigade, or the water main, the fire—in the here and now—began to sizzle and then to smoke. As she watched, it turned to harmless steam. She stared at its transformation, unable to believe what she saw.

"The fire is going out," Elias whispered.

She looked at him, unable to speak, only to nod.

When Mr. Jasper joined them, the thunder sounded again, but it had become a muffled boom, like distant cannon fire. Lightning flashed again but didn't hit the ground.

The three of them stood in the downpour, soaked through, water running down their faces. Elias wiped his face with his sleeve. "Is it out?" he asked, his voice raspy from the smoke.

Mr. Jasper smiled and gestured toward the sky as the rain

began to slow. "Hand of providence," he said. "We're all right."

WHEN LYDIA ROSE the next morning, she remembered the bright blaze of the flames and the sluicing deliverance of the storm, and she shook so badly that she couldn't hook up her corset.

Elias, already dressed, came to her and put his hands over hers, resting them on her waist. "Let me help you."

She shook her head.

"You don't have to be all right."

She leaned back to look at him. She was still shaking. "I will be."

"You know you don't have to put on a show for me," he said.

"No, it's for me."

He reached for her hands. "Soldier's heart," he said. "Worse after the battle than during it."

"Even soldiers of light and love?" she asked. She was still shaking too badly to dress.

"Yes," he said, and when she leaned against him, he folded her into his embrace.

The shaking subsided as the storm had. She said, "Why do I think I smell smoke?"

He laughed softly. "It's in your hair."

She said, "That I can fix."

After they breakfasted, he put on his frock coat. "I'm going to the office," he said.

Even though he no longer did any business.

He read her thought. "I'm going to talk to James Dorsey," he said. "About filing Narcissa's suit."

After Elias left, Lydia stood at her front window. Their street was undisturbed, save for a few leaves torn from the live oak trees. The earth was saturated. The air smelled of the rich loam that grew cotton, a clean odor that momentarily washed away the murk and the mud of the city streets.

A hansom drove up. Cassie alit from it. Lydia opened the door, and Cassie smiled at her. "Did you know I was coming?"

"You know I don't have that talent. I saw you drive up. Come in."

Cassie looked refreshed, as though she'd slept well.

They sat. "I heard about the fire at the school," she said. "And I heard that the rainstorm put it out."

Lydia asked, "Who told you?"

Cassie smiled.

Lydia said, "Mr. Jasper, I'd guess. Or one of the men on his fire brigade."

Cassie smiled again.

Lydia said, "Mr. Jasper told me that it was God's will that the storm extinguished the fire."

Still smiling, Cassie said, "Do you doubt that?"

Lydia suddenly felt dizzy. "It seems that God has company in the heavens," she said. "As you well know."

Cassie nodded.

"Did you ask for her help? The African goddess of vengeance?"

Cassie said softly, "I can ask. But I never know if she'll answer."

Lydia said, "You did ask."

Cassie inclined her head.

"And she answered." Lydia felt dizzier than ever. She closed her eyes against the image of fire—not last night's, tamed and extinguished, but the fire of two years ago. And she felt the weight of the pistol in her hand as though she held it now, in her own living room.

Cassie was no longer smiling. She said, "I see a cloud of death around you. Not your late husband's. Something darker."

Lydia opened her eyes. "Do the spirits tell you so?"

Cassie reached for Lydia's hand. "No, your face does," she said, her voice soft.

"What does it say?" Lydia asked.

"Tell me," Cassie said, and her voice was a caress.

Lydia heard the words as though they'd been spoken aloud. *Because you want to.* "Two years ago—" she said, and then she faltered.

Cassie nodded, as though she understood. "What happened that night?" she asked.

Lydia looked away. During the war, a cloud of death had surrounded Cassie, and she had resisted Lydia's effort to find out why. Now Cassie hinted that she knew something that Lydia never wanted anyone to know.

Cassie's luminous eyes were full of sympathy. "Tell me," she repeated, her voice the merest whisper.

Because you want to. Lydia trembled. Suddenly there was nothing she wanted more. "The night of the massacre—as I watched the school burn—burn to the ground—" She faltered again, and Cassie waited.

Lydia remembered the first time she had met Cassie, who knew that she was a widow, and whose sympathy made Lydia tell more than she wanted to. Cassie hadn't changed. She still knew how to beguile that way.

I haven't changed, either, Lydia thought. The truth was too heavy to carry. She let the burden go.

She said, "A man came at me, out of the darkness. He grabbed me and began to tear at my dress. He wanted to outrage me, and I believe he wanted to kill me afterwards." She took a deep breath as her hand stole to her pocket. She looked up. "I shot him. I used every bullet in my pistol. I shot him dead."

Cassie said softly, "You defended yourself. No one would fault you for it."

Lydia forced herself to remember the rest. "Then I dragged his body toward the flames. As close as I could get. I hoped the fire would consume him and he would never be found."

She put her hand to her face, surprised to feel the moisture on her cheeks. She raised her eyes to Cassie's. "And he never was. I murdered a man and lied about it. Like so many during the massacre. I am no better."

Cassie said, "Would he have murdered you? If he could?"

Lydia took a deep breath. She raised her eyes to Cassie's and they looked at each other for a long moment. "I have no doubt."

"That's your answer," Cassie said.

THE WAY OUT OF NO WAY

A FEW DAYS LATER, LYDIA RECEIVED A SUMMONS FROM CASSIE, in the form of a note as elegant as an invitation to a ball. She showed it to Elias, telling him, "I wonder what she's up to now." She had been uneasy about her confession from the moment she made it.

He clasped her hand. "You don't have to see her."

She sighed. "Or do what she asks."

When Lydia arrived, Cassie ushered her into the séance room, curtained and candlelit, even though the afternoon sun shone brightly outside. Lydia blinked in the darkness and asked, "Can we open the curtains a little? Since we aren't having a séance?" She sounded too irritable, she knew.

Cassie rested a hand on her arm. "Bear with me," she said. Lydia shook her head as Cassie directed her to the table, where Narcissa already sat, her hands folded before her. Narcissa raised her eyes as Lydia took her seat. The low light deepened the hollows in Narcissa's cheeks and the dark circles under her eyes. "I didn't expect to see you," Narcissa said. She sounded sharp.

"Likewise," Lydia said, forcing herself not to respond in

kind. She wasn't annoyed with Narcissa. "How are you? You look tired."

Narcissa said, "Worse than tired."

Lydia felt a surge of sympathy. "I can imagine," she said.

Narcissa looked up. "Can you?"

Cassie said, "At least the school was spared."

Narcissa was even sharper. "Yes, this time. Are they gone? Are they finished? I doubt it."

Lydia sighed.

Narcissa continued, "My brother is still dead and still wronged." She glanced at Lydia. "Will there ever be a suit? I doubt that too."

Lydia reminded herself not to snap at Narcissa. "We don't know that."

Narcissa turned her gaze to Cassie. "What do you think? Have the spirits told you otherwise? Is that why you've summoned us, both of us?"

Cassie sat. At the round table, she seemed to take a place at its head. Her eyes, always luminous, were bright orbs in her face. In the artificial darkness, dressed in unrelieved black, she gave off a glow. She said, "I summoned you here to talk about John Beardsley."

Lydia couldn't help herself. She snorted. "And what are we going to do about John Beardsley, Cassie?"

"We have all suffered at his hands." Her huge eyes settled on Lydia's face. "You and your husband. And the school you hold so dear." She moved her gaze to Narcissa. "You and your family, still wronged, still grieving." She leaned forward. "John Beardsley has intimidated us and threatened us. He has done worse. He has done murder." She reminded them, "The police have done nothing. They are complicit. And the courts? We will never see justice in the courts."

Neither Lydia nor Narcissa spoke.

Cassie's voice dropped to a low, beguiling tone. "If we were men who were Union veterans, if we lived out in the countryside, if we were menaced like this, if we had been wronged like this, we would take the matter into our own hands."

The smell of sage and lavender was oppressive in this dark room, where the closed curtains didn't make the air any cooler. Lydia's head began to ache. "What are you suggesting, Cassie?" she asked.

The faintest smile played over Cassie's lips. Was she thinking of her African goddess of vengeance?

Lydia suddenly thought of the vengeful deities of Greek myth, the Furies, and their sisters, the Fates, who spun and cut the thread of a human life. She drew in her breath.

Cassie said, "What do you think?"

In her exasperation, Lydia was blunt. "Are you suggesting that we murder him?"

Narcissa drew in her breath, stifling her shock.

Cassie didn't reply, and Lydia thought of the accusation from five years ago, about the man Cassie hated, who had supposedly fallen into the river by accident.

Cassie turned to Narcissa. "Don't you want justice?"

Narcissa sat up straight. Color returned to her cheeks, and her eyes flashed with anger. "Through murder? Are you mad?"

"Yes, in every way."

"Do you really think I'd help you murder John Beardsley? Take revenge like that?"

"You're certainly angry enough."

Narcissa said, "I don't deny it. And I'm heartbroken, too. But what good would it possibly do if he died by our hands? Would it make the Beardsleys repentant? Would it end slavery, which still exists in another form? Of course not."

Lydia said, "And why would you ask me for help? Do you really think I would say yes?"

Cassie smiled. "Because I know you're a good shot. Handy with a derringer."

Cassie knew her worst secret, and Cassie had been no one to confide in. Lydia felt sick to her stomach. "And I've been praying for forgiveness since the last time I raised that pistol," she said. "Which you also know."

Narcissa asked, "What does she mean?"

Lydia shook her head. "Later. Maybe."

"Who did you shoot?"

Lydia shook her head.

Narcissa turned to Cassie and her voice rose. "If Lydia shot John Beardsley, she'd be arrested. Tried. Convicted. And hanged. If I shot him, no one would wait to take me to prison or the courthouse. They'd just kill me, and they'd very likely kill my mother and my surviving brothers and sisters. Do you really think I'd put everyone I love in such danger? All for revenge?"

Lydia closed her eyes for a moment, then opened them again.

Narcissa leaned forward, as menacing as she could manage to be. "I don't want revenge. I want a judge to listen to the way I've been wronged by the law. I want a jury to decide what is just and what is fair. I don't want to take my retribution in a dark alley. I want justice in a courtroom, in full daylight."

Cassie said, "Do you think it would do any good? Do you think the Beardsleys, father and son, would allow it?" She leaned forward, and her whole body seemed to expand. "They won't be satisfied until I'm hanged for murder. Until you and Lydia are dead, and if you're lucky, you won't be outraged first. Until the school is a smoking ruin, and they don't care if all the children die as it burns to the ground."

Lydia's hand went to her pocket to curl around the handle of her derringer. She thought of the night of the massacre. She thought of the man who had wanted to outrage her and murder her. And she thought of herself, the woman who had done murder. She laid her hands on the table, splaying her fingers, seeing the new prominence of her veins, a sudden sign of aging. She met Cassie's eyes. She couldn't speak, but she shook her head.

Narcissa said, "To meet threat with threat? Fear with fear? Murder with murder?"

Cassie leaned forward. An aura shimmered around her entire body, turning her black dress the color of moonlight. Cassie took her time in replying. She lifted her eyes to Narcissa, who held herself away from the table, her hands knotted on the tabletop, her spine rigid with her disbelief. Cassie dropped her voice, and it took on a beguiling croon. "What do people say? That we must make a way out of no way?"

"That is not the way, Cassie, and you know it," Narcissa said.

Cassie crooned again. "This is the way."

Narcissa's expression didn't soften, nor did her voice. "That's not justice. That's the way to hell, and you're welcome to it."

Cassie reached out to put her hand over Narcissa's. "Oh, Cissy," she said, reminding Narcissa of the bond they had shared since the days of slavery. "Here and now, this is the only justice you are going to get."

Narcissa pulled her hand away as though Cassie's touch burned her. She rose. "If you want to murder John Beardsley, you'll have to do it without my help." She left the room, and they both heard the door shut behind her.

Lydia took a deep breath. Then she rose too. "You'll have to excuse me," she said. "I can't help you either. You'll have to get along without me."

Narcissa stood in the yard, still gray with emotion. She looked up as Lydia approached and stood near her, unspeaking. Narcissa said, "Don't tell me you understand. Because you don't."

Lydia said, "No, I won't. But I can see you're suffering, and it causes me pain." She reached for Narcissa's hand, but Narcissa drew her hand away.

"It isn't enough," Narcissa said, her face as set as a judgment.

"It's all I have," Lydia replied, and she couldn't keep the pain from her own voice.

Narcissa looked up. She took a deep breath. "Did I hear Cassie right? You've already shot a man?"

Lydia shook her head. "I can't tell you about it. I won't. Not now."

Some of the color returned to Narcissa's face. "Will you?" she asked, her tone less harsh.

Lydia felt faint with guilt, worsened by the midday heat. "Sometime. Soon. But not yet."

Narcissa said, "I'll hold you to it."

ONCE HOME, Lydia sat in the parlor. The pistol in her dress pocket felt like a live coal, and she removed it to set it on the lamp table. Such a pretty, deadly thing. She thought of how much she hated John Beardsley and everything he had done. The room felt hot and airless, but she shivered. Fever or guilt? It didn't matter. She pulled out her handkerchief and wiped her wet forehead, even as she felt cold to her bones.

The door opened, and Elias walked in. He came home at noon every day now, since he had nothing to keep him in his office. He looked sweaty and disheveled. He took off his hat and his frock coat and loosened his cravat as he sat down.

She composed herself. "It goes no better?"

He shook his head. "What's the matter, dearest? You don't look well."

She took a deep breath. "I called on Cassie."

"What did she have to say?"

"She wanted to talk about John Beardsley."

He asked, "What does she hope to do?"

"To make things right."

"And how will she do that?"

"I believe she wants to kill him," she said.

He was silent for a moment, then he said, "It wouldn't be the first time," he said.

"As we both know."

He rubbed his face. "But it's a crazy idea," he said. "And why would she ask you to help her? Whatever makes her think you might?"

The guilt rose up in her like sickness. She covered her face with her hands, and when she uncovered them, Elias was beside her on the settee, cradling her hands in his. "What is it?"

"Elias, there's something I've kept from you."

"What is it, my love?" he asked, his voice full of tenderness.

"It's awful," she said.

"Nothing is too awful to tell me," he said.

She swallowed hard. "I have already stained my soul, Elias."

"You? How?"

"I have already shot a man." She raised her eyes to his. "I killed him."

"When did it happen?" he asked. "And how?"

"During the massacre," she said. "When the school burned." And she told him.

He listened. Clasping her hands, he said, "That was no more murder than war is."

She stifled a sob.

He touched her cheek. "No jury in the country would fault you," he said softly.

She forced the words out. "I fault myself."

"As a soldier, as an officer, I'd forgive you in a heartbeat."

"And as a husband?"

He put his arms around her and held her close. She felt his heart beating against her chest, a steadier beat than her rapid one. "Even more so."

CASSIE DREAMED. She was in the alley again, with the man who wanted to kill her. This time she held a gun, too. As she raised it and aimed at him, she woke up in a sweat.

She rose quietly, not wanting to wake TJ. She drew on her dressing gown and slipped downstairs to sit in the séance room, where she breathed in the scent of lavender and sage. She lit a candle against the darkness, and sat before its small, flickering light. Her sweat had dried and now she shivered, even though the room was close and warm.

Help me, she thought, staring beyond the candle flame into the darkness.

The voice was low and kind, a mother's voice. *You know I'll do my best to protect you*, it said.

No, more than that. Something else. She shuddered. *Something worse.*

Not another curse.

No. She took a deep breath. *I want your help in taking vengeance.*

Did she hear a human-sounding sigh? *It don't help your soul to do that, you know.*

She told the voice, *I'm not worried about my soul. I'm worried about my life. And the lives of my sons.*

That I understand.

Cassie let her thought become a plea. *Then will you help me?*

She heard soft footsteps on the stairs and a soft tap on the doorframe. It was TJ, in his dressing gown. He ran his hand through his sleep-tangled hair. He sat, and she raised her head. He took her free hand as he asked softly, "Bad dream?"

Her voice low and hoarse, she replied, "The dream about the alley. About John Beardsley."

He didn't speak. He waited.

"We all want justice, Lydia, Narcissa, and I," she said, her voice scarcely above a whisper. "We'll never get it in the courtroom or in the prison. I suggested something different to the two of them."

She told him what it was.

He sighed and shook his head. "You have every reason to be furious," he said. "But this notion—"

She thought of the voice's inability to promise her help. "How many times have I called on the goddess of vengeance? How is this different?"

"I don't have to tell you," he said.

"Lydia is a better shot than you know," she said.

His mouth twitched. "Yes, I've seen the pretty little gun she carries. What does she think about this?"

"She hates it. She wouldn't even discuss it. And Narcissa—"

"You raised this with Narcissa?"

"She was furious with me."

He shook his head again.

She let the spirit of vengeance fill her, goddess and Fury. She knew how to appear twice her height and twice her size and fill a room with fear. "I want to hurt him as badly as I can," she said.

TJ had seen her use her glamor, but now he looked at her in surprise. He tried to reach the woman he knew. "Cassie," he said softly. "Cassie, this is madness."

She didn't throw off the glamor. She poured it into her gaze. "I know how to use madness," she said.

He knew that she did. "You don't need a gun for that," he said.

She took a deep breath and looked down. When she looked up again, she had taken the glamor away. She put the slightest plea into her voice. "Will you help me?" She reached out her hand.

He sighed and rested his fingers in her palm. "Will someone go to prison for it?"

"If it goes as it should, then I expect not."

"What are you thinking?"

She told him.

LATER THAT DAY, when Will came home from school, he slipped into the séance room, where she sat, with her head in her hands. "Mama?" he asked.

It was still sweet to hear him call her that. She looked up. "What is it, Will?"

He sat next to her. "I want to help you."

She drew her brows together. "How?"

"To fight Mr. John Beardsley."

She asked sharply, "How do you know about that?" Why was she asking? He was as adept at eavesdropping as she was.

"I didn't ask TJ. Or listen at the door. I just know."

She was again startled by how much he resembled her. She touched his cheek. "No," she said. "I need you to stay safe, to stay in school. I need you to grow up to go to college. That's how you can help me."

He was quiet, thinking about it.

"What is it, Will?"

He surprised her again. He asked, "Isn't it a burden to see and know things other people don't?"

"Yes," she said.

"How do you bear it?"

"I've learned to," she said. "And you can as well, if you want to." She cupped his cheek. "In that, I can help you, if you'll let me."

He didn't reply. He didn't make a promise. But he inclined his head to lean into her caress.

THAT NIGHT, Cassie woke. One word echoed in her head, and she wasn't sure whether it was the voice or the remnant of a dream.

Hunter.

It wasn't dark. Moonlight shone through the drawn curtains. Beside her, TJ started in his sleep, as though he heard something, too. She raised herself on her elbow and his eyes fluttered open.

Even half asleep, he was still a scout for danger.

"I'm sorry I woke you," she whispered.

He blinked. His voice was thick with sleep. "Is everything all right? Did you hear something?"

"Only inside my head."

He sighed and closed his eyes. Then he opened them. He had the look of a man who never slept deeply enough. "Your voice?"

"I think so."

He turned to face her. "What did it say?"

"Hunter." Her eyes searched his face. "Does that mean anything to you?"

"More than one thing," he said. "What does it mean to you?"

"The Hunters out in Shelby County. Neighbors to the Beardsleys."

TJ said, "John Beardsley's friend and drinking companion."

"His confederate," Cassie said.

"Yes, I know," TJ said. "In every respect."

Startled, she said, "Do you know something?"

"Not more than you do," he said.

"How well do you know Hunter?"

Suddenly TJ smiled. There was no mirth in that smile. "Well enough to make him very angry," he said. "Drunk and with a gun in his hand—"

"Aimed at who?"

"I have a good idea," TJ said.

She heard a sound inside her head, halfway between a chuckle and a growl. *Hunter,* it repeated. She laid a hand on TJ's cheek. "Do what you can," she said.

"Yes," he replied.

~

SHE WAITED. A day. Another. And yet another. TJ didn't come to see her. As she waited, she couldn't sleep. She sat in the séance room in the middle of the night, listening for the voice. But the voice didn't come, either.

She thought of all the deaths that shadowed her. Her fiancé during the war, a white Union officer who had loved her. Everett Mason, the man who had abused her in slavery and fathered her sons. Dolly, whose heart had given out.

She couldn't pray for another death. But she could hope for news of it.

She laid her head on the table, and despite the discomfort of pillowing her cheek on its oak surface, she must have fallen asleep, because the sound of a key in the lock of the side door woke her.

It was TJ, his hat gone, his coat unbuttoned, his cravat askew. He had the haggard look she recalled from the war. She started up to cry out, "Are you all right?"

He sat and pulled her down to sit. "Hush. Yes. Unhurt."

"Where were you?"

"At the saloon where Beardsley drinks."

"What happened?" She remembered to muffle her voice. Will slept as fitfully as she herself did, and she didn't want him creeping downstairs to ask why TJ had come here in the middle of the night.

"Barroom brawl," he said.

She grabbed his arm. "What happened?"

He said, "Ease up and let me talk."

She forced herself to loosen her grip. "How did it start?" she asked.

He lifted her eyes to hers. His gaze was limpid. He said, "I may have had something to do with it."

"What?"

"Hunter was drunk. On edge. Beardsley asked him why

the school was still standing. Hunter got up and stomped to the bar to ask for another drink. I followed him there. While we were standing at the bar, I said to Hunter, 'Why is it up to you? Why do you do his dirty work for him? Is he too much a coward to do it himself?' Hunter stared at me. And back at the table, he said to Beardsley, 'You coward, why don't you burn the place down yourself?' Beardsley said, 'Are you calling me a coward?' And Hunter said, 'Yes, I am.' They got up and started to push and shove, and the barkeep told them to take it outside."

"Into the alley?"

TJ nodded. "I followed them outside, but it just got worse and worse. They both drew their pistols." He shrugged, as though he were talking about a day at the horse races.

She drew in her breath in a hiss. "Just tell me," she said.

"Hunter shot Beardsley in the chest. Wounded him. A bad 'un. And Beardsley managed to shoot Hunter."

"Where is John Beardsley now?"

"I didn't stay to find out. I assume someone took him home."

"What about Hunter?"

"Hunter's dead."

"It's a murder?"

"There's no doubt that Beardsley killed him."

For a moment she wondered if Hunter's family would take legal action. She looked down, thinking. "How is John Beardsley?"

"It was a bad wound," TJ said. "In the war, it would have been touch and go as to whether he'd recover."

"He might die," she said slowly.

He said, "Maybe. Maybe not." He met her eyes. "Your hands are clean."

"Our hands are clean," she said slowly.

THE PAYMENT

CASSIE WAS TOO WELL-DRESSED TO GO IN THE BACK DOOR OF the Beardsley town house in Memphis, but she knew better than to knock at the front. She strode to the back door and knocked.

When the door opened, a middle-aged Black woman wiped her hands on her stained apron. "Who are you?"

Cassie said, "I served the family before the war."

The woman stared at her. "What do you want?"

"I'm here to see Mr. John Beardsley," she said. "He'll remember me. I worked in the house."

"He's too sick to see anyone."

"I nursed him once," Cassie lied.

The woman stared at her again.

"I'll be quiet. And I won't stay long. Just enough to let him know I'm sorry he's ill."

There was no reply.

"Where is Missus Beardsley?" Cassie asked.

"She's sick, too. Doctor gave her laudanum. She's sleeping."

"Very quiet," Cassie said. "I won't bother anyone."

The woman looked away, and as she did, Cassie pulled a dollar from her reticule and folded it in half. The woman saw her do it and turned her head to look. Cassie smiled. "Please?" she asked, transferring the money into the woman's floury palm.

She nodded. "Come on in. Follow me. And be quiet."

The woman led her into the main house and stopped before the staircase that led to the second floor, as straight as an arrow. "Up there," she said. "Second room on the left."

Cassie smiled again. "Thank you," she said, and she lifted her skirts to clear the steps and ran lightly to the second story.

The door to John Beardsley's room was open. He lay unmoving in the bed, the coverlet over him despite the heat. Above his white nightshirt, his face was an unhealthy grayish pallor. The room smelled of something sweet and rotten under the odor of lavender water. Cassie had worked at the army hospital at Fort Pickering during the war, and she recognized the smell.

Touch and go, TJ had said, and he was right.

There was a plain wooden chair at the bedside, and Cassie gathered her skirts about her to sit.

He opened his eyes and groaned softly.

"You know me," she said, taking off her gloves.

He turned his head and blinked at her in surprise. "Cassie?" he whispered.

"I was called Cassie, once," she said. "When you were a boy."

"Everett's doxy," he said, his voice raspy.

She shook her head.

He said, "Everett's dead." He was feverish and in pain, not completely anchored to the here and now.

"Yes, I know," she said, smiling a little.

"Why are you here?"

"I wanted to see you," she said.

"Shot," he said. "Bad."

She reached for the coverlet. "May I look?"

He didn't answer.

She lifted the coverlet, but all she saw was the bulge of a dressing under the nightshirt, and she smelled the powerful odor of putrefaction that presaged death. She touched it and he gasped. She let her hand rest there.

She said, "It was you, wasn't it? Framing me? Threatening me?" She spoke in the low, caressing, beguiling voice she used to coax the spirits.

He closed his eyes and didn't reply.

"Following my boy Will?"

No reply.

"Sending those notes to the school?"

Silence.

She smiled, even though he couldn't see her. In the same beguiling voice as before, she said, "Trying to set the school on fire?"

His eyes fluttered open. "That wasn't me," he said, his voice a soft croak. "That was Hunter."

She nodded. "And Hunter is dead, isn't he?"

Again, he closed his eyes.

"You shot him, didn't you? You killed him."

He didn't move.

"Like you shot Titus Armstrong." She paused. "Murdered Titus Armstrong."

He was silent again.

Now she pressed hard against his wound. He groaned in pain.

She whispered, "I know what your father says about you. Everyone knows."

He groaned again.

"That you're drunk, dissolute, and a disappointment to him." She pressed harder and he groaned, a deeper sound than before. He was suffering. She made her voice low and seductive. "He thinks you're a failure. And you are. The task you set yourself—to hurt me and mine and the school—in that you failed, too." She bent down to drop her voice lower. "The school still stands. My boys are untouched." She pressed the wound with all her strength. "I'm alive, and you're dying."

He closed his eyes.

And then she spoke in a suggestive whisper in his ear, as intimate as a kiss. "If you die, you'll be free of all of it."

He jerked his head away from her. "Get away from me," he said in the thready whisper of a man at the end of his strength.

She leaned back and stood, brushing her skirt as though something had soiled it.

A young Black woman in the dress of a servant put her head in the door. "Who are you? What are you doing here? Leave him be. He's sick!"

"I was just leaving," Cassie said, smiling, as though this had been a pleasant social call. The smell of death was stronger than ever. She turned to go, and she ran lightly down the steps as though she expected to greet a friend at the door. Instead, she made her way to the back door. In the kitchen, the woman who'd let her in said, "You saw him?"

She nodded.

"He's bad, isn't he?"

"Yes," Cassie said. "He is." She opened the door and stepped into the heat of the yard, which smelled of the roses that grew in the back and the manure that filled the street.

～

Two days later, in the warm light of a late summer afternoon, Cassie sat in her front room, waiting for business. She looked up at the sound of a heavy tread on the stairs from the rooms above. A low voice said, "You ready to do this?"

Her uncle, talking to her aunt.

They both entered the front room and stood before her table, casting shadows in the bright light. Her uncle said, "We want to talk to you. Private. Can we go in back?" They both looked gray and grim.

"Yes," she said. She rose and they followed her. Once in back, she shut the door and gestured to the table. They all sat in the artificial darkness of the séance room.

She asked, "What is this about?"

Moses Hayes said, "John Beardsley died last night."

She nodded. "I know."

Matilda Hayes asked, "Who told you?" Her voice was accusatory. "Don't say it was the spirits."

"No, it was TJ."

"You didn't have a hand in it, did you?" her uncle asked. He sounded like his old self, the police chief of Camp Shiloh, interrogating a suspect.

Cassie looked down at her well-tended hands. *Your hands are clean.* She looked up. "TJ told me that his best friend shot him in a bar fight, and that's what he died of," she said.

Matilda said, "Too many men close to you are dead."

She gazed at her aunt, then turned her eyes to her uncle. "You both know why," she said.

Her uncle didn't flinch. "It's time for you to go."

She asked, "To keep myself safe? To protect my boys? Or to spare the two of you?"

Her aunt said, "All of it."

"TJ and I will take the boys with me."

There was a long, painful silence. Finally, her uncle said, "For their sake—"

Her aunt said, "Just go."

~

A FEW DAYS after John Beardsley's funeral, Narcissa told Lydia that she wanted to talk to Elias about the lawsuit, and Lydia invited her to call. Elias, who no longer bothered to go into his office, asked James Dorsey to join them. They assembled in the Aronson parlor, the business at hand masked by coffee and cake.

Narcissa said, "So John Beardsley is dead. At the hand of his best friend, I hear."

Elias said, "The friend is dead, too. Beardsley shot him, and it was fatal."

Narcissa regarded him with an uncanny calm and spoke to both lawyers. "There's no longer a reason for the suit, is there? Or a case we can take to court?"

Elias said, "There are still grounds for a civil suit against the police, for their negligence in investigating your brother's death. But the matter is much less compelling now that the murderer is dead." He looked at Dorsey. "What's your opinion?"

"Oh, we could file a suit, and it might come to Municipal Court. We could recover something in damages. But we certainly can't try or convict a man who's dead. We couldn't even do much to besmirch his memory."

Narcissa said, "So that's not the way forward."

Elias looked at Dorsey again, and they both shook their heads.

Narcissa said, "But there is another way. A way out of no way."

Lydia asked, "What are you thinking?"

Narcissa leaned forward, her body suddenly taut and tense like a soldier awaiting battle. "Let's call on William Beardsley," she said.

"To what end?" Elias asked.

Narcissa said, "Not to offer our condolences. We have something else to propose."

WHEN WILLIAM BEARDSLEY'S reply arrived at the Aronson house, addressed to Elias, Lydia said, "What does he say?"

Elias looked up from the note. "He asks me to call on him this afternoon at his office."

"Did you mention that you're bringing Narcissa?"

"No. We'll ambush him."

Lydia laughed.

William Beardsley looked as though he had aged ten years since his son's death. His face was newly lined, and his eyes were bloodshot. Even his hair, usually bright gold, seemed drained of color. In a hoarse voice, he invited Elias to sit. He stared at Narcissa but didn't acknowledge her as she sat, too.

"Sir, my deepest condolences," Elias said.

Despite his appearance, Beardsley's voice was curt and cold. "Save your breath. I know you had a hand in this."

Elias thought, *Good. He's rattled. We aren't.* Carefully, politely, he said, "Sir, your son and I were adversaries, but my only intention was to settle our differences in court."

"You miserable pettifogger. That woman Cassie. You plotted with her—"

"No, Mr. Beardsley, I gave her legal advice, sir, nothing more."

"Colonel Beardsley." He glared at Narcissa again. "Who the devil are you?"

She smiled and said, "I'm Miss Narcissa Armstrong. I teach at the Phoenix School."

He shook his head. To Elias, he said, "Why did you bring this stranger here?"

Without losing her composure, Narcissa said, "Oh, I'm not a stranger, sir. Don't you recognize me? You owned me before the war. I was called Cissy then."

He shook his head. "That doesn't mean a thing to me. I had a hundred slaves in the field, and I never knew their names." He stared at Elias. "And why the devil did you bring her here?"

She folded her hands in her lap as though she were in church. In a tone of unruffled calm, she answered, "Because I know that your son murdered my brother."

He laughed, a bitter sound. "Should I believe that? Coming from you?"

"It's the truth, sir."

He looked at Narcissa with rage on his grief-stricken face. "How dare you try to hurt my family from beyond the grave."

She sat up very straight. She looked him in the eye, a whipping offense in the days of slavery. "Sir, you have hurt my family more than I can ever say."

To Elias, he said, "He's dead. Without my son to speak, you have nothing to take to court."

"Not to a criminal court," Elias said. "But we could still file a civil suit about police negligence."

"They won't hear it."

"They might."

Narcissa leaned forward to interrupt. "Sir, we don't want to go to court."

Beardsley looked at Elias instead of Narcissa. "Then what in hell do you want?"

Elias said, "Repentance, as you reckon it. And you might think of recompense, too."

With scorn, Beardsley said, "You mean money, don't you?"

Elias replied, "Money can help, sometimes. But it doesn't right the wrong."

"Get out of my office," he said.

Very quietly, Narcissa said, "John Beardsley wished me and my family very ill. As you do. But I can't rejoice in a man's death."

"What do you want?"

Narcissa said, "Search your conscience, sir."

"Get out," Beardsley said.

WHEN LYDIA and her teachers returned to the school, Lydia expected the sign and the scent of neglect. But the floors had been washed and polished, and in the classrooms, the desks had been dusted. Mr. Jasper said proudly, "We got a whole crew of ladies in here to clean for you."

Lydia had to blink back tears. "Mr. Jasper, I can't begin to thank you for everything you've done," she said.

He said, "Mrs. Aronson, don't even mention it."

She said, "It's over, isn't it? Hard to believe, but it's over."

He said, "Hand of providence again."

"Even though it took a death."

He said, "Ma'am, I was a soldier, and in my heart, I'm still a soldier. I'm not surprised by death."

She nodded.

She went into her office and sat at her desk, which had

been untouched since the day she departed. She rested her hand on the report she had been drafting for Superintendent Barnum. She left it there, and thought, *My time here is over, too*. It was safe to return the school to the hands of the Black community. It was safe for her to go elsewhere, wherever that was. She and Elias would talk about it and plan for it.

Mr. Jasper tapped on the door and the look on his face drove all thought of safety away. Narcissa was right behind him and came into the room with him. "What is it, Mr. Jasper?" Lydia asked.

He held out the envelope.

But as soon as she took it, she said, "It's not the same as the others." She hefted it. "Heavy stationery. And it's addressed to the school." She opened it.

There was no letter inside. She stared in astonishment.

"What is it?" Mr. Jasper asked.

She said, "It's a pile of greenbacks." She removed them and fanned them out. "Ten hundred-dollar notes. A thousand dollars."

Mr. Jasper was a hard man to astonish. But this astonished him. "A thousand dollars!" he said. "Who would give us a sum like that?"

She looked down at the money and shook her head in disbelief.

Narcissa said, "I can hazard a guess."

"Who?" Lydia asked, still holding the bills.

"Mr. William Beardsley," Narcissa said.

"Why would he—?"

Narcissa said, "We asked. This is his answer."

~

AFTER LYDIA DEPOSITED the money in the school's bank account, Elias returned to his office, and he was surprised when the door opened to admit Cassie. Despite the heat, she wore a black dress, as though she had decided to mourn the man she had hated so much. He invited her to sit and asked, "How are you, Mrs. Auburn?"

"Quite all right," she said.

It was wrong to say "He's gone." Or to ask "Did you have a hand in it?" Instead, he treated her as he'd treat anyone who came to consult him. "How can I help you?"

She said, "It's a matter of business. Legal business."

He nodded.

She reached into her pocket and drew out an envelope. It was unmarked, but it was thick with paper. "This came to me today."

"What is it?"

She opened the envelope and carefully removed the contents. Greenbacks. She fanned them out on his desk to show him. They were one-hundred-dollar bills.

"Twenty of them," she said.

"Two thousand dollars," he said in surprise. "Quite a sum. Who—"

"Oh, Mr. Aronson, I think we can both guess, can we not? Even if the donor hopes to remain anonymous."

He met her eyes. They were huge and luminous, and they gave nothing away. "I'm not a banker," he said. "Why bring it to me?"

"I want to use it for my sons' education. I don't know how best to secure it for that purpose. I thought you might."

That was easy. "You could set up a trust," he said. "You can dedicate the funds for education. It's not difficult to do."

"I'm not planning to stay in Memphis," she said. "Mr.

Randolph and I intend to return to New York, and we'll be taking the boys with us. Does that make a difference?"

"You'll want a lawyer in New York. It will be easier to manage the trust that way."

"I have one."

"Then why ask for my help?"

She smiled. "An apology."

He shook his head. "Talk to your own lawyer in New York."

"I can't sway you?"

"No," he said, and it was freeing to tell her that.

She sighed, very delicately. "Are you planning to stay in Memphis?"

He said, "Have the spirits informed you otherwise?"

She gave him a knowing smile. "I'd think there isn't enough to keep you here. And you and Mrs. Aronson might be happier in New York."

"We might," he said.

Before she rose to go, he asked, "Mrs. Auburn, may I ask you a question?"

She inclined her head.

"How did Everett Mason die?"

And at that she smiled, a very knowing smile indeed. "He died by accident, as you well know," she said.

"You were there. You know for certain."

She shook her head as she rose. "He slipped and fell. He died by accident. Good day, Mr. Aronson."

THAT EVENING, as Lydia sat in the parlor, Elias walked into the house with a jaunty step. He was smiling. She rose and met him in an embrace, then leaned back to take in his expression. "You look pleased," she said, leading him to sit on the settee, where they were agreeably crowded together.

"I did some business today," he said. "Cassie came to see me."

She laughed. "Don't tell me she wants to sue John Beardsley's ghost."

He laughed too. "No, no, it was some perfectly legitimate business. The kind of financial dealing that lawyers need to be involved in."

"I won't pry, because I know you'll tell me it's confidential."

"It's not, because I referred her to another lawyer."

"Good for you," Lydia said.

"She's returning to New York."

"I'm not surprised. The whole ensemble?"

"Yes. Evidently. And then she asked me if we were moving back to New York, too."

"Did the spirits tell her so?"

He smiled.

She said, "How thoughtless of them to tell her first."

He laughed.

"Are we moving back to New York, Elias?"

He smiled. "We could."

She laughed. "New York! Where you can support the party of General Grant, and practice as a lawyer, and even go to Temple Emanuel-El, without fear of being shot in the street!"

He reached for her hand. "But what about you?"

She twined her fingers through his. "Until now I haven't felt I could leave the school," she said. "But now I know I can. When I relinquish the principal's spot, I'll put in a good word for Narcissa with Superintendent Barnum."

"He won't like that."

"I'll remind him that the Phoenix School has a thousand dollars in its bank account, thanks to her."

"In other words, business as usual in Memphis," he said.

Lydia said, "So Cassie and TJ will be our neighbors in Manhattan, so to speak."

"Manhattan is a big place, sometimes."

She said, "In other words, God willing, we'll never see them."

"What would you do? If we left Memphis for Manhattan?"

"Didn't you once promise me a whirlwind of pleasure there, if we got through—whatever we just got through?"

"I know you want more than that."

"We can start there," she said, feeling mischievous. "And then I want to get my bearings."

He leaned close. "And then?"

She leaned closer. "And after that, I'll find some other trouble to get into. Do you think I can find it in New York?"

He whispered in her ear, his voice full of tenderness. "I know you will."

She laughed. "Then I will look forward to it. All of it."

THE END

The event that shadows this story—the Memphis Massacre of 1866—was as bad as I have depicted it in fiction. In 1866, Memphis was the scene of one of the worst racial massacres of the Civil War and Reconstruction era. While it is largely forgotten today, it was shocking news at the time, and the subject of an extensive Congressional investigation shortly after it occurred.

On May 1, when the last Black soldiers in Memphis were mustered out of the Union army, a shooting altercation developed and quickly became an excuse for white residents and local police to rampage through Black neighborhoods. Over the next several days, a mob attacked and killed both Black soldiers and civilians and set fire to homes, churches, and schools in the Black community.

According to the report by a Congressional committee, at which eyewitnesses described what they had seen (and suffered), the damage to persons and property was substantial and horrific. More than forty Black people and two white people were killed. Seventy-five Black people were injured, and in testimony unusual for the nineteenth century, witnesses called by the commission attested to the rape of five Black women. A hundred Black people were robbed and ninety-one homes were destroyed, many of them by arson. The mob targeted Black institutions; every Black church and school in Memphis was burned to the ground.

The local police did nothing to quell the disturbance; in fact, they abetted the mob and participated in its excesses. Federal troops were sent to restore peace.

While about a quarter of Memphis's Black population left the city after the massacre, those who remained were swift to rebuild. Within two years, churches and schools had been restored. The Phoenix School really did exist and its motto was in fact "We have risen from the ashes."

Several of the people described in this book were historical figures. James Dorsey was based on a Tennessee lawyer and legislator who really existed, even though he was active in the 1880s rather than during Reconstruction. His name was Josiah Settle. He was born enslaved in East Tennessee and was educated at Oberlin College, where he, like the character based on him, really did play baseball. He received a law degree from Howard University, taught there, and was admitted to the bar in Washington. In the 1880s, he lived in Mississippi, where he was active in Republican politics and served as a member of the state legislature. In 1885, when he moved to Memphis, he was appointed the Assistant Attorney-General of Shelby County. In 1887, when his term ended, he went into private practice, and his cases included a challenge to segregation on Memphis streetcars—sadly, it was unsuccessful.

Joseph Barnum, the superintendent for the Black schools of Memphis, was a real person, as was John Eaton, who edited the Memphis *Post*, the only newspaper in Memphis that reported fairly on topics of concern to the Black community.

I regret this book's portrayal of the Memphis police, many of whom were of Irish ancestry. It is part of the historical record, described by the testimony to the commission investigating the massacre. The antipathy between the Memphis police and the Black community existed in 1868, as in decades hence, and in our time as well.

The rest is fiction.

THANK YOU FOR READING THE
OTHER SHORE!

If you want more tales of the Civil War, you might like:

The captivating, enthralling, sweeping Georgia series, starting with the award-winning *Sister of Mine* at https://mybook.to/SisterofMine. Rachel is a slave. Her half-sister Adelaide owns her. Slavery them made kin. Will the Civil War make them sisters?

For another tale of love and courage at the time of the Civil War, you'll enjoy *Charleston's Daughter*, at https://mybook.to/CharlestonsDaughter, first in the Low Country Series. Emily is a tormented Southern belle. Caro is a rebellious slave. In South Carolina in 1858, no friendship could be more dangerous…

Want more mystery in Memphis? Take a look at the contemporary Memphis series, starting with Soul of Memphis at https://mybook.to/SoulofMemphis. Nat Raskin is an antique dealer with a broken heart. When she finds a Stratocaster guitar with a secret, what will it cost her to reveal the long-lost truth?

Sign up for my newsletter, The Latest on the Past, at https://www.sabrawaldfogel.com/sign-up, for exclusive giveaways and sneak peeks of new books. I greatly appreciate your help in spreading the word about this book, including telling a friend. Reviews help readers find books. Please leave a review on your favorite book site.

ABOUT THE AUTHOR

Sabra Waldfogel, who is not from anywhere in the South, studied history at Harvard University and got a PhD in American history from the University of Minnesota. Since then, she has been fascinated by the drama of slavery and its long shadow in American history.

Her first novel, *Sister of Mine*, published by Lake Union, was named the winner of the 2017 Audio Publishers Association Audie Award for fiction. The sequel, *Let Me Fly*, was published in 2018. Since then, she has written a duology about South Carolina at the time of the Civil War. Her most recent work is *The River's Edge*, the fist book in the Historical Memphis series, and a series of mysteries set in contemporary Memphis.